Fate's Falls

Volume I

MATED TO THE MINOTAUR
THE GRUMPY DEMON'S SUNSHINE
A REAPER IS FOREVER

KARLA DOYLE

CONTENTS

MATED TO THE MINOTAUR

THE GRUMPY DEMON'S SUNSHINE

A REAPER IS FOREVER

Mated to the Minotaur

Mated to the Minotaur

KARLA DOYLE

MATED TO THE MINOTAUR

When my cousin calls, distraught because her parents won't accept her fiancé because "his skin is a different color," I give her the "we ride at dawn" support she needs and deserves. Then say yes to being her maid of honor at the wedding that's in three weeks.

Booking a flight across the country and getting a dress that's "any color other than green" are doable. Making arrangements in a town Google can't locate is more challenging. Time isn't on my side and my cousin seems to be too busy to respond to messages, so I make use of the best man's contact info.

Constantine is happy to help. And his voice...it's enough to make me swoon. After one phone call, I might be more excited to meet him than I am for my cousin's wedding. I don't know what Constantine looks like, nor do I care. I'm not superficial or a racist like my cousin's parents. I'm as open-minded as it gets.

Turns out, I need to be. Fate's Falls isn't any small, mountain town—it's populated with literal monsters, including the man I'm crushing on. The hulking Minotaur could crush me in one of his massive hands. Logically, I should be scared, but I'm the opposite. I assume it's because I'm long overdue for some adventure, and more than a little curious to know if the hunky Minotaur is monstrous *all over*.

Constantine insists our connection is deeper than physical attraction. He believes we're mates. As in, fated mates. Forever.

My previously boring life just got a whole lot more interesting...

CONTENT NOTES
MATED TO THE MINOTAUR

- low conflict
- fated mates who fall in love immediately
- a cast of secondary characters
- humor
- explicit consensual sex between a Minotaur man and a human female
- oral sex, anal play
- size difference
- cum-feeding/eating
- stretching
- and yes, they do make it fit. ;)

Chapter One

NATALIE

The calendar is not my friend. I have a commission piece to finish this week and I'm still in the initial sketch stage... and it's Thursday. I'll finish it before the next job is scheduled to come in, but it'd be easier if my creative mojo wasn't on an unauthorized sabbatical. I'm still getting the work done, but lately, that's how it feels—like work. I miss the days of feeling endlessly inspired. When drawing was as natural as breathing.

When did the joy of creating disappear? It's not because I'm doing commissions; I actually love drawing from a prompt. If I had to analyze it—and that's really no hardship, I'm a big fan of *over*analyzing things—I'd say my mojo left town when my parents did. We still talk almost every day, but phone calls and FaceTime aren't the same as spending time together. I miss the warm fuzzies I always get when I'm with them. That's right, I'm a twenty-eight-year-old mama's and daddy's girl. And not ashamed of that fact one little bit.

Even after they grabbed early retirement by the horns and drove off into the horizon to embrace full-time RV life, I still had Ro in my daily life. Until she, too, got hit by the wanderlust bug. Or in her case, the *lust* bug. She went on a road trip to British Columbia to meet some builder she started talking to via her online metalwork store—then stayed out there permanently. That was a year ago.

Surrounded by millions of people, yet I feel alone.

So, when the phone lights up and starts playing my cousin's ringtone, my looming deadline can suck it. Rosetta hasn't voice-called me for over two weeks. We're still best friends, but since moving to British Columbia, she's been hit-and-miss with communication. When we do talk, the reason for all the "misses" becomes apparent. She's in love. Wildly in love.

Born two days apart, we grew up together, more like sisters than cousins. Basically, we've been best friends since birth. Despite being extremely close, we're very different people. I'm the romantic, the believer in fate and fairytale endings. Ro is the "I make my own fate," try everything once, balls-out adventurous type. Minus the balls, of course. She's the va-va-voom redhead chick who turns heads no matter where she goes. And leaves a trail of broken hearts behind her.

Driving to the other side of the country to hook up with a guy she met online totally fit with her carefree nature. Putting down roots with him shocked the hell out of me. A year later, I'm still surprised every time she says she loves him. Honestly, I didn't think it'd last, no matter how great the sex is. And apparently, it's pretty great. Another way my cousin and I are opposites—she's having all the amazing sex and I'm having none. Not even bad sex.

I wait one more ring before answering. I always let it go a few before picking up. My cousin has been known to accidentally hit the *Call* button, and some of the heavy breathing I've heard because I answered scarred me for life —and made me green with envy. Unless fate sends someone directly to me, the odds of me getting *any* action are low. Like, single-digit percentage. Sadly, my life has not found its fairytale groove, and none of the men in line during my daily coffee runs have provided the epic meet-cute I know I'm destined to have. One day. One day.

"Hey, stranger," I say by way of answering. "How's the wild life?"

"Amazing. Mostly. Everything except for my idiot parents." A big, hiccupping sob comes through the line. Super out of character for Rosetta. She's cried around me exactly twice in her life—at age ten, when our grandmother on our mothers' side died, and when our grandfather followed a few months afterward.

Her parents can't be dead. If something horrible had happened to them, my mom would've called me right away. Plus, Ro would've led with that news if her parents had passed away. She wouldn't have used the word *amazing* in any sense, even though they're not close and have always butted heads.

I've often wondered if we were accidentally switched as newborns. As infants, we both had fair peach fuzz for hair and could've been twins. Hospital mix-ups happen. I'm more reserved, like her parents, whereas, she's more free-spirited, like mine. Mix-up or not, I'm glad I got my set of parents. I wouldn't trade them for anything.

"What's happening with your parents?" I ask.

"They're close-minded assholes."

That's a known fact. This isn't the first time they've clashed, and I doubt it'll be the last. "What are they being close-minded about?"

"My fiancé."

"Your *fiancé?*"

A squeal from her end of the call nearly pierces my eardrum. "Shocking, right?"

"Um, yeah! This guy must be one of a kind, getting you to put on the ball and chain. Never thought I'd see the day you'd want to commit to one person for the rest of your life. Unless—are you guys doing the open-marriage thing?"

"Hell no," she says on a riotous laugh. "Dak is not a sharer. I'm his, full stop. Even his best friend doesn't talk to me alone without letting Dak know first."

"And you're really okay with that? Being with someone so possessive? Because that's kind of got 'red flag' written all over it."

"He's possessive, not controlling. Zero red flags, I promise. Dak would do anything for me, just like I'd do anything for him. We're unbreakable."

"Ro the ho becomes the ultimate monogamist," I tease. "You sound pretty sure about it."

"I used to make fun of you for believing in finding your one true love, I know. But that saying 'when you know, you know' isn't a load of horseshit lonely people cling to. It's legit. When *the one* comes into your life, you just know."

Envy tightens its greasy fingers around my heart. "I'm happy for you, Ro, even if I haven't seen you in a year because this guy stole you from me."

Another laugh rolls into my ear. "He didn't steal me from you. You're still my favorite human in the whole world."

"Second favorite, you mean. Since your fiancé is obviously at the top of the list." The awkward silence I receive is out of character for her. I wouldn't have thought my comment problematic, but obviously, I touched a nerve. "Look, I don't care where I fall on the favorites list. If you're happy, I'm happy. I miss you so much, though! When's the big day? The wedding will be back here, I assume?" More silence. Enough to make me wonder if she's still on the call. "Ro?"

"Sorry, just calming my shit down over here because we've circled back to the asshole-parents part."

"What's their issue? They should be jumping for joy. Their 'I'm never settling down' daughter is going full-on domestic."

"Oh, they were happy I'm getting married. They didn't even care that the wedding's in three weeks, and that we're having it here."

"Wait, what?"

Ignoring me, Ro continues. "So, they asked for a video call with us, since they haven't met Dak."

That'd never happen with my parents, but they're nothing like Ro's. They're not the type to fly across the country to see their daughter and her boyfriend. Plus, they've probably been waiting for the breakup to happen—because Ro isn't the settling-down type. Or, she wasn't.

"And they didn't like him? From one video call, they made up their minds?" It wouldn't surprise me, honestly.

"They didn't even try getting to know him, Nat. The moment they saw him, they freaked out because he's not a basic white dude. They refuse to come to the wedding and say they'll disown me if I marry him."

"They're *racists?*" I whisper the despicable word even though there's nobody who could possibly hear it.

"What else do you call people who judge others by their outward appearance?"

"I'd call them a lot of things, none of them favorable." I knew my aunt and uncle were old-fashioned about a lot of things, but racist? "Do you want me to go over and try to talk sense into them?"

"No—definitely not. But there *is* something I really, *really* want you to do, if you're willing."

"Of course, Ro. Anything. Name it."

"Be my maid of honor?"

"Well, duh! Of course, I'll be your maid of honor. I'd be pissed if you chose anyone but me!"

"Ooh, Natalie gets spicy!" Ro says on a big laugh. "It suits you, babe! Keep it coming. And on the subject of coming, can you head out here early? I'll send you money for the flight. You can even upgrade to first class on my dime."

Before I can answer, she starts in on me, the way she did when we were kids. Like the times I wanted to dress up our Barbies so they could go on fancy dates with our Ken dolls in the house, but she wanted to ditch the Kens and the clothes, take naked Barbies out in the backyard, and make them do *things* with my brother's assortment of dragons and other creature figures.

"Please, please, *pleeeeease*... It'll be fun, I promise."

I couldn't say no to her then. Because I love her. Also, because I was secretly intrigued by Barbie doing unspeakable things with monsters. As for now... I can't let her down. Especially not when her parents have bailed so completely. "The fun will be in limited amounts because I have deadlines. I'll have to bring work with me. And how early is early?"

"I'll take whatever you can give me," she says. "At least a week before the wedding, though. Two would be even better."

"You said the wedding is in three weeks. So, I should drop everything and come now, basically?"

"Perfect!"

"I was kidding, Ro. Has the mountain altitude clouded your sarcasm detector?"

Her genuine laughter bubbles through the speaker. "Love has! But the air here is amazing, Nat. You'll never want to leave, trust me."

I always have, and she's never been wrong. Even about Barbie's unspeakable adventures. "Send me the info. I'll be there as soon as I can swing it."

NATALIE

There is no "instant" messaging with my cousin. She's notorious for leaving me on read, sometimes until the next day, sometimes indefinitely, because she gets distracted and forgets to reply. There's a three-hour time difference between Ontario and British Columbia, but Rosetta only gets to use that excuse when I send early-morning texts. Which I should stop doing because it only increases my frustration level. But will I change my ways? Probably not. Unlike Ro, I'm a morning person. Always have been.

Hence, why I'm up, dressed, and have put in the equivalent of half a day's work by the time the sun is rising on the west coast. I have a long to-do list before I catch my flight to Kelowna two days from now. Questions that need answering. Since my cousin isn't likely to reply in a timely fashion, I'm going with option number two—the groom's best friend and best man, Constantine. Reaching out to a total stranger for help isn't in my comfort zone, but I'd rather suffer a moment of awkwardness than the anxiety of not having plans firmly in place. Time to find out if the guy who'll be accompanying me down the aisle is an early riser.

> Hi there! ☺ This is Natalie Somers. I'm Rosetta's cousin and her maid of honor. She gave me your number. I hope she's mentioned me and told you I might be in touch about the wedding, but with Ro, it's possible she forgot, so this might be coming out of left field... •• I'm hoping you can help with some long-distance planning I need to do before I head out west in a few days. You can text me or call me at this number. Thank you!

The phone rings before I can second-guess myself. I don't usually answer *Unknown* calls, but the timing would have to be a huge coincidence, so I take the chance and pick up. "Hello?"

"Hello, this is Constantine Tavros. Am I speaking with Natalie?" His voice is *so* deep. Smooth and rich, I can almost feel it wrapping around me, like midnight-blue velvet.

That's right, midnight blue. Not just any color of velvet. My brain is oddly specific about stuff like this. Also, I'm going to need Rosetta to send me a picture of this guy. For now, I'll use my imagination. He's tall, dark, handsome, and built. *All over*, of course.

"Yes, that's me," I say, pulling myself together before I end up sounding like a phone-sex operator. Notebook and pen in hand, I move from my desk chair to the couch. "Thanks for getting back to me so quickly. I know it's early there; you must be a morning person, like me. If I sound tinny, it's because I put you on speaker so I can write things down."

"Your lovely voice is perfectly clear."

Lovely? I assume he's just one of those innocently flirtatious guys, but in *his* voice, the compliment gives me the warm fuzzies *and* the tingles. It has been a while since I had a date. Even longer since I had a memorable one.

"To answer your text," he says, "I was expecting to hear from you. I told Rosetta to give you my number."

"Oh, I didn't realize. That's so thoughtful. Thank you."

A rumble even deeper than his voice comes through my phone's speaker, making it vibrate where it's propped against a cushion. It isn't a laughing rumble, nor is it an angry sound. It's something else. Something...primal.

No, Natalie, it's not. Get your head out of the bedroom, you sex-starved fool.

I give my head a shake and clear my throat as covertly as possible. "I'm sure you have things to do, so I'll try not to take much of your time."

"You're welcome to as much of my time as you want, Natalie."

Another ripple of *yes please* runs through me. Most people shorten my name to Nat, which is fine, but I like the way my full name sounds in Constantine's voice. He says it as if he's tasting it. And liking it.

"Rosetta didn't give me the name of any hotels. No matter how many internet searches I try, I haven't found a single listing for hotels, motels, or inns in Fate's Falls. I don't want to chance it by just showing up, only to find there's no vacancy anywhere. Since she didn't invite me to stay with her and Dak, I assume she had somewhere in mind, but I'm open to your suggestions."

Silence follows. Only the faint sound of breathing and a

sense of awareness I might be imagining tells me he's still on the other end of the call.

"There are no hotels, motels, or inns here," he says, finally.

"A bed-and-breakfast? A hostel with shower facilities?"

"None of those, either. Fate's Falls is a small town and fairly secluded. There's never been a need for any short-term rental places."

"Okay... can you tell me the name of the nearest town?"

More silence. Weird silence. "There are no towns nearby. We're quite isolated."

There's no logical reason for the shiver that ripples through me. So, the town's isolated. Way up in the mountains. With no accommodations for visitors. Ro lives there, and is blissfully happy, so it must be a nice place. I'm looking for trouble where none exists.

I gather a calming breath, releasing it quietly, so the man on the other end of the call won't hear it. No need for him to know I'm a chronic overthinker who's having a little internal freakout right now. "Okay, do you know where Ro planned for me to stay during the two-plus weeks I'll be there?"

"With me."

"I'm sorry, what?" There's no way I heard him correctly. Or that Rosetta would think this is okay.

"I have several empty bedrooms. I offered them to Rosetta for her family's use. As her parents have declined to attend the wedding, you'll have the largest guest bedroom and a bathroom to yourself."

"Will anyone else be there? Your wife? Girlfriend?

Boyfriend? Parents? Kids? Other boarders?" I clamp my mouth shut before any more rambling escapes.

"I have no romantic attachments, no children, and my parents live out of town. I live alone, and there will be no other guests. Only the two of us. But I have a large home. You'll have as much privacy as you want."

Just me and the deep-voiced stranger—who happens to be single and nobody's baby daddy—alone in his house for two weeks. I should politely decline, say goodbye, then call Ro and put her on blast. Either she lets me sleep on her couch, or I bow out of the wedding. Not an unreasonable request, unlike what she expects from me. This *huge* thing she didn't even tell me about, choosing to let Constantine drop the bomb instead. She's in so much shit when I see her. So. Much. Shit.

"It's incredibly generous and kind of you, opening your home up, especially for a lengthy stay. Let me know how much I can give you for your hospitality."

"I don't want your money, Natalie." Somehow, his voice sounds even deeper. The comment is innocent, but the way he says it...

I would swear there's silent innuendo in those words. Like, he doesn't want my money, but he wants something else. Something my body is all tingly about. Which is ridiculous because I have never met this man. I know nothing about him, have no idea what he looks like. His voice, though—I know I like that.

"Have you reserved a rental car at the airport?" he asks.

"Yes, one with all-wheel drive, even though it's summer. Rosetta said there's a lot of uphill driving, and some roads are on the rough side. She hasn't given me directions, but I'm sure the rental will have GPS."

"Some of these small mountain towns don't show up in the satellite mapping. I'll send you detailed directions that'll bring you to the main road into town. There's an outpost there, and it's a good spot for us to meet. After that, you can follow me into town. And if you run into any confusion along the way, I'm just a phone call away."

"Wow, you really take this 'best man' job seriously."

His chuckle is warm and genuine, and I find myself biting my lip to hide a smile he can't see. "Helping people is always a pleasure for me, never a job."

"You must be single by choice." The comment is hanging in the air as fast as it entered my mind. "Sorry, *that* thought was supposed to stay *inside* my head. It's none of my business why you're not romantically attached."

Another deep and delicious chuckle comes through my phone's little speaker. "I'll tell you anything you want to know. Ask away."

"Tempting," I say, switching to handset mode so I can have his voice directly in my ear. "But I should probably save the personal questions until we've known each other longer than a few minutes via a long-distance phone call."

"I'm looking forward to that."

"Me too." Because he seems nice. That's all. Not because I've developed a sight-unseen insta-crush on some guy I know next to nothing about. "Oh, I think you have another call waiting," I say, when a muted double-beep sounds in the air between us. "I'll let you go so you can take it."

"It can go to voicemail—unless you need to get going."

"I don't. I'm a freelancer and work from home. Nobody's clocking my break time."

"Rosetta has shown me some of your work online. Impressive. You're a talented artist."

"Thank you."

Interesting. There are only two reasons Ro would talk about me to her fiancé's friend. One, because she needed to, since the man is offering to house me in his guest room. Or two, because she's got matchmaking in mind. I should hope it's the first option. *Should.*

"I wish I could say I know something about you," I say, "but when Ro and I talk, it's usually about her and Dak. Honestly, looking him in the eye, knowing the things I know, is going to be a struggle."

Constantine's rumbling laugh sends ripples of heat through me. "Do me a favor and don't share any of that information with me."

"So, you don't want to know about the dildo set Dak sent for her to—"

"Stop," he says through a choking laugh. "Show some mercy for the guy who *does* have to look Dak in the eye later."

Light laughter bubbles up from my chest as naturally as breathing. This is nice. I can't remember the last time I found it this easy to talk to someone new. And to a man who interests me—never. Probably because this is a zero-pressure situation. Even if I find Constantine attractive when I meet him, even if he feels the same and we have amazing chemistry, it wouldn't lead anywhere. We live thousands of kilometers apart. But a short-term fling while I'm out there... that's a possibility. If I can pause overthinking long enough to let it happen. Going to have to fight my nature for that to happen.

And now I've gotten *way* ahead of myself. "Do you work with Dak in his construction business?" I ask, wiggling down into my collection of throw pillows, some of which are midnight-blue velvet. Not that that's a sign or anything.

"I help with heavy lifting when he needs an extra pair of hands, but that's the extent of my involvement. My line of work is less grueling. I own a couple of businesses in town. *The Brew* is a coffeehouse in the daytime and a brewpub in the evening. My other business is related—it's a small-batch craft brewery called *Bullheaded Brew*."

"Wow, that's amazing. Were they turnkey businesses, or did you start them from scratch?"

"Scratch, but with a lot of community support. We're big on that in Fate's Falls."

"Rosetta always says it's incredible there. It's the one thing she finds time to slide into her otherwise X-rated conversations."

"Which you're not going to tell me about."

"No." I giggle. "Not until my last day there, anyway."

"Maybe you'll fall in love with the place like your cousin did, and you won't have a last day here."

"Ro fell in love with a person, not a place. She would've been happy to live anywhere with Dak." Hopefully, the envy in my voice isn't as obvious to Constantine as it is to my ears.

"He's completely dedicated to her also, if you had any doubts."

"I don't know him at all yet, but I don't have doubts. Ro has gushed about Dak since they were still in the long-distance talking stage. I'm shocked she's settling down with one person for the rest of her life, but she's madly in love with him, so I'm happy for her."

"What about you?" he asks. "Your cousin says you aren't involved with anyone. Are you in the 'single by choice' category like Rosetta used to be, with no desire to settle down?"

Again, why is Ro talking about me to her fiancé's buddy? It's one thing to tell him how I spend my workdays. Totally another to tell him how I'm *not* spending my free time.

"No, Ro and I were never in the same dating category. Even when we were little, we wanted different things. While her Barbie dolls were out doing the wild thing with wild things, mine always put on the white gown and walked down the aisle. And now she's walking down the aisle."

"And you're out doing the wild thing?"

The snort that bursts from me couldn't be less delicate if I tried. And I did it directly into the phone's microphone. Because, of course, I couldn't have done that while I had him on speaker.

"I take it that's a no," he says, chuckling. At least he didn't seem to mind my unfeminine noise.

Not that I should care, one way or another, but I'm relieved he didn't recoil. "No, I'm a diehard 'white picket fence' girl. I may never find Mr. Right, but I'd rather be alone than work my way through a string of Mr. Wrongs." A brief, awkward laugh involuntarily leaves me. "Not very optimistic or exciting, I know."

"Nothing wrong with choosing to wait for the right person."

"Oh—no, I'm not *waiting*, waiting. Not the big waiting. You know what I mean, right?" God, I hope so. I really don't want the deep-voiced man I'm going to be bunking with to think I'm a twenty-eight-year-old virgin, saving herself for *the one*. That'd really put a damper on any potential fling.

"I know what you mean, yes." No outright chuckle this time, but his tone definitely leans toward amusement.

"I should probably exit this conversation before I divulge any other embarrassing details of my life. But I'm looking forward to meeting you, and seeing everything Fate's Falls has to offer in the weeks I'm there. On that subject, is there a salon in town where I can make a hair and nail appointment for the wedding? I asked Ro, but like the hotel thing, she failed to answer. I know she's excited and busy and stressed, but all I'm going to be is stressed if I don't get some firm plans in place."

"I'll send the salon's number over with the driving directions. Need anything else? Dress shop? Shoe store?"

"I have my dress and shoes already, but do you know if any of the local shops sell lingerie?" I should tell him I'm asking because I haven't had a chance to buy my cousin a bridal shower gift, but when his deep rumble fills my ear again, I bite my tongue. I really like that sound.

Another call-waiting beep makes itself known on his end, and this time, he doesn't brush it off. "That's my manager at the coffeehouse calling from her personal number. She wouldn't call unless it's important, so I better take it."

"Of course. Thank you for all your help."

"We'll talk again soon, Natalie." The confidence in his smooth voice sends another little thrill through me.

Fortunately, he ends the call before my breathy "bye" slips out. I'm not a superficial person, but I should at least see a picture of the man before I work myself up too much. Except, I don't want Ro to send me a picture of Constantine. Pictures aren't always an accurate representation of who someone is. When I see him for the first time, I want it to be real. Personal.

When I woke up this morning, I was panicking about *only* having two days before flying out to British Columbia. Now, those two days are going to seem like the longest ever.

Chapter Two

CONSTANTINE

The addition Dakgorim is building is sided with wide wood planks milled from local trees. Today, he's installing windows and French doors that open toward what was once wild forest, but is now a manicured clearing, complete with a fenced-in area where his future children will play. The addition to his home, the one he now shares with Rosetta, is a nursery.

I'm happy for him, but envious. As full as my life is, it still has a void. One that can only be filled by a mate.

"Looking good," I call, from across the yard.

Neither the compliment nor the notice of my approach are necessary. Dak knows his craftsmanship is top-notch, and the big orc's hearing is even better than mine. Like Minotaurs and many other non-human creatures, orcs have heightened senses. We also share the need to live in secrecy.

Humans have lower levels of vision, hearing, strength, and various other qualities than most "monsters," yet they are our greatest threat.

Not all humans, of course. A number of them live among us in Fate's Falls, including Dak's mate, his soon-to-be bride. Gauging humans' intentions based on appearance was possible many centuries ago. Not now. They no longer favor pitchforks and torches for their attacks. If it were only fear because we're different, it could be managed. The real danger lies in humans' desire to capitalize on our species' differences, and technology has given them the means to be stealthy and targeted in their aggression.

To exist in peace requires hiding in places humans can't access—something nearly impossible in this day and age. Towns like Fate's Falls, shielded and governed by very old, powerful magic, allow us to hide in plain sight.

Grateful as I am for our safe haven, living within the protected boundaries makes it difficult to connect with new people. Not an issue for those who desire solitude or have already found their mate, neither of which applies to me. Platonic and casual relationships were enough until I reached prime breeding age. Now, the urge to be with my one true mate has made living without her very...uncomfortable.

Dakgorim doesn't pause when I reach him. He doesn't even look up, just continues working. Head down, focused, unstoppable. He's been that way all the years I've known him. But this project has him wound tighter than I've ever seen.

"At this rate, you'll be done before the wedding," I say as he lifts a large window into the framed opening with ease.

He grunts, narrowing his eyes at me. "I will finish before Rosetta's cousin arrives."

There's only one reason that would be necessary. "Do you need the room finished because Natalie's staying here?"

Dak's lips curl in a way only an orc's can. A terrifying expression, but I know it's involuntary, not intentional. "This room is for our child, not...*guests*." He says the last word as if it's unpleasant. To him, it probably is. Before Rosetta entered his life, Dak kept to himself. If I hadn't essentially bullied him into friendship years ago, it wouldn't have happened. "Rosetta wishes to use the nursery to tell her cousin about our unborn orcling. She would have been happy with the framed structure, but I will ensure it is completed."

No surprise there. Dak has worshipped the ground Rosetta walks on since she set foot in Fate's Falls. True to his orc nature, he's also very possessive of the ground under Rosetta's feet, the air she breathes, etcetera. Hence why I'm out here talking to him when he's not the person I need to speak with.

Since I *am* out here with him, I can't help replaying parts of my conversation with Natalie earlier. I cut Natalie off from going into detail, but I have a pretty good idea why Dak would've sent Rosetta a set of dildos. Orcs are much larger than humans. In every way, including the size of their cocks.

The same can be said of Minotaurs. As much as my hope for a relationship with Natalie makes me curious about how Dak and his fiancée handle their disproportionate anatomies, I can't broach the subject. Natalie and I will have to find our own way in the bedroom—if we get there at all.

Even though I know she's my mate, it's still possible she'll take one look at me and run as far away as possible.

"Did you come all the way out here to stare into the forest?" Dak's voice snaps me from my thoughts. He hasn't stopped working to speak to me, but his attention darts between the level he's checking and my face. "Perhaps you should sell that too-large house in town and have me build you a one-bedroom cottage with a nice view of the pine trees." It could be a legitimate offer, or Dak's particular brand of dry sarcasm. Likely a bit of both.

"I came out here to talk to Rosetta about her cousin."

Thick eyebrows rise over eyes so dark they're impossible to read. "She is in her workshop. I do not allow her in the construction area. Her safety is paramount, especially now."

We both know his use of *do not allow* isn't literal. Rosetta may be petite, but her attitude is far from small. If she wanted to hang around and watch him build the nursery, she would. Of course, then he'd stop working on the addition to build some sort of safety station to protect her from all the things he deems hazardous. That's probably why she abides his request to stay out. Well, that and the near-seamless way their dynamic fits together.

I've only taken a single step toward the large, rectangular outbuilding that houses Rosetta's metalworking shop and Dak's construction equipment when he says, "Your respect is appreciated."

Pivoting, I give him a nod. Even an orc's best man knows better than to approach his mate without permission. Formality out of the way, I continue on to the shop.

Because of the noisy machinery, a loud chime sounds and lights flash when I open the door. Safety precautions

Dak installed when Rosetta began doing her metalworking in here.

Rosetta kills the power at her workstation, sets her cutting tool down, and flips her safety visor up. "Hey, Constantine. What's up?"

"Your cousin contacted me this morning. By text. I responded by calling."

"Not surprised." She glances at my hands. "I don't know how guys like you and Dak use cellphones at all, since they're all made for human hands. One of your fingers takes up half the screen's width."

"I use a stylus for texting. But I called Natalie because I wanted to talk with her as directly as possible, so she'd feel more comfortable staying in my home." I would never use an ill-tempered tone with Dak's mate, but I do cross my arms across my chest. "A plan she wasn't aware of."

"Oh, yeah, about that..." She shrugs and raises her hands, palms up. "Oopsie?"

"Unconvincing."

"You're right. I totally avoided answering questions that might cause her to cancel her trip. She's been my best friend since we were born, and she's the only member of my family who'll be at my wedding. I couldn't risk it."

"You weren't concerned that having a man she's never met tell her she'll be living with him for two weeks might bring her plans to a screeching halt?"

"Any other man, yes. But I knew you'd have no problem wooing her."

"Convincing her, you mean."

"No, I meant *wooing* her." Rosetta moves away from the vise holding a strip of metal with three pieces of rebar protruding upward. She leans one hip against the end of the workbench and mimics my folded-arms stance. "I saw the way you looked at her picture on her website's bio page. There are plenty of beautiful females in Fate's Falls, and I've never seen you get moon-eyed over anyone. Hell, I've been here for a year and you've never gone on a single date, that I'm aware of."

"That's correct, I have not." And it's been a lot longer than a year.

"I knew it." She nods at the verification. "Tell me you didn't go home and immediately stalk Nat's socials."

"I didn't." I huff out a breath when she narrows her gaze. "Not immediately. I had to stop at the brewery and do some work first."

"Ha! I knew it."

"Natalie is very attractive."

The snorted laugh Rosetta makes is similar to Natalie's during our telephone conversation this morning. I found Natalie's adorable. Charming. Rosetta's has no effect on me whatsoever.

"Do you disagree?" I ask.

"Oh, no. She's beautiful. It's the way you said her name that made me chuckle. *Nat-a-lie*... each syllable drawn out, like it's the prettiest name you've ever had the privilege to say. All reverent and shit."

"It is a lovely name."

Rosetta removes the welding helmet and sets it aside. Her red hair sticks out in every direction, having long since escaped a bun, and she makes no attempt to smooth it. "Look, there's no denying you're the reigning Mr. Congeniality in Fate's Falls, but let's be real here, okay? Just between us girls," she winks, "you've got a little crush on my cousin, don't you?"

"I do not have a crush. I'm intrigued. At this point in my life, I should only be attracted to one woman."

"And you're attracted to a bunch? Look, I've been there. I used to have my eyes on lots of guys at the same time, so I'm not judging. But that won't sit well with Nat. Even short-term. She's not boring or a prude, but she is traditional. Definitely someone who wants to stay inside the white picket fence, not someone who plays the field. You're a good friend to Dak and me, and I like you, but I don't want Nat to get hurt. So, this is me asking you to look elsewhere, instead of at my maid of honor. In fact, I'll head into town now, before the dayshift ends at *The Brew*. I know Dela has a one-bedroom apartment, but she's a sweetheart. I bet she'll let Nat crash on her couch for a couple of weeks."

"No," I say, blocking her forward motion. Totally out of character for me, and the wide-eyed expression on Rosetta's face is enough to make me step aside immediately. "I apologize. And now I'm requesting you don't find other accommodations for your cousin."

"Give me a good reason not to. How do I know I can trust you with the closest thing I have to a sister?"

"Because when I said I should only be attracted to one woman, I meant that I am only *able* to be attracted to one woman. Once a Minotaur reaches a certain point of maturity, our biology demands we find our mate. I reached that age fifteen years ago, and haven't been attracted to anyone since. Believe me, I've tried, I've looked—a decade and a half is a long time to go without...companionship. I don't get to choose my mate; Minotaur pairings are governed by innate forces. By fate. I'm attracted to Natalie—and only to Natalie."

"Are you saying what I think you're saying? You think she's your fated mate? From looking at a picture?"

There's no way I'm telling her it began earlier than that. "Any doubts I had disappeared when I heard her voice."

For a moment, Rosetta covers her mouth with her hand. Then she shakes both out at her sides. "Shit, she's going to freak the fuck out."

"Because I'm a Minotaur."

"Well, yeah, that's part of it. I haven't told her there are non-humans here, or that I'm in love with an orc. All I said is that my parents disapprove of Dak because of his skin color. Which is not a lie," she says, raising her index finger. "But I think she's going to be okay with the whole 'monsters are real' jazz once she stops hyperventilating and meets everyone."

"Then why do you believe she'll freak out about being my mate? Both you and Natalie have told me she's a permanent, committed-relationship type of person. Wouldn't that make her inclined toward a positive response?"

"She wants a happily ever after, but she's planning to *choose* who she spends her life with, not be *told* she's someone's fated mate."

"Do you feel you chose Dak? That finding each other had nothing to do with fate and your mate bond?"

Though he's not one to engage in extended or deeply personal conversation, Dakgorim has stated a firm belief that fate led him to find Rosetta's online metalworks shop. At the time, he had no projects that required unique, hand-made metal fixtures, yet he searched the internet for such, anyway. And found Rosetta's creations—and his mate.

In front of me, Rosetta makes a sound that's part sigh, part harrumph, the noise accompanied by a narrowed gaze and hands on her hips. "This has nothing to do with Dak and me."

Meaning, I've made my point. But this isn't the time to gloat or tease. I need Rosetta's support, not her ire.

"Even if Nat is attracted to you," Rosetta continues, "she's only going to be in town for a couple of weeks. Boring as I think her life in Toronto is, she's a creature of routine. I had no issue packing up and changing venues, but I don't see her uprooting from everything she's known for twenty-eight years to stay here. Plus, it sucks that my parents are dicks and I may never speak to them again, but it's not even a sacrifice to me because I have my life with Dak. Nat, on the other hand, is super tight with her parents. There's no way she'd lie to them, or give them up—either or both of which she'd have to do if she moved her to be with you. I'm sorry, Constantine, but there's no way she can be your fated mate."

Arguing is pointless. But I know the truth. There's no way Natalie Somers *isn't* my fated mate.

Chapter Three

CONSTANTINE

The people who work in my businesses are incredibly good at their jobs, and my presence is rarely required. I hired Shay Winterlock when she moved to Fate's Falls. *The Brew* was relatively new back then, still in its first year of operation, and only a coffeehouse at that time. In the beginning, I worked in the business full-time. Didn't matter that I, the owner, was on-site and technically the manager. Shay quickly assumed the role. She saw ways to improve operations and forged forward without permission or assistance, tweaking things to make them more appealing, efficient, or profitable. She's a doer whose decisions always have a positive effect.

Fifteen years later, I still drop in at *The Brew* a couple days a week, but spend most of that time in the kitchen or back office. Shay and Dela keep the customer-facing side running like a well-oiled machine. My bulky presence behind the counter tends to be more of a hindrance than a help.

Today's visit isn't about offering to help or staying out of the way.

Mid-afternoon is a steady time. A continual but light flow of customers, nobody in a hurry, generally speaking. There are three people in line when I enter through the front door. A shapeshifter named Trace from the outpost, Razbunare, a vengeance demon who I'm sure is here to soak up Dela's presence more than he's here for the coffee, and Lexi, the little witch who owns *Every Witch Way*, an online sex-toy business that's earning a tidy residual income for many of Fate's Falls residents.

I give them all a casual wave as I pass, then head behind the counter toward Shay, where she's cleaning an espresso machine as if the equipment needs plague-level decontamination. "Did we have another malfunction since you called this morning?"

There's not much Shay can't handle without me, which is why I cut my call with Natalie short this morning, when Shay called for a second time. Our usual tech wasn't picking up when she tried him. She was this-close to asking one of the larger customers in line to carry the possessed piece of equipment out to the back alley.

"No. The new guy you got came by and fixed it. No problems since." The straight-lipped expression on Shay's face suggests there is a problem, even it it's unrelated to the earlier mechanical issue.

After a decade and a half, I'd say we're more than employer and employee. Friends on a level that includes mutual trust and concern, but not close enough to socialize or share our internal stuff. Not close enough that I feel comfortable asking what's wrong, even though it's obvious something is. Maybe she'll talk to Dela later. They seem to have become good friends since Dela moved to town seven months ago.

A glance over my shoulder confirms Dela has the customer traffic under control. Clearing my throat to prepare for the uncomfortable reason I'm here causes me to huff in a distinctly Minotaur way.

Shay's attention snaps up to my face. "You okay, boss?"

"Yes. No. I hope so."

Her green eyes open wide, all traces of irritation gone from her face. "This is a first. You're not one to hang around in the gray zone. I take it there's some way I can help, but you hate being in a position to ask for it."

"Exactly."

She waits a few beats, grinning when all I manage to get out is another bullish huff of breath. "You're going to have to tell me. I'm not a mind reader."

"But you are a seer, and that's the help I'm here to ask for."

Smile, gone. Green eyes, shuttered hard. "Then I can't help you."

"I know you don't like to use your magic—"

She cuts me off with a raised hand. "Remove the words 'like to' from that sentence. I *don't* use my magic. Period. By choice—my choice."

If anyone in town knows the reason Shay turned away from magic, I've never heard about it. "I apologize for overstepping." Seems like my day for that. Another damn huff escapes while I'm rubbing the back of my neck. Embarrassed as I am that my bullish nature is getting the best of me, the involuntary response appears to take the edge off of Shay's intensity.

"Let's finish this conversation in the office," she says, then cranes her neck to see around me, toward Dela. "I'll just be a few minutes."

"No problem," Dela says, as cheerfully as always.

Shaking my head at Shay, I wave off the opportunity of a private conversation. If I can't say it to her out here, it should probably remain unsaid, as my request should have. "No need, thank you. And I sincerely regret asking what I did. I've got something important coming up, and I'm in unfamiliar territory. Guess I just wanted a cheat code, to make sure I'm on the right path."

Shay gives a small laugh. "There are no cheat codes. Even if I used my powers, I might not get the answer to whatever your specific question is. I never know what part of someone's future I'll see when I touch them. But if you want to *talk*, run your concerns past me, I'll give you my unbiased opinion. That's a skill I'm always willing to share."

My turn to laugh now. Interesting as Shay's unbiased opinion about my situation might be, I'm not going there. "Appreciate it, thanks. But it's probably best I let things unfold however fate intends."

"Wise choice. No point fighting fate."

With every cell of my being telling me my mate will soon

be part of my life, I couldn't agree more. All I can do now is wait and hope Natalie feels the same way.

Two days later

CONSTANTINE

Since our first conversation two days ago, I've spent more time on the phone with Natalie than I have with everyone I know combined, probably for the past year, if not longer.

She replied to my emailed driving directions by saying how much she enjoyed talking to me, and suggested I call her again, anytime. Fortunately, I was alone when I read that message, because I celebrated the invitation with a bellowing rumble. Then wasted no time accepting the invitation. I called her later that day and we talked for an hour. About her art. My businesses. Conversation came easily and the minutes flew by. I only let her go when she sighed and said she had to buckle down and finish a commission piece so she could stay on schedule, adding that she was already stressed-out because she was running late.

If she were here, with our mate bond established, I would do everything within my power to ensure she never experienced stress. She wouldn't have to take on more work than she can comfortably accomplish. She wouldn't have to *work* at all. I would happily provide for all her needs, so she had time to create whatever she wanted, on her own timeline. And I would satisfy all of her intimate needs. Even without meeting her in person, I know we'll have chemistry in the bedroom. Fate wouldn't pair us if we weren't compatible in every possible way.

After saying goodbye at the end of our second conversation, I resisted the urge to call her again later that night. With her impending work deadline, the three-hour time difference, and knowing she's an early riser, I was surprised when her name lit my phone as I was settling in bed for the night. Talking to her while I lay naked in the dark made it impossible to keep my hand off my cock, which hardened the moment I heard her voice. I ended up taking our conversation to the living room, with all the lights on, to keep the growling need out of my voice. Even after an hour of conversation about our favorite foods, recreational activities, and other innocent topics, I was still hard for her.

The following day brought a couple more phone calls. The first one, brief and casual. The nighttime one leaned into flirtatious territory—on both our parts. Subtle comments. Suggestive meanings. Though it wasn't a long conversation, it ended with a deep rumble I couldn't contain and I'm sure she heard. And from her end, a breathy goodnight that left me no choice but to take the edge off after the call. I've never come so fast in my life.

This morning, I awoke to a text she'd sent in the wee hours, after checking in for her red-eye to Kelowna.

Natalie

Sitting in the terminal at Pearson with my jumbo latte! My flight leaves in two hours. I should probably try to keep this message low-key and casual, but I'm just tired and wired enough to say things I shouldn't. I can't wait to meet you in person. Is that saying too much? If it is, just tell me. Save me from making things awkward. (Or more awkward.) ☺

She was in the air with her phone powered off by the time I saw the message. I replied immediately, telling her it's not awkward and I feel the same way about her. Then I sent a separate text to let her know Rosetta and I would meet her at the outpost I'd noted in my directions.

Rosetta wasn't part of my original plan. Having her there is insurance. A way to soften the shock that might cause Natalie to get into her rental car and drive straight back to the airport after seeing me. Because I don't know what I'd do if that happened.

Natalie texted when she landed; just a quick one to let me know she was safely on the ground and headed my way. No more mention of her excitement to see me, but the triple blushing face emojis were a good sign. Women have a definite advantage when it comes to emojis.

"You're awfully quiet over there," Rosetta says from the passenger seat of my pickup truck, where we're parked at the outpost.

The outpost sits just outside of Fate's Falls and is staffed by shapeshifters. They predominantly assume human form while manning the station. Most of the time, their job consists of coordinating deliveries with our in-town drivers, since all mail and packages are processed through the outpost. Sometimes the outpost staff act in a park ranger capacity, redirecting travelers who've taken a wrong turn on the mountain roads. They never have to act in a security capacity because only those approved by the Oracle are able to pass the boundary. Those who aren't won't even see the road leading into town.

"You're quiet too," I say, keeping my eyes on the empty road ahead.

"I guess we're both nervous about Nat's reaction. Maybe I should've met her here by myself, instead of with you."

That would've required Rosetta making the offer, which she didn't, but now isn't the time to point out her lack of consideration where Natalie's travel plans are concerned.

"I'm surprised you didn't pick Natalie up at the airport," I say instead, though it's another criticism that's been on my mind since Rosetta told me her cousin was coming to Fate's Falls for the wedding, and that she hadn't disclosed we're a town full of non-humans.

"Because I want the baby news to happen at my house, and I knew I wouldn't be able to hold it in during the long drive, during which Nat would undoubtedly ask a million questions."

"Understandable. I've talked to her a lot in the past couple of days, but always making sure I steer the conversation away from anything that could lead to questions I don't want to answer honestly until we're face-to-face."

Rosetta gives a small, commiserative smile. "Soon it'll all be out in the open."

"And you firmly believe Natalie will accept everything she's about to discover?"

"If I didn't, I wouldn't have asked her to take a five-hour flight across the country, followed by an hours-long drive into the mountains to a town she wouldn't have been able to see or enter." Rosetta's mouth twitches from side to side, then she sighs. "Okay, I haven't fully disclosed everything to *you* either. I consulted the Oracle before I called Nat. I had to know if she'd be allowed past the boundary to attend my wedding."

"That was very responsible of you."

She rolls her eyes. "I'm not *completely* self-absorbed."

"Of course not," I say, though it's not a completely honest opinion. Rosetta merrily goes about her life without pausing to consider others, the exception being Dak. She has always prioritized his happiness. That gets her a pass in my books. "With the wedding and baby stuff, taking that preemptive measure with the Oracle could easily have fallen through the cracks."

She narrows her gaze at me. *"Riiight."* Self-absorbed though she may be, she's still damn perceptive when she pays attention. She knows I'm being consciously neutral. Sucking up, if you will.

"What did the Oracle say?" I withhold the other question I want to ask—why she didn't tell me this information sooner. As in, during our conversation in her workshop two days ago, when I revealed that Natalie is my mate.

"The Oracle said there are no visitor passes for Fate's Falls. For a being as old as time itself, she's pretty snappy. Doesn't miss a beat."

"What else did the Oracle say?"

"What makes you think there was more?" Rosetta's intentional torment and obvious amusement in dishing it causes my tail to whip upward. She glances at it in the space between us in the front seat. "I always forget you have a tail, but not during this little blip of a trip."

Tail movement is primarily involuntary, and more noticeable when emotions are heightened. Everything has been running higher since I spoke with Natalie. All of my instinctual Minotaur traits are amplified.

When my only response is a bullish huff, Rosetta laughs, at which my tail whips sharply to the right.

"It's pretty. So floofy at the end."

"It is not *pretty*. Or... *floofy*."

"Chill, Constantine, your masculinity is intact; I was only talking about your tail. But you know what?" She twists on her seat, tapping her cheek while her gaze wanders over my clenched-jaw expression. "Now that I'm stuck in this truck with you, getting a good, up-close look, your hair is pretty, too. So shiny. Looks like you don't have a single split end on those long, wavy locks. Tell me your beauty secrets. Do you deep condition?"

There's no withholding yet another gruff release of breath, this one louder than the last. "Is this how you speak to Dakgorim?"

"God, no. He'd lose his shit. But I have told him he's cute plenty of times. And sexy, of course."

I can't imagine the word *cute* sits well with the massive, permanently scowling orc, and I have no desire to lead her into further conversation about his *sexiness*.

"Oh, look, there's a car coming!" Rosetta sits up straight,

pointing at the road beyond the windshield. "That has to be Nat."

The minor irritation Rosetta stirred up vanishes, replaced by a buzz of anticipation. With each second, my heart beats faster, harder. My body and soul know my mate is nearby. My wait is almost over.

Chapter Four

NATALIE

Thank goodness Constantine sent detailed directions. He told me some of the small mountain towns don't show up on the satellite map and he was right. There were no results when I typed "Fate's Falls" into my rental car's GPS. Literally none.

I love Rosetta like a sister and a best friend, but Constantine's number is the only useful information she's given me for this trip. Her text replies have fallen into three categories: brief, evasive, and emoji. Not a big deal if I were back home, going about my normal, predictable life. But I'm here, thousands of kilometers from my safe little studio apartment on the third floor. I'm driving up an actual mountain, on a narrow road bordered by trees as tall as my apartment building. Maybe taller.

If I took a wrong turn or had some sort of freak automotive failure, I'd be screwed. There hasn't been a single town since I began my ascent. But there have been plenty of wildlife warning signs. Deer. Moose. Bears. No thank you to those and all others. I'm not a fan of big furry things.

So, yes, I'm a bit peeved with my cousin for leaving me hanging. For potentially putting my life in danger. Even so, I'm still relieved she's going to be there with Constantine when I arrive.

I haven't stopped thinking about my phone calls with him. It's likely I've built our connection up in my head, made more of it than it actually is. Rationally, I blame my recent lack of dating. Of course, I'd respond to a friendly, helpful, deep-voiced man. I'm only human.

Still, we spent hours on the phone the past couple of days. He called multiple times. We texted too. They weren't just casual conversations between two people whose best friends are getting married. Honestly, we barely even talked about Ro and Dak. We talked about my art, his businesses, our likes and dislikes for lots of day-to-day stuff. Lots of getting to know each other. Yet, even from the first call, it felt as if I already know him.

The way we connected so naturally... that's how I've always expected a real relationship to feel. The long-term, there's no doubt it's going to last forever, kind.

I definitely need to leave my apartment more. Interact with people, face-to-face. Put myself out there, in the dating trenches, until I find somebody I'm comfortable with. Someone who'll be easy to talk to *and* give me tingly feelings. Somebody like Constantine.

Sighing, I glance at my phone where it's sitting in the dashboard mount I brought along. According to the route I manually programmed into the map app, the Fate's Falls' outpost should be directly ahead.

"Continue on this road for five-hundred meters, then your destination is on the right." By the time the artificial voice has finished her instructions, there's a single-story building within view.

I assumed it'd be a small gatehouse at the edge of town. I assumed wrong. The closer I get, the larger I realize it is. The front portion of the building looks like a log cabin—like an old-time outpost—but the rear section is sided with metal and there are two large bay doors, the kind you'd see on a warehouse. This isn't just a security guard's station for a gated community.

Maybe I'm in the wrong place. Seems unlikely, given the specific directions I received, but out here in the middle of nowhere, it kind of feels like anything is possible.

Heart racing, I pull into the parking lot, the gravel crunching under my tires as I park across from the only other vehicle in the lot—a large, dark, four-door pickup truck. With its tinted windows and the sunlight shining in my eyes, I can't make out the passengers in the front seat of the cab. I hold my foot on the brake pedal and keep the engine running.

My pulse kicks even higher as the truck's passenger door opens. Then everything in the world is right because my cousin is running across the parking lot, waving her arms, calling my name. I put the car in *park* and turn off the engine, hopping out as she reaches the driver's door of my rental.

"You're here!" Squealing, she pulls me into a hug before I can even close the car door, bouncing me around in a semicircle before releasing me and standing back, still holding my hands. "I didn't realize how much I missed you, but holy shit, I've missed you!"

"You've been too busy being in love to miss me, which I'm very happy about, and I'm sure your parents will be, eventually, too."

The twist of her previously smiling lips tells me I should've left her parents out of this reunion moment.

"Sorry. Forget I mentioned them. The next couple of weeks are all about you," I say, checking her over, head to toe, then back again. "Mountain air, love, and constant boinking agree with you, Ro. You're practically glowing."

A laugh lighter than the brilliant sunshine overhead floats from her fresh smile. "I have literally never been happier. And every day when I wake up, I'm even happier than the day before. I didn't know life could be like this."

I should be overjoyed for her, not overflowing with jealousy. Green is not a good color for me. I'll get over it. A deep-voiced distraction would help, though. "Is Constantine just going to wait in the truck?" I ask, attempting to twist around to face the vehicle that's now behind me. "I know you're going to think this sounds silly, but we've talked a lot the past few days, and I'm excited to meet him in person."

Rather than let me shift position, Ro blocks me. "It's not silly at all, and I know he's super excited about meeting you, too, but there's something I need to tell you before he comes over."

"What is it? God, Ro, you should see your face. It must be horrible. Is he—" *No.* I refuse to say any of the superficial words aloud. "Is his great personality compensating for something beyond his control? It has to be something external if you think you have to prepare me for it. You wouldn't have me staying at his house if he's a monster."

Ro makes a strangled sound, her fair complexion burning bright red. "Boy, do you know how to pick the words." Shaking her head, she retrieves her phone from her jeans' pocket, swipes and taps a few times, then takes a deep breath. "First, I'll show you a picture of my fiancé."

"Seriously? You're going to dangle that mysterious comment, then leave me hanging while you show me a picture of your fiancé?" This is getting weirder by the minute. I already know Dak's not a garden-variety white guy, otherwise her parents wouldn't have taken issue with his skin color.

Constantine must be the same nationality as her fiancé. Though, why she thinks she needs to ease me into it is beyond me. There's not a racist bone in my body. She knows that. Probably better than anyone.

I can't help cracking a smile when she hands me the phone, displaying what's obviously a Halloween party picture. "He's really tall and built like a brick shithouse— definitely your type. It's great that you found someone with a fun-loving personality to match yours. But why aren't you in costume, too?"

"I'm not in costume because he's not in costume." Her expression is stone-cold serious when I look up from the image. "He's an orc. For real."

"Very funny, Ro."

"Scroll backward and forward. You'll see."

There's no way she's serious. She's setting me up for something.

"Nice try. No matter how much you rave about it, I do

not want to see a picture of his dick. I'm happy to accept your word for it being enormous."

"You have to see it to truly believe it, but you're just going to have to take my word for it because there are no pictures of Dak's dick." She makes a swiping motion with her finger. "Scroll."

"I just flew across the country, then drove up a damn mountain. I'm exhausted. Too drained to joke around. Can we please just go into town so I can clean up and relax? We can play your 'I'm marrying a big green monster' game later."

"Just scroll," she says, sighing. "Please."

"Fine." Since I'm already expecting more of the man-in-costume pics, it doesn't surprise me when that's what I see. Except, there are a lot. Like, *a lot.*

Based on the backgrounds and Ro's various outfits, the pictures span multiple seasons. Her clothes range from her shop coveralls to jeans and sweaters, a puffy parka, shorts and tiny tanks, and plaid pajamas. There's even one where they're both wearing dressier clothes—Ro in a body-hugging purple dress and him in black slacks and a dress shirt. Dozens of photos, and in all of them, he's green. Literally green. Head, hands, arms...green. Then there's his flat, inhuman nose and distinctly pointy ears. Eyes so dark they appear completely black.

"I don't understand," I say, meeting her eyes. "This isn't a joke? How can it be anything other than a joke?"

"The world we live in is home to many species of sentient beings. Some of them can pass as human and choose to live in the mainstream. Those that look different have to live in secret, sometimes in towns like Fate's Falls, where they're protected from outside threats."

"This is insane, Ro. Either you're playing the biggest joke of all time on me, or you've wandered past the edge of sanity, and I need to get you off this mountain and into therapy."

"I'm perfectly sane, I promise. And not joking. Not lying." She takes the phone from my trembling hand and stuffs in her pocket, then pulls me into a hug. "Maybe I shouldn't have brought you out here. I could've told you I'd gotten married after the fact. I could've kept everything from you for the rest of your life. If you want to turn around and go back home, I'll understand."

I ease back from her embrace so I can look at her. Inspect her. Ro has never had a good poker face, mostly because she doesn't bother lying. She's as transparent as they come. *Transparent.* I gasp, covering my mouth. "Are invisible people real?"

"Um...maybe? There are none in Fate's Falls, but it's not like we have one of every flavor on the monster menu."

"You call them monsters? That doesn't sound politically correct. Kind of seems like it'd be a derogatory slur."

"Are you saying you believe me?" she asks, ignoring my question about whether it's politically correct to call non-human species monsters. Her delusions are rubbing off on me.

Now *I'm* the one who needs therapy. "I don't know what I believe."

"That's okay. This is a lot to take in." Clasping both my hands, she nods. Gives me a gentle smile. "Do you want to see for yourself? In person. Not pictures on my phone."

"See what? The monsters?" The laugh that bursts from me sounds like a crazed cackle. "Who should we see first? Bigfoot? A werewolf? Your *orc* fiancé?"

"How about a Minotaur?"

My snickering lips snap shut. Eyes wide, my blood flowing hot and cold at the same time, I turn toward the deep voice coming from behind me. "You," I whisper. That's all I can get out while standing face-to-face with a hulking creature who definitely isn't human. But his voice... "Constantine?"

"Yes, Natalie, it's me."

It really is him. But how is it possible? Everything inside me says yes, that's the man from the call. The man I've been thinking about nearly every waking minute for the past two days. The urge to go straight into his arms is overwhelming, as if that's where I belong. Him being a hulking monster with horns and hooves doesn't even bother me. Why doesn't it bother me?

"I think she's going into shock," Ro says, wrapping her arm around my waist firmly. "We should head over to your place so she can lie down."

"Good idea." His amber eyes stay locked with mine. At the end of his wide, flat nose that leans toward being a bull-like snout, his black nostrils flare.

Is he...scenting me? Does he like the way I smell? God, I probably reek after a day full of traveling. Maybe Minotaurs don't find sweat distasteful the way humans do? I have so many questions, the main one being why I'm struggling to stay away from him when all I want is to be wrapped up in his massive arms.

"Come on, Nat. I'll drive your rental car. Constantine

will meet us there. Then we can talk about everything while you're comfortable and safe."

My legs could be steadier and my pulse is still hammering, but I'm not on the verge of fainting. I wriggle free of my cousin's hold and take two tentative steps toward Constantine. "You're really not a man?"

"Not a human man, no."

"But a man," I say, rather than ask. Because there's no question that he's *manly*.

Taller than any human male I've been around. The blue button-up shirt he's wearing looks stretched to its absolute limits across shoulders broader than a football player in pads. His jaw is wide and strong, and his brown skin definitely looks like short, velvety fur. Except on his hands, which are huge. As in, he could crush me with one of them, probably without batting his big, amber eyes. Or, he could do much better things with those big hands. With those long, thick fingers.

A wave of heat washes through me. I very much need to get a grip. "I've been on the go for over ten hours, and I feel grimy from traveling. I could really use a cold drink, a comfortable chair, and a hot shower, in no particular order."

Ro steps to my side, her blue eyes opening wide. "You're okay with...everything? With Constantine being a Minotaur and me marrying an orc? You just flipped a switch and went from borderline hysteria to cool as a cucumber?"

"I definitely don't feel cool." I'm looking at Constantine when I say it. Flirting with him, whether he can read between the lines or not. Maybe I am still a little hysterical. "But yes, I'm okay," I say, turning my attention to my cousin. "You're healthy and happy. I'm sure I'll probably freak out a little—or maybe a lot—when I'm surrounded by all the different types of non-humans, but at the end of the day, they're still people, right? As long as they're not dangerous, their appearance shouldn't matter."

"Out here," Constantine gestures around us, "there are no guarantees of safety. All creatures are potentially dangerous, monster and human alike. But inside the boundaries of Fate's Falls and other places like it, violence and intentional harm are impossible. The land is protected by very old magic, and only those who are pure of heart and have reason to be there can enter. Everyone within the boundary is safe."

"Monsters and magic and secret towns only selected people can enter..." I push down the burgeoning hyena-like laugh bubbling inside me. "None of this is possible. I'm having the wildest dream of my life."

"You're not dreaming." Ro's hand against mine is warm, solid. "This is all very real, and I'm so happy you're here."

"As am I," Constantine says, his wide, black lips curving upward as he holds my gaze.

Definitely the wildest dream ever. I hope I don't wake up too soon.

Chapter Five

CONSTANTINE

"Maybe I should wake her up and say goodbye before I leave." Outside the closed guest room door, Rosetta taps her toes on the hardwood floor. She told me Natalie fell asleep almost immediately on the short ride from the outpost to my house. No conversation whatsoever. Natalie didn't ask for additional details. She simply got in the passenger seat of her rental car, closed her eyes, and passed out.

Unsurprising, after a long day of traveling and the revelations we dropped on her. She remained asleep after Rosetta parked in my driveway. After I opened the car door. She slept through Rosetta's gentle urgings that they'd arrived at my house. Stayed asleep while I carried her inside. *That* was concerning. Enough so that I called the doctor to pop by and check on her.

All vitals good, the kindly telepath assured us. A quick peek inside Natalie's mind confirmed plenty of brain activity, though the doctor wouldn't disclose what was going through Natalie's unconscious mind. Doctor-patient confidentiality applies, even though Natalie didn't know she was under medical supervision. Dr. Schaefer agreed with exhaustion and acute stress as likely causes for Natalie's current deep-sleep state, advising us to let her rest as long as necessary for her body and brain to catch up.

"The doctor said to let her wake naturally," I remind Rosetta, who has been impatiently waiting it out in my living room for the past two hours. "She said forcing Natalie awake could add additional trauma."

"Then I either go home and you call me as soon as she wakes up, or I can tell Dak to come here and wait with me, even if it's all night. You have that other guest room we can use, right?" She wiggles her ginger eyebrows.

I narrow my gaze at her. "Dak is always welcome in my home, as are you, but surely you can keep your bodies separated for one night."

"Wrong-o. Sex with your mate is like oxygen. Gotta have it."

It has been fifteen years since I engaged in any type of sexual activity. Thinking about physically joining with Natalie has my cock thickening to uncomfortable proportions, which is neither convenient nor appropriate right now. "I'll call you when Natalie is awake."

"You don't think she'll freak out when she comes to in a strange house with a Minotaur for a host, and I'm nowhere to be found?"

"I'm not a stranger, and much more than a host. I'm confident she'll be okay."

Stepping away a stride, Rosetta takes stock of me. "You still think she's your mate."

"I know she is." Sitting idly in the truck earlier was impossible because the pull toward Natalie was so strong. Waiting outside her bedroom is almost a physical struggle.

"Okay, so she's *your* mate. What if she doesn't feel the same way about you? Are you going to be able to stay cool?"

The fur on the back of my neck bristles. "I'm a Minotaur, not an animal. Natalie is safer with me than anywhere on earth. There's literally nothing I wouldn't do to ensure she's safe and happy. My need to protect and care for her is ingrained."

"That's what I wanted to hear," Rosetta says. "And she must trust you too, since she still agreed to stay here, even after she saw that you're not human."

That's because some part of Natalie feels our fated connection. Whether she accepts it—and chooses to stay in Fate's Falls—remains to be seen. But that's not a conversation to have with her cousin.

"Okay, but she may wake up groggy and confused." Rosetta sighs. "Maybe I should just stick around. I'll call Dak and tell him that's my plan."

"Or you could record a short video for her to watch, telling her everything is okay and you'll be back as soon as she needs you."

"Ooh, good idea." Taking her phone from her pocket, Rosetta motions down the hall, toward the living room. "I'll go do that, then head home."

"I would give you a ride, but—"

"No, I'd hate for Nat to wake up completely alone," she says. "Dak will pick me up."

I t's wrong to be happy when the front door closes after Rosetta's departure. I should do whatever is necessary to provide comfort for my mate, and having her cousin here would undoubtedly increase her comfort level. But I can't help wanting Natalie all to myself.

After a couple of quick calls to both businesses, letting them know I'll be unavailable for anything less than an extreme emergency, I pour a glass of cold water and head quietly to the guest room door. The sun has disappeared below the treetops, and I don't want Natalie to awaken in total darkness. That's the reason I give myself for opening her bedroom door and entering without consent.

Her scent fills my head the moment I step inside. Light and natural, like fresh rainfall. Whatever travel griminess she felt before falling asleep is unnoticeable and irrelevant to my senses.

I inhale deeply and hold it. Breathing her in this way isn't enough, but it will have to do for now. I tread as lightly as possible, in this moment cursing my choice to forgo carpeting in the guest rooms. Even my most careful steps cause noise; hooves against hardwood will do that.

"Constantine?" Her sleepy voice floats in the darkness.

"It's me. You're in my guest room. I didn't mean to disturb you. I was going to turn on a night-light so didn't wake up surrounded by darkness. Rosetta had to go home, but she'll come back whenever you call her."

"You're not disturbing me, and you can turn on the light. The normal light, not a night-light."

"Do you remember meeting me in the parking lot?" The silence that follows hangs heavy, broken by the sound of my tail swishing against the back of my pants. At least she can't see it. Yet.

"I remember," she says, finally. Softly. "You're a Minotaur, and I'm in a magically protected town full of creatures I'd rather not refer to as monsters, since my cousin is marrying one, and I don't think of you as one."

That's good. Very good. My hand is on the table lamp, but I still don't press the switch. "Before you got in the car with Rosetta, you thought you were dreaming."

"It was a lot of unbelievable information to take in all at once, but I'm okay. Really." Her eyes find mine the instant I turn on the light. Then she smiles, and it brightens the room more than any light source could. "Hi. See? Not freaking out even a little bit."

"I wouldn't blame you if you did, but I'm glad you're feeling more relaxed." I set the water on the bedside table. "Thought you might wake up thirsty."

"Thank you." The blanket Rosetta draped over her falls away as Natalie shifts to a seated position with her back against the headboard. Her delicate chin tips up while she takes a long drink.

Watching her, even in the simple, innocent action of quenching her thirst, stirs the urge to provide for her needs. Food, water, and shelter. Also, her intimate needs. She feels our connection—I know she does. Her scent changed when she heard my voice. Then changed again when our eyes met.

Every breath I take brings more of her sweet arousal to

my nose. I would bury my face between her legs and lick her to completion right now if she consented.

Her eyes go wide at the huff that rumbles from me. "Are you okay?"

"Yes. I control my Minotaur traits to the best of my ability, but nature has its way at times. The bullish huffing, snorting, and tail swishing are involuntary physiological responses. Frightening as they may seem, I promise you'll never be in danger with me, with or without the protection spell over Fate's Falls."

"I'm not scared," she says, rising from the bed. "There's this part of my brain that keeps lighting up with 'this can't be real!' warnings, but it's only a small part, surprisingly."

"I'm very happy to hear it." Standing by the bedside table already put me in close proximity, but now that she's in my personal space, looking up at me, it takes all my willpower not to touch her, especially with her scent filling my nose. Foolishly, I breathe deeper. The effect is as expected—my cock hardens further, straining painfully inside my jeans, and another animalistic huff pushes from my nostrils. "I apologize—"

"Don't. That sound doesn't bother me. Well, it does bother me a little, but not in a negative way." Even in the low lighting, the soft-pink coloring her cheeks is visible. "I'm not turned off by the sound. At all." The rapid fluttering of her eyelashes, the way she pulls her bottom lip between her teeth, then licks her lips afterward... She's turned on. If her other body language wasn't proof enough, her scent is. Her arousal is undeniable; so heady, I can almost taste it.

I haven't been sexually intimate with a human woman before, but Natalie's biological responses seem well attuned to mine. The temptation to pull her against me is almost too great to resist.

"Are you hungry?" I ask, forcing my mind to places other than the big bed just a few feet away, where I could spread my mate's legs and devour her. "My kitchen is fully stocked, and I'm a passable cook for most things. Or I can take you out instead, if you'd like to get a glimpse of the town. We can order in, pick something up, or I'm sure your cousin would love to have you over. Whatever you prefer."

If her beautiful smile is any indication, Natalie doesn't seem to mind my obvious, overachieving desire to please her. "I'll send Ro a quick message to know I'm awake and not freaking out, but I'd rather stay in this evening, if that's okay with you. I don't expect you to cater to me, though. Pretend I'm not even here."

"That would be impossible, nor is it something I want to do. Catering to you anytime would be my pleasure." Coming on too strong? There's nothing I can do about it if I am. Doesn't matter that she hasn't consented to being my mate. She is mine, and I'm committed to her. I couldn't turn it off if I wanted to.

"In that case, I'm starving. Not picky either. I'll gobble up whatever you put in front of me."

There's no preventing my nostrils from flaring. Not while I'm picturing Natalie on her knees, lapping at my cock. It's too big for her to take into her mouth, but the thought of her exploring every rigid inch, sliding the tip of her tongue over my skin, tasting the milky cum that leaks out...

"Would you mind if I grab a shower first?" Her question snaps me out of my desire-induced imaginings.

"Not at all." A bit of solitary time to pull myself together would be good. "The guest bathroom is directly across the hall, and you'll be the only one using it during your stay, so feel free to make yourself at home. There's plenty of empty space in the cabinets if you want to settle in."

"That's incredibly generous, thank you."

"My home is your home." A statement truer than she's aware, but I'll let her think it's spoken from a place of hospitality. For now. With a nod, I make my way out of her bedroom and head for the entryway, where I left her larger piece of luggage after bringing it in from the car.

While I'm reaching for the suitcase, my phone buzzes in my pocket. A quick check reveals two texts from the evening manager at *The Brew*. Not emergency issues, but questions I should respond to sooner rather than later, so I do.

Once work is out of the way, I collect Natalie's bag and head to her bedroom.

The shower is running behind the closed bathroom door. The guest room door is open wide, so I enter and turn to the right, toward the closet. I set her suitcase beside the dresser, then pivot to leave—exactly as Natalie zips into the room, wearing nothing but a towel.

She shrieks, literally jumping on the spot, clutching the towel tight and causing it to rise higher up her legs—and it was already at the top of them.

"Sorry." I point at the newly deposited luggage. "I heard the shower running and thought it was safe to drop off your large suitcase. I didn't bring it in earlier because I didn't want to risk waking you with any unnecessary noise."

"Oh." That's it. That's all she says while taking stock of me. Batting her eyelashes. Licking her lips.

Knowing I should keep my eyes on her face doesn't mean I do. My gaze drops to the bottom edge of the white terry cloth where it's skimming the apex of her thighs.

She hasn't showered yet and gods help me, I can't resist inhaling. I'm not even trying to hide that I'm breathing her in. The scent of her arousal hasn't waned in the minutes since I left the room. She smells delicious, like the only thing I want to taste for the rest of my life.

Pretty sure my cock has never been harder than it is right now.

"Are you—are we—" The blush on her face deepens. Spreads downward, to the base of her neck, to the swell of cleavage above the towel. "Never mind me, I'm just mentally overloaded and imagining things."

"You're not imagining things."

"How can you say that when you don't know what I was referring to?" Her voice is so soft. Not in a shy way, just beautifully soft.

I grip the back of my neck with one hand, rubbing at the tension there. If I say too much, too soon, I could ruin everything. Maybe irreparably.

"I should get in the shower before I run out all the hot water without getting a drop on me," she says, when I fail to answer her question. "I just came to grab my carry-on bag so I didn't have to put my travel clothes back on." She angles her chin down, then meets my eyes again. "Not sure how I'm going to carry it without losing my towel, though."

My gaze follows hers to the small bag beside the bed. "I'll get it for you. I'll put it outside the bathroom door. You can pull it in after I'm safely out of this part of the house."

"I'm not worried about my safety around you." A laugh

bubbles out of her lips and she shakes her head. "That's ridiculous, right? We've talked on the phone a lot the past couple of days, and you're not a *complete* stranger, but…" Again, her gaze travels over me. "You're not human. And you're massive. You have horns on your head and you could probably crush my skull in one of your huge hands. Yet, here I am, not only staying in your home, but standing in front of you, nearly naked. And I'm not even the tiniest bit afraid. What does that say about me?"

"Do you want an honest answer, or casual reassurance?" Best way to know what direction to go is to ask.

"Honest answer."

"You might want to sit," I say, gesturing at the bed.

"I'm visiting a magically protected town filled with monsters and I'm talking to a Minotaur, who I'm interested in, and not in a general curiosity way. At this point, I doubt there's anything you can say that's going to shock me."

We're about to find out. "The ease you feel around me is because you're my mate."

"I'm sorry," she shakes her head, "what did you say?"

"In each Minotaur's lifetime, they have one true, fated mate. You are mine. And while humans aren't bound by the same forces, some do experience the mating bond with species different from their own."

"And you think that's what I'm feeling? You think we," her index finger wags back and forth between us, "two people who've literally just met, are destined to be together?"

"Yes."

"You say that as if you're dead serious."

"Very much alive, and entirely serious, yes."

"Okay, maybe I do need to sit down." One hand on her forehead and the other clutching her towel, she takes a few small steps toward the bed and sits on the edge, unaware that doing so shifts the towel even higher up her hips.

The low lighting in the room casts enough shadow to prevent me from truly seeing between her legs. Thank the gods for that.

Her hand drops from her head to her lap, where she adjusts the towel, maximizing what little shielding it provides. "I really don't know what to say."

"You don't need to say anything, Natalie. Not now, not at any time. I'm here for you, to give you whatever you need. As your mate, I do mean that literally, so never feel shy or awkward to tell me what I can do for you." I wait for her to look up at me. "I'll never pressure you to do or feel anything. I promise you that."

"Okay," she says in that soft voice that makes me want to wrap her in my arms and never let go.

"I'll be in the kitchen whenever you're ready to eat."

There are no defenses shuttering her expression. Her eyes swim with questions and emotions, her lips forming only the faintest smile. "I'll be there soon."

Nodding, I leave her alone in the room, fighting every instinct to do the opposite.

Chapter Six

NATALIE

Despite my earlier comment about using all the hot water, it didn't run out during my shower, even though it may have been the longest one I've ever taken. I've always done my best thinking in the shower. Not this time. There's too much crowding my brain. I can't imagine how shriveled I'd be after a shower long enough to sort through everything I've learned since arriving.

My texts to Ro didn't prove helpful, either. She answered my first message immediately, relieved that I'm awake, mentally sound, and sticking around to be her maid of honor. As soon as I changed the subject to Constantine's "you're my fated mate" confession, the conversion changed. Ro sent a big-eyes emoji, followed by a shrug emoji, said we'd talk about it in person tomorrow, then ghosted me.

Talking tomorrow would be fine if I weren't bunking *here*. Sure, I could hide out in my bedroom for the rest of the night. I don't *have* to join him in the kitchen. I'm hungry, but I'm not going to die if I go without eating for one night. If I didn't want to seem totally rude, I could text him and say I'm going to bail on food because I'm exhausted. A reasonable excuse.

That'd only buy me tonight. Tomorrow's Saturday. It's possible he doesn't work on the weekend, or he took the day off to be a good host. What am I going to do if he's out there in the morning? Hole up in my bedroom until Ro finds time to come rescue me? And rescue me from what? Someone who seems perfectly nice and totally accommodating?

Not just nice and accommodating. He's a hunky Minotaur who thinks I'm his fated mate. I may not feel the certainty of a fated-mates bond, but I do feel something. And lots of it. Attraction like I've never experienced—for a man who's not human. I knew there was a spark from the first time we talked on the phone. Our easy connection was a turn-on, even without knowing what he looked like. With each call, each minute spent talking, the connection grew. So did the sparks.

I came here planning to act on those sparks if opportunity presented. To break out of my overthinking mode and have some sexy-times fun during this two-week break from my plodding life.

Well, opportunity has certainly presented. Constantine didn't make a move on me, but the "you're my mate" thing should be an open invitation to get down to it.

Except I don't think it is.

I've never met a human male who'd balk at a quick fling

with a predetermined expiration date. No-strings-attached, commitment-free sex is every human man's dream.

But Constantine isn't human. The concept of having one true, fated mate in a lifetime sounds like it has more strings than a marionette. More than a harp. Heck, a marionette playing a harp. And getting caught up in all those strings could make disentangling myself very difficult. Also, it wouldn't be fair to him.

So, decision made. No finding out if Constantine is massive *all over*. My body is going to have to keep on jonesing. I didn't pack my vibrator out of fear I'd be selected for some random luggage inspection. Maybe there's a sex-toy shop in town. That's a question I'm sure Ro will be happy to answer tomorrow. Tonight, I'm going to be a friendly houseguest. It's the least I can do.

Determined to appear more uninterested than I truly feel, I opt for sweatpants, a baggy hoodie, and fuzzy socks. No makeup. Hair in a loose, basic braid. This is the head-to-toe version of granny panties. If I were asked to label this look, I'd call it "man repellent" or "the attraction vaccine."

It's a short trek down the hall to an open-concept kitchen, dining, and living room area. Just like the guest room, everything in here is light, airy, and noticeably over-sized. Monster sized.

Constantine is leaning over a large, granite-topped island, focused on a flat-screen TV on the opposite side of the living room. *The Sports Network.* Apparently, some things are universally "guy," no matter their species.

His rapt attention on the highlight reels gives me a moment to check out this new-to-me backside view of him. He's still wearing the blue button-up shirt, only now the sleeves are rolled up to his elbows. His forearms are the thickest I've ever seen. There's something about a man with solid arms and rolled-up shirtsleeves. Constantine wins this category by a landslide.

Maybe the clothing here is magically enhanced, too. It must be, because the way his shirt is stretched taut across his unbelievably wide back would be too much strain for normal material and stitching. His long, dark hair lies in neat, shiny waves that end in a tidy line at shoulder-blade level. I shouldn't want to touch it, but tell that to my fingers, twitching at my sides.

There's a subtle V shape to his upper body, but only because his shoulders are so damn wide. He's definitely not thin at the waist. He's deliciously thick. The kind of body that could give protection or the world's best cuddle.

With how snug his jeans fit over what is undoubtedly a solidly muscled butt, the belt he's wearing must be for fashion, not function. And it works. It *all* works. So well, in fact, I'm a heartbeat from sneaking back to my bedroom to make use of my fingers and one of the extra-fluffy pillows while I mentally undress him in private.

Until he turns to face me. "I didn't hear you come in," he says, using the remote to turn off the TV without taking his attention off of me for a split-second. "Feel better after the shower?"

"All cleaned up and fresh. Head to toe and everything in between." I snap my mouth closed. So much for my decision to keep things platonic. I might as well have invited him to inspect my freshness, up close and all over. At least I'm dressed to un-impress. That'll save me from my uncontrollable, galloping libido.

Leaning back against the island, his gaze sweeps down and up my body. When his eyes lock with mine, he doesn't look unimpressed by my clothing choice or lack of fancying up. Heat swirls in his amber eyes. One of his bullish huffs follows, and this time, he doesn't apologize for it.

Likely because earlier, I all but told him the sound turns me on. Which it did. It does.

"Hungry?" His question could be literal or innuendo.

Either way, my answer is the same. "Starving."

"Let's get you filled up."

Yes, please. Fill me up, Constantine. Fill. Me. Up.

Squeezing my legs together does nothing to relieve the building tug of need. There's no hiding it from him, either.

His big, strong jaw ticks and he draws a deep breath, his nostrils flaring as he undoubtedly catches the scent of my arousal. Tail flicking at his side, he pushes off from the granite and takes a step toward me. *"Natalie."* The deep, rumbling way he says my name sends another ripple straight between my legs.

"Yes?"

"I need you to know that no matter how much I crave you, and even when your body is crying out for me to claim you as my mate, I won't act until you tell me you want me."

I could play coy, tell him I don't know what he's talking about. But we'd both know it to be a lie. "I don't know what's happening to me. I'm a slow cooker at the best of times. I'm attracted to you, but I literally *just* decided it'd be best for us to remain platonic. I'm only here for a couple of weeks and I don't want things to get messy between us. Then I walked out here, checked you out, and bam, I'm heated to maximum. I'm ready to do all kinds of things I'd never do on a first date. And this isn't even a date; I'm just a guest in your house."

"You know you're much more than that. Attempting to deny or avoid it won't change what fate has in store for us, but we don't have to figure it all out here, now. How about we round up some food, kick back on the couch, relax, and get to know each other. No pressure for more. We can even make a mutual promise that it *won't* turn into more tonight."

"Even if I have a moment of weakness and tell you I want more?"

His dark lips curve into a warm smile that matches the affection in his eyes. "Even then."

"I'd like that. Very much."

"Good," he says, extending one arm toward the living room area while moving toward the kitchen cabinets, where he takes out a serving platter. "Go and get comfortable. I'll bring over a plate."

"Okay." The weight of his attention follows me while I peruse the seating options as if I were Goldilocks. "I don't want to take your favorite spot," I say, looking over at him. "Where do you usually sit?"

To my surprise, he points at one end of the large sectional. "There. But I don't mind switching it up. You might disappear in the divot I've made in that seat cushion, though."

It's so easy to laugh with him. "I'm not *that* small."

"Compared to me, you are." The flare of his nostrils is clear, even from across the room. He's thinking about our size difference in ways that have nothing to do with innocently sitting on the couch.

I know it because I'm thinking about it too. The size of his cock likely matches his big body, and if so, it's huge. He's sure I'm his mate, so sex must be possible. God help me, I want to find out. I have so many questions to ask Ro when I see her tomorrow.

Before the heat between us rises any higher, I turn away, then settle on the best part of any sectional sofa—the inner corner. The earthy-gray velour and pillowy cushions welcome me like an embrace. Fatigue rushes in, not over-taking my arousal entirely, but subduing it. If I close my eyes, I'll be out within seconds.

Not wanting to fall asleep, I shift to a more upright posi-tion as Constantine joins me. "Ooh, that looks amazing," I say, my empty stomach making itself known while I attempt to not drool at the contents of the large, wooden serving tray he places beside me.

"It's all yours. Dig in." The couch doesn't shift when he sits, but the depression of the cushion beneath him is defi-nitely visible.

"How much do you weigh?" The question pops out of my mouth as it enters my head. "Sorry! That's too personal a question."

"Between us, there's no such thing. I'll tell you anything and everything you want to know." Again, the heat flickers in his eyes, as if he knows the particular things I was wondering moments ago. "To answer the question you asked, I'm around 180 kilograms. Just shy of 400 pounds."

Three times my weight. He'd crush me if he were on top. Only, I know he wouldn't, because he'd be careful while fucking me.

Stop thinking about him fucking you, Natalie! Especially while he's sitting right there!

Desperate to be something other than being horny for the horned Minotaur, I focus on the food. A selection of sliced meats and cheeses, crackers and quarter slices of some sort of grainy bread. Assorted cut fruits and raw vegetables. A wedge of pâté with a spreading knife. Little bowls of dip. There are even pickles. Very specific pickles. In fact, everything on the platter looks deliberately selected.

Picking up one of the little green cornichons, I meet his gaze again. The pickle is crisp, tart, and sweet, and I can't help making an *mmm* noise when its flavor bursts in my mouth.

His smile widens. "Good?"

I lick my lips to catch any lingering juice. "Very. Those are my favorite kind of pickles. Did you take notes during our conversation about foods we like and dislike?"

The deep chuckle he makes might as well be his fingers on my clit. "No note-taking required. I remember every detail."

"Your memory is better than mine. I always have a note-book on the go—tabs for work projects, personal stuff, banking, etcetera. On top of that, I have online spreadsheets. Every aspect of my life has to go in a list or a spreadsheet. I can't imagine how much I'd forget if I didn't record it all. I write everything down."

"I hope you left a lot of pages for your Fate's Falls section." He drapes one beefy arm along the back of the couch, the tips of his fingers nearly reaching my shoulder.

The serving tray on the cushion between us prevents me from subtly shifting closer. But I want to. Even though my hoodie would be in the way of skin-on-skin contact, I'm still tingly at the thought of feeling his touch.

I focus on the charcuterie board while I attempt to settle the flutter low in my abdomen. "I think Fate's Falls is going to need its own notebook." Unable to resist, I look at him from beneath the fringe of my eyelashes—and find him staring at me. "Is there a stationery or other store in town that sells pretty notebooks?"

"The notebook has to be pretty?"

"Of course." My body temperature is on the rise again, and it's not from the cozy sweats I'm wearing. The over-sized, nondescript sweats I'm now regretting. I'm not the shapeliest woman around, but my body is decent enough, and I'm kinda wishing he could see it, even though we agreed tonight was just for relaxing and getting to know each other. It wouldn't hurt for him to get to know what I look like when I'm not hidden inside boxy fleece coordinates. Too late now.

"Yes, there's a store. *Fae-vorite Things.* It's downtown, near my coffee shop. Stationery, trinkets, lots of pretty things."

"Is it owned by a non-human?"

He nods. "A fairy named Flora."

"A *fairy?* For real?" Appropriately, or inappropriately, I'm gaping like a fish. "Does she have wings?"

"She does, yes."

"Is she tiny, like a butterfly?"

"No," he says, chuckling softly. "Pixies are small like that. Fairies are human-sized." He says it all as if it's totally normal. Which it is to him.

"Are there pixies here in Fate's Falls?"

"Several families of them. Quite a few fairies, too."

"Wow, that's...it's all so..." Completely unbelievable. But I'm hearing it from a Minotaur, which makes it as possible as anything. Still, I make a mind-exploding gesture and *kaboom* sound, at which he chuckles again—a sound that makes me smile. "I can't wait to see it all."

"And I can't wait to show you everything."

Warmth washes through me as he looks into my eyes. I should be making these plans with my cousin, not him. I'm here for Ro, not to play *fake dating your alleged Minotaur mate* with Constantine. Except, it wouldn't be fake. And every minute I'm with him makes it feel less alleged.

His smile widens while watching me line up three crackers, then layer each in production-line fashion, until they're perfectly equal mini towers of identical deliciousness. "How much trouble would I be in if I said you're cute?"

"Zero trouble. I never understood women who get bent out of shape by the word cute. Did your last girlfriend have a problem with it?" Now I'm the one whose mouth is going to get them in trouble. "Not that I'm comparing myself to anyone who's had girlfriend status."

"You shouldn't."

It's as if my stomach has a trap door. "Of course not," I say, returning the loaded cracker I'm holding to the tray.

His dark eyebrows draw together, his eyes flaming with intensity as his gaze focuses on the frown tugging my lips downward. He shifts, dropping his arm onto the seat cushions and capturing my hand, where it lies like a dead fish beside the serving tray. "You're my mate, Natalie. Whether you accept what fate chose for us or not, you will always be beyond comparison."

How sad is it that's the most romantic thing anyone's ever said to me? A short time with this man, this Minotaur, is already proof I've dated nothing but duds until now.

Until now. Well, that thought sprang out pretty darn naturally. Is this the beginning of dating Constantine? Am I really going there while I'm here?

Not before we discuss the bigger issue. The one that goes *way* beyond dating.

"How long have you thought I'm your mate?" Attempting to make the moment more casual, I pluck a perfect cherry tomato from the platter and pop it into my mouth.

"I've *known* since I heard your voice. I was fairly certain when I saw your picture. And I've had a sensation in my chest since the first time Rosetta mentioned your name."

The tomato feels like a rock stuck in my throat. I pull my hand from his and beat my fist against my chest, choking the tomato down. "You're kidding about the 'since you heard my name' part."

His gaze stays on my face as he makes a slight head-shake. "I'll never lie to you, and I wasn't exaggerating."

"Did Ro know about all this 'mate' stuff when she arranged for me to stay here?"

The dark-brown fur of his face makes blushing impossible, but the set of his mouth seems like an equivalent. "The accommodations were my idea. My offer of guest bedrooms to any of her family who could attend the wedding was sincere, but I was motivated by more than a sense of friendship or goodwill. I wanted *you* here. And no, I didn't tell her you're my mate at the time. Not until after you and I spoke on the phone. When I mentioned it to her after that, she suggested having you stay with a female friend instead of me."

"Why did she change her mind? And then change it back, obviously, since I'm staying here."

"She knows the intensity and permanence of a mate bond. She doesn't want you to get hurt emotionally, but agreed to let you stay at my house because she trusts me to take care of you." He grips the back of his neck and massages it with his big hand. "And because I pleaded with her."

My eyes go wide at that little truth nugget. "You pleaded with her? That's pretty intense, you know. Like, red-flag intense." My heart's thumping a mad beat against my ribs and I swear the temperature in the room just rose five degrees. "Why am I not seeing red flags?"

"Because you feel our mate bond, even if your conscious mind hasn't accepted it yet." What should be a ballsy statement holds no cockiness whatsoever. It doesn't sound irrational, either.

Maybe the magical aspect of this town is affecting my ability to think logically.

"I can tell you're unsettled," he says. "What can I do to ease your mind?"

"I'm not sure that's possible with everything I'm trying to digest." I smooth my hand over my forehead and crown, then slide my fist down my damp braid with a subtle tug, attempting to snap myself out of whatever this is. It doesn't work. The feelings, wild as they are, refuse to be broken. "Okay, explain to me how you're so sure I'm the one."

"I just know. That's how it is with Minotaurs. But that's not the real question you want answered, is it. You want to know why you think I might be right." He's so calm, seemingly at complete ease with this conversation.

"Maybe," I hedge.

Smiling, he offers me his hand, palm up.

I don't hesitate. Placing mine on his is automatic, and I gasp the instant we touch. His hand is warm, firm, soft. The sensation of his fingers closing around mine is electric, but also soothing. My body temperature rises with each second of contact, but it's not just arousal. It's lightness, comfort, excitement, and calm, all at once. More than a physical response. There's a connection.

The amber of his eyes shines brighter than before. "You feel it."

"I feel something, but I already knew I felt something for you. I'm not seeing a 'this is your mate' banner light up in my head. Is that how it is for you?"

The soft lighting casts a shimmer on his dark hair as his body shifts while silently chuckling. "There's no flashing banner. Nothing that literal or tangible."

I give him the single-raised-eyebrow expression. "You're suggesting I should embrace the woo-woo?"

This time, his chuckle is audible. Deep. Super sexy. "If that's the same as relax and be open to possibilities instead of searching for answers, then, yes."

"The woo-woo, like I said. Totally my parents' schtick; it's just never been mine." A smile tugs at my lips, then I exhale and let my eyelids flutter closed. "Okay, here goes." Taking a deep breath through my nose pulls his scent into my lungs, my head. Earthy, masculine, virile. Warmth flows through me like a gently rippling wave. My skin tingles and a soft, golden glow brightens the insides of my closed eyelids. It's like being immersed in pure energy. And he's there. Not as a picture in my mind, as a presence. I feel like I could touch him...

"You're reaching for me."

"No, I'm not," I say, opening my eyes. "See? I haven't moved."

"You heard that?"

"Of course I did. I had my eyes closed, not my ears."

"You wouldn't have heard it with your ears, Natalie. I didn't say the words out loud."

"Bullshit." I yank my hand back to clap it over my mouth. "Sorry, that's probably offensive because of your, um, heritage. God, saying that probably made it worse."

The deep laugh I remember from our phone conversations rumbles from him. Then he shifts position, moves the serving tray to the coffee table, and gently removes my fingers from my face. "You're fine. No offense taken by any of it. Minotaurs share history with bulls, just as humans do with primates. Would you be offended if I used the term 'apeshit'?"

"No, I'm not a psycho," I say, smiling as tension loosens its grip on my shoulders. Questions about the origins of the other non-human residents in town pop into my head, but I push them aside to make room for more important things. "I distinctly heard you say 'You're reaching for me.' Your voice was crystal clear. You must have said it out loud."

"I didn't. My word to the gods, Natalie."

"Then how? I'm not a mind reader."

"But you are my mate."

"And mates can read each other's minds?"

"Not all mates, but some."

"I don't want anyone knowing what I'm thinking all the time. Have you been reading my mind since I got here?" My face feels hot enough to burst into flames. "Do you know what I'm thinking right now?" I pinch my eyes closed and mentally repeat one word over and over in my head: *Pickles. Pickles. Pickles.*

"Natalie," he says, softly laughing. "I don't know what you're thinking."

"You're sure?" I crack one eyelid open. "You promise?"

"Yes, and yes, one hundred percent. Plus, it was *you* who heard my thought, not the other way around."

"Oh shit, you're right. I don't think I want that kind of power." Still, I can't resist closing my eyes and trying again. Several deep breaths later, all I have is a calmer heart rate. "I don't hear anything now. And it doesn't feel like you're in my head."

He's smiling at me when I open my eyes. "Because I'm not. The first time, I opened myself to you so the mate bond could flow between us. You did more than accept it, you moved into it. Picture opening a door and walking into my mind. It's sort of like that. Though, you hearing my thought was unexpected."

"I'm so sorry. I had no idea I was invading your privacy like that."

"You weren't. I welcomed you there. I always will." Taking my other hand, he gently caresses both while holding my gaze. Sparks skitter through me. Awareness and arousal immediately, then the other sensations return. "Do you feel it now, without closing your eyes?"

"Yes," I whisper, afraid to shatter the feeling by speaking louder. Like before, warmth floods me, wraps around me.

And he's there, in my head, like a comforting presence. It's different than before, though. Looking into his eyes makes it extremely intimate. I hope he doesn't let go. Doesn't stop whatever he's doing to make this happen, because I never want this feeling to end.

But it does end, when my phone vibrates in my pocket at the exact moment Constantine's doorbell rings.

Groaning at the inevitable, I slide my hands out of his. "That has to be Ro."

"Did you ask her to come by?" he asks, rising from the couch.

I shake my head while checking my phone. Sure enough, there's a new text from my cousin.

> **Ro:**
> Dak and I are at the door. Thought you might appreciate some backup to reduce the awkwardness. Constantine is a great guy, but I know I should have waited for you to wake up before I took off. Sorry! Here now though! Let us in! Seriously, let us in. I can't wait for you to meet Dak. Don't be scared, okay? He looks like a brute, but I swear, he's really a big green teddy bear.

If she'd sent that message immediately, when I texted her before leaving the bedroom, I would've jumped at the offer. Now, I wish she'd stayed home. Sighing, I return the phone to my pocket and shrug my shoulders while looking up at Constantine. "Better answer the door. I'll go with you." My intention is to tag along behind.

He clearly has other ideas because he takes my hand to help me up, then keeps it.

"We really shouldn't be holding hands when we open

the door," I say as we reach the entryway. "I don't want Ro to think we're together."

"She wouldn't disapprove."

"I agree." Stopped at the door, I wiggle my fingers free of his big, warm hand. "But she'd get her hopes up that I've agreed to be your mate, which would mean I'm staying in Fate's Falls."

"You *are* my mate, Natalie. That won't change if you decide to leave after your cousin's wedding."

After what I experienced with him, I really can't argue the "you are my mate" point. I felt it. I liked it. But declaring it is a lot of pressure, especially so fast. Even if I did, I'm not ready to make a decision about the rest of my life. Maybe it's a good thing Ro and her fiancé are here. If Constantine and I had continued down the path we were on, I probably would've agreed to be *his* fiancée before the end of the night. Part of me—a significantly sized part—thinks that would be the best thing ever.

"You didn't hear my thoughts just now, did you?" I ask, when he gently squeezes my hand before releasing it.

"No. I may never be able to, and for it even to be possible, you'd have to open yourself to me—mind, heart, and soul. That can't happen while you're feeling uncertain."

"Wait." Stopping him before he reaches for the door handle, I place my hand on his forearm. The short fur covering his thick muscles is soft beneath my fingers, and I can't resist stroking it. Is the fur on the rest of his big, solid body the same? I want to feel it all. Beneath my hands. Against my naked body. It could be raw physical attraction. I could be having some weird post-traumatic response thing. Or it could be that he really is the one I'm meant to be with.

Nothing about this makes sense. Does it have to, though? It's time I took a page out of my cousin's book, stopped overthinking, and just went with it. Rosetta found true love with a monster. Maybe I will too if I don't close myself off from the possibility. If I open myself to him the way he did with me.

Closing my eyes, I take a deep breath, push my fears and doubts aside, and imagine myself opening a door, hoping he's on the other side. *I'm certain I want you.*

His deep rumble and sharp, bullish huff snap me back to where my mind needs to be. Heat blazes in his eyes. His nostrils flare wildly.

"Did it work with me touching your arm? Could you feel it?"

"Yes, Natalie, I felt it."

I shouldn't expect that he heard the thought I tried pushing toward him, but I'm disappointed that he didn't. "We better answer that," I say, when the doorbell goes off multiple times in succession. Unquestionably my cousin's doing. "The sooner we let Ro in, the sooner we can kick her out."

His body shakes with silent laughter. "I like the way you think."

Chapter Seven

CONSTANTINE

When I say, "I like the way you think," she's unaware of the depth of those words.

I didn't just feel the connection she initiated. I heard her voice in my head.

I'm certain I want you. She's only certain of the physical aspect right now, but the rest isn't far behind. She believes in the bond. She's just not sure she can accept it.

She will, if I can rein myself in and give her space to get there.

Forcing a genial expression into place, I take a breath, then open the door.

"That took way too long." Rosetta's eyes open wide as her gaze flips between me and Natalie. "Holy shit, were you two *in the middle of something?*"

Natalie's beautiful face flushes bright pink. "We were talking."

"Must've been one *hot* conversation." Rosetta steps inside and pulls Natalie into a hug. "I want all the details tomorrow. Every last one," she whispers against Natalie's ear.

But I hear it, as I'm sure Dak does. Not that his face gives anything away. Orcs are known for their nearly permanent scowl, and Dak is no exception, even in the presence of his beloved mate.

"Get you something to drink?" I ask once he's inside. "Beer? Mead?"

"Water." His dark-eyed gaze slides to Rosetta.

Ah. The pregnancy secret. If I were the betting type, I'd wager Rosetta spills the beans tonight instead of waiting until she shows Natalie the brand-new nursery. "Come on in." I wave them toward the living room. "I'll grab some glasses and a pitcher of ice water. Can I get you something, Natalie?"

"Do you mind if I look at the options?"

"My fridge is your fridge."

Rosetta snorts while leading Dak to the couch, and Natalie follows me into the kitchen. The open layout doesn't give us privacy, but having her near me is a plus just the same.

She inspects the refrigerator's contents while I get a tray, pitcher, and four glasses from an upper cabinet.

"Can't decide what you want?" I ask, standing behind her, close enough that I can breathe her in. Her hair smells like roses, but it's her womanly scent I can't get enough of. I would prefer we come together with our future together resolved, promised to one another. But I will never reject my mate. Whenever and however she wants me, she will have me. Even if I lose her in the end.

"What's in the unmarked can?" She points at one of many beverages in tidy lines on a middle shelf.

"A new beer we're developing at the brewery."

"That's so cool. How's it different from your other beers?"

"It's a Berliner-style Weisse wheat beer, and we've infused it with rose hips to give it a hint of unique, sweet and tarty flavor."

"Wow, I have no idea what any of that means," she says, looking over her shoulder at me. Her wide hazel eyes are so pretty, so clear and sparkly. And her lips, curved up in an easy smile, are the most tempting thing I've ever seen.

My hooves click against the tiled floor as I shift from foot to foot. "It means I sound like one of those annoying craft-beer nerds who talk over people's heads."

The giggle she makes is light and effortless. "Well, you are *literally* talking over my head, because you're so tall. But I didn't take it in a condescending way at all. You sound like someone who's really into the product they're creating. I'm the same way when I'm in a good creative groove."

"I look forward to hearing you talk about your work."

Her happy glow fades. "Well, lately, everything feels more like work than good creativity, so you may have to wait a while."

The urge to tell her we have all the time in the world teeters on the tip of my tongue. Instead, I go with, "Maybe the change of scenery will spark things for you. If not the mountain landscapes, then all the colorful monsters. Like Dak, for example." I tilt my head toward the living room.

She laughs softly, covering her mouth.

If we were alone, I'd take her hand away so I could see the smile she's hiding. Hear her laughter unmuted. We'll get there. I know we will. "Want to be my first non-employee taste tester?" I point at the plain white can again. "If you don't like it, you can dump it and get something else."

"You can't count my opinion because I'm not much of a drinker in general, and definitely not a beer connoisseur, but I'd love to try it."

Leaning in to get the can is an excuse to press my chest to her back. To breathe her in from close up. There's no stopping the huff of breath I make or the wild swishing of my tail. I'm rock-hard for her and I'm sure she feels my cock against her lower back.

She doesn't move away though. The opposite. She leans against me, presses more of her small, delicate body to mine. "Are we still mutually promising nothing will happen between us tonight?"

"We probably should," I say, grazing the shell of her ear as I force myself to do the right thing. "I don't want you to wake up with regrets."

Looking deep into my eyes, a sigh leaves her rosy lips. "I wouldn't regret being with you, but I would regret it if I hurt you."

"You won't." I cup her chin and sweep the pad of my thumb over her soft skin.

"Ahem..." Rosetta calls from the living room. "We're still here, you know. And we're thirsty. Though clearly not as *thirsty* as the two of you..."

Shaking her head, Natalie ducks out from in front of me to look directly at her cousin. "It's good to know that true love and fresh mountain air hasn't changed you."

"Oh, it has," Rosetta counters, pushing up to her knees and hanging over the back of the couch. "But you're never going to know how if you don't stop flirting with the Minotaur and get over here so we can talk."

"Go join them. I'll bring the drinks over."

NATALIE

I should want to throttle Ro for the embarrassing comments, but there's not a lick of anger in me. Despite the fire raging beneath my cheeks, I'm not truly embarrassed either. I can give her a little shit, though. The world wouldn't be right if I didn't.

"Hey, brat," I say, dropping onto the couch, facing her. That's the extent of my giving her shit. As soon as I hug her, all I have are sappy feelings. "I've missed you."

"Ditto, *snore*."

Tears prick in my eyes at the use of our younger-years' nicknames for each other.

Squeezing me tight, Ro whispers, "I know it's selfish, but I hope you fall in love with him and decide to stay."

It wouldn't take much to fall for him. Heck, it's already happening. Which is bonkers and unlike me. I need to slow down. I just don't want to. "Let's focus on making the most of the next couple weeks."

"Right, of course. We're going to have so much fun, I promise." Her nose is rosy and her eyes are glassy when she sits back. Ro's not the weepy type. Her red hair bounces wildly as she shakes her head. Then her usual sassy expression is back. "Introduction time!"

Aside from wrapping his massive arms around her, the orc beside her doesn't react when she climbs onto his lap, wiggling and grinding as she makes herself comfy. Now that I'm truly face-to-face with her fiancé, there's no denying that he is, in fact, an orc.

"Dak, this is Nat. Nat, Dak."

The huge green monster nods at me. "Nice to finally meet you. My Rosetta speaks of you frequently, with love and admiration."

Ro said he's possessive, but the way he says *my Rosetta* seems worshipful. No red flags detected here, either.

I smile, aiming for one that's normal-ish. Not that anything about this is normal. "It's nice to meet you, too. I've heard a lot about you, all very good."

Constantine chokes back a laugh while setting the drinks on the coffee table.

I bite the inside of my cheek because I know he's thinking about the stuff I alluded to during our phone conversation—that Ro likes to tell me spicy stuff about Dak. Now that I know what the guy looks like, it casts those details in a whole new light. Because Dak is huge. Usually, I just listen and giggle when Ro tells her sex tales. Now I have logistical questions.

There's not much space between me and the armrest, but Constantine takes it, rather than sit on the fully available other branch of the L-shaped couch. I scooch over, toward Ro and Dak, but Constantine's hand on my hip halts additional movement.

One of Ro's ginger eyebrows rises and a smile curves her

lips. No mystical mind-meld bond required to know her thoughts. She thinks it's a done deal. That I'm one good Minotaur dicking away from calling Fate's Falls home forever.

She might be right.

Heat from Constantine's body seeps into mine, increasing when he leans forward, his chest pressing tight to my back while reaching for a drink from the table.

I really want that good dicking. To hell with our mutual promise to behave.

His hand is so big, he easily holds the white can and a pilsner glass at the same time. "I wasn't sure which way you wanted it."

"In the can is good."

Ro snickers openly. "You might have to work up to that."

"Ro!" The heat of a thousand suns flares inside me.

Behind me, Constantine's body shakes with amusement.

Even Dak is smiling. Sort of.

Just great. We're all thinking about me getting fucked in the ass by my Minotaur mate.

My Minotaur mate. Not *a* Minotaur, not *the* Minotaur sitting next to me. *My Minotaur mate.* I just mentally claimed Constantine—as my mate.

How would that look in reality, once the euphoria wears off and the rest of the world creeps back in? *Mom, Dad, this is my boyfriend, Constantine, my fated mate, who happens to be a Minotaur.* When I think about saying those things...they don't feel weird. Maybe the magic that safeguards this town really has affected my brainwaves.

The sound of the aluminum tab cracking open jolts me from my thoughts.

"Thank you," I say, accepting the can from Constantine. I take a big mouthful, hoping it'll cool me off and give the others space to start a new line of conversation. Beer isn't my usual drink of choice, but this doesn't taste like ordinary beer. There's no bitterness at all. It's light and creamy, with a distinct fruity tang. Yummy enough for me to take another big swallow immediately.

"Better slow down," Ro teases. "Unless you've been boozing it up a lot since last time we drank together at my farewell night out? The Nat I know is a lightweight."

"I'm just having one." If it gives me a little buzz, that wouldn't be the worst thing. I take another sip, then offer the can to her. "It's one of Constantine's new brews. So good. Honestly, the best beer I've ever tasted. Try it."

"No thanks."

"You'll like it." I squint when she shakes her head. "Worried about cooties from the outside world?" I tease. "I can put some in a glass for you."

"No, I'm good with water."

"You never drink water. You always say it's a waste of your taste buds. This won't be." I'm bordering on asshole territory here, but something's off. Ro's not a lush, but she never shies away from a good time or new experiences. "Come on, try it."

As I jiggle the can, Dak splays his hand over her abdomen. Holy shit. Ho. Lee. Shit.

I never get the chance to make Ro squirm; I've only ever been on the receiving end. This is going to be fun. I crank the drama dial high, pushing my bottom lip out in a pout. "I came *all* the way across the country for you, and you won't even take a sip of this delicious beer I'm sure you'll like? You *have* changed." I fake a sniffle for extra effect.

"Oh shit, you figured it out, didn't you?"

"Figured what out?" I ask, exaggeratedly fluttering my eyelashes.

Ro rolls her eyes, then the biggest smile I've ever seen spreads across her face. "That I'm pregnant, dork!"

The two of us squeal in unison, like we used to do as kids. As teenagers. As young women stepping into adulthood for the first time.

"Oh my god, Ro!"

Constantine grabs the can from my hand as if we planned the move. Then I'm hugging my cousin, squeezing her tight. But not too tight, because her "I swear, he's really a big green teddy bear" fiancé is giving me major stink-eye over her shoulder. Or at least I think he is. With his dark eyes and perpetual scowl, it's hard to be sure. But it feels like a stink-eye occasion for some reason.

"Role reversal. You're the brat now," she says, smacking my shoulder after releasing me. "I had a whole amazing plan for telling you about the baby. Tomorrow, at my house, in the beautiful nursery Dak busted his ass to finish, solely for that reason." She cranks around to face him, cupping his green jaw and kissing him, protruding tusk teeth and all. "Sorry, baby. I'll make it up to you."

Baby? She calls her hulking, monster fiancé *baby?*

And he doesn't seem to mind. Not that I'd be able to tell if he did.

She plants a deeper kiss on him, one that has him pulling her back onto his lap, where he not-so-subtly rocks her back and forth while they make out as if Constantine and I aren't sitting right here.

Okay, then...

I inch backward until I connect with Constantine, but pervy me can't stop staring at the extreme PDA in front of me. Angling my head up and back against his chest, I whisper, "Should we leave the room?"

He tips his face down, close to mine. "If we do, they'll have sex on my couch, and that's a mess I'd rather not have to clean up."

"I heard that," Ro says, breaking her lip-lock to look at us and stick out her tongue. She really hasn't changed since moving here. Falling in love with a monster and getting pregnant with his baby don't seem to have mellowed her sass at all. "Since you look plenty comfortable and not traumatized *at all*," she makes a circular swirling motion toward us, "Dak and I are going to head home."

"But you just got here." There's not a lot of life in my protest, I admit.

Ro's snicker tells me our year apart hasn't diminished her ability to read between the lines with me. "We'll have some bestie time tomorrow; it's all arranged. Constantine's going to take you to his coffee place at nine-thirty, and we're meeting up with Dela, another human who lives here now. She's a sweetheart, you're going to love her. From there, we'll do a bit of shopping while you check out everything Fate's Falls has to offer." One eyebrow rises over mischievously twinkling eyes. "Well, *almost* everything."

"You're still a brat," I say, rolling my eyes at her while pushing up from the couch.

She takes my hand and lets me pull her to her feet, then bear-hugs me. "You wouldn't want me any other way."

It's true. If Ro didn't tug me out of my comfort zone, I'd probably never leave it. Right now, that means I'd still be back in my little apartment, alone and lonely as I plod through life, wishing for things I'd never find there.

Things I've already found here.

Generic conversation is passed around as we all head for the front door. One more hug from Ro, then she and Dak are on their way home, likely to fuck each other's brains out. If they can't keep it under control sitting next to us on the couch, I can't imagine what they're like in private.

The energy in Constantine's house changes as soon as he locks the door behind them. All the sexual tension from earlier comes rushing back the moment we're alone.

"I'm going to clean up the food and drinks," I say, trying to focus on anything other than wanting to climb him like a tree.

He shakes his head. "I'll take care of that later. Can I get you anything? Another drink, different food?"

Your body rubbing up against mine would be good...

"No." I shake my head emphatically, probably looking like a weirdo in the process. "I think I'm ready for bed. Alone," I add, heat rushing to my face and between my legs. "Even though I'm tempted to ask you to break your promise that nothing will happen between us tonight."

"I'm not sure I could deny you if you did."

The pull between us is magnetic. I move closer, stopping with little more than a hairsbreadth separating us. "I'm not sure I can deny myself." Unable to resist, I place my hands on his big chest. "I swear I'm never like this," I say, looking up at his non-human face while sliding my palms over every inch of his shirt-covered torso. "I don't do stuff with someone I just met. I've never been someone to rush into things. But with you, I just want to jump in and do it all."

A rough huff of breath accompanies a deep rumble in his chest. "Doing it all will take time."

"It's not *that* late…" Am I doing this? Going for it? I think I am. "And I'm not tired anymore."

"Not time as in hours." He cups my waist and pulls me tight against him, so my soft body molds around the very large, hard bulge in his jeans. "Time meaning preparation."

Oh. "But it's possible, right?" I bite my lip, fighting the urge to reach down and touch him *there*. "A Minotaur and human can…fit together?"

"I've never been intimate with a human, but there are many recorded couplings."

"Recorded? As in cross-species porn videos?"

His body rocks with deep, low laughter. "I should have said 'documented,' as I was referring to historical records of mated couples."

I groan, pressing my forehead against his chest to avoid looking him in the eye.

One of his large hands cups my chin and tips my head up. The smile is still on his face, but it's less amusement, more seductive. It matches the heat in his gaze. "But there are videos of the type you mentioned."

"Oh," I say, another wave of heat rolling through me. "Have you watched any?"

He gives a single nod. "Only after discovering I have a human mate."

"Curiosity about the fitting thing?"

Another nod. "Are you curious?"

"Very. Where can I see them?"

"There are some websites you won't be able to access unless your device has our enhanced settings and protections. You can use my computer if you'd like to—"

"Yes," I say, cutting him off. My face couldn't be any hotter than it is right now. The rest of my body matches, too. "I know porn isn't reality, but I need to see how it'd work if we—*have sex.*"

Nostrils flaring, he steps back. "I'll get my laptop and bring it your room so you can have privacy."

"Okay." I nearly stumble while walking away. Not from the beer I drank, the lightheadedness is purely adrenaline. I'm about to watch monster porn on my Minotaur mate's computer, so I know what to expect when we have sex. Who am I and what is this reality I'm suddenly part of?

In my bedroom, I don't know what to do with myself while waiting for him. Should I wait at the door? Sit on the bed? *Lie* on the bed, patting the mattress? I glance down at the outfit I'm wearing. Definitely not the third option. This isn't a seduction scene; it's research. Really freaking sexy research.

I nearly jump out of my skin when he raps on the doorframe.

"Didn't mean to startle you," he says, offering the laptop across the threshold. "There's no password, and it's queued up if you want to watch one of the more romantic videos. If you change your mind, you're welcome to use the computer for whatever you want. You can look at all your regular human internet stuff, too, and nobody outside of Fate's Falls will be able to track your activity."

"Because of the magic?"

He nods. Winks. "Best firewall there is."

"I'm not sure if I'll watch the video." Awareness sizzles through me when our fingers brush while I take the laptop from his hand. Who am I kidding—I'm watching it the second I'm behind a closed door. The way his eyes are twinkling, he totally knows it. "I'll see you in the morning?"

"Anytime you want, Natalie. My room's at the other end of the hall if you need anything."

If I open my mouth to speak, who knows what'll come out. What I'll tell him I *need.* Instead, I nod and smile. Hope he can't tell how turned on I am. How eager I am to see what a Minotaur cock looks like, so I know what's in store for my ghost town of a pussy.

Chapter Eight

CONSTANTINE

Sleep may not be possible tonight.

My mate felt our bond, didn't deny it, and openly voiced her sexual attraction and the difficulty she's having containing it. Down the hall, she's watching video of a male Minotaur fucking a human woman. And she's enjoying it.

I probably should have been forthcoming about my Minotaur senses. Told her that my hearing and olfactory receptors far exceed those of humans.

Even with two closed doors and many meters between us, I heard the video when she pressed the *play* button, heard her gasp of embarrassment, and the sharp stabbing at the keyboard as she muted the volume. Now I can hear her soft moans. I can smell her heightened arousal.

I couldn't fall asleep now if my life depended on it. Not

with my cock harder than it has ever been, throbbing with need for my mate. I don't dare take myself in hand. Natalie wouldn't require heightened senses to hear me. Minotaurs are not quiet when sexually engaged. That's all I need— for Natalie to knock on my bedroom door because she hears me lowing while I relieve the pressure in my heavy balls.

Closing my eyes only serves to heighten my other senses. Lying on my back, I grab fistfuls of bedsheets as the sound and scent of her climax—the third one—fill my head. A cold shower won't help, but I'll take one anyway. The pounding water may drown out the sound of things I crave to experience up close.

Light tapping on the door stops me in my tracks as I'm crossing to the en suite bathroom. I glance at my raging erection, then at the door. There's no way to hide my physical state. I could pretend I didn't hear the knock, but I did tell her I'd be available if she needs something.

I pull on a bathrobe and cinch the belt tight, restraining my cock in an upward position against my body, then open the door.

"I watched the video," she says before I can ask what she needs.

My gaze drops from her glassy eyes and flushed cheeks. The baggy sweats from earlier are gone, replaced by a pale-pink bathrobe that ends above her knees and molds to her body. The hard points of her nipples strain against the thin material, proof that she's not wearing a bra underneath.

Like a glutton for punishment, I inhale deeply, unable to prevent the animalistic huff of breath from rumbling out of me when her scent fills my nose. I should apologize, but I can't. Holding back from touching her takes every resource I possess.

"I—" Her gaze trails down from my face, following the front edge of my robe to the V where my furry chest is exposed, then lower, to the bulge of my cock behind the ties. "I don't think I'll be able to have sex with you." Her eyes flick back to mine. "Not if your... *equipment* is the same size as the Minotaur in that video."

It's bigger. But I'm not about to tell her that and send her running. "I'll never pressure you to do something you're not interested in."

"But I *am* interested." The tip of her pink tongue darts out to moisten her lips. "I'm very interested. In you. Like, uncontrollably interested. Going-out-of-my-mind interested. Is there something about this town that causes that reaction in human women? Because, obviously, my cousin is experiencing the same thing, after I watched her practically going at it with Dak, right in front of us."

"It's not the town, it's the mate bond."

"Theirs?" she asks, and I nod. "And... ours?"

"Yes. And ours."

"The mate bond is why I'm standing at your bedroom door when I *know* I should have stayed in my room? Why I feel like we've known each other forever, even though we've just barely met?"

"That's how it is with mates, yes."

"So... there's nothing I can do to stop what's happening, to control these feelings and urges I'm having for you? Fate decided we're supposed to get together, so it's inevitable?"

Getting everything I want might be as simple as telling one small lie she'd never have to know about. But she would never be truly mine that way. "There is a way for you to be rid of the feelings you're experiencing." Tightness twists in my chest, in my gut, making it difficult to say what needs to be said. "You can reject me."

"It's that simple? Just say I'm not interested, and it all goes away?"

"A little more formally than that, but yes, it'd be that simple for you."

"What about you?"

I shake my head. "If you reject me as your mate, the bond is broken for you, not for me."

Her delicate eyebrows draw together. "But you could reject me, too, right? Then we'd both be free to fall in love with whoever we choose."

"I assume you, as a human, would have that option. If our bond is broken, I could have sex with others, but I would never find another mate. I'd never love someone. Fate gives each Minotaur one person for that."

"You're saying if I reject you as my mate, you lose any chance at love?" The air goes out of her in a *whoosh* when I nod. "If I don't want to commit to a fated mate bond I didn't know existed until today, I'm robbing you of your only opportunity at a happily ever after? That's a huge amount of pressure."

"Don't let my feelings or future affect your decision." I tuck a strand of hair that's worked free of her braid behind her ear, then trail my fingers along her cheek. "I want your happiness more than my own."

"Let me guess," she scrunches her nose, "that's because of the mate thing."

Even with everything hanging in the balance, and her

obvious frustration, I feel light enough to smile. "Yes, but also because I'm a pretty decent man."

"You are pretty," she says, laughing softly. "And from what I've heard and seen so far, decent, too."

"Nobody's ever called me pretty before." I tilt my head. "Well, aside from your cousin, but she only said it to piss me off."

Once again, she pinches her eyebrows together. "I meant it as a compliment."

"And that's how I took it." Touching her after the heavy conversation might be pushing it, but I do it anyway, capturing one of her hands and weaving her fingers between mine.

"What if, after you get to know me better, you realize I'm going to drive you crazy with my grab bag of quirks? Because I've got lots. Would you reject me then?"

"Of all possible mates, fate chose you for me. Made me wait fifteen years for you. I already know you're exactly right for me. I promise you, now and always, I will never reject you."

"Then...would you walk me to my room and kiss me goodnight?"

"It would be my honor and pleasure." Shifting my hand to the small of her back, I guide her down the darkened hall, my cock hardening more with each moment I feel her warmth beneath my palm.

At her bedroom door, she faces me and gently curls her hands around the front edges of my robe. "I like you." Color rises on her cheeks as she slips her fingers beneath the fabric and through the short fur of my chest. "And you know I'm attracted to you."

"Both good things and feelings I share," I say, wrapping my arms around her snugly enough for my cock to make itself known against her belly.

"But everything about this is new to me, and it's all happening so fast. I have a lot to think about before I do something that will permanently affect both our futures."

"I understand. And I'm grateful you're willing to take some time before you decide."

"Is there a line I should know about? A limit to how far things can go between us before the mate bond kicks in officially? If we kiss, are we sealing it? Or if we have sex, if that's even possible, is that what makes it final? I would hate to hurt you later because I got caught up in the heat of the moment, and unknowingly committed to more than I'm aware of."

Whether she's ready to admit it yet or not, she is my perfect one. She's willing to sacrifice pleasures she obviously wants if that pleasure would make *my* future painful. Fate chose well.

"Whether we enjoy each other sexually or never share a kiss, we're already mates. We will be until the end of our lives, unless you break your bond."

Her lips part as she blinks up at me. "Then...kiss me. Not a goodnight kiss. The kiss you'd give me if it were the only kiss we'd ever share."

Desire to please my mate roars to life inside me. Sliding my hands up her back, I find the end of her braid and tug the elastic away. Her hair is damp around my fingers as I thread my fingers through it and let it sift free. "Beautiful." I lean down and press my nose to her crown, breathing in the floral scent of her shampoo. "Lovely, but nothing compares to the scent of your arousal."

A soft gasp rises between us, then a sharper one when I wrap her long locks around my hand and gently tug, causing her head to tip back.

"Are you sure you want me to kiss you as if I only have one chance?"

"Yes," she whispers. "God, yes."

"Then I hope you aren't in a hurry to sleep." Angling above her, I inhale the scent of her skin, of her breath, then seal my wide mouth to her smaller, softer one.

She opens for me instantly, welcoming my tongue with a moan that drives me to kiss her deeper, harder. The tip of her small tongue touches mine, igniting sparks that race straight to my cock. Soft, breathy sounds rise to my ears like sweet, sexy music. And the taste of her—gods, the taste of her. One kiss will never be enough.

Inside my robe, her hands glide over my chest, up to my shoulders, then down to my abdomen, as far as our position allows. Close enough to feel the head of my cock where it protrudes above the level of the robe's belt.

She gasps again, whispering against my mouth, "I know I told you to kiss me, but can I see you?"

"You can have whatever you want, Natalie. In all ways, for all things, I'm yours." Releasing her hair, I ease back to give her full access to do whatever she wishes.

Looking up at me with glassy eyes, she unties my robe and slides it off my shoulders. "I—" Whatever words she thought to say morph into a choked gurgling sound as her gaze travels over my naked form. "You're huge. Everywhere. So, so, *huge.*"

Pride at impressing my mate brings my bullish nature to the forefront. A loud, assertive huff pushes from me, my hooves scrape against the floor, and my tail swishes like a flag in the wind. And my cock—it juts tall and hard, the wide, bulbous head shiny from the milky precum beading out.

I step closer, cup her face in one hand while cradling the back of her head with the other. Then I taste her lips again, teasing them apart with my tongue.

She melts beneath me, her body pressing to mine as her hands explore my fur-covered muscles, my waist, then, finally, my cock. Her fingers curve around the shaft—both hands, the tips barely meeting.

I groan into her mouth as she strokes me, and when she drags one fingertip through my leaking slit, the groan turns into a near-feral growl. I break our kiss, capture her tiny wrist, and draw her hand up between us. "Taste," I say, guiding her finger to her lips.

Her tongue peeks out first, tentatively obeying. Her eyes open wide, then she sucks her fingertip between her lips, humming until her finger pops free. "It's sweet." A laugh bubbles up from her glistening lips. "If all men tasted like you, there'd be no more complaints about not getting enough blowjobs." She lowers her gaze to my cock. "Though I don't think giving you one is within the realm of possibility for me."

I tip her chin up so our eyes meet. "There are many other ways we can enjoy each other."

Holding my gaze, she releases the tie at her waist, slides the robe off, then brings my hands to her bared skin. "Show me."

Chapter Nine

NATALIE

I've never been a sexual initiator. Or sexually adventurous. Or quick to engage in any kind of intimate activity. I've absolutely never done things the first night I was with someone. And it goes without saying that I've never been with a Minotaur.

If all of this were a dream, it would be the wildest, best dream anyone could have. But it's real. I'm naked with Constantine and our kiss is about to become a whole lot more.

"Natalie." The way he says my name sends warmth to every cell of my being. "So beautiful, my perfect one." He slides one thick, powerful arm around my back and pulls me flush against him, then dips down to kiss me again. His mouth is much bigger than mine, but our lips fit together as if they were meant to.

I run my hands all over him, sparks skittering through me as the short fur covering most of his body tickles my palms, my breasts, and every other bare, sensitive part of me. I'm being thoroughly and properly kissed by a monster. His tongue is long and broad and should feel like too much when it strokes into my mouth, but it's perfect. Warm and tickly and firm. Each kiss, each sweep of his tongue, tightens the longing tug between my legs. The achy emptiness I'm desperate for him to fill.

But that cock... holy hell, that cock. I could barely circle it with both hands. And it's so freaking long. There's no way it can fit inside me. But I want it to. God, I want it to.

The couple in that video had no problem fucking. That Minotaur wasn't as thick as Constantine, but he was still huge, and the woman didn't just take it—she took it like, well, like a porn star.

"That video," I say, breaking our kiss. "The couple, do you think they're bonded, or just having sex?"

"They're mated."

I pull back a little more so I can see Constantine's face. "How do you know?"

"Their bio was in the video description."

God, he's cute. Massive and sexy, yes, but cute. "You're probably the only creature on the face of the earth who reads the video description on a porn site." I squeak when he scoops me up into his arms. The position puts his arm directly under my ass, his fur teasing between my legs as he strides to the bed.

I expect him to lay me out, but instead, he sits me on the edge, parts my thighs, then drops to his knees between them. I can't even remember the last time a man voluntarily went downtown. I do know it wasn't in a fully lit room. And never like this, with me sitting up, watching. Yet I'm not the teensiest bit self-conscious. When he leans in, takes a deep breath, then one of his bullish huffs wafts over the place I want his mouth, I feel desired more than I ever have before.

Fire blazes in his amber eyes as he takes my hands and brings them to his horns. "Grip me hard and pull me in. Ride your bull's face until you come."

Oh. God. He's *so* dirty. And it works. It *so* works.

His horns are hard and coarse against my hands. I tighten my grip pull his face closer to my pussy. Eyes on me, he drags that wide black tongue across my sensitive pink flesh. I gasp at the immediate rush of need he stokes, pulling him tighter against me to get more. And he gives it.

My head falls back as his tongue burrows inside me, wiggling and thrusting, pressing against places that make me moan and squirm. Holding his horns, I rock against his face to take his tongue deeper, to feel his nose press against my clit. Squelching wetness and ravenous slurping fill my ears and I almost come from the deliciously dirty sound of being eaten out by my Minotaur mate.

He's my mate, and god, I am *so* his.

Would it work this way? The bond? Eyes closed, I open my mind to him. Clear away everything except him and me and the way he's making me feel. Warmth like before flows through me, and then he's there, in my mind.

Suck my clit.

His mouth rumbles against my pussy, then his tongue slides up to my clit, circling, circling, before he sucks it hard enough to send me over.

Moans and squeals and babbled curses fly out of me as I

jerk and writhe against his face, coming for what feels like forever. When I can't take any more, I let go of his horns, but he doesn't stop. He keeps suckling. Circling. Nuzzling. Until I'm coming again, this time long and gently, like a rippling wave.

My perfect one.

The words in my mind are as clear as if he spoke them aloud, and I snap my eyes open to find him watching me. He lavishes one last, long lick before rising between my legs.

"I heard you again," I whisper. Zero shyness about what we just did, but my heart is racing because of hearing a few words through our bond. A connection *I* initiated—while his face was buried in my pussy.

"I heard you too."

"I kind of figured, since you immediately did what I thought." My face must be the color of a fire engine. "Sorry that the first thought of mine you heard was a sex command."

His deep chuckle makes all his muscles dance. His cock too. "I welcome your sex commands anytime, mental or spoken aloud, but that wasn't the first time I heard your voice in my mind. Before we answered the door earlier, you thought, *I'm certain I want you.*"

"I didn't think you heard that. You didn't tell me."

"Your cousin was trying to beat the door down at the time, then we never circled back to it." The way he looks at me while stroking my face makes my heart want to beat its way right out of my chest.

"This is all so surreal. I can't believe any of it is really happening."

"Do you wish it wasn't?"

"I have no regrets." I smile up at him, happiness blooming inside me like the most beautiful flower. No more denial. I want this. I want him, even though I have no idea how to make it work, long term. That's something to worry about another day. "Is that normal, hearing your mate's thoughts so early and easily?"

"Honestly, it's unexpected, with you being human. But it would seem it's normal for us, and I welcome it."

"It freaked me out the first time, but... I like it."

"That makes me very happy," he says, dipping down to kiss me.

Tasting myself on his lips and tongue strikes a match inside me. "Keep kissing me," I say. "I want to try again, like this." It's trickier this way, but as we find our kissing rhythm, I relax and open the door in my mind.

He's right there, his mental presence as big and warm and addictive as his physical being.

Can you hear me? I want to taste you again. Feed me your cum.

The kiss ends with his rough rumble vibrating through me. Heated gaze locked with mine, he guides both my hands to his cock. "Stroke me. Milk me so I can feed it to you."

So very dirty.

Giving a two-handed hand job is a first, but my inexperience and irregular strokes don't seem to turn him off. His massive, dark cock responds to my ministrations, quickly pulsing beneath my palms. I glance down, my mouth watering at the steady beads of precum leaking with each upward stroke.

"Open your pretty mouth for me," he says in a husky

voice, then, "Gods, you're perfect," when I do exactly what he wants.

Because I want it too. I asked for it. Through our bond.

"Squeeze harder. As hard as you can, you won't hurt me." He makes a sexy-as-hell bullish snort when I double-down on the stroking. Behind him, his tail swishes wildly from side-to-side. His hooves stomp at the floor—once, twice. Then his mouth forms an oval and he lows, long and loud, while warmth coats my fingers and rolls down my hands.

Holding my gaze, he reaches down, then brings two loaded fingers to my mouth and spoons the thick, milky substance into my mouth. Tapping my chin, he watches me close my mouth and swallow.

This is definitely the dirtiest thing I've ever done, but it just feels right. "I want more," I say, holding my mouth open like a baby bird. I swallow the next mouthful as quickly as the first, then lie back on the bed, lightheaded and spinny, licking the cum off of my hands like a kid would with cake batter after scraping the mixing bowl. "What did you mean when you said 'doing it all' would require preparation? What kind of preparation?"

The bed shifts as he settles alongside me, propped on one arm and looking down at my face. "Stretching exercises."

"Like yoga?"

"No," he says, smiling. "Not like yoga."

I gasp as he touches between my legs, at the thickness of his single finger sliding inside me. *Ohhh... stretching exercises. For my vagina.* I hum when he withdraws, using my slickness to lubricate my clit while he teases it. "This is my kind of exercise."

"This isn't the stretching part, just the warmup."

"Never skip the warmup." Giggling at my own wittiness, I slide my hand down his body. His cock is still hard, or hard again, I don't know which, and sticky with cum. Wasted cum. "Why does this taste so good?" I ask, lifting my hand toward my mouth.

He catches my wrist before I can lick my fingers. "Because you're my mate. And I love watching you enjoy the taste of me, but Minotaur semen is good for other things, too."

"Making baby Minotaurs? I'm on the birth control pill to regulate my periods, so we don't have to worry about that."

The rumble he makes and the emotions swirling in his eyes tell me he wouldn't be worried at all if he got me pregnant. That he'd like it.

And that turns me on almost as much as everything else about him. "Aside from breeding, what else is Minotaur semen good for?" Saying the word *breeding* makes me desperate to feel him inside me. Desperate to come again.

"It's known to heighten sensation." He guides my fingers between my legs. "Try it here."

Apparently, I've become an obedient little naughty human, because I get busy on my clit without having to be convinced, and I have never, ever, masturbated with an audience. Not even in front of a mirror. But I don't even blink about doing it in front of Constantine. And that sensation-heightening thing? Oh yes. I'm already so close, I'm not sure I can stop. "Touch me again..."

On his side, he presses against me, his deep rumble

sending vibrations rippling through me. His hard cock lies heavy across my legs, its fat tip leaking milky white cum that runs down the inside of my thigh. "Gods, Natalie, you're so fucking beautiful," he says, sliding one thick finger inside me again. His single finger is nearly as big as a human cock—but not nearly as big as *his* cock.

"One more," I pant, rolling my fingers back and forth over my clit, my gaze lowering to his hand between my legs as he withdraws, coats two fingers in pearly precum, then enters me again. The fullness forces my eyelids to flutter closed. Whatever it is about his semen that's a sensation enhancer goes to work immediately, setting me ablaze with the need to come. Broken words and breathy panting are the extent of my communication as he moves those two huge fingers deep inside me, tapping them against a place no man or vibrator has ever found. I cry out, high-pitched, coming in a never-ending hot wave of pleasure.

When my body raises the white flag and I'm boneless and breathless, he slides his fingers from my pussy, then sucks them into his mouth. Growling. Nostrils flaring. *"Natalie,"* he warns when I curl my hand over his huge cock and slide it along the shaft.

"I want you."

Heat flares in his amber eyes. "Your pussy isn't ready for my cock."

"Then make it ready." At the end of a stroke, I gather a generous amount of precum and rub it between my legs. "That will help, right?"

"Yes, it will help, but—" A rough, bullish huff pushes cuts off his words as I tug his hand to my pussy again, positioning three of his thick fingers at my entrance.

"Get me ready."

"Even if you can take all four of my fingers tonight, I won't fuck you afterward, you'll need time to recover."

"Four?" The word squeaks out of me.

Raising his hand, he groups his fingers together, showing me the size of them, then lowers his hand, placing it alongside his cock.

Oh god. His cock is...bigger.

"I..." That's never going to fit inside me. I want it to, but there's just no way.

"It will fit."

"You heard my thoughts?"

"Not this time," he says, smiling, gently cupping my face. "But they're written all over your beautiful, terrified face."

"Not terrified, just..." I bite my lip, then sigh. "Okay, mildly terrified, because that thing is massive."

The upturn of his thin black lips and the bullish huff he makes are undeniably male pride. Then his expression gentles, and he draws me against him, my back to his front, that giant battering ram of a cock nestled between us. "I will happily spend my life pleasuring you with my tongue and fingers only."

I tilt my head to see his face. "You'd be okay with never having actual sex? For the rest of your life?"

"I would be happy just to be with you, Natalie, with or without sex of any kind."

It'd be an unbelievable claim from any human man I've ever met. Given Constantine's obvious sexuality and prowess, it should be unbelievable for him, too.

My heart tells me it's true.

"You don't have to go," I say, when he presses a kiss to my hair, loosens the arm wrapped around me, and he begins to move away. "I mean... I don't expect you to stay. But you can. If you want to."

"I want to." Despite his big, bulky physique, he shifts us between the sheets smoothly, almost effortlessly. He ensures my head is on one of the soft, cool pillows, my hair tucked neatly behind my shoulders. Then his big arm wraps around me again, and he snuggles in tight behind me, cradling me with his soft, furry body. "Are you comfortable?"

Covering his hand with mine, I close my eyes and open my mind to him. *More than ever in my life.*

His deep rumble vibrates against me, an unspoken confirmation that he heard my answer through our mate bond. "Sleep well, my perfect one."

Chapter Ten

NATALIE

"I'm sorry Rosetta is late," I say to Dela, glancing at the wall clock for what has to be the tenth time since she joined me at my table in Constantine's cozy-yet-hip coffee shop—right on time, which was half an hour ago. "You don't have to stay. I'm sure you'd rather not hang out in your workplace on your day off."

Dela, a semi-new-to-town human who is one of Constantine's full-time weekday employees here at *The Brew*, smiles while shaking her head. "I'm happy to wait. Constantine is a great boss, and my coworkers and the customers are so nice, being here never really feels like work. I often come in for coffee on the weekends."

"Ask her if that has anything to do with hoping to catch a glimpse of a certain red hell demon she has the hots for," a woman's voice says from behind me, then its owner turns one chair at the neighboring table toward us and sits.

Based on the full-face glowing blush on Dela's face, that comment hit the bullseye.

"Wait a sec," I say, looking back and forth between them. "There are hell demons here?"

"A few," the woman who's sort of sitting with us says, a playful smile curving her full, plum lips. "But the one Dela has a crush on won't be here today, because he knows she's not working."

Dela rolls her eyes, but there's a noticeable uptick in her expression. "He comes in for the coffee, Shay. Not because of me."

"You are in such denial." The woman's dark curly hair bounces with her light laughter, then she turns her attention to me. "I'm Shay, Dela's coworker slash self-appointed life coach."

"Shay's being gracious. It'd be more accurate to say I forced her into the position because I constantly need help." Warmth and sincerity fill Dela's voice, matched by an expression of genuine affection as she smiles at Shay. "I basically made Shay adopt me when I moved to town seven months ago."

"Girl, I'm only six years older than you." Shay crosses one high-booted leg over the other. "But I love you like a sister, and because of that, I get to tease you like one, too."

"You two sound a lot like Rosetta and me. We're cousins, but we've always been more like sisters. I'm Natalie, by the way." I offer my hand to shake, but Shay salutes me with her takeout cup instead.

"I make a point not to touch people," she says. "Everyone, not just you. It's a me thing." Her green-eyed gaze appraises me. "You and Rosetta being close explains how easily you're handling all the monster stuff." She tilts her head toward a naga and a goblin having coffee a couple tables over.

"Oh, I didn't know anything about the existence of non-humans until yesterday afternoon, when I got here, and met Constantine." Just saying his name stirs warmth in my chest. Between my legs. After being wrapped up in his arms all night, I woke up alone in bed this morning, my stomach growling at the aroma of the breakfast he was cooking in the kitchen. We kissed good morning—long enough that he had to remake the eggs that shriveled in the frying pan—then ate together like an old married couple. If old married couples have chemistry that feels like magnets being pulled together, that is. If I didn't have plans to meet Ro, I'm pretty sure Constantine and I would be naked in bed right now, working on those *stretching* exercises.

"Earth to Nat. You in there?" Ro snaps her fingers in front of my face.

My cheeks heat to inferno temperatures at the realization I've been caught daydreaming. "Oh good, you're finally here," I say, attempting to shift everyone's focus to my tardy cousin. Because they're currently all staring at me.

Ro, Dela, and Shay all sport smiles of various types. Shay's is pure amusement. Dela's smile is more of an "awe..." type of warm and friendly smile. Ro's is a total "gotcha" grin, her lips stretched to maximum width while her eyes twinkle with the torment she's undoubtedly planning to dish. Hopefully, she'll wait until we're alone.

"I don't have to ask where your mind was," Ro says,

settling on the chair beside me. "The question is, how far did you and Constantine go last night?"

"*Ro!*"

"Because I drove past him, walking down the street a few blocks down," she continues, "and he looked like one very happy Minotaur. And he always looks happy, but this was next-level."

"Can confirm," Shay says, nodding and raising one hand. "Had a little chat with him in front of the bakery. That man is on cloud nine. Vastly different mood from the last time I talked to him, a few days ago."

"The day he stopped in here to talk to you?" Dela asks, leaning closer. "When things got kind of tense?"

"Mm-hmm." Shay nods, then settles her gaze on me. "Brief moment of tension, that's all. Something was weighing on his mind, and I'm going to take a guess you're the something, and that everything is working out the way fate intended."

"There's that word again," I semi-mutter. "Does everyone in this town believe in fate?"

All three women nod.

"And everyone's okay with having fate determine the course of their lives?" I ask, fiddling with the empty paper cup in front of me. "Because to me, fate sounds like lack of free will or the option to choose. Oh sure, you *can* choose, but going against fate will ruin someone else's life."

The women go silent, all traces of smiling, teasing, or good vibes snuffed out by my opinion.

Dela, sweetheart that she is, reaches across the table and squeezes my hand. "Sounds like your welcome packet included a lot of big stuff."

Ro's snort rips through the tension I unintentionally created. "And now we're back to my earlier question. Just how big was his *stuff*, and how welcoming was your packet?"

Raising both hands as if in surrender, Shay rises from her seat. "I'm out. I cannot be having work conversations with Constantine if I know about his sex life. Though, for the record, I'm happy he's happy, and hope you will be, too." She points her gloved hand at me before giving us all a wave and walking away.

"Is she germaphobic?" I ask, once the coffee shop's door closes behind her. "The no touching, sitting away from us, wearing leather gloves inside during the summer..."

Dela's lips turn down. "Nothing like that. She's a witch. A seer, specifically. When she touches someone, she sees their future and, well, she doesn't want to."

Beside me, even Ro looks serious.

"So, she never touches *anybody?* You know, even personally," I whisper, and they shake their heads. "Wow. That's rough."

"You know who else hadn't touched anyone in a hell of a long time?" One of Ro's ginger eyebrows rises. "Constantine." She nods as if to confirm her own story. "The day he told me you're his mate, he said that once fate has chosen a mate for a Minotaur, they literally cannot be attracted to anyone else, even if they haven't located their fated mate."

Uneasy as the constraints and repercussions of fate make me, my heart picks up speed, knowing I'm that one special person for him. Because there's no denying his attraction to me. Or mine to him. "Did he mention how long he's been waiting for me?" It's a question I should ask him directly, but I'm too curious to wait.

"He said it's been a decade and a half, Nat. That man has gone without for fifteen years."

"Holy shit!" I clap my hand over my mouth, but not before every head in the place turns in my direction.

Across from me, Dela giggles. "For once, it's not me blurting something out and turning red because of it."

"So, last night...?" Ro makes the gimme motion with both hands. "Did you put an end to his long-ass drought? Tell us everything."

Dela makes a lighthearted pouty sound while pushing her chair back from the table. "It's been forever since I've had girl time like this, but I think I have to take a page from Shay's book. I can't be blushing and averting my eyes every time my boss is around."

"Oh, don't go. Please? We'll talk about something else." I give Ro the stink-eye. *"Right?"*

A bubbly laugh rises from Dela's model-perfect, luscious lips. "That's sweet, but you two need to roll with this convo. Plus, I always call my mom on Saturdays, and I found out she has plans later, so I need to catch her before I miss a day. Believe me when I tell you that you never want to take a single day for granted." Coming around the table, she leans in and gives me a quick hug. "It was so nice to meet you. Text me anytime and no pressure, but I vote for you to stay in town after the wedding."

"Thanks, it was great meeting you, too." I smile until she leaves the coffee shop, then it's just me and Ro, finally. "Your friends seem nice."

"Everyone in town is nice. I'm probably the least nice

person here," Ro says with a snort. "You're way better suited to the vibe than me."

Talk about a perfect segue. "Um, on the subject of vibes, is there a store here that sells them?"

"Heck yeah, there is." She's out of her chair before the last word has left her mouth, hauling me up along with her. "You are going to lose your freaking mind when you see the stuff Lexi sells."

I toss my empty cup in the trash on the way out of *The Brew*, the brilliant morning sun blinding me when we step out onto the sidewalk. I was more than a little distracted with Constantine on our walk over here. Now that I'm taking a good look at the downtown, I see all the things I didn't notice earlier.

The main street is a hub of bustling activity. No empty or rundown stores; everything is pristine and eye-catching. Manicured trees and raised flower beds dot the edge of wide, well-maintained sidewalks. Angled parking lines both sides of the street—hatred of parallel parking must be universal. In the center of it all, there's a large parkette with lush green grass, gardens, and benches. A beautiful fountain sits in the middle, and there's a large raised gazebo near one end, its wide stairs facing the length of the park.

I point at it, asking, "That's where the wedding's happening?"

"Yup. But we can talk about the wedding stuff later. Right now, I want to hear the Natalie stuff." Ro hooks her arm with mine, guiding me down the street. "Especially the parts that include you getting your mate bond on. Or *not* getting it on, since you want to buy a new vibrator."

"Why can't it be both? Are you telling me you haven't used a vibrator since moving out here to be with Dak?"

"Damn straight. He insists on being the giver of all orgasms. Literally, *all*." Grinning at me, she wiggles her eyebrows in a hubba-hubba motion. "Even those times when I just want a quick little release O, he takes care of it. The man knows his place, Nat, and that place is between my legs."

Well, I can't say that sounds horrible. And I wouldn't be surprised if Constantine offered for things to be the same way, though I think he'd be less intense about it than Ro's orc fiancé.

Ro halts in front of a small, green-and-purple shop with a gold window decal that reads *Every Witch Way*. "This is it."

"Are you sure? With a name like that, it sounds like an occult shop."

"Oh, there's magic stuff—for getting you magically stuffed," she says, tugging the door open and essentially shoving me inside.

One glance is all it takes for my eyes to feel as if they're going to pop out of my face. There are dildos everywhere. All kinds of sizes, shapes, and colors. "Holy —" I snap my lips closed before embarrassing myself. Again.

"Not so holy, though I do have an angel's cock model that I guarantee you'll find quite heavenly, and some incredibly realistic angel-wing feathers which are fantastic for sensual touch play." The response comes from behind a counter, then the voice's owner pops into view. "Oh! New girl alert! And Rosetta, hi!" The young, green-skinned woman hurries out to greet us up close, thrusting her hand forward. "I'm Lexi, the person to see for all things sexy and wonderfully bewitched."

My gaze drops to her green hand with slim fingers and long, purple nails, waiting for me to take it. "You don't mind shaking hands?"

"Of course not." She grabs hold of my fingers the instant I tentatively raise them. "Why in the realms would I mind shaking hands?"

"She met Shay this morning," Ro says.

"Ah. Well, Shay is a seer, and I'm not, so no visions for this witch." She gives up pumping my hand to gesture at her face, tilting it this way and that, the way a cosmetics model might. "Plus, this is Goodwin green, whereas Shay is a Winterlock. Totally separate covens. Different styles of magic. Mine is more fun." She winks. "What brings you ladies in this morning? Shopping for something magical to spice up the bedroom, or just touring around?"

"Just touring." I jump in before Ro can throw me under the embarrassment bus.

Lexi's ebony hair shimmers with her nod. "Take your time and check everything out. All my products are made from body-safe materials, so if you're wondering about insertion in any or all possible orifices, the answer is, yes, you can." Her laugh seems to bounce in the small shop. "If it fits, of course. Some of the models are rather large, after all!"

My gaze drifts to a massive, heavily ridged, dark-green dildo on a nearby shelf. It must be twelve inches high, and that's not including the big set of balls at its base. It makes Constantine's cock look average in size.

Following my focused stare, Lexi moves to the shelf and strokes the appendage lovingly. "Forest giant. Isn't he marvelous?" A blissful sigh leaves her lips. "Vern moved from Fate's Falls a few years ago, unfortunately. But his licensing agreement is indefinite, so at least we'll always have his majestic cock in stock."

Wait, what? I can't get any of the questions out because my bottom lip is hanging down.

"Show her what they do, Lexi." Ro gives me a shoulder bump. "This is the coolest."

Lexi gives up caressing the huge dildo to position her palms on either side. "The motions will vary, adapting to the user's physical responses during each use, so this is just for demonstration purposes." The next words she says are in another language. Then the big green dick begins rippling and moving side to side.

"There are no batteries," Ro says. "It's infused with magic."

"But...how? And I mean that in every sense of the word. How?"

A brief utterance later, the dildo stills, and Lexi smiles over at us. "All the models are anatomical replicas created from live volunteers who've entered into a licensing contract. Some people choose a set term, others go infinite, like Vern did. Forest giants live a long time, but by signing an endless agreement, his estate will receive the royalties as long as *Every Witch Way* is in business. It's all legally airtight, and the licensors are paid generously. A mold is made of whatever body part we'll be selling, then the products are individually hand-poured by moi, and imbued with a pleasure-giving spell."

"And you sell enough of them in a town as small as

Fate's Falls to make a living?" The struggling artist in me can't wrap my head around how that's possible.

"Not even close!" Lexi laughs again. "The big money comes from the website. Humans can't get enough monster-inspired sex toys, but you probably know that, right?"

Once again, my cheeks heat. Thank god this particular witch doesn't read minds. Nobody, not even Ro, knows about the tentacle toy I bought last year, after reading a series of super-steamy Kraken romance books. That hunk of silicone went from box to bed to bin in a matter of one day. The definition of disappointment.

"How do you sell to humans outside the protected area without being discovered? And without you there to start them with a spell, how do the products know when to move? And when to stop?"

"The website uses a standard URL humans can access, and the Oracle's magic makes it impossible to track back. The outpost sits just outside the boundary area. It has a variety of valid shipping addresses. They process all the packages going in and out of Fate's Falls. There are lots of businesses here that do very well beyond the border. As for how the magic works... witchcraft doesn't have to be doom and gloom. Human customers believe they're cordlessly rechargeable on the dock provided with each unit, and activated by body heat. It's bullshit, but nobody questions it because the products always work perfectly. Lots of very satisfied customers out there!" she says with a wink. "I'll leave you to explore the goodies."

I wait for Lexi to return to whatever she was doing, ducked down behind the counter, then drag Ro to the farthest corner of the little store. "This is—" When words escape me, I throw my hands up.

"Wild, right? I was so tempted to send you something from here, but I could never decide what kind of monster dick you'd prefer." Again, Ro wiggles her eyebrows at me, then turns her head toward the counter, and calls out, "Lexi, do you have a Minotaur model?"

"*Ro!*" I hiss under my breath.

"Sure do, ladies!" One green arm shoots up, pointing toward a shelf on the opposite side of the shop. "It's one of the bestsellers!"

Ro drags me in the direction indicated by Lexi's finger. She scans the decorative placards sitting in front of each item, her lips moving as she silently reads the creature descriptions until she gets to the one I'm already staring at. "There it is, Nat. The Minotaur. That's pretty damn big."

"It is."

"There's no name on it—for privacy reasons, I'm sure—but maybe it's Constantine's."

"It's not." *Shit!*

Her head whips in my direction, her eyes popping wide open when she sees what I'm sure is a crimson blush on my face. "You've seen his cock! And had a good enough look to know it's not this one," she says, snorting, dodging when I try to cover her mouth with my hand. "No more withholding—did you fuck?"

"Can you please keep your voice down?" A pointless ask, I know. Rolling my eyes, I sigh. "None of this—" I make the hand gesture for intercourse. "But yes to other stuff. Good stuff. *Really good.*"

The high-pitched squeal Ro makes has Lexi popping up

behind the counter. "If there's celebrating happening, I want in!"

"Natalie and Constantine are mates!" Ro hugs me tight enough that I'm gasping for air within seconds.

"Not," I sputter, "officially." I take a deep breath when she pulls back, holding me at arm's length. "Don't get your hopes up for me to stay."

"Why *wouldn't* you stay? You hit it off before you'd even met. You've obviously got physical chemistry if you did 'really good stuff' with him the first night, and you never get down with a guy on the first date. Hell, you rarely even get down with a guy."

"Thanks, Ro. Always nice to be reminded I'm uptight."

"Stop that." She gives me a mock slap on the face, complete with sound effects. "I bet it's because you're his mate. Part of you has been waiting for him all this time. And now you found each other. Just...fall in love, make adorable furry babies, and stay here forever. Please..."

"We'd have to have sex to make babies, and I'm not sure it's possible." I tilt my head toward the Minotaur dildo and whisper, "He's bigger than that."

Ro's eyes go round. "Oh my. Well, maybe Lexi has some training dildos you could practice with."

"I do," Lexi says, appearing at our sides, as if out of thin air. "But I don't think you'll need them. Not if fate has mated you to a Minotaur." She reaches for a jarred product on the shelf below the imposing dildo. "Minotaur semen is a known aphrodisiac. It's one of my fastest selling products."

Not much makes Ro pause, but even her mouth is hanging open as she points at the small container between

Lexi's thumb and index finger. "Are you saying that's a jar of Minotaur jizz?"

"With a pinch of magic to maintain its shelf life. No artificial preservatives here!"

"It's a pretty small jar," I say, remembering the amount of cum Constantine produced, and the flow that continued afterward. I probably swallowed three times as much last night.

"Because Minotaur ejaculate is highly potent. Only a small amount is needed to achieve intense sexual results."

Oh shit. "How is it, um…" I try clearing my throat, but there's no getting rid of the sensation there. The memory from last night is so vivid, I can almost taste Constantine's cum in my mouth, feel its silkiness sliding down my throat. "How do people use it?"

"Topically provides wonderful results. It's absorbed into the dermal layers immediately and heightens sensation instantly."

"Damn, Nat," Ro says, grinning widely. "You lucky bitch."

I shoot her the side-eye, then reach for the jar in Lexi's hand.

"You won't need this." Lexi draws her hand back. "Your mate's semen will prepare your vagina for penetration."

This is the wrong place to be getting turned on, but how can I not with images of Constantine smearing his cum onto my pussy running wild in my mind? "Oh, I was just wondering if there were any other directions or warnings on the label."

"The only risk is exhaustion from extreme pleasure!" Lexi laughs while returning it to the shelf, then leans in close enough to whisper in my ear. "Ingestion is completely safe and very exhilarating, but it won't help make his cock fit inside you—you'll need to massage it around down there for that."

"Thanks," I choke out.

"Anytime," she says, winking as she walks away.

I snag Ro by the arm and tug her toward the front of the shop. "Let's continue on the tour."

"What did she say to you back there? And I thought you wanted a vibrator?"

"Not a magically enhanced one that's molded from someone's actual cock," I say, low enough that I hope only Ro hears.

No such luck, if Lexi's laughter as we open the door is any indication.

This town is going to take some getting used to.

Chapter Eleven

CONSTANTINE

It's the best kind of surprise finding Natalie in my backyard when I get home from putting in a few hours' work at the brewery. The urge to head out there directly so I can soak up every possible minute with her is strong. But when I see what she's doing under the cover of a broadleaf maple tree, I pause with my hand on the sliding glass door.

She's drawing. Legs crossed on a canvas lounge chair, back hunched, left hand holding a large tablet in place on her lap, right hand moving quickly across the screen. And her face—gods, her face. Rosy cheeks, pink lips parted, eyes wide open and focused on whatever she's drawing.

She mentioned having to work on commission pieces while she's here. More than once, she also said creativity hasn't been coming easily.

Watching her now, she seems completely engrossed. I should leave her alone to continue, not disturb her groove, but I can't help myself. The next thing I know, the house is behind me and I'm crossing the flagstone patio, my mate in my sights.

Her head rises and turns, an instant, beautiful smile curving her soft mouth. "Hi."

Unable to resist, I dip down for a taste of her lips. An assumption, yes, but she responds by opening for me, not only inviting my tongue into her mouth but also sliding hers into mine. She hums as I thread my fingers through her hair. Softly moans when I cup the back of her head firmly and deepen the kiss. I'm tempted to scoop her into my arms and take her to bed right now, in the middle of the afternoon, and never let her leave.

"Your way of saying hi is much better," she says, when I force myself to break away.

"Think you could get used to it?" I'm pushing, something I keep saying I won't do. I'm beginning to think it's impossible not to push. I want her to be mine, and I know she wants to be.

"I don't want it to stop. Can that be enough for now?" Reaching up, she traces my features, leaving sparks in the wake of her touch, then strokes my hair where it lies in front of my shoulder. "I'm not saying I've decided to leave after the wedding. There's just so much for me to digest before I make a decision that changes both our lives. But I'm really thinking about everything, I want you to know that. When I decide, it won't be impulsive. I'll be sure."

"I couldn't ask for more than that." I curl my fingers around hers and bring them to my lips, pressing my lips to the soft skin on the back of her hand. "I thought you'd be gone most of the day with Rosetta and Dela, checking out the town."

"Dela bailed before we left the coffee shop. Ro's X-rated talk scared her off."

Settling on the end of lounger, I make a show of covering my ears. "Remember—no details about Dakgorim."

Laughing lightly, she leans over her tablet—which powered off sometime during our kiss—and pulls my hands from my head. "Actually, she started talking about you and me. Asking pointed questions. Making guesses based on my face's various shades of pink. Dela and Shay both said they'd rather not know those kinds of details about their boss's personal life."

"Good." The image of them scurrying makes me chuckle. "I'd rather they don't know, too." But I'm damn curious to know how much Natalie shared with her cousin. "What did you and Rosetta do after that?"

"She took me in a few shops, then out to her place to show me her workshop and the baby's room. The workshop is amazing, the best space she's ever had to do her metal-working. And the nursery Dak built is stunning, though I'm still in shock that Ro's pregnant. That she's in love and getting married. I never in a million years thought she'd want those things in her life."

"She found her mate. That changes everything." It needs saying, as many times as it takes. Greeted by silence, it's clear I pushed too much. "Did you get a pretty new note-book at *Fae-vorite Things?*"

Her expression lightens at the subject change. "We didn't get there. I'll go by myself. Maybe tomorrow."

That's a good sign. I want her to feel comfortable here. Like part of the community. But I also won't sacrifice an opportunity to spend time with her. "I'll join you, unless you'd prefer I didn't."

"I'd like it very much if you joined me," she says, sliding her hand across the chair toward mine. "Not just for shopping."

"Whatever and wherever you want, I'm in."

"About being *in*..." The roses in her cheeks are in full bloom now, her irises blown wide, despite the bright afternoon sunlight. "One of the places Ro took me was a shop called *Every Witch Way*."

There's no containing the chuckle that scene inspires. "You met Lexi."

The highlights in Natalie's auburn hair shine with her nod. "She seems like she'd be a fun person to hang out with." No mention of Lexi being a witch, or having green skin. Natalie's initial surprise at the reality of monsters seems to be fully behind her. Behind us.

"Lexi definitely favors fun," I say, stroking Natalie's small, soft hand. "I've always known Lexi to be friendly, easygoing, and good-natured. She's smart, too."

"So, I could trust the information she gave me to be accurate?" That's a loaded question if ever there was one.

"I don't know her on a level where I feel comfortable giving a blanket yes or no answer. But I'd believe anything Lexi says about her products or business. She's very passionate about them, and thorough."

"Then I think you should clear your calendar." Moving her drawing tablet to a side table, Natalie smiles, then climbs onto my lap. "Because she told me that Minotaur semen is an extremely potent aphrodisiac, and that if you massage enough of it into my pussy, I'll be able to take your cock."

My bullish huff is strong enough to ruffle her hair, which makes her laugh and snuggle closer. "Consider my calendar clear until you beg me to stop making you come."

Her arms wrap behind my neck as I push up from the chair. "Apparently, if I swallow enough of your cum, that might be never."

"You probably shouldn't have told me that, my sweet little mate. Not when you know how much I want to make you mine forever."

She doesn't answer. Not with words. But the way she clings to me, nuzzling my neck and stroking my hair while I carry her into the house... those actions speak volumes. She may not be consciously ready to commit to being my mate, but the desire is there.

"We're going to your room?" she asks when I turn down the hall opposite the guest bedrooms.

Our room. One day, that's how she will describe it. Until then... "Larger bed. More room to spread you out and pleasure you."

"I really can't argue with that." She smiles up at me as I lay her on the bed, my kneeling position spreading her thighs.

The flowy dress she's wearing pools just below her waist, the material thin enough to see her bra beneath, and my mouth waters at the sight of her breasts rapidly rising and falling. I didn't worship them as I should have last night. Time to change that.

"Having trouble?" She gives me a playful, coy look as I

struggle to manipulate the tiny pearl buttons running down the front of her sundress.

"There are far too many of these," I say when even the first one proves too challenging for my big hands.

"Then take it off another way, however you need to. I have other dresses."

She doesn't realize the instincts her suggestion provokes—an uncivilized desire to ravage her, to breed her. This isn't the time, but maybe one day, after she has claimed me for her mate, I will let the bullish part of me have his way.

For now, I skim my fingertips along the neckline of the pretty blue dress she won't get to wear again, then curl my hands around the front edges and rip it open in one swift motion. The sound of buttons bouncing across the hardwood floor seems distant compared to the rumble rolling up from my chest.

"*Natalie.*" I trace the top edge of a pale-blue lace bra, then drag my finger down the middle of her body, to the front of her matching panties. "You're so beautiful. I want to look at you forever."

With one hand, she opens the front clasp of the bra. The material falls away and her breasts spill free. I cup them, one in each hand, learning their weight, stroking the deep-rose nipples with my thumbs until both are tall, hard peaks.

"God, yes," she says when I take the first one into my mouth. "Your tongue feels so good. And your teeth scraping my skin when you suck... and your fur..."

I give the other breast the same treatment, going back and forth between them until her skin is red and slick with my saliva. I would spend hours teasing her breasts, but the scent of her arousal is irresistible. I lick and kiss my way down her body, tugging her panties out of the way when I reach her hips.

She wiggles to help me get rid of them, placing one delicate foot in the middle of my chest as soon as the scrap of material clears her toes. "Now you. I want you naked."

Shirt, pants, and the rest hit the floor in under ten seconds. My cock is hard as a tree trunk, and when she licks her lips while staring at it, every bullish instinct kicks in simultaneously. Rough huffing of breath, stomping of hooves, my tail swishing wildly. Physiological responses I wasn't sure a human mate would be able to get past, but Natalie doesn't just accept them, they arouse her. I see it in her glassy eyes. Her parted lips and shallow breathing. But mostly, in her scent. I could come just from the scent of her pussy.

Cupping her feet, I open her wide, drape her legs over my shoulders, then kneel between her spread legs. "Gods, Natalie. Your pussy is the only thing I want to eat for the rest of my life." I mean to go slow. To tease and draw out her pleasure. But the instant I taste her on my tongue, have my nose pressed tight against her slick, silky folds, there is no slow. No teasing. No control. Just my ravenous hunger for my mate's heat.

Her soft moans and twitching hips spur my need for her to come on my face. I reach down, stroke myself until my fingers are coated in precum, then spread it over her entrance. Her back arches as I burrow my tongue inside her, fucking her with it while I nudge and rock my wide nose against her clit.

I gather more precum, withdraw my tongue and replace

it with two well-coated fingers. Her walls squeeze them, resisting, then relax.

"I want some," she says, holding her mouth open while her hips rock against my face, my fingers.

And I want to feed it to her. All day and night long. Feasting on her pussy, I look up at her, press my precum-covered fingers between her parted lips, growling when she moans. My cock is too big to experience the sensation of her sucking it, but I swear I feel it between my legs when she sucks my fingers deeper into her mouth.

I slip my fingers from her pussy, coat them in precum, then slide three inside her while licking and flicking her clit. The air is thick with her scent, her breathy moans. She's ready to come. Desperate for it. But my mate also wants my cock, and I need to ready her. To stretch her for what's next.

I'm already throbbing for her. Leaking a steady stream. I dribble more into her mouth, then cover my hand with it and ease all my fingers between her swollen pink pussy lips.

"Oh god," she pants, as I push deeper. Deeper. Until the base of my fingers sit at her entrance. She moans low and long as I begin to fuck her with my whole hand while doubling-down on her clit. A sharp, high-pitched cry replaces the moan as she tangles her fingers in my hair. Grabs my horns. Bucks against my face, panting and babbling as she rides my mouth, my fingers, my nose.

Even when her grinding stops and her body goes flaccid, I keep devouring her. Twisting my fingers inside her, I find that spot that drove her to orgasm last night, and press on it while rolling my tongue fast and hard over her clit.

Her body arches like a taut bow, then she cries out my name, rocking against my face until her panting turns to soft, breathy laughter. "Tell me I'm ready," she says when I rise between her thighs. "Because I want to be ready."

If I could look at every part of her at once, I would. In this moment, I can't look away from her pussy, stretched and glistening. I guide my cock to her entrance, using the fat tip to spread precum all over her.

She's so small. Even with the stretching, the head of my cock is wider than her opening. But she'll take me. We'll fit. She'll come with my cock buried inside her, and I'll coat her walls with my cum.

She tenses as I press in, rocking forward, forward, trying to push past her body's defenses. Beneath me, her hair moves against the blanket as she shakes her head. "You're too big."

Pulling back may be the most difficult thing I've ever done. For her, I'd do anything. Including not give up.

I lean in and kiss her. Softly at first, then deeper, sliding my shaft over her clit in a matching rhythm, until her legs wrap around my back and her hips rock upward to meet my thrusts.

Her body twitches and tenses, jerking beneath me as she comes again, moaning my name against my lips. "Try again, please, I want you inside me."

"You'll have me there, my sweet one. I promise you." I ease out of her hold. Kneeling before her creamy thighs again, I stroke myself hard and fast, until my balls are hot and tight, my cock throbbing with the need for release. "Taste me."

She reaches down, catching the first small surge of cum, her eyes closing as she licks her fingers clean.

"Again, Natalie." I growl as she happily, greedily, swallows another mouthful. "Watch me fuck you," I command, looking into her lust-drunk eyes when she stares up at me. "Watch us mate." My tail whips as the last trace of control snaps.

She catches it, brings the tip to her breasts, tickling her nipples with the fur. Lips parted, eyes wide, she watches cum spurt from my cock.

I paint her pussy with it, drenching her folds, her entrance, then grip her hips and push inside. No resistance this time; her pussy is ready, pliant. But still so tight. So perfectly godsdamned tight.

Holding anything back is impossible now. My head tips back, a long, loud low leaving my mouth as I sink deeper inside her body.

She cries out, panting, grabbing my hips, her nails digging in. "*Yes, ohh...*"

Buried as deep as her body can take me, I lean forward, rocking, pressing against her clit until her walls squeeze me while she comes. "Gods, Natalie, you feel so good. So fucking good, my mate." Growling, I kiss her as deeply and thoroughly as I'm fucking her, getting lost in the taste of her, the feel of her, the lines between us blurring, meshing.

My mate. Her voice is crystal clear in my mind. The words unmistakable. Her arms wind behind my neck, her fingers thread through my hair, and her gentle sigh fills my mouth.

Breaking the kiss only because I want to look in her eyes, I ease back that small bit, fighting the words that are desperate to leave my mouth. The questions. The declarations. The promise to love her for eternity.

"Did you hear me?" Her cheeks tint with an adorable

blush. "In your head, I mean. I'm sure you heard all the other things."

"I heard it all. Your beautiful, sexy sounds and your words through our bond. I loved all of it."

"I did too. And I meant it, meant those words. I know you're my mate, just as much as I'm yours." Emotions swirl in her eyes as she pulls her bottom lip, still puffy from everything we shared, between her teeth.

"But you still haven't decided what the future holds for us."

"I need more time. To sort through things. Not things about us. I know *how* I feel, just not what I'm going to do with those feelings. And until I do..." Her soft fingers trail along my face, my nose, my lips. "It wouldn't be fair for me to commit yet, to claim you as my mate."

Whether she formalizes it or not, verbalizes it or doesn't, I am hers already. I always will be. Telling her that would seem like pressure. So, in this moment, I do what's right for her. I kiss her. And I wait.

Chapter Twelve

CONSTANTINE

The past week went by with the smoothness of silk. Mornings of waking up with Natalie in my arms. Days divided between me showing her around Fate's Falls, or putting in some work while she and Rosetta dive into wedding prep for the upcoming event, or Natalie tapping into what she describes as fresh creative mojo. Hours can go by in a blink when she gets in a drawing groove. And I could sit and just watch. There's something magical about her all the time, but practically glows when she's drawing.

All evenings have been spent together. Some, we grabbed dinner at one of the restaurants in town. Others, I cooked for my mate, pride roaring inside me when she moaned in delight at the food I fed her, especially when she allowed me to hand-feed her.

I love feeding her. Food. My cum. Especially that. I knew it was part of some species' mating practices, but I never had the urge to do it until I met Natalie. Watching the thick, milky substance puddle in her mouth before her lips close, hearing her hum and moan as she swallows... it stirs primal instincts I didn't know I possessed.

Every night together is passion and pleasure, each time easier and deeper than the one before. Preparation no longer required. Her body welcomes mine, eagerly stretching to take me inside. Molding to my cock, milking endless cum from my balls.

Everything is perfect—except waiting for Natalie's decision. With half her planned time here gone, the clock is running down. I swear I hear the hands ticking in my mind, moving faster with each day that passes.

I don't know what I'll do if she leaves. If she let me, I could follow her back to Toronto. Live in seclusion, venturing out under the cover of night, hiding what I am beneath hoods and other coverings. I'd be with her, but I wouldn't be the mate I am now. Would that version of me be enough for her? It shouldn't be. She deserves someone who can take care of her, not an oversized house pet.

"Hey, boss—whoa," Shay says, popping her head inside the back office at *The Brew*, mid-Monday morning. "I was going to tell you Natalie's out front, and that you should pack up whatever work you're doing to go check on her because she looks kind of down, but you look just as bad off. Everything okay on the home front? I have no basis for giving relationship advice, but I'm here if you need a sounding board."

"Appreciate the offer, but it's just something I have to wait out."

Shay nods. "Gotcha." There's a good chance she knows what's going on, without me saying more. Natalie and Rosetta share every detail of their lives, and much of that recent togetherness has taken place in the coffee shop, under Shay's watchful eye and misses-nothing ears.

"Thanks for letting me know Natalie's here."

"Sure thing. I've got your back, you know. Here at work and as a friend."

"Ditto, Shay." I give her a nod, close the programs I was too distracted to actually use, then tuck the chair under the desk and head out front to the customer area.

Every cell in my body wakes up when Natalie enters my view. Her gaze snaps to mine, and she brightens, but not before I see the expression Shay described. Even Natalie's beautiful smile doesn't entirely hide the clouds in her eyes. Doesn't matter that we've only known each other a short time, we've spent it learning about each other. Even without our mate bond, I'd be tuned-in to her emotions. Something's weighing on her. If I can alleviate that weight, I will. Whatever it takes.

"Hi," she says as I pull the nearest chair as close to her as possible and take a seat. Her hands rest on the table, and I cover both with one of mine, completely engulfing them.

I lean in for a brief kiss. Not the kind she prefers, but publicly appropriate. "I thought you were working on a commission piece this morning."

"I was. I started to, anyway. Then I got a call and now I'm here."

"Rosetta wants to do something?"

Soft hair moves like an auburn wave when she shakes her head. "No, it wasn't Ro on the phone. It was my mom."

It's as if a rock dropped into my stomach. I know she's close with both parents, even though they don't live near each other anymore. "Is everything okay?"

"With them, yes. They're healthy and happy, loving their RV life."

"Then why are your beautiful lips curved down instead of up?" I ask, tracing the line of her mouth.

"Apparently, when I told them I was coming out to British Columbia for Ro's wedding, they decided to change course and head in this direction so we could have a visit. A fun surprise because they miss me. Under normal circumstances, I'd be thrilled to get extra time with my parents. They've developed a serious aversion to city settings since they became full-time RVers—" A small, genuine smile tugs at her lips, disappearing just as quickly. "Now, I only see them a few times a year. But they don't know about non-human species and magically protected towns. They won't be able to find Fate's Falls. So, I won't get to see them *and* I'll have to lie to them. I hate both those things. I don't even know what lie I can tell that won't have them calling the police because they think I'm under duress."

"Did you call Rosetta to get her opinion?"

Again, Natalie shakes her head. "Her wedding is this weekend and she just started having morning sickness. I'm not going to add my parent troubles to her plate, especially when hers have dickishly disowned her. Talk about twisting the knife."

"Then we'll solve it together." I cup her face in my hands and look into her eyes. "We'll find a way to make it work."

"I don't know how that's possible. They're near Kalispell, Montana now. They never take the most direct route, but even so, they'll be in Kelowna tomorrow."

Not a lot of time, and honestly, we have limited options. But we do have options. "Come on," I say, standing and drawing her up with me. "Let's go for a walk and talk."

The mid-morning sunshine wraps around us when we exit *The Brew*. Taking her hand, I lead her toward Amazra's bakery up the street. Sugary baked goods won't fix the problem, but a treat might coax a temporary smile to Natalie's face.

"Have you considered telling your parents the truth about Fate's Falls?" It's the question I've wanted to ask every day of the past week. I know fear of estrangement from her parents is the primary reason she's hesitant to commit to our bond. Unfortunate as the current situation is, it has provided the perfect opportunity. "You told me they're both free-spirited, open-minded people. There's a chance they may accept everything that exists, like you did."

"And if they don't, then what?"

"You meet them in a nearby town to have your visit, then return to Fate's Falls for your cousin's wedding."

"And *then* what, Constantine?" Though she's never voiced it specifically, I know it's fear of losing the close relationship with her parents that's holding her back from staying here.

Stopping on the sidewalk, I wrap my arms around her, nuzzling her hair, kissing her head. Delaying the conversation because I'm afraid where it'll end—with the end.

"We should talk about this." Her soft voice is muffled against my chest, but I feel the hitch in her breath. She sighs as I rub her back, then tips her head back to meet my eyes. "We need to talk about what happens after the wedding."

"Have you made your decision?"

"No," she says quietly.

"Then anything I want to say will sound like I'm pressuring you. And I'm trying very hard not to do that, even though it's killing me not to do everything in my power to convince you to stay."

She buries her face against me, squeezing me as tight as her petite arms around my bulky frame can. Then her muscles relax and her breathing levels out, and I feel her warmth inside me as well as out.

I don't want to lose you.

"You won't," I say, answering the words she spoke through our bond. "We'll find a way. I promise you."

Her eyes hold unshed tears when she eases backward and looks up at me. "You shouldn't promise something that's beyond your control."

"I don't need to be in control of this. Fate is. And I'm sure fate didn't send you to me just to tear you out of my life after I've fallen in love with you."

She blinks slowly, her lips parting and closing, parting and closing. "You're in love with me?"

"Completely."

"Because of the mate bond?"

I shake my head. "Being mated brought us together, but I fell in love with you because you're you."

She jumps into my arms, wrapping herself around me, right there in the middle of town. A pair of vulpine folk make their species' equivalent of a wolf whistle as they walk by, one of them issuing a good-natured "Get a room" loud enough for any monster in the vicinity to hear.

"Sorry," Natalie whispers in my ear, then wiggles her way back to her feet.

"Never apologize for showing me how you feel." I press my lips to her crown, inhaling her scent until it fills every corner of my senses.

"I'll show you in detail at home." Bright pink floods her cheeks. "At your house, I meant. Obviously."

"'At home' works for me." Capturing her hand, I weave our fingers together, using them to point at the store before us. "Let's stop in here first. You never got the pretty pink notebook you wanted."

"To keep track of all the monster information I need to remember," she says as I hold the door open for her. "Do you think me buying one will signal fate to work in our favor?"

I don't get the chance to answer. The moment she crosses the threshold of *Fae-vorite Things*, the fairy who owns the shop makes a beeline—or more accurately, a fairy line—straight for Natalie.

Flora's brilliant-green eyes widen as she hovers in front of Natalie, her iridescent wings moving fast enough to make a faint buzzing sound. She does a circle around Natalie, pausing at her back, then zips in close, lifting Natalie's hair to inspect her ears. "You look fully human."

"Um...because I am?"

"You're part human, for sure, since you have no wings and your ears appear naturally round." Flora settles in front of us, her wings stilling, but remaining open. "But there's no mistaking that scent. Where in your lineage is your fairy family member? Or members? Can't be too far back. It's strong enough that I smelled it as soon as you stepped inside."

"It must be my shampoo or body lotion you're smelling. I don't have any fairy family members."

"You absolutely do." Flora's wings whir, lifting her off the floor again. "Come with me," she says over her shoulder, "we'll look them up in the registry."

Instead of following, Natalie leans in to me and whispers, "Is this a joke she plays with new people?"

"Only if it's a new joke."

"She didn't do this with Dela or Ro?"

"Definitely not with Dela. You'll have to ask Rosetta next time you talk to her."

"Let's go do that now." Natalie turns toward the door, only struggling a little when I wrap my arm around her waist and prevent her from escaping. An adorable *hmph* pushes through her lips. "I'm getting a weird vibe in here, and the only non-human I want to vibe with is you."

I manage to contain the audible part of my amusement, but not the smile on my face. "We'll go straight home after this, and I'll give you all the vibrations you can handle."

"Fine," she says, grudgingly taking a step toward the rear of the shop, where Flora is waiting with a big smile. "Let's get this crazy over with."

Flora claps as we reach the counter. "This is so exciting. We haven't had new fairy blood in Fate's Falls in over four decades. I'm Flora, by the way." She shoves one delicate-looking hand out. "Ooh!" Her pointed ears twitch when Natalie accepts the handshake. "Did you feel that little spark?"

"The static electricity shock?"

Fairy laughter has a certain lightness to it, and Flora's practically floats. "No, sweetie, that was fairy magic!"

Natalie backs up tight to my body, tilting her head to give me a *help me* look. I wrap my arms around her, covering her hand with mine and squeezing gently.

"What's your full given name?" Flora asks, fingers poised over a computer terminal keyboard.

"Natalie Aine Somers. Natalie is the basic spelling, nothing funky. Last name is spelled s-o-m-e-r-s and the middle name is a-i-n-e."

"What a lovely Irish spelling. Is that from your human side of the family, I wonder, or the fairy side?"

There is no fairy side.

I bite back a chuckle at the words Natalie pushed to my mind. Even in my head, her frustration is clear.

"Of course there is," Flora says, looking up from the computer. "I've got the information right here."

Natalie goes stiff as a board in my arms. "Wait—you heard me? You—*heard me?*"

"Well, you did broadcast it, sweetie. Toward your mate, yes, but when in the company of fairies, anything you push his way might as well be through a loudspeaker. Something to keep in mind, so you can keep your private things private." She winks.

The tension goes out of Natalie's body. As in, all the tension, all at once.

"Uh-oh, I think I short-circuited her." Flora rises higher above the counter to get a closer look at Natalie's rag-doll slumped position in my arms. "Take her into my apartment at the back, Constantine. I'll get her a cold drink."

I scoop Natalie into my arms, holding her tight as I

follow Flora through a door and down a short hall that opens into the living room of Flora's small apartment. By the time I settle on the couch with Natalie on my lap, she's blinking and looking around. "I'm here," I say, "you're safe."

"Is it true? Am I part fairy?"

"You fainted before we got details, but it sounds like it." I stroke her hair, everything in me warming when she leans in to the touch. "It would explain how naturally we're able to share thoughts with our bond."

"I do like that part." Her soft lips curve in a smile. "I like all the parts."

"As do I."

"Okay, here we go," Flora calls before fluttering into the room. Giving us a little heads-up, no doubt. She hands Natalie a highball glass of clear, bubbly liquid. "Plain old sparkling water. Not even a pinch of fairy magic."

A strangled sound leaves Natalie's lips, then she croaks out, "Thank you." With each sip, Natalie perks up a bit more, her normal rosy tones fully restored by the time she reaches the bottom of the drink.

"Feel better?" Sitting sideways on the opposite end of the couch, Flora's wings move in slow, gentle rhythm. "Ready to explore your fairy roots?"

"My fairy roots." Natalie shakes her head. "Of all the things I've learned since I got here, I think this is the most unbelievable."

"Well, believe it. Fairies are fastidious record-keepers. We write everything down."

My chuckle gets both women's attention. My smile is for my mate. "You said that to me the first time we talked. 'I write everything down.' Maybe it's the fairy genes."

Across from us, Flora beams. "Could be! Natalie, your great-grandfather on your father's side, Alfred Somers, is a full fairy. He was born and raised in Wildefell, Montana, a magically protected mountain town like this one."

"Montana?" Natalie jerks upright, staring at me wide-eyed. "Is it coincidence my parents just spent a week there?"

"Your great-grandfather still lives in Wildefell," Flora says. "Maybe they were visiting him."

"I have a living great-grandfather? And he's a full fairy?" She's not technically screeching, but with each question, the pitch of her voice gets higher. "Wait—do male fairies have wings too?"

"Of course," Flora says, fluttering her wings fast enough to lift her off the couch. "Even being only half fairy, your grandfather had wings. But then he mated with a human woman, further diluting the fairy genes, and by the time your father was born, there wasn't enough fairy DNA to produce wings. It's noted in the records."

"Holy shit." Natalie flops back against my chest. "Just... holy shit."

"What about Rosetta?" I ask. "Is she part fairy too?"

Natalie shakes her head. "No, we're related on my mom's side. Oh my god, do you think my mom knows about my dad's fairy heritage?"

I can't send a telepathic message to anyone but my mate, but the look I give Flora above Natalie's head seems to do the trick, because Flora doesn't speak, though I'm sure she knows the answer to Natalie's question. "I think there's one way to find out," I say, rising from the couch and guiding Natalie to her feet. "Let's go home and call your parents."

Chapter Thirteen

NATALIE

"Did you know your grandfather? The half-fairy one?" Constantine asks as we step inside his house. He's been peppering me with questions all the way here.

I think he's trying to make sure I don't pass out again. Apparently, shock and I don't mesh well. "I only ever talked to him on the phone. He and my grandmother lived far away. My parents said they couldn't travel, and I always assumed it was for health reasons. Now I know it was because my grandfather had wings. Wings!" I recognize the hint of hysteria in my laugh. I had it the day I met Constantine. After everything that's happened, you'd think I'd be handling this better. "They told me he died, but I wonder if he's still alive, too." Okay, not the best train of thought for remaining calm.

"From everything you've told me about your parents and your relationship with them, if there was any dishonesty on their part, I'm sure it would've been to protect the family, not to deceive you."

"I know." I lean in to his side, my arms circling his waist as much as possible while we walk through the house. "This is just so much to absorb. My family includes *fairies*. It's..."

"Amazing. Exciting." In the living room, he wraps me in an embrace, his big hand stroking my hair while turning my ear to his chest. The steady thump of his heart calls for mine to slow and match it. "And good news for us, I hope."

It could be, if the conversation with my parents goes the right way. But even if my mom is aware of my dad's unique lineage, she may not know about all the other non-human species in existence. Aside from wings and pointy ears, fairies basically look human. My Minotaur mate, on the other hand...

Making the call, broaching this subject matter, is a risk. One I don't have to take. I could lie to my parents, tell them Ro and her fiancé eloped, that there's no wedding to attend. I could meet them in Kelowna for a visit, come back here for the wedding, then go back to Toronto without breathing a word of this reality to my parents. I could reject Constantine officially, freeing us both to move on, separately.

Even if I leave here, I won't forget him. I could never replace him. I don't want to.

I know what I *do* want.

Tipping my face up, I meet his waiting gaze. His strong jaw is clenched, his black lips in a straight line. I don't have to ask if he heard my thoughts. He wouldn't have, since my mind is the furthest thing from open to him right now. I've been locked up tight in my own head since we left Flora's. No more of that. I want to share everything with him. Always.

Placing my palms on his big, broad chest, I inhale deeply and open myself to him. Light flickers in his amber eyes, then warmth flows through me, igniting sparks of arousal and calm comfort at the same time. Our bond. Our connection. Reaching deeper, I picture the door between us. Open it.

I decided. I'm staying with you.

His eyes widen. "Gods, Natalie. Tell me I heard you correctly." The smile that breaks across his face when I nod is like no other I've seen.

"I wanted to tell you before I call my parents, so you know I choose us, that my staying isn't because they approve. I'm staying because I want to, whether it's easy or not. I hope this call with my parents goes smoothly, but I know we'll sort things somehow. I'm not going to lose them because I love you. Tell me what I need to do to make it official. How do I accept you as my mate—no, how do I *claim* you as my mate? Because I want to. I love you."

That open door in my mind feels like it blows off the hinges, leaving a wide-open archway in its place. Where there was light before, there's a beautiful, perfect, endless glow.

"You just did," he says, then dips down, sealing his lips to mine.

The call can wait.

His chuckle rumbles against me.

I don't have to ask if he heard my thought. I know he did. Everything is clear now. Right and perfect.

Claim me as your mate.

Mine. His single unspoken word takes all the space in my mind, sending my pulse rocketing, the heat between us flaring. The pressure of his kiss intensifies, his growl vibrating through me as his tongue slides between my parted lips.

Our hands bump and tangle as we scramble to get rid of the physical things between us. Clothing hits the floor, some intact, some shredded by Constantine's big, impatient hands. Clothes are replaceable. Time with him isn't.

After a week of seeing him naked, you'd think I'd be used to the sight. Wrong. I can't take my eyes off him. He's huge. All over. Wide and thick, solid from horned head to hooves. Dark-brown fur covers nearly every inch of him, and I run my hands over it, spreading my fingers. The soft fur tickles the tender skin in the V between each finger, and I swear a feel it between my legs too. Longing tugs beneath my clit and deep inside me. I need his huge cock filling me. Making me come. I'll never get enough of him.

His tail lashes wildly behind him, his hoofs stomping against the hardwood as I grip his cock with both hands and stroke it hard. An actual blowjob is impossible, but I drop to my knees and do the next best thing, licking up and down his long, impossibly thick shaft, sucking each of his big, heavy balls between my lips and tugging until he groans.

One hand threads through my hair to cradle the back of my head. With the other, he grips his meaty cock and angles it toward my mouth. "Open for me, my sweet little mate. Taste me."

Starved for him, always, I open wide, humming when the first drops of sweet, milky cum hit my tongue. He presses the bulbous head of his cock against my lips and presses, forcing my lips to stretch wider. Wider. As open as my mouth can go, leaving no gap for air. Breathing through my nose fills my head and lungs with his rich, earthy, masculine scent. I wait until thick warmth coats my tongue, all the way to the back of my throat. Then I close my lips before anything seeps out, moaning as I swallow it all down. The light, buzzy sensation hits me faster than the times before. Because we're truly mated. Because I love him.

Looking up at him, I stroke him again, gathering precum on both hands, then spread it over my nipples and between my legs, where I rub my clit until my hips are rocking against my fingers. I'm drunk on him. Desperate and so, *so* ready.

His nostrils flare, his breath pushing out in a rough huff. My sexy Minotaur doesn't attempt to hide his bullish side from me now. He knows it turns me on. Everything about him does.

He reaches for me, helping me to my feet, then lifts me onto the couch, placing me on my knees, facing away. The firm pressure of his palm on my heated skin as he bends me over the backrest sends anticipation rippling through me.

I'm expecting him to fuck me, but he doesn't. He pushes my knees apart—wide apart—then settles between them, face up. His thick, furry arms wrap around my thighs and he pulls me down onto his face. My eyes roll back in my head as his long, wide tongue pushes inside me, so incredibly deep. Another bullish huff pushes from his nose, the heat of it tickling my sensitized skin.

I moan as his tongue finds that magic spot and moves against it, pushing me toward the peak. Reaching down, I take hold of his horns, gripping them hard while I rock against his face, rubbing my clit hard and fast on his wide nose.

Wet warmth slides down the crack of my ass, then the pad of his finger is there, massaging my anus with his precum. Getting it ready to take his thick finger.

Leaning forward, angling so I'm open wider, I moan as he presses the tip past the tight ring. "More," I pant, "I want all of it." I moan as his finger fills my ass—deeper, deeper, then I cry out, riding his face hard while I come and come and come.

"Gods, you undo me, Natalie," he says, rubbing his precum-covered cock head up and down my pussy after positioning himself behind me. Holding my hips, he pushes inside, huffing, his hooves clomping. Driving me wild with all the primal tells of his desire for me.

Knowing he'll fit doesn't make the absolute stretch of it any less thrilling. My panted moans join his rough grunts of pleasure. Every inch feels like it must be the last, but there's more. So much more. It should be too much, but I want it all. Inhuman sounds leave me when he bottoms out, his furry abdomen pressed tight to my ass cheeks and heavy balls brushing my inner thighs.

He folds over me, his chest to my back. Slips his hand between my legs to stroke my clit. "You take me so well. I crave you. More than air, I need you." His normally smooth voice is husky with tightly held need. "Come for me, my sweet mate. Squeeze me, milk every drop from me."

Stars explode behind my closed eyelids as I come hard, panting his name, writhing against his fingers on my clit, my skin tingling beneath his hot, ragged breath on my neck.

His deep, long low fills my ear as he comes. His massive

cock throbs inside me, then I'm coming again, my body flying high on cum coating the deepest parts of me.

His cock slips out of me, and what feels like endless cum oozes from me, running down the insides of my thighs and—

"Oh no, the couch," I say, shifting quickly, but it's too late. Puddles of white are all over the earthy-gray velour. "Yikes. That's going to leave a mark."

Constantine's rumbling silent laughter vibrates through me as he pulls me against him, then onto the other side of the L-shaped couch, where he lays us out together in a beautifully entwined embrace, nuzzling my hair and neck before kissing me softly. "All that matters is the mark you left on my heart, sweet Natalie."

"It matches the one you made on mine," I whisper, snuggling in, soaking in the rightness of being with my mate.

The call, and everything else in the world, can wait a while longer.

The next day

NATALIE

"They're still not picking up," I say to Constantine after my third attempt to call my parents. "Twice yesterday, and now this. I keep getting their voicemail."

"But they replied to your text last night. They're probably going through spotty service areas."

Nodding, I set my phone down. Logically, I know he's right. My parents have never been the kind of people to be glued to their phones. Tech is a convenience, a means to be in touch with me, not part of their daily lives. Especially since they downsized their possessions and stress levels and hit the road. More than ever, they're all about slowing down, taking the path less followed, and connecting with the world around them. They'd probably love it here in Fate's Falls.

I may have inherited some fairy DNA from my dad, but I did not get the "relax and be chill" gene from either parent, so I pick up my phone and check it again. No missed calls. No new voicemails. I tap the group text I have with both of them, rereading our exchange from last night. Well, *their* exchange, really. They're honestly the cutest.

> Hi, Mom! Hi, Dad! I can't wait to hug you! And I have news. Great news. Call me when you get to Kelowna so we can arrange a place to meet.

Mom:
Hi honey! We're planning to do some night
driving so we can get to you sooner.
Love you!

Dad:
Don't worry, I'm doing the night driving, not
your mom. The wildlife population is
counting on me.

Mom:
It was one raccoon, fifteen years ago. And
it ran out in front of my car as if it had a
death wish. My poor little Toyota was never
the same.

Dad:
I'm still doing the night driving.

Dad:
See you tomorrow, sweetie! Can't wait to
hear your news!

Constantine is right. My parents are fine. They're not avoiding my calls, just driving along and watching the world go by. They'll phone when they get to Kelowna, then I'll head down and meet them. I'll tell Dad I know about his fairy heritage, then share my great news—I have a fated mate! I'm in love with a Minotaur! No big deal. Except it's a huge deal. A tall, furry, horned and hooved, huge deal.

I slump over the kitchen island, my forehead pressed to the cool granite. Constantine's hand on my back settles my anxious mind instantly, each gentle pass up and down my spine further easing the tension.

"Are you expecting Rosetta?" he asks when the doorbell chimes.

I sit up straight, checking my phone again to see if I missed a message from her. "No. We're not getting together until tomorrow afternoon to make wedding favors."

His heavy brow lowers over narrowed eyes. "I don't know what 'wedding favors' are. That must be a human thing."

"Or just a chick thing. Flora and Shay knew."

A smile takes the place of his perplexed expression. "I'm happy you're building new friendships."

"Me too. I already have more friends here than I did in my entire lifetime when I lived in Toronto." I scrunch my nose when he smiles wider. "What?"

"I like hearing you describe it as 'when I lived in Toronto.' Putting it in the past tense. No longer calling it 'back home.'"

I hop off the counter stool and wrap my arms around him. "This is my home now."

"I'm glad you feel comfortable in Fate's Falls."

"I do, I really love this town, but I was talking about you. Wherever you are, that's my home."

"And you are mine." He dips down, brushing his lips over mine. The beginning of a kiss that could quickly become more—if the doorbell didn't chime again.

Groaning, I ease backward from his arms. "Sorry, that has to be Ro. With everything happening in her life right now, I don't want to leave her hanging, even though she didn't let me know she's coming."

"I'd never want you to." He presses a kiss to my forehead. "I'm glad she has you, and she's always welcome here. Just don't give her a key."

"Um, never." My body heats at the thought of all the things I wouldn't want anyone to walk in on. So many perfectly dirty things. "I better get the door," I say, when his nostrils flare and his tail swishes side to side. I don't need to hear his thoughts to know he can smell my arousal, that he'd like nothing more than to make me come right now.

"Natalie." A bullish huff of breath follows my name. "The door or our bed. Five seconds."

Giggling, I take one more look at his big, beefy deliciousness, then hurry to the door. I don't even try to tone down the love-drunk smile on my face as I grab the handle. Ro will take one look at me, give me a "get it, girl," then turn around and leave us to our insatiable mate bond. I'll make it up to her. I have all the time in the world with her now.

Only...it's not Ro's face I see when I open the door.

"Surprise!" my parents say in unison, complete with jazz hands.

I shriek at the sight of them—and not in a good way. My distress call brings Constantine thundering to the door, the sound of his hooves clapping against the hardwood practically echoing.

He pulls up just shy of barreling into me, his big arms wrapping around me protectively. Warmth flows through me from a place deeper than his physical embrace. Our bond. *Everything will be okay.*

What should I do?

"Introducing us would be good," Dad says, giving me a big smile while openings his arms. "Hi, sweetie. We sure have missed you."

Happy tears roll down my cheeks as I go from the arms of my mate to those of my father. Two men I love and trust. Both here in this strange, wonderful place where unbelievable things make perfect sense.

"Dad," I say, hugging him tight. Then, "Did you *hear* my question?"

"I did. Only to break the ice, since you seemed pretty flustered. I'll do my best to block your internal voice, but do your old dad a favor and try not to share any overly personal thoughts with your boyfriend while I'm around."

Choking on a laugh, I ease out of the hug. "Okay, but he's not my boyfriend. Constantine is my mate. My fated mate."

Mom's eyes open wide, then she takes her turn at attempting to hug me to death. "That's wonderful, sweetheart. Your dad and I are so happy for you."

"You are?" I ask as we break apart.

"Of course we are," Dad says. "Finding your other half is the best kind of magic." He wraps his arms around Mom, gazing at her as if he's seeing her for the first time. "I knew your mom was my fated mate immediately."

"We both knew," Mom says, touching his face and drawing him in for a kiss.

Watching them share a kiss isn't awkward at all. They've never hidden their affection for each other. Knowing what I know now about the mate bond, it's a miracle I never had to witness more than G-rated shows of love.

"Love you," Dad says to her, then turns to me again. "Now that you've found your special one, your mom and I will always know you're happy, safe, and loved, whether we're on the opposite side of the continent or parked in your driveway."

I glance past them to the RV—the first one I've seen in Fate's Falls, with good reason. "How did you find me? How did you find Fate's Falls?"

"You told us where you are. Fate's Falls may not be on human maps, but it's on fairy ones, which are much better kept, for the record."

"Of course they are," I say, feeling lighter and luckier than ever in my life. "We fairies write everything down."

"That we do, sweetie." Dad extends a hand to Constantine, a warm grin in place as they shake. "Jonas Somers. And this is my wife, Siobhan. We're honored to meet you."

"The honor is mine entirely," Constantine says, nodding at each of them. "Thank you for creating your beautiful daughter. I will treasure, respect, and protect her for the rest of my life."

Who needs a wedding when your mate makes a vow like that on the front doorstep? Though...Constantine would look hot in a tux, and I can't even imagine what honeymoon sex would be like.

Marry me and find out.

Biting my lip doesn't hide the big smile overtaking my face. Nothing could. My life is officially the best fairytale ever.

Epilogue

Eight Months Later

CONSTANTINE

I f Dakgorim had his way, Rosetta and their new baby would be off-limits to everyone but him. His protective nature went into overdrive when Rosetta got pregnant, ratcheting even higher when their orcling arrived. Delivery by home birth, and if not for having a female physician available, Dak might've insisted on playing doctor in addition to head of security.

That was a week ago. It's taken Rosetta seven days to convince Dak to let us visit.

Natalie has been climbing the walls at being kept away. No amount of cute pictures would satisfy her—and by gods, there've been a lot of them.

But we're here now, bearing more gifts than any single

baby needs. Dakgorim will undoubtedly scowl at the sight of so many bags and boxes. Orcs are minimalists by nature. Pretty sure Rosetta wouldn't give a damn if we brought a truckload or came empty-handed. She just wants to see Natalie.

My mate is practically vibrating beside me by the time I knock on the door of the small wooden home in the forest. Her smile falters a bit when Dak opens the door. They don't dislike each other, but he's not the easiest person to get close to, whereas Natalie is warm and open to everyone. Including Dak. Even now, while he's scowling and sniffing the air around us, giving us the orc equivalent of a black-light check over.

"You may enter," he says, stepping aside.

"Congratulations!" Smiling—genuinely, too—Natalie offers him a light-blue envelope, which he takes after an awkward moment of silent glaring.

"You may leave the packages out here." He points toward an empty corner. "No clutter in the nursery."

"Okay, sure," Natalie says, as the two of us set our armfuls of gifts in the designated space. "Is Ro going through another feng shui phase?"

Dak's thick black eyebrows draw together, then he jerks his head toward the addition he built last summer. "Follow me."

Natalie catches my hand, squeezing it while opening herself to me. *She must love him for his huge dick.*

My body shakes with silent amusement at the thought she sends me. I know she doesn't really believe her cousin is with Dak for his cock. In the eight months she's been in Fate's Falls, she's witnessed the bond between Dakgorim and Rosetta many times. She's seen how naturally they click, despite their many obvious differences in personality. Fate chose well for both of them. And now they share more than their mate bond. The urge to have that with Natalie has been there since our first night together. Maybe one day, when she's ready.

Dakgorim enters the nursery ahead of us, moving to stand behind Rosetta where she's lifting the swaddled baby from the crib Dak made. The orc's facial expression softens as he looks at his wife and child. He even smiles, as much as an orc can.

A soft gasp leaves Natalie's lips as she moves toward them, tilting her head to get a better look at the sleeping green orcling in her cousin's arms. "Oh, Ro, he's so beautiful."

"Want to hold him?" Ro asks.

"Of course, I do." Instead of taking the babe from Ro's arms, she looks up at Dak. "I will be as careful with him as I would with my own child." Not asking permission, per se, but an offer of respect. She really has gotten to know the big orc.

"I know you will," he says, nodding.

Happy tears roll down my mate's face as Ro places the infant in Natalie's arms, arranging his blanket just so. "Oh, Ro... he's utterly perfect. And he smells so good."

"Come back when his diaper's full." Ro snorts. Then sighs, stroking the red hair that lies across his small forehead. "I'm kidding. Even his toxic-level poop doesn't bother me. I love him so much, Nat. I can't even describe it."

I move closer, pressed to Natalie's back, one hand on her hip, the other on her shoulder. I offer congratulations to Dak and Rosetta, keep my focus on the baby in Natalie's arms, but ignoring her scent is impossible. Arousal. Love. And... ripeness?

I stopped taking the pill. And I'm ovulating.

It takes conscious effort to control my Minotaur physiology. To hold my tail and hooves still. To prevent my breath from huffing out.

My mate feels it all, though. Her soft laugh rings in my mind, as clear as if she released it in the room.

Take me home and put a baby bull in me.

My cock feels hard enough to break down the walls. My heart, so full it could burst. But this could be an impulsive decision made in a moment of baby lust. As much as I want to see her grow round with our baby, I don't want her to have regrets. *Are you certain you're ready?*

Tipping her face up to look at me, she smiles. *I'm ready for everything with you.*

And that's what I will always give you, my mate. Everything.

The Grumpy Demon's Sunshine

THE GRUMPY DEMON'S
Sunshine

KARLA DOYLE

THE GRUMPY DEMON'S SUNSHINE

RAZBUNARE

I was born in the fires of hell, created to grant humans' selfish wishes for revenge in exchange for their souls. I exist only to fulfill my purpose. After eons of meting out vengeance, both petty and dire, something sparked inside me—an emotional response. Vengeance demons do not *feel* things. And yet, I did.

Rather than return to the hell realm, I wandered the earth before settling in Fate's Falls, a protected place where monsters of all types reside in harmony. There are even some humans in town, including one female who stokes flames inside me that put hellfire to shame.

The lovely coffee barista is too soft. Too small. Too filled with sunshine and goodness to be attracted to a towering, red-skinned, hell-born demon. She will never know my feelings, never return them, but Dela is my purpose now. I would kill for her. I would die for her. But I cannot stay away from her.

DELA

After dying at the hand of my ex-boyfriend, then being returned to life by a reaper, I follow his advice and escape to Fate's Falls. Not only are reapers real, so are all kinds of fantastic creatures, many of whom reside in the secret small town surrounded by mountains and forests. I'm not afraid of the monsters here, but I didn't expect to be attracted to one. Especially not a massive, red demon who barely speaks and has the most intense case of resting-grumpy face I've ever seen.

When a coincidence—or fate—gives me a chance to get to know Raz, the attraction quickly becomes something deeper. And it's mutual. Turns out, the hotter-than-hell demon isn't so grumpy after all. He's sweeter than a cinnamon roll, and he's mine for as long as I want him, which might be forever...

Content Notes

THE GRUMPY DEMON'S SUNSHINE

- a hell-born vengeance demon who develops emotions and turns out to be an adorable cinnamon roll hero
- I will kill for you and die for you vibes
- size difference (but don't worry, it fits!)
- he puts his long tongue *everywhere* (yes, everywhere)
- explicit sexual acts between consenting adults
- sweet happily ever after

Please be mindful of the following sensitive content:

- mentions of previous psychological and emotional abuse (of the heroine by her ex-boyfriend)
- mentions of violence that occurred in the past
- mentions of mental health struggles & death

Chapter One

DELA

"Oh, Dela..." my coworker singsongs from the opposite end of the café counter. "Your favorite customer just walked in."

Nope. Not giving Shay the satisfaction of a response or reaction. And I'm definitely not turning around to confirm who she's talking about. Besides, I don't have to. The temperature is easily several degrees higher than before the bell over the front door jingled, and that's not because the furnace kicked into overdrive.

Raz is the hottest monster in town. Yes, yes, phoenix shifters literally burn, but that's once every what, five-hundred years? Dragon fire is *technically* hotter than Raz, too, but again, that's not part of a dragon's day-to-day, out-in-public existence. Neither of those creatures, nor any of the others in town, affect the coffee shop's room temperature.

But Raz does. Heat radiates from the towering red demon. Even without seeing his brooding face and curved black horns above the heads of the other patrons, I feel his presence every time he comes into The Brew.

Shay says she doesn't feel the increase in room temperature. I call bullshit on that, but the more I dispute her claim, the more enjoyment she gets from pushing my buttons. She's my favorite person to work with, one of my new best friends, and I don't mind the teasing when Raz *isn't* within earshot. But honestly, who knows how far that range is? He's a revenge demon, for goodness' sake. His life's purpose is to hear vengeful wishes and make them happen. Odds are, his hearing is pretty damn good.

Right now, all *I* can hear is my pulse pounding a heavy beat. Based on its increasing speed, he's getting closer to the counter. Meaning, I'm going to have to face him momentarily. There are only so many sugary sprinkles I can add to the birthday-cake iced latte I'm making before I have to turn around and hand it off to the customer patiently waiting for her order. On that note, I hope fairies can't get diabetes.

I force myself to return the sprinkle shaker to the shelf, then draw a deep breath. Overloaded iced latte in hand and smile in place, I make the necessary swivel. My focus should be the fairy with beautiful, iridescent wings and wide green eyes. The person whose drink I'm holding—or, more accurately, *withholding,* since I haven't set it down. It's become my personal security drink. When I turn it over to its rightful owner, Flora will flutter away and Raz will move up, one step closer to the counter. Before I know it, he'll be directly in my face.

After I tip my head back to look up at him, that is. Which I'll have to do because he's a customer. Something I'll want to do because what Shay said is true—Raz is my *favorite* customer. My favorite monster. My favorite man.

To him, I'm just a coffee barista. An unremarkable human who chose to live in a town full of monsters. He probably assumes I moved to Fate's Falls because I have a monster fetish. I came here to escape a monster of the worst kind—a human man who tried to hurt me.

Despite its population filled with some potentially deadly creatures, Fate's Falls has a zero-tolerance policy for aggression of any kind. The monsters who choose to live here may do heinous things outside the town's boundaries, but never within. There hasn't been a single occurrence. As a survivor of some ugly shit, when presented with the opportunity to live without fear, I jumped. Not literally, I was too broken and weak at the time. But internally, mentally, I did more flips than an Olympic gymnast.

If Fate's Falls didn't have its guarantee of peace and harmony, I still would have moved here. It's far away from the city where I lived with Doug. Even if he tried to hunt me down, the odds of him finding this small town nestled between mountains and forests are slim. Maybe even impossible, if the stories I've heard are true.

As for monsters... It never occurred to me I might be attracted to one. My unexpected interest is irrelevant because I'm riding the celibacy bus now. Okay, that and my vibrator, which yes, *is* oversized and red. Coincidentally. Or subconsciously. Maybe I was thinking of Raz when I ordered it online. But whatever. That's as close to his cock as I'm ever going to get. Assuming he has a cock. That's not information you can fact-check via Google, after all.

"Here you go," Shay says, prying the birthday-cake iced latte from my grip, then passing it to my extremely patient fairy customer.

Snapped back to reality, my cheeks flame with embarrassment. Everyone in the café just witnessed me completely zone out while thinking about riding my Raz-inspired vibrator. Here's hoping none of them have the ability to read minds.

"I'm so sorry for your wait," I say to Flora as she rises from the floor, takeout cup in hand.

"No problem, sweetie." She winks before fluttering away. Not a general, friendly wink; it's slow and exaggerated, a knowing kind of wink.

Oh shit, can fairies read minds? The better question is, *can* revenge demons? Because there's one directly in front of me now. How did he get to the head of the line, anyway? I could've sworn he was at the back, near the door.

A glance to my left gives me the answer. Shay opened the second register—probably while I was off in hell-demon dreamland—and all the customers between Flora and Raz abandoned my line for hers. I have no idea if there's anyone standing behind Raz. He's not the largest being in Fate's Falls, but he's pretty huge. If I didn't tilt my head upward to look at his face, I'd be talking to his abs.

"Sorry for the delay," I say, grateful my voice sounds normal when I pull myself together enough to use it. "What can I get for you today?"

"Are you unwell?" he asks, ignoring my apology and question.

"No, I'm fine." I wrangle my features in to an appropriate, neutrally friendly smile. No easy feat with Raz's stare drilling holes in me. "Can I get your usual, or would you like something different?"

"Usual?" His pronounced, permanently furrowed brow rises the tiniest bit.

My customer-service smile morphs into one that's genuine. I've watched him enough to know he's always in control of his expression. Of his voice. Of everything about himself, I assume. Seeing that control waver, even infinitesimally, because of me...that's enough to make my day.

"You always get the cauldron of doom, extra-hot." The darkest coffee we make, it's the closest liquid to a true black color that I've ever seen, and it packs a wallop with over 600mg of caffeine per hundred milliliters. That's more than double what the strongest brand made for humans contains.

"I have never ordered a *cauldron of doom*. You are confusing me with another customer."

"Um, no," I say, letting my gaze rise all the way up to the top of his wavy black horns, then do a slow wander downward until I meet his glowing eyes again. "Zero confusion."

"Then you are simply making a mistake. In my existence, words are crucial; I remember all which I have spoken."

I should've known better than to attempt casual conversation or humor with him. In the half-year-plus I've worked here, he's never given me any indication either would be welcome. My ex gaslighted me about a lot of things, but he was obviously right when he said I'll never learn, because here I am, attempting to start fresh, yet inexplicably drawn to another closed-off man.

"You're right. You always order 'the largest capacity of the strongest coffee.'" I make air quotes around his customary words. "Which is a cauldron of doom. *Cauldron* equals extra-large in our lingo, and *doom* is our name for the most jacked-up brew we serve. I took the liberty of adjusting the serving temperature to make it extra-hot once I learned your core temperature is higher than, well, nearly everybody's. You didn't complain about the change—in fact, you started coming by more frequently, so I assumed you enjoyed it, and I continued to prepare it that way."

"I was unaware."

Is that a hint of sheepishness on his resting scowl face? Pretty sure it is. It's hardly an apology—not that he owed me one—but it's something. And his comment, well, it makes me wonder if maybe...

I lean forward over the counter, hoping to keep my next words private. "I'm happy to read you the menu options anytime. English is a human language. I wouldn't expect everyone in Fate's Falls to be able to read it."

A low rumble rolls from him, his lips becoming an even straighter line than normal. "I understand every language that has ever existed on this plane, written, spoken, or communicated by action."

Offending a hell demon can't be a good thing. I inhale deeply and hold it in. On the job with a customer staring me down isn't the ideal place to engage in the affirmation techniques my therapist taught me, but I manage to re-center myself before dizziness sets in.

With my pulse back where it should be, I exhale and give him a smile. My feelings, desires, and grab-bag of issues aren't his fault. I'm not going to hold a harmless miscommunication against him. Nor am I going to apologize for being considerate, even if it was misplaced. All that aside, we're two entirely different species—if *species* is even the right word for demons. I'm not about to ask Raz that question. Honestly, there's only one question I should ever be asking him. "What can I get for you today?"

He's silent, his strong brow line lowering as he stares at me. If it were possible to see behind his eyes, the gears would undoubtedly be turning, likely as he wonders what kind of frail-human malfunction I'm having.

I bite my tongue and hold my smile in place. Definitely not going off-script again. I'll wait him out, one way or another.

"A cauldron of doom," he says in his ever-present deadpan. Then, his lips twist into an unfamiliar shape—it's not an actual smile, but a hint of upward tick is there. "Extrahot, if it is not an inconvenience to ask for your usual preparation."

"Coming right up." Heat blooms on my cheeks, even though there's no way in hell—or on earth—that he's flirting. The fact that he's making this out-of-character and kind-of-clunky attempt at friendliness is enough. For now.

RAZBUNARE

It is fortunate when she turns away to prepare my beverage, because I find myself unable to force my gaze from Dela's face. Increased adrenaline has widened her capillaries and brought blood closer to the surface of her facial skin. A physiological response she cannot control, brought on by any number of stimuli. Fear, anger, embarrassment... the reason matters not. She is radiant; even more so than the dozens of other times I have observed her. Red suits her.

Most humans fear me on sight. Because of my size. My red skin and glowing eyes. The long, dark horns curving up from my cranium's frontal bone. I was created to intimidate, to ensure the humans who choose revenge in exchange for their soul are aware there will be no release from the bond.

Dela has never shown any sign of fear in my presence. She meets my gaze directly, though to do so requires she tip her head back to its maximum angle. Her voice does not waver when she speaks to me—even just now, when my inability to engage in comfortable communication would have made any other mortal shudder.

Embarrassment or anger are the logical causes for the color of her delicate cheeks. Either or both are possible after the exchange we just shared.

I must refrain from attempting conversation. Especially with this human who intrigues, confounds, and arouses me in equal measure. She is a curiosity I should not indulge. Yet I am unable to focus my attention anywhere else.

In the vast span of my existence, I have encountered countless human women, many very pleasing to the senses. However, I could not individually recall a single one. None captivated me beyond the fraction of time they spent in my purview.

Until Dela.

She lingers in my mind when I am not in her presence. Her full lips with their pale-rose hue—natural, not falsely painted, like most modern human women favor—and their pronounced bow shape. Her eyes, as blue as the clearest earthly sky, are always wide open and never shuttered. Looking into them brings a lightness unlike anything I have experienced and cannot resist returning to. And, in the moments when I am alone, free of the noise of the worlds above and below, memories of her voice flow through my mind, flooding me with an unfamiliar combination of peace and longing.

I did not think myself capable of those... *feelings.*

"Here you go." The music of her voice pulls my focus from futile thoughts.

I hold up a payment card as she sets the takeout cup in front of me.

Her hair shimmers as she shakes her head. "This one's on me."

"I have ample financial assets."

The upward curve of her mouth increases and her eyes twinkle as if filled with stars. "It's a friendly gesture, Raz, not charity."

I was born in the fiery depths of hell, yet hearing her speak my name, even in its shortened version, creates a different kind of heat within me. "Friendly." I repeat the word no one has ever used in regard to me.

"Yes. If that's overstepping, I—"

"It is not." I try once again to arrange my lips in a position she will interpret in a pleasing manner. "Thank you," I say, lifting my cup from the counter.

The delicate brown arcs above her eyes rise. "Anytime."

Behind me, an orc called Dakgorim loudly grumbles his displeasure that I have not relinquished my position in the line.

"Choose a time," I say, ignoring an additional huff from the orc.

Dela's head tilts slightly to the right. "A time?"

"A convenient time for me to purchase a beverage for you, when you are not performing the duties of your employment."

"You want to buy me a coffee when I'm off the clock?" she asks, a rouge deep enough to rival my color rising on her cheeks and quickly spreading down her neck and into the neckline of her yellow shirt.

The sight of it nearly causes me to crush the paper cup in my hand. My desire for her is irrelevant. Speaking out of turn in an environment where she is not permitted to respond freely or to escape has made her uncomfortable, yet again. "I wish to return your friendly gesture. My nature requires balance be maintained."

"Oh," she says, her countenance falling. "Then I guess our natures are completely opposite, because when I give, it's freely. I never expect something in return."

Though I doubt she intended her comment to scathe, it does just that. Shame is not familiar to me. Though made to mask the true intent of my offer, my statement about balance was accurate. Even in delivering the darkest of reckonings, I have felt no regret. Vengeance is my reason for existing, and I have always behaved within the boundaries of my agreements. But today, I acted on *my* desires. Perhaps not forbidden, but a mistake.

Further words are unnecessary. I was foolish to have spoken so many already. Even my nod before turning is more than I should give.

Next time, I will hold my tongue. But later, when I am alone, I will call up the memories created today. Visions of her tinted cheeks, the way her lovely lips curved for my eyes only, and the sound of my name in the song of her voice.

Chapter Two

DELA

My feet and lower back are screaming at me by the time I toss my barista apron in the laundry bin at the end of today's nonstop-busy shift. Since I have no plans to change jobs, I should invest in a better pair of sneakers for work. A high-quality pair.

I can afford them. Even though I had to start over in every aspect of life when I moved to Fate's Falls, I have money in the bank. Enough to buy whatever I need and still have a safety buffer. My boss is generous with our pay and the customers tip well. Going to work is never a hardship—except on my body some days. But that can be remedied with new shoes. A massage would help, too, if I could work up the nerve to go to the spa in town.

My hesitation isn't because the local masseuse is a multi-armed naga. The monster part doesn't bother me at all. It's the idea of lying in the dark, completely vulnerable. Seven months after waking up from what Doug intended to be my final sleep, I'm still kind of wobbly in the trust department.

I'll get there. My therapist says I'm doing great, and she's right. The past still bites me in the ass sometimes, but those bites become smaller nibbles every day. I've never been mentally and emotionally stronger. I like who I am now. And it only took being murdered by my human ex-boyfriend, returned to life by a reaper, and welcomed by a community of monsters to get to this point.

Life is too precious to waste a step of it wearing mediocre shoes.

"Bye," I say, tossing the black sneakers in the trash can. Well, in the direction of the can, which, unfortunately, is on the other side of the doorway. "Watch out!" My warning comes too late.

One shoe connects with Shay's shoulder as she walks into the staffroom. Shrieking, she bats the second projectile away. "I'm going to assume those weren't meant for me," she says, collecting the sneakers from the floor and dangling them from her gloved hands. "Garbage?"

"Yes." I give her an apologetic grimace. "Thanks."

She waves one hand below her nose as she drops them into the can. "Good call. Even my ninety-eight-year-old grandmother doesn't have a spell powerful enough to exorcise that much evil."

Hand place dramatically over my heart, I suck in an exaggerated breath. "Well, I never."

"Never what, washed your sneakers?" Shay winks at me while tilting her head toward the trash can. "Believable."

"Meanie," I say, enjoying our easy camaraderie. "Thank you."

"For what?" She drops onto the chair across from me and we both pull on our street shoes—mine, a pair of basic canvas flats that cost about an hour's wages, and hers, knee-high leather boots that sound like foreplay when she zips them.

"For your friendship. For taking me under your wing here. Showing me the ropes around town. Making me feel comfortable, both at work and outside of it. You didn't have to do any of that, but you jumped in and did. Seven months later, you're still looking out for me when I have a flaky moment, like earlier today."

Shay's eyes shine. "If you don't know by now that I love you like a sister, you never will. And because we're on the sister level, I'm not afraid to call bullshit on your *flaky moment*," she says, making air quotes. "Girl, you done lost your lady shit over the big red demon today. It was written all over your pretty face how much you want to grab him by his big old horns and ride him until he fills you with his hellfire."

"My mind did run away a bit today."

"Today?" One of Shay's perfect dark eyebrows rises as she snorts. "It's been running wild since the first time you laid eyes on him. But today was definitely extra. As soon as he walked into the café, you looked like you were going to burst into flames."

"Oh god."

"Hon, I think you're praying to the wrong deity on this one."

Groaning, I fold forward, elbows on my knees, cover my

face with my palms and peek at her through my fingers. "Do you think Raz knows?"

A robust laugh leaves Shay's full plum lips. "Not sure what answer you're hoping for here, but Raz was probably the only person in the place today who *didn't* know what was going through your head."

Pushing my mortification aside, I sit up so I can see her eyes again. As dark as they are, they convey a lot. Not that Shay ever has an issue with verbally revealing exactly what's on her mind.

"It's not great that everyone in the café this afternoon could tell I was... *distracted* by Raz. But why wouldn't *he* know? He's been dealing with human desires for eternity, literally. Why doesn't he know mine?"

The volume out front increases noticeably, signaling the arrival of the staff from next door who always flood The Brew after their shift ends. The Brew has two faces—coffee shop by day and brew pub in the evening. Even though it's pretty laid-back when the taps are flowing, I'm still glad to slinging coffee-house beverages instead of alcohol.

Shay and I are usually gone by now, and the noise out front requires she rise from her spot and move to the chair beside me so we can hear each other speak. Angling her body to look directly into my eyes, she says, "I told you I don't use my magic anymore, so when I answer your question, take it as years of insight, not as *I know*."

I nod rather than speak. Shay's magic is a touchy subject —literally and figuratively. As a seer, she can see the future of people she touches. She hasn't told me what she saw that made her decide never to touch anyone ever again, but it must've been horrific for her to spend the rest of her life without personal contact. I like and appreciate her too much to even nudge her in a direction she doesn't want to go.

"There are a lot of different kinds of demons out there, and I don't claim to be an expert on any of them," she begins. "Raz is a revenge demon, and based on everything I've been taught, that means his entire nature is fine-tuned to that purpose." She sighs at the squinty expression I feel my face forming. "What I'm saying is, if you're not wishing for revenge, you're not going to ping on his radar. Not officially, anyway. Though, watching him with you, it's safe to say you *are* on it."

"You think so?" God, I sound like an infatuated teenager, not a twenty-nine-year-old woman with enough life experiences to make me feel over-the-hill most days.

Affectionate amusement shines in Shay's eyes. "You're really into him."

"I'm attracted to him, certainly. But maybe that's all it is? I've discovered the tall, red, and grumpy type turns me on a little?" I raise my hands in submission when she gives me the stink-eye. "Fine, a lot."

"So, do something about it, girlfriend. Take charge of the situation."

"I wouldn't have a clue how to do that. I'm not bold and confident like you. I'm—" I snap my mouth shut. I am not all the things Doug made me believe.

Close your eyes. Deep breath in. Hold on to the truths. Exhale and release the lies.

My therapist's technique calms my mind, but it would be nice if I didn't have to use it every day. And if I had more truths than lies. Seven months into the healing process, and I'm still not sure who I really am.

"You okay?"

Opening my eyes, I find Shay's hand hovering a couple of inches above mine. Even with gloves on, she avoids touching people if she can. I must look every bit the mess I am for her to get that close.

"I'm okay. Thanks," I say, and she eases back to a comfortable distance for her. "I told you the gory details of my last relationship and how it would've ended—how *I* would've ended—if the reaper who came for me hadn't directed me here instead."

"Reapers get a bad rap; they're just doing their job. Still, I'm glad it was Kohl who got the call when your number was up. He's one of the good ones."

Asking how she knows Kohl is pointless; I've gone there before, when she's made similar comments. For as much as she's told me about her past, I know there's even more she hasn't.

"Is Raz one of the good ones?" That's the question I really need answered.

"Depends how you define 'good.' I'm not trying to patronize, but you know what he does, right?"

"He grants people's revenge wishes."

"The kind of revenge people are willing to trade their *soul* for, Dela." Arm draped across the back of her chair, she crosses one sexy-booted leg over the other, making me squirm a little with her serious tone and stare. "We're not talking about wishing for someone to step in a massive pile of shit, or get dumped by their girlfriend. Though I'm sure there are losers who'd give up their eternal soul for paltry crap, I doubt those are the typical kind of requests Raz deals in."

"You're saying he's probably caused bodily harm. Or... killed people."

"No probably about it."

"Is that something you *know*?"

"As in, from a touch?" Shay waggles her fingers. "No. From my coven's history books, yes. It's information I'm willing to share, if you're sure you want to hear it." She watches as I shake my head. "I don't blame you. But if you're looking for someone who doesn't have blood on their hands, literally, you should stop looking at Raz."

"I'm not looking for anyone. I don't want to be looking at anyone in that way."

She uncrosses her legs and leans forward, elbows on her knees, hands tucked carefully between them. "And yet, you are, and it's Raz you can't tear your sweet little eyes from. What does that tell you?"

"That I should move to an isolated cabin on the edge of town and get a job that doesn't require I interact with others."

Shay rolls her eyes. "Too late for that. Even if it wasn't, I think fate might still have put Raz in your path somehow."

"You think I was meant to meet Raz?" Of all the many, many things my mind has churned up and spit out, that was never one of them. "You believe in fate?"

"*Girl.*" Shay shakes her head. "You thought the 'Fate' in Fate's Falls was just for the sake of pretty alliteration?"

"Actually, I thought it's because the waterfall is so high and steep, someone probably died there. Yes, I'm a bit on the morbid side; my mind always goes to death. A side effect of narrowly escaping being a homicide victim." I shrug. "Honestly, the town's name is one of the few things I haven't overthought. You're telling me I should add it to the list?"

"Gods, no. Besides, this one is simple. Only those who are supposed to be here find their way here. If you're in Fate's Falls, it's for a reason. I'm not saying Raz, specifically, is your fate. Maybe he's just part of the bigger picture—how you get back on the horse." Sitting straight, she spreads her hands apart. Widely apart. "I bet it's a really big horse, too."

"*Shay!*"

"Don't even try to deny that you've thought about it. I don't have to be a telepath to know what you're thinking when Mr. Tall, Red and Horny walks in."

"You think he's horny?" Dammit, why did that have to come out sounding so hopeful?

"*Horn*-y." Hands at her head, Shay gestures upward. "As in his horns, you dirty girl."

I groan as she dissolves into laughter.

"Oh, that was good," she says, fanning her face after her full enjoyment of my faux pas subsides. "As for your fate, only the Oracle knows why you're in Fate's Falls. Best advice I can give you is don't try figuring it out. Just enjoy your life here and let it unfold."

"That's a lot to unpack. I have so many questions."

"You always do," Shay says, smiling as she stands. "You get *one* more, then I have to go."

Guilt twists its gnarly fingers inside me. "Sorry, I didn't mean to keep you from something important."

"Stop that. I'd have already left if it was. So, what's it going to be? The most burning question in your mind right now."

There are so many. About the Oracle. About Fate's Falls.

"Same question as before, and I know you can only give me your opinion, but, is Raz one of the good ones?"

"If you can accept the actions he takes within the code of his existence, then, yes, he's one of the good ones."

"Would you accept them?"

Shay waves her index finger. "That's two questions, and the answer is irrelevant, anyway. Raz doesn't come to The Brew for me. He comes here for you."

"He comes for the coffee," I say as she walks to the door.

Stopping in the staffroom doorway, she looks over her shoulder at me, a coy smile on her face. "He's lived in Fate's Falls for two years, but he never set foot in The Brew until you got here."

"Coincidence."

"Maybe." She winks. "Or maybe it's fate."

Chapter Three

RAZBUNARE

My dwelling on the outskirts of Fate's Falls is equipped with all the amenities of this era, including running water. The standing-room-only shower lacks pressure, but I have become accustomed to its convenience. Sometimes, I make use of the natural water near my cabin. A place where I am not confined, and the water does more than cleanse my exterior.

Today is one of those times. I crave the power of thundering water against my skin, so I cut through the woods surrounding my cabin until I reach the small clearing with its ninety-five-foot-high waterfall. The moon and sun are exchanging possession of the sky, bathing the crest in a pale, pre-dawn light. I will be back in the privacy of my cabin before the sun has fully risen.

After divesting myself of my pants, I stride into the river.

The cool water laps against my skin, only reaching mid-thigh level in the bubbling pool at the base of the falls. I stand beneath the plunge, eyes closed, letting the turbulent water crash over me, pummeling my skin, roaring in my ears. Yet it does not clear my mind. Dela remains there, where she has been since our interaction in the coffee shop yesterday.

During that visit, she did not just serve my beverage. At her initiation, we conversed. She spoke to me with humor. She smiled for me, not merely at me, in the obligatory manner employees must with customers. She offered genuine kindness. These things linger in my thoughts, but above them all, the lovely color of her skin when she blushed.

In turn, I insulted her and made her uncomfortable. Even if I had not behaved in that manner, her demeanor toward me will never extend beyond friendliness. Wanting more is foolish and futile.

If the pounding water will not beat the yearning from me, I will find another source. I could ask one of my hell-born brethren in the other realm to torture me. There would be no question of why—inflicting such measures is their purpose. But that would be physical pain without meaning. A personal element is required for this to succeed. I need a punisher with motivation to rid me of my desire for Dela.

Her employer may be useful for this purpose. The well-respected Minotaur has looked out for Dela since she arrived in Fate's Falls. I will speak to him today and divulge the unbecoming thoughts I have about Dela. Given the Minotaur's protective nature, my admission may entice Constantine to use his significant bulk to deploy force against me. Certainly, he will forbid me to visit his coffee establishment again. If all else fails, I will leave town. Return to hell, where I belong.

The thought of never seeing Dela again rips through me like a jagged blade, and I roar loud enough to drown out the pounding rush of the falls crashing around me. Enough of this.

I step forward, opening my eyes as I exit the curtain of water and halt immediately.

Dela stands at the water's edge. The sun's morning rays wrap around her lovely, soft form. Her full lips are parted, her wide-eyed gazing bouncing between my face and my exposed body—including my cock. The tip is hidden beneath the water, but only momentarily. The sight of her is enough to harden my shaft. Having her attention on me causes it to rise above the water's surface with zeal, giving her a full and clear view of the flared, spade-shaped head.

"Why are you here?" I speak loud enough to project my question over the din of the water.

"I... I came to look at the waterfall." The tilt of her chin and the degree to which her mouth opens indicate she is also attempting to be heard.

My hearing is superior to any human's. She could have whispered and I would have understood every word. I have no need to move closer, yet I do. I cannot stop my legs from striding toward her, just as I cannot will my cock to return to its slack position.

Any other human would have fled. If not the moment they saw a demon standing beneath a waterfall, most certainly when the demon's cock rose at the sight of them.

Dela does not run. Does not flinch when I step out of the

water and stand before her—unclothed and undeniably aroused.

"Do you want to put your pants on?" she asks, glancing at the garment I discarded.

"Demons do not feel modesty."

Her gaze once again drops to my cock, her skin taking on an appealing red hue when she tips her head up to meet my eyes again. "That's... yes, well... um..." The air temperature is not hot by human standards, yet she wipes her palm over her forehead and exhales. "*Would* you put your pants on? It's hard—" a small strangled sound rises from her lips, "it's *difficult* to concentrate while you're naked."

"I do not find it difficult."

"For me. It's difficult *for me*. Your..." She gestures in the vicinity of my cock while looking off toward the waterfall behind me. "Your *parts* are hard—*difficult*—to ignore."

"I will cover myself. Then I will escort you out of the woods. It is not safe for you to be out here alone."

Her eyes meet mine again. "Why not?" she asks, her gaze trailing me as I move to gather my pants. "This area is still within the town limits. The no-harm rule protects me."

"The animals who reside in the woods are not bound by that rule." I step into the pants, acutely aware of my cock bobbing, and Dela watching it, as I wrestle the garment upward over my wet skin. Finally, though not easily, I am able to tuck my cock aside and zip up. "Not the shifters who live among us; they won't harm you, even in their animal forms. The lesser beasts, if hungry or feeling threatened, would not hesitate."

A shiver ripples through her, and she wraps her arms around herself. "I was so grateful to be safe from malice, I never considered not being safe from the environment." She turns toward the waterfall and sighs. "Guess I won't come out here again."

Now that my lower body is covered, I join her by the water's edge, the need to protect her from any and all things building inside me. "Safe from what malice?"

"I shouldn't have said that." Her bright eyes dim, and she turns her head away, staring off at the waterfall.

"Was it untrue?"

"No, it's true," she says, her voice quiet, as if far off in the distance. "Impossible to believe when I look back on it, but I'm here, surrounded by proof that impossible things are true."

I have inquired about Dela's arrival in Fate's Falls. Not directly, those are not questions for a customer to ask a coffee barista. Not when the customer is a hell-born demon, and the barista is an innocent human. I asked the Minotaur. If Constantine had information, he was unwilling to share it.

"You can trust me." Looking down at her, I wait to gain her attention. "If it is within my power to deliver, you have only to ask."

Her eyes widen. "Do you mean for revenge?"

The thought of delivering vengeance in Dela's name stirs sensations in me unlike any I have experienced. For her, it would be more than fulfilling my purpose. I would do it to please her. "If you wish for it, even silently, I will ensure you are satisfied."

She gives me one slow blink, then a smile pulls at her lips. "I don't want revenge. And it's a good thing you can only hear *those* thoughts, or I'd be in a heap of trouble."

Humans' wishes for revenge come to me without bidding; I do not have to listen for them. This has not prevented me from opening my mind, hoping to hear Dela's voice in my head. Day and night, I find myself probing, searching for even a small wish from her. And have encountered none.

"I would like to know your thoughts," I say. "I assure you there will be no trouble of any quantity."

A short, sweet laugh leaves her smiling lips. "I don't think that level of disclosure falls within the nature of our relationship. No matter what Shay says."

"Who is Shay?"

As Dela tilts her head, sunlight paints her hair with streaks of gold. "Shay Winterlock. Another barista at The Brew. We both work the dayshift; she's always there while I'm there."

"I have not seen her there."

"*Raz*. Come on. You've never seen the other coffee barista?" When I fail to respond, she sighs, then continues. "The really beautiful woman with long, curly hair, green eyes, smooth brown skin, nice boobs, a great butt, and legs for days?"

"I have not noticed her."

Dela rolls her eyes. "Okay, this is ridiculous. Shay's gorgeous and it's literally impossible that you haven't noticed her all the times you've been in The Brew. There's no shame in admitting you find a woman attractive."

"That is your true feeling?" I ask. Humans are notorious for deception, both intentional and subconscious.

"Yes, of course."

"I am attracted to you. Your beauty is all I see."

The openness of Dela's eyes and lips indicates I have spoken out of turn again. Though she is not trapped by the duties of her workplace, her options of escape are limited, nonetheless.

"You are disturbed by my admission."

"I'm...surprised," she says. Though her voice is calm, her physiological responses are not.

"I have tried to rid myself of the attraction, but it has not been within my control. I will speak to the Minotaur who owns the establishment where you work and have him restrict me from entering. As I have no need of anything from town, you will not have to see me again."

"What if I *want* to see you again?"

The quickening of her pulse is visible in the column of her delicate neck. "You are frightened." Unable to resist, I place my fingers over the beat, eliciting a gasp from her full lips.

She captures my hand before I can draw it away, molding my fingers to the gentle curve of her neck. "I am, but not of you." Her gaze briefly drops to the space between us. "Okay, maybe one *part* of you."

"You fear my cock."

A sputtered laugh rises from her lips, and her cheeks bloom with fresh color.

"It is a reasonable fear. I am much larger than any human male, and you, my sweet Dela, are so very soft and small."

"If that's meant to scare me off, it's not working," she says, moistening her lips as she moves closer. "Kind of the opposite."

"Your reaction is not uncommon. Throughout time, many humans have expressed curiosity about fornication."

The glow leaves her face, deep creases forming at the bridge of her nose as she steps away from me. "It was you referring to me as 'my sweet Dela' that made me feel... never mind." She makes a throaty noise that matches the cloudy expression she wears. "This soft, small human isn't interested in *fornicating* with you or anyone."

"My words were merely a statement of fact. It does not matter to me if you wish to discover how much of my cock fits inside you, or if you have chosen a life of celibacy. You affect me beyond carnality, my sweet Dela."

She crosses her arms over breasts that make my fingers flex with the urge to touch. "Did you say 'my sweet Dela' again so I wouldn't be angry at you?"

"Manipulation is never my intention. Not with anyone, but above all others, not with you."

"Then I accept your apology," she says, the tension leaving her posture as she lets her arms fall to her side.

"I did not apologize."

"Yes, you did." Her lips curve into a full smile as she looks up at me. "In your unique way, which I appreciate."

"I am glad to have pleased you so the smile could return to your face." I may never know the sensation of her mouth against me, but I can no longer resist touching her lips. Gently cradling her chin in my hand, I trace the lines of her mouth. The upward curve of her full bottom lip. The peaks and dipping valley of her upper lip. "Your smile puts the sunshine to shame."

"That's beautiful." The softness in her eyes gives way to

twinkling amusement. "Not very 'statement of fact,' but beautiful."

"It is factual to me. I always see sunshine when I look at you." I step back before taking an action she will not forgive as easily as my direct manner of communication. "Let us return to the reason you are here. The literal sun of this realm has risen fully, and you are likely to be safe from wildlife. Still, I will wait nearby while you look at the waterfall."

"You could look at it with me if you want. I'm enjoying this time with you." Once again, her cheeks flood with rich color. "Or I can leave now, rather than make you wait around. I'm sure you have other things to do."

"Nothing I would choose before you."

"For a demon who barely wanted to grumble his coffee order to me for the past seven months, you're pretty good with words." She brushes her hand against mine, weaves our fingers together, then smiles so beautifully, she renders me speechless.

If I cannot provide a verbal response worthy of this gift, I will show her.

She shrieks when I scoop her off the ground with a single arm. "What are you doing?"

"Giving you a view of the waterfall it is unlikely you have seen."

The light fabric of her summer dress does little to mask all her soft, womanly curves. Her breast presses against my chest, her rounded hips and ass against my arm where she's perched. The toes of her cloth shoes graze my abdomen, and her hands have a tentative placement on my shoulder and chest.

My cock is hard again, straining to be free of the pants. To be inside my sweet Dela, a place it will never be. I will gladly live with perpetual, unsated desire if it allows me to have her close. "The climb is not smooth, but I will keep you safe."

"The climb? We're going to the top of the waterfall?" The excitement in her voice is like music.

"Yes. You should hold on to me. Firmly."

Twining her arms behind my neck brings her lush body tighter against me and her lips within inches of mine. "Is this okay?"

Kissing is a behavior I have not experienced, nor desired, before this woman. Dela's mouth has consumed my thoughts since the first time I saw her, and I have to fight the urge to know how it would feel against mine.

"The ascent is steep and rocky. Your current grip may not be adequate. Do not hesitate to hold my neck, head, or horns directly."

"Are you sure?"

"I will not lie; your hands on my skin and horns will give me pleasure. But that is not why I suggested you hold me in those places, and I will always contain my desire for you."

"I hope not *always*..." Her tone is breathy, her pupils dilating beneath rapidly fluttering eyelashes.

"You have only to wish for it. There is nothing I would deny you, but anything other than revenge, you must express aloud."

"I will, I want to, but... I need you to know that when I tell you I'm ready for...*things*, it's not because I'm curious about having sex with a non-human, it's about you. And I trust you, but I'm not sure I trust myself yet."

"I have eternity to wait for you, my sunshine, and so I will. There is no other creature in this realm or any other who could prevent me from doing so."

"You won't have to wait that long."

I suppress a groan when she slides one hand over the back of my head, up to my right horn, then curls her fingers around it. Though her hands are small and her touch light, the sensation stokes the fire within me in a way no other being has. "Do you feel secure?"

"More than I ever have before," she says, then presses her lips to mine.

Chapter Four

DELA

I'm kissing a demon. Four words I never in my life expected to string together.

Raz's body tenses as I press my lips to his, and for a second, I almost pull back and apologize. Muscle memory is a long-lasting bitch.

Then his grip on me tightens, and the blunt ends of his dark fingernails press firmly against my leg. Not enough to hurt me—I know he'd never allow that to happen. Just enough that I feel his reaction to the kiss. To me.

Past me can go to hell because present me isn't pulling back from kissing my demon.

He doesn't take control of the kiss, just goes with it, following my lead and giving back in equal measure. I lean in closer, parting my lips and touching the tip of my tongue to his. The inhuman sound he makes vibrates through me, and it's hot—literally hot. My entire body heats as if I'm too close to a fire. Only, the fire is Raz, and all I want is to get closer. To slip my dress off my shoulders and feel his heat directly against my breasts. His arm is firm and warm beneath me, his hand positioned so close to where I want it. If I arched my back and opened my thighs a little, would he take the signal and slide his fingers between my legs?

No, he wouldn't. And I'm not ready to tell him what I want. I won't put him in a position where he has to choose between breaking his word or rejecting me. I'm not sure I'd emotionally survive either thing.

I ease back from the kiss until a hair's breadth separates our mouths. "I haven't kissed anyone that way in a very long time."

"I have not kissed anyone."

"Ever?" I ask, pulling back more, enough to see his full face.

"That is correct."

"You're kidding."

"Vengeance demons do not tell jokes."

"It's an expression, a colloquialism." I bite the inside of my cheek so I don't let my smile become a laugh. "It means 'you can't be serious.'"

"Vengeance demons are always serious."

A small laugh slips free, but only a quick one that tapers into a sigh.

His strong brow descends over demon-serious eyes. "I frustrate you."

"Sometimes, yes. But not right now. In this moment, I'm thoroughly enjoying how '*you*' you are."

Raz's stoic facial expression isn't prone to much variation, and this moment is no exception. "I am incapable of being anything else," he says, looking into my eyes with unflinching intensity.

"I like you the way you are, Raz. Steady, direct, consistent, honest. I need those things in my life."

For the briefest moment, his eyes flicker with something unfamiliar. "I wish to be everything you need. For that reason, I must inform you of inaccurate information I gave yesterday at your workplace."

A knot forms in my stomach at the thought of him lying to me. I can't be with someone who'd deceive me. Not even casually.

"After stating my desire to buy you a beverage at a time outside of your working hours, I told you I wished to return your friendly gesture, to maintain balance. While those things were true, they were not the full reason. I wanted to share personal time with you. Your physiological responses indicated discomfort, so I focused on the aspects you would find tolerable."

I knew it! The butterflies in my stomach *weren't* wrong. "You were asking me on a date?"

"That is the current human term." The permanently serious, more-than-a-little intimidating hell demon is the eight-foot-tall-plus-horns embodiment of adorable.

"This human would have said yes if you'd asked directly. And since we're admitting things, the physiological responses you noticed weren't negative. Surprise first, but also excitement." I snuggle in closer, watching the glow in his eyes flicker as I slide my hand higher up the horn I'm holding. Interesting. Something to revisit later, when I'm feeling braver. "I've been attracted to you for months, since the first time I saw you, but wasn't sure I should act on it."

"Because I am a demon."

I shake my head. "Because the last time I was drawn to someone, he turned out to be a monster in the most sinister sense."

"Is he responsible for the malice you mentioned?"

"Yes."

Again, Raz's grip on me tightens. "Vengeance is my purpose; I hold no stake in the transactions. But this is... personal. Whatever retribution is due, I will take pleasure meting it out."

A shiver ripples through me as images of Raz physically destroying Doug flood my mind. Flaying him. Setting him on fire. Things I've never imagined, never considered. Now, any one of them could become a reality. "Do you know what I'm thinking now?"

"No. I will only hear if you seek vengeance."

"I don't want vengeance. If one of the things that just flashed in my mind happens to leak out, it's an accident—I don't want you to act on it. As horrible as he was to me, I don't want you to do anything, okay?" When Raz's response is to clench his jaw and stare a hole through me, I place one hand on his cheek and give him the best smile I can call up with all this heavy stuff going through my head. "Believe me when I say that by living, I'm personally meting out the best possible revenge."

"Your life is a precious gift."

"Help me make the most of it by taking me up the escarpment for that special view of the waterfall," I say, sliding my hand to the back of his neck for the firm hold he advised. "And after that, I'm free all day, if you want to continue our date..."

"This is a date?"

The smile on my face now is as big and real as they come. "I kissed you, and you kissed me back. Unless you turn away or tell me I have bad breath, there's going to be more kissing at the top of the waterfall. So, yes, Raz, this is a date."

"Your breath is the sweetest thing I have tasted." His lips curve up—not a lot, but enough to label it a smile. "So far."

Did he just flirt with me? I think he did. But it's Raz, so maybe not? "Are you talking about food or drinks we might have later?"

His mouth returns to its standard, straight line. "No."

"Good," I say, as heat floods my cheeks and butterflies take flight in my stomach.

"I can be specific to prevent confusion."

I choke on a laugh, then let it run free, giggling against his warm skin. "Let's save that for the next date."

RAZBUNARE

I do not possess a heart. My liege created me to fulfill a singular purpose, and did not burden me with unnecessary physical attributes.

This morning spent with Dela confirms I do not require

a beating heart to experience emotions. Sensations that sparked inside me the moment I looked upon her face seven months ago, and have grown every time since. There is more to my attraction than a desire to enjoy the pleasure of her soft flesh connected with mine. I care about her. For her.

Emotions are humans' greatest weakness, the reason I am able to contract their souls to my liege's hell realm. They are ruled by their feelings. I have never wished to experience life as they do. I could not, as wishing is an emotional response.

Now, with Dela, I am filled with wishes. How, after eons, did this single, fragile human elicit changes to the very makeup of my being? I have no directive to follow for such an occurrence. No knowledge of how to repair what has broken inside me.

Knowing I should not be this way does not motivate me to seek a solution. I would sooner cease to exist than be rid of these feelings. An irony, as that is the precise thing I had determined to do before she found me at the waterfall.

As I instructed her to do, she clung tightly to me while I climbed the rough escarpment to reach the crest of the waterfall. Having her soft body pressed close to mine and her hand wrapped around my horn were too strong a stimulation to ignore, and my cock remained hard throughout the trek. Releasing her did little to assuage the condition. The moment I returned her feet to the ground, she took my hand, and did not let go for a single second. It is difficult to keep my arousal under control in her presence. Seemingly impossible while we are in direct contact.

Dela drove to the woods this morning. My height prohibits me from riding in any vehicle with a closed top, and Dela's is exceptionally small. After another kiss that left me aching for further exploration of her body, she moved to her car, waved from inside, then left me to walk to town. An action which caused her guilt until I assured her I am incapable of experiencing pain or fatigue. I did not tell her the solitary journey would be a reprieve, an opportunity for my cock to stand down. I have no expectation of sexual contact with my sweet Dela, and she does not need to know the full extent of my desire.

It did not take as long as expected for my cock to lose its rigidity. Without Dela's presence to consume my mind, wishes for revenge bombarded me. I heard none during the hours spent in her company. After eons of constant inundation, I should have noticed the lull.

These wishes are my reason for being. I have ignored the voices before, but only briefly. Since the day I was drawn to the coffee shop, the first time I saw Dela, I have been more selective of the revenge I fulfill. Weighing the validity of wishes, considering the consequences to all involved—actions I am not meant to take. My liege requires souls in his realm, and delivering as many as possible is my duty.

Yet, I have not done so in the past seven months. I have satisfied enough vengeful wishes that I have not been recalled to hell. But I have contracted no souls today. Meeting Dela and sharing more time with her is my priority. My duties as a vengeance demon will wait.

Despite having the faster method of travel, Dela is not in sight when I reach our agreed-upon meeting place in town. The central downtown square is more populated than the times I have passed it on my way to Dela's workplace. Most days, there are two or three residents present, sitting on the immaculate parkette's benches or on the edge of the decorative, bubbling fountain.

Today, there are over a dozen people crowding the area. Though I rarely interact with the other residents of Fate's Falls, I recognize most who are in attendance. Normally, I would not spend more time on people than it takes to be aware of my surroundings. But two romantic pairings hold my attention.

Dakgorim, the orc who built many of the structures in Fate's Falls, including my cabin, stands at the bottom of five stairs leading to a raised gazebo. Behind him, and a couple of steps up, a human female has her arms wrapped around the sizable orc. The smile she wears never falters. Her chin rests on his shoulder and she presses kisses to his cheek at regular intervals. Much like me, orcs are not given to smiling, as humans do. But his affection is obvious, nonetheless. One of the orc's large hands spans both her forearms, his fingers curled possessively around them.

The Minotaur who employs Dela stands a couple of feet from the orc. At Constantine's side, a human woman is tucked under one of the Minotaur's thick arms. His substantially sized hand rests near the top of her breast, with her much smaller one absentmindedly stroking his fingers. Like the female hugging Dakgorim, the woman with Constantine appears happy and comfortable.

The orc and the Minotaur share similar stature with me. Their women are significantly smaller, much like Dela. I have anatomical knowledge of all sentient species in this realm. Like mine, orc and Minotaur cocks are double, if not more, than those of human males. Perhaps Dakgorim and

Constantine are abstaining from sexual penetration with their women.

"Hi, I'm here, finally." Dela's voice at my back pulls my attention from the gathering near the gazebo. "I always call my mother on Saturday mornings. I did that when I got home to drop off my car because I didn't want her to worry, and the conversation ran longer than usual. Sorry I kept you waiting."

"An apology for dedication to those you care about is unnecessary," I say, when she reaches my side. "And you are worth any wait." The vengeful wishes retreat to the back of my mind, and, yet again, my cock tests the confines of my pants. As it does every time she is in view, and more so, now that I have tasted her mouth and felt her softness against me.

She slips her hand against mine, smiling when I fold my fingers to encompass all of hers. This lovely creature is not only touching me, she is doing so where anyone may see.

I did not think it possible for her to desire my company. My touch. My kiss. Nor did I think my response possible. These sensations of lightness, anticipation, and contentment. Never have I experienced any of the three. To have them all at once, woven together inside me, should be concerning enough to have me returning to hell for guidance. For extermination. But I do not wish them gone, these emotional responses. Only for them to grow stronger. With her.

"They must be going over the plans for Dak and Rosetta's wedding in the square next weekend." She nods toward the assembly of creatures socializing near the gazebo. "Are you going?"

"I have no knowledge of a wedding."

"Oh. I noticed you watching them; you were staring at them the whole time I was coming up the street. I thought you must be friends with Dak or Constantine, or both."

"Vengeance demons do not have friends."

"You know, I've heard a lot about what vengeance demons don't do and don't have, but... it seems like you're at a place in life where you're ready for some changes."

"Vengeance demons do not—" I snap my mouth closed. "You are correct."

"Do you mean that?" she asks, then immediately holds up her other hand. "I already know the 'statement of fact' answer—vengeance demons do not lie. What I mean is, how do you feel about the changes?"

"I would tell you that vengeance demons do not feel things, that we are not burdened by emotions, and until recently, the statement would have been true. I have no explanation for this change you brought about, but this is the first day of my existence when I understand what it means to be happy. And if that is a burden, it is one I wish to continue bearing."

Dela always shines, but as she wraps her arms around me, the light within her practically glows. The top of her head barely reaches my chest. Despite my higher-than-human body temperature, the warmth of her cheek pressed against me seeps into my skin. She, too, is happy. And I am part of her happiness.

The people looking at us are unaware of this new mutual state. Their straight-faced expressions and narrowed gazes indicate concern. A hell-born demon who has lived among them for two years, yet had minimal interaction with anyone, is embracing a gentle, pure, human female. Their concern is understandable.

"I'm sorry," she says, easing back from me. "I shouldn't have thrown myself at you in public. Not without discussing the boundaries of our relationship. I shouldn't even assume that's what it is. I'm doing it again."

"Doing what?"

In front of me, she twists her hands together, her lips losing their pretty smile. "Wanting something to be a certain way so much, I convince myself that it *is* that way, even if it means ignoring signs to the contrary."

"Though I speak every language in this realm and in hell, I do not understand ambiguousness."

She sighs. "After the time we spent together at the waterfall, I thought... I thought it was the beginning of something between us. A relationship. Then I felt you tense up while I was hugging you, and I realized I had over-stepped, made assumptions about what you want."

"Assumption is unnecessary. I have been direct with you, and I will continue to be, as that is what I know. I desire to be with you in all ways that please you. That will not change. Only at your request will I leave you. The increased muscular tightness you sensed occurred because others were observing our embrace. I noted the apprehen-sion on their faces. I am vengeance, a creature created for darkness, and you are sunshine. We do not belong together."

The tension in her expression and posture fades, but the smile does not return to her face. "Is that what you really think? That we don't belong together?"

"Yes. But it is not how I *feel*, my sweet Dela."

The light returns to her eyes. To her skin. "So... it's okay with you if I show affection in public?"

"I welcome your touch in any location or manner you wish. And I would never tell you how to conduct yourself, not in public or in private."

"You have no idea how much that means to me," she says, placing her palms and chin on my chest, her face tipped up to look at mine. "I'd kiss you right now if I could."

"Then I will make an adjustment to accommodate your desire." I lower to one knee, bringing us face-to-face. The attention of anyone other than Dela means nothing to me. That does not mean I am unaware of it. "Everyone is watching. Many will have questions if you kiss me."

"Let them ask." She wraps her arms behind my neck, grips one of my horns, and presses her soft lips to my mouth.

It has only been an hour since she last kissed me, but having this contact again makes me crave more. When she breaks away, it is difficult to let her put space between us. I want the opposite. If I could, I would carry her to my cabin in the woods and keep her with me always.

"I have a question for *you*," she says, as I rise. "And I don't want you to feel pressured to answer a certain way."

Vengeance demons do not feel pressure from humans, though many have tried through the centuries. This is not what she needs to hear. Also, it is possible that Dela could pressure me, as she has affected me in other impossible ways. "I will answer you honestly."

Nodding, she draws a deep breath. "Would you like to be my date for the wedding next Saturday? It'll be here in the square, just before sunset, then there's a drop-in reception at The Brew afterward. Open bar courtesy of Constantine, and delicious finger foods. We can make a brief appearance or stay as long as you like."

"You need not use food or beverages as enticement. If you want me by your side, I will be there."

"Perfect." She weaves the fingers on one small hand with mine. "This whole day is perfect. So much so, I'm afraid I might be dreaming the whole thing."

"You have dreamed of me before?" I say, as she leads me away, toward the shops lining one side of the square.

"Yes." The smile on her face when she looks at me is one of a different kind. "They were good dreams too, but in a different way."

"They were sexual dreams."

"A bold assumption," she nudges me with her shoulder, "but yes, they were."

The knowledge that her sleeping hours have included sexual fantasies about us has my cock standing at the ready. "You did not fear my cock in the dreams, as you did at the waterfall?"

"I'm not *actually* afraid of it," she says, choking back laughter. "Nervous, sure, but I was flirting when I said I may be a little afraid of it. It was flattery."

"Humans express adulation by falsely claiming fear?"

"Sometimes? Humans are rarely as straightforward as you." She stops in front of one of the many shops I have never entered and faces me. Smiles at me with warmth and affection. "But I'll work on it, so my words are more accurate to my thoughts. To what I want."

"That will make giving it to you more efficient."

"The giving shouldn't be one-sided, Raz. If I'm going to be direct about what I want, then you should do the same. Tell me what *you* want."

"I have already done so."

"Yes, you have, but I meant it as in, specifically. You know... when the time comes that we're alone together in private."

"You wish to know my preferred sexual activities."

The color rises on her cheeks again. "Yes, that would be helpful. Because you're not human, and also, because in my last relationship, I—" She closes her eyes longer than a normal blink, drawing a deep breath.

Patience is part of my nature, yet waiting for her to continue requires conscious effort. The more I know, the better I can care for her.

She exhales slowly, then meets my gaze again. "I wasn't good in the sex department, and my ex was human. If I couldn't get it right with someone in my species..." Her next exhalation is a sigh, her shoulders visibly dropping. "I don't want to disappoint you."

"That is impossible." I have much to learn about interpreting her expressions and reactions, but my declaration does not appear to assure her. "Tell me why the smile has not returned to your face."

"There's a question in my head, and I want to ask it, but I'm not sure I want to hear the answer."

"Humans are a very conflicted species."

"Aren't we just?" Her words ride a self-deprecating laugh. "Okay, I'm going to ask, and find a way to deal with the answer, whatever it is." After releasing my hand, she takes another deep breath, but appears no more relaxed upon exhaling.

Unease is another new sensation for me. This one is not pleasurable.

"Have you—" A small rumble rises from her throat as she shakes her hands where they hang at her sides. "Have you had sex with a lot of humans?"

"That is the question causing you distress?"

"Yes," she says. "And the fact that you didn't give me your usual straightforward answer and a distinct number isn't helping alleviate the feeling."

"I will supply the information you requested, but it has no relevance."

"Oh, great, it's a big number. And because I said I'd try to be more direct, by 'great,' I mean not great at all. Because it's a human thing to say the opposite of what we mean."

Breathing is not necessary for me, but at this moment, I mimic the deep intake and release of air I have watched Dela do. It has no effect on me. Why I thought it might when it does little for her, I do not know. Perhaps the combination of new emotions and the renewed push of voices seeking fulfilment of revenge have affected my logic.

"I have had no human sexual partners."

Her eyes open wide, then reduce to narrow slits. "This morning, you said many humans have been curious about having sex."

"That does not mean I satisfied their curiosity."

Brightness returns to her eyes, only to be clouded again within seconds. "But you've had sex with non-humans?"

"Yes. With other demons in hell."

"That might be even worse," she says, turning her attention toward the street.

"I do not understand why this information is causing you discomfort." When she responds with a slight shake of her head, I gather her chin in my hand and gently direct her face to meet mine. "I have existed for as long as humans have inhabited the earth, and in that time, have engaged in activities normal for my kind."

"I know. Of course. I'm being oversensitive, worrying about things that are none of my business, making things about me when they're not, like I always do. I'm sorry, I know it's annoying."

"Vengeance demons do not get annoyed." I wait for her to laugh or smile, as she has the other times I've made such comments, but it does not happen. "As you have expressed an intent to be more direct, I will try to communicate in a way that is less 'statement of fact,' while remaining truthful. For eons, I have existed. With you, I am living. I have engaged in activities normal for my kind. For you, I feel desire. I wish to please you, to see you smile, to hear you laugh. I wish to protect you from all that could cause you harm or unhappiness. I had no wishes for these things—no wishes of any kind—until you. There is no comparison between the time before you and this time with you."

A choked gasp leaves her parted lips. *"Raz,"* she whispers, beaming up at me.

"Are you at ease now?" I ask, lowering my hands and clasping one of hers.

"How could I not be after that? Thank you for being patient with me. I didn't mean to unpack all my emotional baggage." She looks up at me as we resume walking. "I'm probably the worst first date ever."

"I am not dissatisfied."

The sound of her laughter is lighter than the air it inhabits. "I'm lucky you haven't had any other first dates."

"Nor will I have any other."

"You believe that?"

"Yes." Simple and straightforward is not the type of answer she wants. Humans prefer more words. Only for her am I willing to use them. "I never sought human companionship. I did not give thought to humans at all, beyond answering their need for revenge and fulfilling my purpose. One day, I was drawn to town, to the coffee shop. I had never been inside and could think of no explanation for my urge to enter. Vengeance demons do not act impulsively. Then I saw you and experienced a sense of lightness. Vengeance demons do not feel things, and I did not realize then that the sensation you invoked was an emotion, as I do now. But I knew you were the reason I had been drawn there. Though I could find no logical reason for it, I continued to visit, to have those few minutes with you."

"Maybe I'm just the beginning of a change within you. It's possible you'll be drawn to someone else. It happens. I hope it won't, but it might, since it happened with me."

"It will not. I cannot give you factual proof, only that I know."

"That's good enough for me," she says, leaning her head against my arm as we continue down the street. She halts our movement in front of a bakery and points to its large, protruding window showcasing shining trays of small edible items of varying sizes and appearances. "Have you ever had the spicy scones Amazra makes? They're made with Carolina reaper peppers and cinnamon. Way too high on the Scoville scale for me, but I always think of you when I see them."

She thinks of me while shopping. Dreams of me. Touches and kisses me without caring who sees. This delicate, perfect woman chooses me when she could have any other. It makes no sense. However long or short a time this lasts, I will do all that is possible to make her happy. Revealing another simple truth will do that, as it provides an opportunity for her to share her enthusiasm with me.

"I have not been inside this establishment."

As expected, her lovely mouth forms a wide O. "You've been in town two years and you haven't set one red foot in Just Baked?" She tugs on my hand while turning toward the door.

I would follow her anywhere, at any time, but the voices I have been ignoring choose this moment to push through, rendering me motionless and immovable. Bound to my purpose, a servant to my singular duty. I have no choice but to process the onslaught of revenge-seeking wishes, right here on the sidewalk, in Dela's presence.

"Are you okay?" Standing in front of me, her soft voice penetrates the din.

I see her. Hear her. Feel her hands squeezing mine. But I cannot answer. Not until I select the soul I will acquire for my liege's dominion.

"Raz?" The warm mouth I wish to feel against mine is down-turned. Above her seeking gaze, her brow is furrowed. "Is something wrong?"

With so many voices crowding my mind, choosing one

should be immediate. But it is no longer simple. No action I take will directly involve or affect Dela, but I do not wish return to her side with blood on my hands.

There. An older male with petty demands against a deceptive partner. He will get his wish.

Locked on to my immediate destination, the other voices subside. For now. With so many seeking revenge, the respite will not last long.

"There is nothing to worry about," I say, focusing on Dela. "But I will have to delay the rest of our date and attend to my duties."

"You mean revenge? You have to go grant someone's revenge wish? Now?"

"It is my purpose. Ignoring it brings consequences, as you just witnessed. Fulfilling my purpose also brings consequences, because it requires I disappoint you. If what I am and the reality of what I must do changes your decision to spend time with me—"

"It doesn't," she cuts me off, reaching up to graze my face with her soft fingers. "Just...be careful at work, okay? I know firsthand how evil some humans can be." She is worried for the safety of a hell-born demon who has committed acts that would terrify and disgust her.

I do not deserve her sunshine. "No harm will come to me." I capture her hand where it rests against my cheek and turn it, pressing my lips to her palm. "I will see you soon."

Walking away from another creature, in hell or in this realm, has never registered as anything other than an automatic action. Solitude is my existence. *Was* my existence, until today. Leaving Dela standing on the sidewalk is not merely a physical movement. Doing so creates an unwelcome tightness inside me.

On the opposite side of the town square, I cannot resist looking back. When I do, she is not there, nor anywhere within the scope of my vision. The tightness increases, pulling all the emotions of this day into a knot only she has the power to undo.

Chapter Five

DELA

By the time I walked home from downtown on Saturday, I had a handful of messages from my friends waiting on my phone, which I'd intentionally left in my apartment after dropping off my car.

> **Rosetta**
> You and Raz! OMG! Call me!

> **Rosetta**
> Guess I'll add a chair for the wedding next weekend? Or will you just sit on his lap? Looks like he'd be more than okay with that seating arrangement. 😉

Shay

I'm across the street and I see you out there with your horny demon!

Shay

You got him down on one knee already? Woot! Told you! Gonna need allll the details, girl! And don't think about waiting until Monday to spill!

Natalie

Welcome to the "we have giant monster boyfriends" club! Maybe we can go triple-dating with Ro and Dak after their honeymoon. (Not that those two need a honeymoon! LOL)

Shay

What's going on out there? You okay? You look kinda upset, and yes, I am peeping on you. #NoShame Want me to run out there and kick his grumpy red ass?

Shay

Why is leaving? I'm literally two minutes away if you need me.

Even my boss—aka, Natalie's newly minted boyfriend—texted me.

Constantine

Hey. Hope I'm not out of line, texting you about non-work things. Just checking to make sure you're okay. Not because I don't trust Razbunare, I just know you've been through a lot, prior to moving here, and want to let you know I'm here as a friend who'll have your back anytime you need it. Text me if you need anything.

It took one message to my boss, a few to Natalie, and two hours' worth of back-and-forth with Rosetta and Shay before my phone calmed down yesterday. But I'm not complaining.

It's been a long time since I had friends. I left the ones I'd made as my younger self behind when I moved to a new city to be with Doug. Once I was far away from everyone who cared about me, he began chipping away at my self-worth, making sure I alienated old friends and lacked the confidence to make new ones, even on a casual level.

I'm fortunate to have made some great connections since moving to Fate's Falls. Rosetta was the first human I met when I moved here, and her high energy was a lot to take in at the point in my life when I just wanted to crawl into a hole and disappear. She refused to leave me alone to wallow, though, and I'm grateful she didn't. We don't spend a lot of time together—her big, bossy orc fiancé keeps her *occupied*—but we've developed a daily texting friendship.

Her cousin Natalie is new to town, but now that she's with Constantine, it's safe to say she's not going anywhere. That works for me because she's one of those people who feel like they've been in your life forever after talking to them one time.

Shay is the kind of friend everyone should have, and I'm so lucky I get to spend time with her five days a week at work.

I never would have gotten close with a coworker in my previous situation. Too risky, letting someone who spends forty hours a week with me have insight into my personal life. In hindsight, if I had, I might not have ended up temporarily dead.

But then I wouldn't be here. And *here* is working out pretty great.

Maybe Shay was right about fate. Something I'm sure she'll remind me of as soon as the opportunity presents, probably in front of customers at work on Monday. I'll take the embarrassment. Today, I need to see Raz.

I hated spewing old insecurities all over our first date. Hated it but couldn't stop it from happening. My therapist says I shouldn't expect a speedy repair for things that took years to dismantle. As much as that makes sense, I hate that I'm still broken.

But Raz was so good about my mini-breakdowns. So patient and accepting. Then our date ended without warning, because he had to go mete out vengeance somewhere.

A shiver rolls up my spine. The vengeance thing is... heavy. I said it didn't change what I want, but it's hard not to think about what he might be doing. Shay told me he's killed before, and I won't judge him for doing the things he was created to do, especially centuries ago. But does he still? If so, can I live with that?

What would that look like if this thing between us

becomes a long-lasting relationship? *Have a good day at work, honey! Don't get blood on your pants because I'm terrible at getting stains out!*

Of course, I've only ever seen him wear dark clothes, so blood stains wouldn't be an issue. But still.

What about the people on the receiving end of the revenge? I'm sure some of them deserve what's coming to them. Doug, for example, would've deserved it, had I taken Raz up on his repeated offers to grant me any vengeance. But I can't stop thinking about the shoe being on the other foot. What if after I left him, Doug had wished for revenge on me? Would I truly be dead now? As much as I want to be with Raz, I need the answer to that question.

To get it requires an in-person conversation because Raz doesn't have a phone. One of the less-serious details I learned yesterday while we were climbing to and from the crest of the waterfall. *Vengeance demons have no need for phones.* Revenge wishes haven't adopted technology yet; they still arrive by brainwave.

Yesterday in the square, he said he'd see me soon, and I assumed he'd find me when his duty was completed. It's possible he doesn't know where I live, though if he's been coming to The Brew several times a week for seven months because of me, the odds are good that he knows where my apartment is. Fate's Falls isn't a big place.

Maybe that's too forward for him. Just because he has no physical modesty doesn't mean he's the make-a-move type. The opposite. If coincidence—or fate—hadn't placed us both at the waterfall yesterday morning, we'd still be oblivious to the other's feelings.

I'm still working on rebuilding the parts of me Doug

broke, but I'm willing to take the leap and go to Raz. Besides, if I have to sit with my thoughts another day, I'll be mentally unraveling by the time I get to work tomorrow morning. Shay is an amazing friend, but she shouldn't have to collect my pieces when I fall apart. New me has much stronger glue than the old me. I'm not the weak, dependent person Doug made me believe I was. I'm strong enough to face my fears head-on. To survive whatever life, or fate, puts in my path. I need to remember that.

R az's cabin, tucked away in the woods, not far from the waterfall, is a five-minute drive from the edge of town. There's no driveway, just a path from the road where I parked to the small clearing surrounding the wood cabin. The structure blends with the trees, looking as if it's been here a long time, though I know Dak built it for Raz. That's why it's taller than your average single-story dwelling. Including his horns, Raz is close to ten feet. He'd have to crouch in my apartment or his horns would scrape the ceiling.

There's no answer when I knock on the massive door. The sound peals through the silent forest, the only response coming from the temporary stoppage of birdsong.

It's been over twenty-four hours since he left me in front of the bakery. Maybe that's a normal amount of time to make someone's revenge wish happen. I didn't think to ask his definition of "soon," assuming it's similar to mine. But "soon" could mean an entirely different thing to a demon who's been around as long as humans have populated the earth.

Waiting for an indeterminate amount of time skates too close to "clingy" territory. I want to be with him, but even if our relationship lasts, I won't become a woman who can't stand on her own. Not again. I'll leave him a note, then head back to town and find Shay. Give her all the details she's impatiently awaiting, then get some of her valuable insight about everything that's happened so quickly.

The cabin's front door has a simple sill, only a couple of inches deep. There's no paved walkway, no place to sit, no smooth surface to write on.

Long-fallen pine needles crunch beneath my feet as I circle the cabin. A single oversized wooden chair sits on a small deck at the back, and I drop into it while removing the notebook and pen I carry in my purse. *It's always a good time to release negativity. If you can't speak the words, write them down.* My therapist's suggestion. It has proven helpful. So has burning the pages I fill. I don't want to look back and re-read those negative thoughts. There's no place in my heart for hatred, even for someone who tried to destroy me.

Today's words aren't negative. They aren't anything— because I can't think of what to write. Pen at the ready, I stare into the woods, my mind as blank as the page beneath my poised hand.

"Dela."

I jump up from the chair at the sound of Raz's voice; the notebook, pen, and my purse clattering onto the deck in the process. "Where did you come from?"

"Hell."

"I meant, just now. The ground is crunchy, but I didn't hear footsteps. Or the patio door slide open. Where did you come from just now?"

"Hell," he says again, taking the seat I vacated, then drawing me onto his knee. "I must visit after each vengeance is fulfilled. The contracts for souls are stored there."

"After three years in a cubicle at my tedious previous job, I guess it's appropriate that there's paperwork in hell." My bottom lip drops when I feel a brief rumble from Raz's chest. "Did you just laugh at my joke?"

"I believe so."

I swivel on his knee, so I'm directly facing him. "You believe so? No 'vengeance demons do or do not'? You're always certain."

"Things are changing." The glow deep in his eyes brightens as he slides one hand through my hair and watches it sift through his fingers, then cradles my chin with his palm. "I am changing."

"You've begun to experience feelings, I know. And laughter is the body's way of expressing an emotion, so that makes sense. It just took me by surprise. How did it feel?"

"Natural. Light. I understand why creatures enjoy this sensation."

"Laughter is one of the best feelings." A big smile breaks across my lips. "I'm so happy you get to enjoy it."

"There is another feeling I would like to enjoy." The hand at my hip pulls me higher up his muscular leg, only stopping when my bare legs are wedged tightly in the V. "Now that I know what it is to kiss you, I crave the feeling of your lips against mine. I hated leaving you yesterday and could not return fast enough."

Serious subjects can wait. I want this moment, just the two of us, without our pasts or whatever the future holds.

"You really are good with words." My lightweight sundress bunches up at my hips when I shift to straddling his lap. "And with your lips and tongue," I say, pressing myself against him everywhere possible as I hover my mouth a breath's width from his. "Show me how much you crave me."

Another rumble in his chest vibrates against me, but this one isn't his newfound ability to laugh. It's harder, a silent growl. Then his hand is in my hair, his fingers molding to my head, holding me in place as he kisses me. This time is different than the others. Yesterday, he followed my lead. Today, he's in control. His kiss is firm, deep, demanding.

I melt against him as his tongue slides between my lips, just enough to touch my tongue, then retreating, a rhythmic teasing dance that has me rocking my hips to match it. Grinding on the hard length of his cock between my legs feels so good. Too good.

He grips my hips when I begin to wiggle backward. "Do not stop."

I shake my head when he settles me back in place. If I keep rubbing myself on him, I'll come. "I'm too embarrassed."

"Modesty and embarrassment are emotions humans have not always felt. It is in the nature of your species to take sexual pleasure."

"I should embrace my prehistoric roots and just go for it whenever the urge strikes?"

"If I am within reach, yes."

I shiver at the possession in his statement. But not out of fear. I know his possessiveness isn't for the sake of controlling me. "I want to let go with you."

"Then do," he says, guiding my body in a slow, firm rocking motion against his cock. "Your desire is mine. Take your pleasure with me."

The spark between my legs increases with every slide over the solid bulge in his pants. I could come like this. But if I'm letting go, I want it to be mutual. "Take me in the house," I say, looking into his eyes. "And I mean that in more ways than just entering the cabin."

The glow in his eyes flares brighter than I've ever seen. "There is nothing I would not do for you, to you. Demon that I am, I require consent in all things. I need to hear you say the words."

"I want... I want your tongue between my legs. I want to taste your cock. I want to feel you inside me." I cling to him as he rises, though I'm in no danger of falling when I'm up in his arms. "I've never told someone what I want before," I say against his neck while he carries me past the glass doors.

"I hope you will always tell me."

Always. That could be another fifty years or so, if he's talking about my lifespan. I don't expect him to want me when I'm old and frail. The way he wants me now is enough. I want it to be enough.

"Your pulse has slowed," he says, sitting on the edge of a massive bed with me cradled in his arms. "And the deep pink has left your cheeks."

"I'm thinking too much. Again. Turning what should be the sexiest moment of my life into a look at lonely, old, future me. I wish I could turn off my brain and just enjoy the sex I want to have with you, but I'm not wired that way. There's all this stuff I can't shut off, even when I'm more turned-on than I've ever been. So, when you've had enough of my messy spiderweb of thoughts and emotions, just tell me to go, and I will."

"A spiderweb is complex, not messy. An intricate collection of individual threads with incredible strength when woven together. If you think I will find your collection of thoughts and feelings anything other than strong and captivating, you are incorrect. You are all I desire, and I desire all of you, including the parts you think I will not. I will never tell you to leave, nor will I force you to stay."

My heart dances a pitter-patter at his beautiful words. "I won't always be young, Raz. I'm going to grow old, get wrinkly, probably saggy, and you'll be exactly as you are now. All I ask is that when I get too old for you to want me, let me go gently."

"I will always want you, my sweet Dela. I was drawn to you before seeing you. You are more lovely than any creature I have laid eyes on, but it is your heart and soul I do not want to be without. When the day comes that your sunshine leaves your body and moves on to the next place, I will return to hell and ask my liege to return my essence to hellfire, so that I do not have to exist one day without you beside me, giving me life."

How to say *I love you* without saying *I love you*.

Is it possible to love someone in such a short time? I think it is, when fate has a hand in finding the one you're meant to love.

Turning in his arms, I place my hands on his shoulders, then resume the straddle position over his lap. "I could listen to your beautiful words forever, and I plan to, but right now, I want your mouth doing other things."

A growl rumbles through him when I grip both his horns

and slide my hands up and down. "You will keep doing that while I lick you until you come." A firm tug on the front of my dress sends the buttons scattering, some onto the soft, yellow blanket covering the bed, some to the wooden floor. His large, warm hands cup my breasts reverently. "I wish to taste every inch of you."

"I wish for that too."

"It is good we are in agreement." His lips curve up in a subtle smile, then he takes a nipple into his mouth. His *hot* mouth.

It felt warmer than human when we kissed, but not hot, like it is now. His lips are like a brand on my skin. Heat ripples through me and I arch toward him, eager for more. His tongue flattens against the underside of my nipple and he begins suckling. It's so good. Never-ever-stop-doing-that good. Desperate to get pressure on my clit, I rock forward on his lap, grinding for more contact, moaning at the spark of an impending orgasm.

He releases my nipple with a wet *pop*, meeting my gaze with fire in his eyes. "On my mouth, Dela. I want to feel your womanly heat pressing against my face. I want to taste your pleasure when you come."

All I can do is nod. Nod, and slip off my dress and panties while he lies back, getting in position for what he wants—me, on his mouth. When I said I wanted his tongue between my legs, I thought *I'd* be the one on their back. I've never done *this* before. Never wanted to. Never had a man command me to press my pussy against his face until I come. Honestly, nobody has ever cared if I came.

Raz cares. My pleasure is his current number-one priority.

I wiggle my way up his body until I'm straddling his neck. He doesn't usually breathe, but the instant I grab hold of his horns, hot air hisses from his mouth, tickling my skin like a light kiss. He grips my hips, the tips of his fingers pressing firm enough to trigger endorphins, but he doesn't pull me higher. No. Without saying a word, I know what he wants. It's in his eyes as he stares up at me.

On my mouth, Dela.

All it takes is one small shift, then my inner thighs are against his ears and I'm hovering above his mouth. His strong, warm hands slide over my skin, caressing every inch he can reach, which happens to be a lot of me because he's so big. Everywhere he touches leaves a trail of tingly sparks, but when his fingers curl around my ass and he draws me down to sit on his face, I feel like I might burst into flames.

I watch his tongue slide up the front of my mound. Long and black against my fair skin, the erotic sight takes my breath away. He presses the tip against my clit, and it takes everything in me not to close my eyes. But I want to watch. He makes me want to soak in the sensation in every way possible.

My body moves involuntarily, meeting the rhythm of his tongue. Within seconds, I'm breathing hard, chasing the building spiral beneath my clit. I rock forward, gripping his horns tightly for support as I grind on his mouth.

Beneath me, he growls, the deep sound vibrating through me, pushing me to the edge. His hand slips between my legs and two long fingers slide inside me, pressing a sensitive spot inside me as he suckles my clit hard.

I snap, crying out as I writhe on him, coming until I can barely breathe. I shudder as the last wave of aftershocks ripple through me. Then his arms are around me, gently shifting me onto the bed beside him, where he strokes my hair while looking at me with a combination of adoration and desire.

"How much time do you require before I can pleasure you again?"

"You want to do that again?" Just thinking about it has my body tingling. I felt like a goddess, riding his face like that. I felt sexy and desired—truly—for the first time in my life.

"I could spend eternity devouring you. A few short minutes is not nearly enough."

"Well, it feels like the bones in my legs melted, so a few short minutes is all I can handle in that position."

"Then I will pleasure you in other positions," he says, continuing to look at me after rolling onto his back again. He pats the highest part of his chest. "Sit here, then spread your legs and let them rest on my shoulders while you lie on top of me. I will draw your sweet center onto my mouth and make you come as many times as your body is able."

My clit thinks it's a great idea, but... "Are you sure you want *that* view?"

"You are worried that I will find your anus unappealing."

I groan, covering my face as heat flares in my cheeks. "That's a bit more 'statement of fact' than I'm ready for."

The warmth of his hand on mine, peeling my fingers from my face, calms my racing pulse. "There is no place on your body that does not appeal to me. When I said I wish to taste every inch of you, I did mean every inch. The pleasure I would give you has no boundaries, though I will respect your desires or lack thereof."

"You want to—" I swallow hard, clearing the way for words I never thought I'd say to make their way to my lips. "You want to lick me *back there?*"

"Yes, but you must want it too." His heated gaze locked on my face, he releases my hand and trails his fingers down my neck, to my breasts, where he strums my hard nipples, one, then the other, until I'm arching toward his touch. "I would give you pleasure in every possible way. My tongue in your ass. My fingers and cock if you wish to be filled with them. But I need to hear you say the words."

Who knew consent could be the hottest kind of dirty talk? "I want." My voice is barely a whisper, rough and breathy because I'm so turned-on. "I want you to do everything to me. And I want to do everything to you."

The glow in his eyes is bright red. He relinquishes my nipples to remove his pants, his huge, hard cock jutting out from his body the instant it has freedom. "Lie on me, my sweet Dela, and open yourself to me."

I'm so tightly wound, the simple brush of my skin against the blanket is enough to make me gasp. My legs shake as I straddle him the way he instructed. Another gasp rushes from my lips as he pulls me toward his mouth, then another when his hand spans my back to guide me to a prone position on top of him.

"You are perfect, my sunshine," he says, lapping and sucking at my clit until I'm desperate to come, not a single care in the world that I'm spread wide, revealing my most private parts, literally right before his eyes.

The fat head of his dark-red cock lies high on his abdomen in front of me. I curl my fingers around it and stroke, exploring the smooth, spade-shaped tip and deep ledge beneath, then the thick, ribbed shaft that's hot against my skin.

Beneath me, against me, he moans, doubling down on my clit until I'm humping his mouth with abandon. I cry out when the tension inside me snaps, and I come. And come. And come.

Over-sensitized, I wriggle off of his body, only to find myself turned onto my back with my legs spread wide and draped over his shoulders as his tongue finds my clit again. Even as I plead, "it's too soon," the climb toward another peak begins.

He reaches for my hand, bringing it to join his tongue at my clit. The combination of his tongue and my fingers is erotic, electric. Then his tongue slides down, dipping between my folds before continuing to my ass.

I flinch at the first light laps, relaxing as the nerve endings adjust to the sensation. "It feels good," I say, rubbing my clit harder.

His rumble vibrates against me. Through me. Then he presses the tip against the tight ring that has never been breached. My body jolts, instinctively trying to get away, but there's no escaping Raz's hot, probing tongue. A different instinct takes over as the tip pushes past my defenses.

I moan, rubbing my clit faster while bearing down to get more of his tongue inside me. White flashes behind my closed eyelids as I come, sharp and fast, a willing, breathless prisoner to the pleasure.

My heart's still racing when he rises to kneel between my legs. I shouldn't want more, but God, I do. I reach for his cock, my mouth watering at the memory of its heat in my hand. "I want you inside me," I say, then shake my head. "No, that's not right. I *need* you inside me."

He takes my hands and guides me to my knees. "It would be safest if you ride me," he says, settling with his back against the headboard, his long, red legs straight and his huge cock standing hard and tall.

My pulse is like a wild, galloping horse as I straddle him.

He groans as I take hold of his horns. "You will never know how good it feels when you do that."

"After the orgasms I just had, I think I have a pretty good idea." I hum as he skims his hands over my body, then fills his palms with my breasts. Reaching between us, I guide his big tip to my pussy, gasping at the immediate flare of heat when it nestles between my folds. He's so thick, even the rounded, spade-shaped tip stretches me as I descend. He's too much, but I want all of him. My body *needs* all of him.

The rumble within him vibrates all over me, everywhere our bodies touch. I can't resist looking down, watching his cock disappear inch by inch into my body as I slide down the cock that never seems to end.

"I want..." Wiggling and rocking, I pant as another inch of him fills me. But there's more, and God, I want to feel all of him. "I want more..."

Cupping my hips, he guides my body up and down, setting a slow, sensual rhythm that seats him deeper inside me with each stroke. "You are taking me so well," he says, then captures one of my nipples with his mouth.

My eyelids flutter closed as he suckles. The sensations send a tight tug of longing between my legs. Then his hand is there, exactly where I need it, rubbing my clit. I rock forward to get more pressure, gasping as my pussy connects with his groin. God, he's in me, all of him, and the heat of him inside me, the exquisite tingling burn of being stretched... *"Raz,"* I moan, grinding on him, then coming apart, panting and rocking and coming. It never ends... the sensation, the waves ricocheting through me.

Then his moan, the low, long rumble I feel everywhere... His cock throbs inside me, and somehow, I come again, or still, I don't know which.

Everything goes white behind my eyelids, then his arms wrap around me, holding me tight and safe, rolling me over to my side as his cock slips out of me. The emptiness after being so utterly full is overwhelming. A shiver ripples through me, and I gulp for air, burrowing against the heat of his body.

"Are you in pain?" There's an edge to his voice I haven't heard before.

"No," I say, opening my eyes and shifting to look into his. "I promise. It was amazing. You made me feel amazing."

"You make me feel everything."

My heart feels as if it's lodged in my throat, pounding so hard I can barely get a whisper past it. "I feel everything with you, too." It's as close to telling him I love him as I can get. I know it's too soon to be real, but my heart, my head, they're both sure that it's real.

Chapter Six

RAZBUNARE

"Hey..." Dela says, raising her head from the position she has assumed, draped over my body. Holding herself up, she looks around the single room of my dwelling. "There's no kitchen."

"Vengeance demons do not require sustenance."

Her eyes open wide as she meets my gaze. "You don't eat?"

"I can consume food and drinks, but both are unnecessary. I have rarely partaken."

"So... all those coffees you've ordered, you didn't actually drink them?"

"I ingested small amounts while I lingered in your workplace for what seemed an acceptable amount of time."

Her Cupid's bow lips form a beautiful smile. "You really liked me."

"Like is an insufficient word."

"Oh?" A rich pink rises on her lovely face.

Though I know the feeling to be true, I cannot lay claim to love yet. She would not believe me capable of that emotion so soon. "I have wanted to be in your presence, and nowhere else, since the first moment, my sunshine."

Sighing, she leans in to my touch as I cup her soft cheek. "I want to say we could've been together if you'd asked me out back then, but I would've said no, even though I was attracted to you. I wasn't ready then."

"I would have waited. Even if you never returned my affection, I would have waited."

She pulls her plump bottom lip between her teeth. Much is going through her mind; I can see it all in her eyes. But she does not share her thoughts. Just smiles and kisses me, taking another look around my dwelling before resuming her place on my chest. "Is this bed the only furniture you have?"

"Yes. For the first year I lived in this cabin, I had nothing. Vengeance demons do not require comfort, as other creatures do."

"You just...sat on the floor? *Slept* on the floor?" Her nose scrunches up and her eyebrows pinch together. "And what did you do while you were awake? Lie on the hard floor and stare at the ceiling?"

"Vengeance demons do not require sleep. Our purpose is to fulfill human wishes for revenge and supply our liege with souls. That is what we should be doing at all times."

She shakes her head, her soft hair eliciting a pleasurable

sensation as it grazes my skin. "So, you're the literal embodiment of 'all work and no play.'"

"We are permitted respite in the hell domains, should we choose." The comment causes her lips to turn down. "I have rarely done so," I add, to direct her thoughts from our earlier conversation about my previous sexual activities with other demons. "And not for many decades."

"Then what *have* you done? Has your entire life just been revenge after revenge after revenge?"

"That is why I exist."

"Not anymore." Her smile returns, then she lays her cheek on my chest and one small, soft hand on my face.

"Not anymore," I say, stroking her silky hair all the way to its ends, near the tempting swell of her soft backside. My cock hardens at the thought of pulling her on top of me and sliding into her warm, welcoming body again. It is too soon. My endless craving will wait until she recovers from taking the full length of my shaft. In all my eons, I have never felt such pleasure.

Her fingers play across my lips, the line of my jaw, the outer shell of my ear. "What made you decide to get a bed?"

"I cannot give you a factual answer."

Shifting position, she rests her chin on my chest and looks up at me, a playful smile lighting up her face. "Excuse me? Vengeance demons always have a factual answer."

For the second time today, I feel the spontaneous, light vibration in my chest.

"I love that you're laughing," she says, pushing up enough to kiss me.

Love. Humans use the word in varying degrees, toward many things. This is the first time I have heard Dela use it, and it pleases me to hear her say it about me, when she has reserved its use.

"I had the bed built after I saw you for the first time."

Her eyes open wide.

"I did not expect you to share the bed with me. I only knew that I wanted to experience your world in ways you do. To be closer to you, even though I would not ever truly be close to you."

"You're pretty close to me now." She wiggles her delicate eyebrows at me. "You were *extremely* close to me a few minutes ago."

The need to get that close to her now roars inside me, louder than any voices ever have. The voices have remained silent since I returned from the hell realm and found Dela waiting. If only they would stay silent for the rest of her lifetime, so I could enjoy every minute with her.

"You look serious. Not in your normal serious way. Kind of...far away. Like outside the bakery yesterday. Do you have to go again?"

"The wishes for vengeance will return. When they do, I can only delay my duty for a short time, then I must fulfill a wish, so that a soul is designated for my liege's dominion."

"It sounds horrible, committing someone's soul to hell. How do you choose?" she asks quietly. "Has it become difficult to mete out revenge since you started feeling things?"

"It is not a vengeance demon's place to judge what is right or wrong. We are not built to experience compassion, guilt, or any other emotion. They are a hindrance to our purpose, one I must continue to fulfill, or I will be recalled to the hell realm. Perhaps to be remade. Or destroyed."

Any remnant of a smile vanishes. "Then you have to do

whatever you have to do. If you're gone one day and don't come back—" Her mouth closes and she swallows hard, blinking rapidly over glassy-sheened eyes. "I don't want to lose you that way."

"You will not lose me any way," I say, wrapping my arms around her. "I will continue to consign souls to hell, enough to satisfy my liege, while also being selective about those whose wishes I fulfil—as I have been for some time." I loosen the embrace so I can look into her eyes. "I will cause no physical harm for the duration of my life with you."

"And there'll be enough non-violent revenge wishes for you to do that for, oh..." Beautiful red roses bloom on high on her cheeks. "Say, the next fifty years?"

"Or more. Fifty years will not be enough time with you, my sunshine."

Chapter Seven

DELA

I've just zipped up the new dress I bought when Raz's heavy knock rattles my apartment door. Butterflies take flight in my chest as I hurry to answer. He promised he'd be back from his demon duties in time for Dak and Rosetta's wedding this evening, but in the short time we've been together, I've quickly realized that he's not always able to gauge or control how long meting out vengeance will take. It's quicker to bludgeon someone or drop them off a bridge than it is to deliver carefully crafted revenge that keeps the scales as evenly balanced as possible.

"You're here," I say, flinging open the door. My jaw drops at the sight before me. I've been attracted to Raz since the moment I laid eyes on his massive red form—which is always shirtless.

Fate's Falls' businesses don't adhere to the common "no

shirt, no shoes, no service" rule found in places primarily populated by humans. Though many of the non-human inhabitants here do wear some manner of clothing, there are too many body types, shapes, and sizes to make it a hard-and-fast decree. And once you get used to it, the assortment of furry, horned, hooved, or other unique body parts you might see around town are no big deal.

Seeing Raz dressed in a white, long-sleeved button-front shirt *is* a big deal. He's hot, my big red demon. Smokin' hot.

Once I've collected my bottom lip from the floor, I pat around my mouth to ensure there's no drool. "You own a shirt."

"I do now."

"It looks amazing. You're handsome and sexy and—" Heat creeps up my neck as I catch myself before saying the next words.

As always, Raz stares a hole in me. His preferred method of getting me to say the things I'm holding back.

"Every female at the wedding is going to be eye-fucking my demon boyfriend."

One of his brief rumbles of internal laughter pulls the crisp white fabric taut across his broad chest. "Had I known the effect wearing a shirt would have on you, I would have purchased one many months ago."

"Oh, I quite enjoyed your shirtless visits. Zero complaints." I trail my fingers over the soft cotton hiding his chiseled physique from view. "Let me grab my purse and we can go."

He catches my hand before I turn. "I wish to tell you how beautiful you are, but cannot find words adequate to describe it."

"Those'll do," I say, using the front of his shirt to tug him down to a level where I can kiss him. Too much time has passed since the last time.

The way he tugs me tight to his body and coasts his hands over my curves tells me he feels the same way. My pretty red dress and his sexy white shirt won't be making an impression at the reception. All of our clothes will be on Raz's cabin floor before the first toast to the bride and groom has been made.

But I don't think I can wait that long. *"Raz,"* I whisper against his lips.

He understands the plea without additional words. Hands on my hips, he ducks low and walks me backward into the apartment, closing the door behind him. He doesn't bother maneuvering us through to my small bedroom; he lowers himself right there, stretching out on his back on my living room area rug.

Hunger flares in his glowing eyes as I lift the silky red wrap dress to expose my bare body beneath. Panties are pointless when I know I'll be alone with him. He's insatiable, and so am I.

"On my mouth, Dela. Now. I need to taste you while you come."

My body is humming, and he hasn't even touched me yet. Feet on either side of his head, I stand over him, giving him an all-access view as I lower myself. His tongue is waiting, and I moan as he pushes it deep inside me as I settle on his face. Grabbing his horns, I bounce on his tongue, the slick sound of it sending sparks racing through me. I love when he tongue-fucks me, but it won't make me come. It just makes me wet and messy, ready for his cock.

I rock forward, moaning shamelessly when he slides his tongue to my clit. I slide my fists up and down his horns, making him growl against my pussy, spurring him to suck harder, flick faster. The orgasm hits me without warning, making me writhe and grind on his mouth until I'm gasping for breath.

This time, Raz doesn't keep going, pushing me into a second wave. He doesn't take me down with gentle laps over my clit. Behind me, the sharp zip of his fly slices the air, then his hands are on my hips, lifting me off his face and centering me over his towering cock.

My head falls back as his hard, fat tip pushes inside me. The heat of him... God, the thickness. Every time is like the first time, stretching me wide, taking him deeper, deeper, until there's no room for more... until there is. A shuddering moan leaves my panting lips as he angles his hips to fit the full, impossible length of him inside me. "Raz, *Raz*..."

"Now," he growls, pressing a finger against my clit and sending me crashing into another spiral of pleasure, his cock throbbing as he follows me over. He catches me before light-headedness has me tumbling off of him. "I have you, my sunshine."

The carpet is no match for his big, soft bed, but the way he looks at me while cradling me beside him would make anywhere feel like home. The way he always looks at me. The realization of it catches in my throat, making me choke on my breath.

"Are you unwell?" The broody set of his brow says the headshake I give him isn't a good enough response.

I can't tell him I love him. That *he's* my home, and I want to pack my things and move to his cabin so we can live every day like this moment. Love isn't part of his vocabulary, even though I know he feels it. And he's been a solitary creature literally forever. He might never want a 24/7 girlfriend. I'm okay with both things. Because I'm not broken like I used to be. My glue is holding. My spiderweb has never been stronger.

"Just thinking about how happy I am. About us, together and individually."

"As am I." He presses a soft kiss to my lips, then helps me to my feet. "I have wrinkled your dress," he says as he follows me out the door. "And I am not sorry. Now all the males at the wedding will know you have been well-fucked by your demon boyfriend."

I giggle while sliding my arm through his. "And all the women will be jealous."

"Their envy would be pointless. I only see you. I want only you."

RAZBUNARE

It has been difficult to keep my secret from Dela. There is no deception in the information I have withheld. I am...excited. An interesting feeling with layers that never settle. After we have finished whatever post-wedding socializing she wishes to do, I will take her to the cabin and show her what I have planned. If she thinks it is too soon, I will wait as many days, weeks, months, or years as she needs. But I do not want to wait. Fifty years will not be enough time with her. I want to live in her sunshine every possible minute. Even being among this gathering of people is bearable with her by my side.

"Girl, let me look at you," one of Dela's friends says, making a *mm-hmm* noise as she surveys Dela from top to bottom. "So gorgeous. And that glow. I'd ask where I can get some of whatever it is making you look so radiant, but I think you've got the source locked down."

Dela laughs, gesturing toward me. "Shay, you know Raz." Then Dela turns to me, giving me a raised eyebrow as she continues. "And Raz, I'm sure you recognize my friend Shay from The Brew."

Vengeance demons do not lie. But humans do not require full honesty at all times. "It is nice to see you," I say, offering my hand to the woman, a human gesture she waves off in rejection.

"Tempting, just to see what I might see, but I'll pass, because of what I might see."

Dela snuggles under my arm, pressing her softness against my side. "That sounds like a riddle, but she means it literally. Shay is a seer."

"*Was* a seer," Shay corrects.

"You still are; you just choose not to practice."

Shay flicks her fingers, then settles her gaze on me. "What about you, Razbunare? Could you choose not to practice the thing you were born to do?"

"No, I would be recalled to hell if I failed in my duty."

"Bummer," Shay says, "having no free will like that."

"Oh, he has free will," Dela tells her friend. "He's particular about the revenge he fulfils now. No violence, no physical harm. He tries to keep things fair and minimize the negative ripple effect. That's why it takes so damn long and I don't get to see him every day."

Shay's gaze swings from Dela to me. "A vengeance demon with a conscience and code of conduct. Interesting. When did that happen?"

I do not fault Dela's friend for wishing to protect her, but Dela does not require protection from me. "Two years ago."

Dela shifts to look up at me. "Before you came to Fate's Falls? I thought you changed your method of meting out revenge after you met me." Though she maintains a pleasant expression, her voice is missing its joy.

"I'm always interested in an origin story," Shay says, when I fail to answer my sunshine's question. "What happened two years ago to bring about the change in your method?"

"*Shay,*" Dela hisses, sliding out from beneath my arm. "That's Raz's business, not ours." Protective of me, despite her disappointment that I was not entirely forthcoming with details from my past.

The space she no longer occupies feels like a cold void. This is not the time or place I would choose for such a conversation, but remaining silent will only deepen her unhappiness. "I did not tell you the exact moment things began to change for me because it involves violence. Though you may know I have been brutal in fulfilling my purpose, I did not want to tell you the details of those transactions, particularly when they occurred in recent history."

"I wouldn't have judged you," she says, taking my hand.

"I never will." The softness of her hand against mine is a strength far greater than the power I embody.

"I came to this realm to transact a soul from one of large cities. The revenge sought by this human male would have been easy to grant—violence has always been the most efficient way to fill the hell realm with souls."

Beside me, Dela shivers, then squeezes my hand, a silent assurance.

"But you didn't do it?" Shay asks. "Whatever horrible thing that evil piece of shit wished for, you didn't do it?"

"I did not. He wished severe bodily injury to a female. The woman with whom he shared a home and a bed. He claimed she had betrayed him by traveling without him, among other men, when he had expressly forbidden her to go. He was prepared to contract his soul to hell in return for the woman permanently losing the use of her legs. He wished her to remain living, but unable to physically walk away from him."

Shay's expression no longer holds a challenge, and Dela's... I have never seen her fair skin so devoid of color.

"You were in Chicago," Dela whispers, her fingers sliding from mine so she can cup both hands over her mouth.

"Oh, girl...no. No." Shay moves toward Dela, her hands out. She pauses, draws a deep breath, then pulls Dela into an embrace. "I'm so sorry." Shay rubs Dela's back, meeting my gaze over Dela's shoulder. "What stopped you from hurting the woman in Chicago?"

"Sunshine. The sky was dark gray that day. Raining and dark as night, everywhere except the place I found the woman. Above her, it was brilliant. Surrounding her so brightly, I could only see an outline of her form. I thought she was an angel, but when I spoke, she did not answer. That meant she was human. She could not hear me because I am a vengeance demon, and she had not wished for my presence. I should not have faltered in my duty, but I could not take an action that would diminish or extinguish such pure light. Nothing was the same after that. I began to see things differently. To want things."

"Wait," Shay says, as Dela backs out of their hug. She removes her gloves and takes both of Dela's hands. "Let me see." Eyes closed, she breathes deeply, smiling as she meets Dela's gaze again. "All clear from here out. Nothing but sunshine and horny rainbows."

The noise Dela makes sounds like a laugh, and she's smiling, but tears roll down her face. "Thank you."

"You don't need these," Shay says, wiping the moisture from Dela's cheeks before pulling on her gloves. "And you," she gives me a nod, "need to ask your woman how she ended up behind the counter at the coffeehouse." Then she walks away, leaving me with Dela, alone, despite being surrounded by people.

"It was me. I was the woman in Chicago. Doug didn't want me to go on a company team-building ski retreat. He said it was because he didn't trust the men around me, but I knew that was a lie. It had to be, because he'd spent years drilling it into me that nobody else would ever want me. He'd successfully cut me off from my friends and moved me away from my mom. He didn't want me to go on that trip because he didn't want me to make any new connections. When I said I *had* to go, he accused me of defying him. He told me I'd be lucky to come home in a wheelchair. You saved my life, Raz."

My insides knot, pressure building in my chest. "I will destroy him, Dela. But I cannot do so without your wish for vengeance."

"I would never wish for that. Even after he attempted to deliver revenge on his own."

I have committed atrocities in the name of my purpose and felt nothing, because I had no emotions then. Now, I feel as if I am burning alive. This is rage, and I would wield it like a lethal weapon if she wished it. "What did he do?"

"He killed me," she whispers. "After I said I might leave, he used my medications to overdose me. I was dead, technically, but a reaper sent me back. I woke up holding a card with a phone number. I snuck out while Doug was sleeping. He thought I was dead, and he just fell asleep, like it was any other night." A shiver runs through her, and she shakes it away. "That number on the card led me to Fate's Falls, and I started over. All I've ever wanted is a happy, safe life. I have everything I could ever wish for now. Here. With you." She flattens her palms on my chest and smiles up at me. "There is one more thing I wished for, actually. Someone to love, who would love me back with their whole heart. I have that with you, too."

"Vengeance demons do not have hearts." It is becoming more natural to arrange my lips in a smile, and the one I give her now earns me one of her affectionate nudges. "But you have made me feel like I possess one. If I had a heart, it would beat only for you. I love you with all that I am, my sunshine."

"And I love you," she whispers, shining brighter than she ever has. "Take me home, Raz."

"To your apartment?"

The silk of her hair glows like a sunset sky as she shakes her head. "To your home."

"I would like it to be our home. I am having it fitted with a kitchen. And I have ordered chairs I think you will find comfortable."

The smile on her lovely lips blooms larger. "You don't need to entice me with food and beverages," she teases, replaying my comment when she invited me to this event. "Or chairs, since we'd both prefer I sit on something else." She shrieks when I scoop her into my arms, drawing the attention of everyone still lingering in the town square.

The eons I have existed do not matter. My life, my eternity, is with Dela.

DELETED SCENE: PROLOGUE
THE GRUMPY DEMON'S SUNSHINE

Dear Reader,

During editing, we decided to delete this prologue scene which happens before Dela moves to Fate's Falls, and instead, to thread the details of Dela's past throughout the main story. And I'm glad we went that route, because it makes the story better. But... I found I couldn't let this scene go to the bin, so if you'd like to read this nugget from Dela's life (and death) before she moved to Fate's Falls, here it is.

Please note that the following scene includes death and mention of psychological abuse and physical harm from the heroine's previous boyfriend.

PROLOGUE

Approximately seven months before Chapter One begins...

DELA

Everywhere I look, there's nothing but light. The purest, brightest light I've ever seen, yet it doesn't make me squint or want to shield my eyes. And I'm moving, I'm upright and can feel my body in motion, but when I glance down at my legs, they look as if I'm standing still.

I must be dreaming. One of those lucid dreams, I guess, since I'm aware of it. But I don't remember going to bed. Or lying on the couch. Wasn't I just eating dinner with Doug at the kitchen table? I'm sure that's right.

When I got home from work, he was already in the apartment. Not only does he never get home first, but he'd picked up my favorite takeout—spicy Tuscan chicken pasta from the nice little indie bistro in the neighborhood—and a bottle of wine I love. I mostly steer clear of alcohol because it doesn't mix well with the cocktail of prescription meds I take, but tonight was worth making a small exception.

After our fight this morning, I wasn't sure he'd come home at all. It wasn't even close to the worst fight we've ever had, but the way Doug had looked at me when he walked out... I burst into tears the moment he slammed the door behind him.

In the heat of the moment, I'd said maybe I should get my own place again, just until we were fighting less, something I've never voiced in our many other rocky moments. I hadn't planned to suggest it and felt ill as soon as the words left my lips. I know I'm not strong enough to be without him, that I need him. I texted him those things throughout the day, repeatedly, even though he never replied once.

We were done, and I'd caused it. I was sure of it.

I was prepared to beg for another chance when I walked into our apartment after work. But I didn't have to beg. Dinner was ready and waiting for me, and so was he—but not primed for a rematch and his inevitable victory. He was smiling. In a good mood. Beyond good, actually.

Throughout dinner, he listened to me, not making even the most subtle backhanded dig or a single negative comment. There was soft touching. Kissing. We were having the nicest togetherness we've had in years.

This morning's fight and my suggestion of taking a break must have had a positive impact. I felt warm inside. From the wine, the affection.

To us, I said as we clinked glasses.

To the future, Doug said in return.

I haven't had that much hope in my heart in a long time.

But now I'm asleep? I must have had more wine than I recall, and passed out. I need to apologize. God, I hope I didn't ruin everything.

Closing my eyes, I take a deep breath and will myself to wake up. When I open my eyes, I'm still in the dream, only now, I'm not alone. An ominous, robed figure stands before me. The size of a large man, the hood of its cloak is deep enough to shadow its face from my view. Wherever I was going in my floaty motion, the figure is blocking the way. I should be terrified, yet I don't have the urge to scream or run. There's no fear inside me at all.

"I need to wake up," I say simply.

"This isn't a dream," the figure answers in a soothing, masculine voice.

"It has to be." I turn my head side to side, surveying the endless white nothingness. "What else could it be?"

"The end."

"The end of what?" The words are barely out of my mouth when the clarity of it all hits me. "You meant, this is the end of *me*, didn't you?" I pat around on my body, hair, and face. I feel solid enough. I can't be dead. But maybe that's what all ghosts think. "Am I... *dead?*"

"Your heart has stopped beating, you're at the crossing. For most, this would be considered death."

"For most? What does that mean?"

"The Oracle says it is not your time to leave the earthly plane. I can take you across to the next place now, but I can also take you back. If you choose to return to your previous form, you should rise from your bed and leave, as quickly as possible, then never return to that life."

It's not cold wherever we are, meaning the chill rippling through me is internal. "Why should I do that?"

In the same floaty way I did, he moves toward me, close enough to see the hint of a male humanlike face in the shadows of his hood. "The one in whom you place your trust will not fail twice."

"Fail twice at what?" I inhale sharply as the last word rolls from my lips. "Are you saying Doug tried to kill me? That can't be right. We weren't fighting. And even if we had been, he doesn't raise a hand toward me when he's angry. He's not a violent man."

"Violence does not always come in the form of a physical strike."

Ice and fire churn in my stomach. I fight the urge to vomit, if that's even possible in my current state of semi-deadness. "You're sure it was him? He's the reason I'm... dead?"

"Yes."

"How? How did he—" I can't force the words *kill me* out of my mouth. "How did I die?"

"Overdose."

"My prescriptions," I whisper. It's a statement that doesn't require the nod of confirmation I receive.

Aside from the occasional acetaminophen tablet, Doug doesn't take anything. I'm the one with a ripe collection of anxiety meds and sleeping pills. He must've laced the dinner or wine. Possibly both.

"But why? To make it look like an accidental overdose? Or suicide? I don't understand. We just made up from a fight. He was being so nice, so sweet. Why would he pretend now, when he never has before? If he didn't want to be with me, why not agree to my suggestion of moving out, and just end our relationship? Why would he want me dead?"

"I am a guide from one place to the next, not omniscient. Though, I doubt you need an all-knowing entity to answer your questions." Again, the man in the cloak moves just enough to give me a glimpse of his face. "It's time to choose, Dela."

I don't bother asking how he knows my name. Either I'm truly on the cusp of death, and he's some sort of otherworldly being responsible for guiding souls, or this is the most bizarre dream I've ever had. In either case, the ominous robed man would know my name. That's the least weird part of this whole thing.

"I want to live."

He gives another single nod, then a human-looking hand extends beyond the flowy edge of his sleeve. Warmth flows through me when I take it. Peace like I've never experienced. Then it's gone, replaced by the crush of day-to-day emotions as the bright white surrounding us morphs into the dimness of my bedroom.

The small table lamp on the bedside table is on, casting a pale glow over everything, including my lifeless body. I'm lying on my back with the sheets neatly pulled up to armpit level, both my arms on top, completely straight at my sides. Not a position I would ever sleep in. I look like a corpse. Which is what I am, I suppose.

The pull to rejoin my physical body is overwhelming, but my motion halts with a single word in my head. *Wait.*

I can't question my guide; I no longer have a voice. Or solidity of any kind. When I glance down at the place it feels like I'm standing, there's...nothing. Am I just a soul, floating around in my third-floor apartment? Is this what it's like to be a ghost? Are ghosts even real?

Watch. Again, his single internal word commands my attention.

My incorporeal eyes snap to Doug entering the bedroom. He goes about his business—undressing, pulling on a pair of gray pajama pants, setting out clothes for tomorrow, scrolling his phone as he sits on his side of the bed.

Maybe the mysterious man from the white place was wrong. Maybe I had some sort of freak allergic reaction during dinner, and Doug thinks I'm sleeping it off. He doesn't realize I'm dead.

He pulls back the covers and slips between. Instead of turning off the light, he rolls onto his side, facing me, propping himself up on one arm.

I hold my metaphorical breath as he leans in to kiss me goodnight. This is when he'll realize I need help. This is when he'll save me.

Only, that's not what happens.

Even in the low light, the contempt in his expression is unmistakable. "You should've known I'd never allow someone like you to leave me."

Screaming is impossible in my current ethereal form, but I hear it as clearly as my guide's voice in my mind when he says, *Remember.*

. . . . .

A Reaper is Forever

A REAPER IS
Forever

KARLA DOYLE

A REAPER IS
FOREVER

SHAY

One seer is born in the Winterlock coven in each generation.
The elders call it a gift, but if I could return or exchange it, I
would. Witches born with the ability to see the future don't
possess other magic, and I can't turn it off. My precognitive
skill is always there, every time I make skin-to-skin contact.
Talk about a relationship buzzkill.

Young, impatient, and frustrated with being the least useful
member of the coven, I left in search of a normal life. Then
money got tight, and I sidestepped the rule about not profiting from magic. It was just an innocent psychic fair in a
hotel ballroom. But the horrific things I saw when I looked
into that man's future... I tried to alter the future I'd seen,
but only changed mine—by dying.

The phrase "you only live once" isn't always accurate. My death was temporary.

After returning my soul to my body, a kind, gentle reaper brought me to Fate's Falls, a secret, magically protected town full of monsters and supernatural creatures. He said I'd be safe here. And I am, physically. But the only protection from my magic is to never touch another living being again. A sacrifice I'm willing to make until the reaper I've been thinking about, fantasizing about, for fifteen lonely years returns to town.

The temptation to let my guard down with Kohl is almost as strong as my self-preservation instinct. As a reaper, he's not a living being. But a reaper is forever, and seeing his future might be the worst kind of vision of all...

Though this book can be read as a standalone story, it is best read after *Mated to the Minotaur* and *The Grumpy Demon's Sunshine*.

AUTHOR'S NOTE
A REAPER IS FOREVER

One of my favorite things about writing paranormal romance is the freedom to make shit up. You might find bits and pieces of theology or mythology in my books, but don't count on me to follow any particular "rules," and you absolutely shouldn't take anything as fact.

This book has a slower burn, lower heat, and the hero is significantly less monster-y than my other monster romances. **There is no funky monster peen in this story, sorry.** I wrote it because Shay deserved a happily after ever, and this is the way her story unfolded from my brain.

Though this book can be read as a standalone story, **it is best read after** *Mated to the Minotaur* and *The Grumpy Demon's Sunshine*, in that order.

If you only read one of those prior to the book, the author recommends *The Grumpy Demon's Sunshine*, where Shay, the heroine in *A Reaper is Forever*, is a significant secondary character, and you get a deep glimpse into her personality and life.

If you've already met Shay, you know that she has...issues. *A Reaper is Forever* reveals Shay's backstory, and takes her on a journey to both a personal happily ever after and a romantic one.

Chapter One

SHAY

A shrill feline yowl breaks the silence in my bedroom as I jolt upright.

"Sorry I scared you." I pat the spot on my bed where my cat just sprang from. "Come here, drama queen. You can bite me and we'll call it even."

Rune returns to the bed, sniffs the finger I offer, but declines the opportunity to sink her feline fangs into my skin. My cat has never shown any sign of being a familiar. Not surprising. I'm the least witchy witch there is. It makes sense for my cat to be just that—a cat. Plus, I found her in the alley behind the coffee shop, and familiars are always received as a gift from another witch. Hope isn't my strong suit, but with the pittance I possess, I thought *maybe* the Oracle had left Rune in that alley for me.

Even without magic, Rune is the best kitty. Always forgiving when I scare the shit out of her with my nightmares, like the one I just woke from. They're less frequent now, but when they happen, I see the visions as clearly and horrifically as I did when I touched that man's hand and saw his future. All those women, some murdered, some on their way to reaching that end.

And him. I still see him, too.

Cold ripples up from my gut, making me shiver. Fifteen years since the night I foolishly set up a table at a psychic fair, but when I have one of the nightmares, it feels like yesterday. Younger me had been so desperate to be independent, something other than the Winterlock coven's lone and never-needed seer. I couldn't get out of Gettysburg fast enough.

But Pittsburg hadn't been the adventure and new beginning I hoped for. Limited and specific as my magic is, it's also impossible to turn off. Wanting to live a "normal" life didn't make it happen. I still got visions every time I made skin-to-skin contact. Talk about a relationship buzzkill. The only normal aspect of my life was the heap of responsibilities and expenses. Everything cost more than I expected. Even working part-time while going to college, I couldn't keep up with the rent *and* eat.

I'd decided to quit the University of Pittsburg and move back home. Start the next semester at HACC. I planned to surprise my mom with the news during what she thought was my Christmas break visit. The best gift I could've given her. But first I had to get home. And I was down to my literal last dollar.

My damn pride wouldn't let me ask Mom for money, so I broke one of the coven's cardinal rules—*never profit from your magic.* I told myself it wasn't a big deal. Touch a bunch of strangers' hands, tell them some vague truths about their futures, make enough cash to buy a one-way bus ticket. People at the psychic fair would assume I was a fake, just like all the other fortune tellers and woo-woo vendors. The coven would never know. Mom wouldn't look at me with disappointment. It was a dirty little secret I could live with. Everyone has at least one skeleton in their closet, right?

Never did I consider that I'd touch the hand of someone with actual skeletons in his closet. That I'd see the future atrocities of a serial killer.

Visions I relived in tonight's nightmare. His bloodied mouth and hands, eyes wild with excitement from the unconscionable acts he'd committed. Then the nightmare switched to my personal memories from that night. The flicker in his eyes when I told him what I'd seen in his future. Somehow, he'd known I was lying. That I had the power to see the evil in him. He enjoyed that I saw the truth.

I'll never forget the rabid glee on his face when our gazes met outside the hotel. He thought he had me, but I was prepared to do whatever was necessary to change the future I'd seen. And I tried. I died trying.

Purring and rubbing against me, Rune pulls me back to the present with a single gentle meow.

"Want to go for a walk?" I ask and get a string of feline conversation in return. "Me too. Let's go."

Rune hops off the bed, following as closely as possible while I throw on clothes and make my way out of the small cottage. It's a miracle she hasn't tripped me in fifteen years of weaving around my legs. Maybe there's some magic in the black cat after all.

Out on the sidewalk, Rune trots ahead of me, quickly blending in with the darkness. Our predawn walks are her time to scope out the neighborhood. Catch up on new scents. She sticks close to our regular route, though, and always returns to my side by the time we round the block toward home.

As usual, the street is empty and quiet. Even the birds aren't awake yet. Four in the morning is too early for a lot of people, but they're missing out. There's a special kind of peacefulness at this time of day. Here in Fate's Falls, anyway. The Oracle's magic protects the town and its residents from harm. Evil doesn't exist here—aside from in memories. There's no escape from those.

Rune's aggravated yowl pierces the silence. Muttering a curse, I switch from a relaxed pace to sprinting, following the sound into Minerva Goodwin's side yard. It's probably just a standoff between Rune and Cookie, Minerva's cat. They have low-level beef. Not the scrapping variety, just feline smack talk. I always imagine Cookie bragging about having a cat door, egging Rune on. Whatever they're saying, it's harmless. But if the noise wakes the old witch, I'll be on the hook to make amends for disturbing the ninety-five-year-old's sleep.

Shining my phone's flashlight around the dense gardens, I say, *"Rune, stop talking shit and let's go,"* in my sternest whisper. "I'm going to have to visit every day for a week if you wake Minerva."

"No chance of that."

I straighten, as if my puppet strings have been firmly

yanked. Doesn't matter that I haven't heard his voice in a decade and a half. It's part of that night. Unforgettable.

In what feels like slow motion, I turn toward the sound. He looks the same as I remember. The only time I've ever seen the reaper. "Kohl."

"Hello, Shay." The hood of his dark robe barely moves when he tips his head. Just like that night. A reaper's cloak is more than just clothing—it's part of their being. "It's good to see you. You're looking well."

"Anything's better than the last time you saw me." Funny isn't my specialty, but I pull it off sometimes. Based on the lack of response my attempted humor gets, now is not one of those times. "Seriously, though. I know I thanked you before, but that apology came from twenty-one-year-old hysterical me. I've thought about you a lot over the years. Even with its limits, I'm grateful for this life. So, thank you for that night and all the nights I've had since."

Rather than answer, he steps closer. Close enough for me to see his dark eyes focused on mine. To *feel* his gaze inside me, searching my soul.

"Um, hello... I feel you poking around in there. Checking to see if I'm still worthy of the second chance?"

Now, his full lips curve upward. Just a little. Even that hint of a smile tugs at my insides. Makes me feel all fluttery and shit. Like a normal woman successfully flirting with an interesting man. Which is not at all what this is.

"I was looking to see if you're happy."

Crossing my arms over my chest, I raise an eyebrow at him. "Ever consider asking?"

"I could have. But I knew your soul wouldn't lie."

My exaggerated, affronted gasp hits the right notes,

netting me another almost-smile. Still, I can't resist asking what his probing found. "So, what's the verdict, Mr. Soul Snooper?"

Before Kohl can answer, Minerva's big orange tabby shoots out from between the hosta plants, with Rune hot on his fluffy tail—until she spots Kohl. Emitting a low, constant rumble, my literal scaredy-cat cowers behind my legs. Cookie, on the other hand, sits directly in front of Kohl, quietly staring up at the dark-cloaked reaper.

"Wow, he seems to like you," I say, unfolding my arms so I can point at an uncharacteristically docile tabby. "And that cat doesn't like a lot of people."

"The attention isn't a matter of 'like.' He's waiting for me to settle Minerva Goodwin's final request."

"Final request?" I clap my hand over my heart. "Oh shit, you're here for her soul. Wait a sec. Why are you *here*, here, in the physical realm? Don't you meet souls in the in-between?"

That's where I met him. He accompanied me back to the mortal realm, then brought me to Fate's Falls, but I know that's now it usually works, unless—

"Is Minerva back from the dead too? Is that your reaper specialty or something?"

Calm and silent, Kohl lets my questions hang in the air. Making sure I don't have more to add to the barrage? Probably. A flash of something less serious plays across his face when I make the zipping-my-lips gesture, then the tickly sensation low in my belly returns.

What does it say about me that I find a reaper attractive? It says my self-preservation instincts are as alive and well as my physical health, that's what. Deciding to avoid skin-to-skin contact for the rest of my life killed pretty much any possibility of a non-platonic relationship. If I'm going to be attracted to anyone, the only safe option is someone completely off-limits. A reaper who exists on another plane certainly checks that box. Maybe that's why I've spent fifteen years fantasizing about this one.

"It is not usual for me to turn souls back to their mortal bodies, though I understand why you might think that, knowing I have done it for someone other than you. Minerva Goodwin's soul has moved on to the next place. It was her time, and she was ready. She passed peacefully, in her sleep."

"The ending we all wish for," I say, my voice coming out softer than usual.

"Most wish for that, yes. Warriors wish for an active death."

"You've met a lot of warriors on their way to the next place?"

"Quantity is a relative thing, but throughout history, I have guided many."

"Throughout history." I take a beat to give Kohl a good look-over. Sure, I've only seen him one time before tonight, and it was during the most terrifying point in my life, but those memories are crystal clear. And what I can see of his face looks exactly the same. Not a single wrinkle on his pale skin. "Exactly how much history have you been around for?"

"What mortals would consider all of it."

It feels as if my jaw has unhinged, it drops so low. *"All of it,* as in, since the beginning of time?"

"That, I couldn't say. I have no firsthand knowledge of what existed before the first sentient mortal being with a soul being died in this physical realm. My existence began when I was needed."

"But you've been around since then? Since the first human died?"

"The first sentient mortal being with a soul," he says, correcting me.

Holy shit. I make the mind-blown gesture, complete with sound effects.

"I would very much like to stay and continue our conversation, but I'm needed elsewhere."

"Of course." I wave a hand in his direction.

"You're not wearing gloves."

"No need at this time of day, when I've got the world to myself and there's zero chance I might accidentally touch someone," I say, then it hits me. "Hold on—how do you know about the gloves?" I started wearing them *after* the night I died, after he brought me to Fate's Falls. After I swore to myself that I'd never to use my magic again.

"Just because you haven't seen me doesn't mean I haven't seen you."

Hands on my hips, I cock an eyebrow. "Are we talking casual observations when you happen to be floating by on reaper duty, or have you been keeping tabs on me?" This attempt at humor gets an actual smile from him. Glorious. Just like in the fantasies I've had about him.

A sorrowful meow rises from between us. Moment broken. But I can't be mad at the big ginger tabby. Poor thing just lost his person, and my guess is that he knows she's gone.

"I have not forgotten you," Kohl says, meeting the cat's

gaze before turning his dark eyes on me. "Minerva's final request was for you to take Cookie."

"*Me?*" I press my fingers to my forehead when he gives a single nod. "What about someone in her family? I realize her daughters don't live in town, but her great-niece does. As much as I'm not a fan of Lexi Goodwin, she is the logical choice to take Cookie."

"But not Minerva's choice."

"Ugh. Why me?"

"I didn't ask the reason."

"You just agreed. Assumed I'd say yes." I throw my hands up when he nods again. The warm fuzzies from minutes ago feel more like hot pricklies now. "Why would you make a promise that *I* have to fulfil?"

"Is it not a privilege to be gifted a familiar by another witch?"

"A familiar? Are you sure she was talking about *this* cat?" I say, motioning at Cookie.

The corner of Kohl's lips twitch. That's his answer.

I tilt my face upward, groaning up at the dark sky. "*My* cat is not going to like this."

"You may be surprised." Kohl's gaze locks with mine the moment I lower my head. "Beautiful relationships can grow from the least likely circumstances."

Warmth ripples through me. Foolishly. He's talking about the cats, or maybe generalizing. Not referring to me—to us. Meeting twice in fifteen years is not a relationship. Even if it could become one, I wouldn't let it.

What a day. And the sun's not even up yet.

"Fine." I heave a pained sigh. "I'll connect with Lexi and arrange to get Cookie's things from Minerva's house. Until then, he'll have to share Rune's stuff. Based on his hefty physique, I assume he's not a fussy eater."

As if he understands every word, Cookie moves from sitting in front of Kohl to rubbing against my shins. Maybe he does understand what I'm saying—he is a familiar, after all. My familiar now.

Before I can speak a reassuring word to Rune, she comes from behind my legs, touches noses with the big ginger, then the two of them are off. Shoulder to shoulder, trotting off toward my little cottage like good old buddies. Seems like Kohl got that one right.

"Guess I'd better follow my *cats*, plural." Rolling my eyes melodramatically doesn't get me a laugh, but his full, pale lips curve upward. Just a little, but enough to ignite a new round of warm tingles low in my abdomen. "I'm glad I got to see you again. You know, before the next time I'm dead." Waving, I walk away before I start rambling again. Not a problem I usually have. I'm always in control of my words. Of everything.

"Shay."

Goddess, my name sounds delicious in his deep, smooth timbre. I stop on the spot, turning toward Kohl, who looks simultaneously ominous and enchanting in his dark, flowing cloak.

"I'll see you soon."

"Well, those aren't good words to hear from a reaper. Are you taking over seer duty now? Giving me the heads-up that my clock's ticking?"

"I'll see you before you're dead again," he says, a smile in his voice to match the one on his face. Then he's gone. No cloud of mist, no dramatic fading out. One second, he's there, the next, he's not. *Poof.* There's just air where he stood.

But I know from experience, when Kohl is on this plane, he's solid. As real as any living, flesh-and-blood man.

What is *soon* to a reaper who has existed for millennia?

Foolishly, pointlessly, I hope I won't have to wait too long.

Chapter Two

KOHL

I watch Shay as she moves toward home. On the sidewalk in front of newly departed witch's house, she jogs to catch up with the cats. Smiles down at them, speaking to them in a soothing but lively tone. Telling them how things are going to be. She advises her black cat not to get any ideas about unrestricted in-and-out access, and lets her new addition know there will not be a cat door, so he'd better get used to living inside except for daily supervised walks. Despite the warning in her words, there's no sign of her earlier annoyance about taking the Goodwin witch's familiar. It's clear she has already accepted the ginger tabby into her life. Her heart.

The walls she erected to safeguard herself from having visions don't prevent her from feeling things. The aloof exterior she curated isn't fake, but it's just one side of her. She cares deeply for others. More than she'd like, because caring makes her vulnerable. That's when her cultivated contentment slips into resignation, and the enormity of her loneliness catches up with her. Even then, she never wavers in her choice to remain separate from others.

I was untruthful when I told Shay I was needed to be elsewhere. Being close to her again, in physical form... the temptation to hold her was overwhelming. I haven't forgotten the sensation of enclosing her in my embrace. Haven't stopped longing to have her in my arms again.

Yearning. Desire. *Love.* Feelings experienced by mortal beings. From birth through death, emotions are what drive them.

I am not mortal. Reapers exist to fulfil an endless purpose. We do not die. We are not meant to feel.

Yet, since the moment I was drawn to Shay's soul, I have *felt.* Endlessly, deeply, but only for her.

While guiding the newly departed to the what lies beyond, I meet souls in the in-between place. The rare times I need to enter other realms, the duration is short-lived. What mortals would think of as a blink.

The night of Shay's death, I was drawn to her soul *before* the transition. I watched her consciously put herself in the crosshairs of a malevolent man, then lure him from a populated area to an abandoned bridge. She ran when he chased her across the run-down structure, but not to escape.

My vision is not affected by illuminance; I saw everything with complete clarity. Shay led the man directly to the gaping hole in the metal sheeting. Her path was intentional. Premeditated.

She was prepared to die that night. Not because she wished to end her life. She acted to save the lives of others.

I didn't know her motivation until later, after I brought her back to the earthly plane. While I held her, her body shaking from cold and fear, she revealed everything she'd seen in the visions. Torture, slaughter, and other heinous acts. She'd sacrificed her life trying to prevent them from happening. And she'd failed. The serial killer hadn't fallen through the hole as she'd intended. Only she plummeted fifty feet into the icy river. What should have been her watery grave.

A mortal's time or method of death is of no consequence to reapers. We do not choose who lives or dies, nor do we deliver judgment. A reaper's purpose is to guide souls to their next place. Then we move on.

I have continued to serve the Oracle, but I have not moved on. Fifteen years is nothing in the span of a reaper's existence, yet every day since leaving Shay that cold December night has seemed like an eternity.

When I began watching over her, I told myself it was concern. For her safety because the serial killer still lived. For her mortal life, because I had altered the natural order of her existence. I tried to convince myself that *concern* was the embodiment of all the emotions I experienced.

As the years progressed, I accepted that my continued close observation had become a fixation. Seeing her face-to-face tonight... I can't deny the truth that has been there all along. The feelings I have go much further than concern or fascination.

If I stopped watching over her now, would my feelings disappear? She doesn't require my guardianship. The

Oracle's magic protects this town—and others like it—from evil and violence. Shay is safe here. And, as the Oracle hasn't corrected my unauthorized action of returning Shay's soul to her body, it seems unlikely to happen. Though, that does raise other concerns for the future of Shay's soul.

Awareness that I am needed draws me to the in-between, the natural plane of existence for reapers. Its purity and light fill me with peace and purpose. This is where I belong. But not where I want to be.

SHAY

Is it in poor taste to thank Minerva Goodwin for dying on a Saturday when it's more convenient for me? Probably, but I also think the old woman would appreciate me being real with her, even in death, so I light a circle of candles in my living room and send out my message. Whether she receives it or not, is another matter.

I don't have normal magic like the other witches in the Winterlock coven do. Like witches in the Goodwin coven do. No, I'm the "once in each generation" Winterlock witch born with seer magic. And only seer magic. Meaning it's anybody's guess if my attempt to contact Minerva on the other side has the desired effect. Or any effect, aside from giving my living room some nice ambiance for a short period of time.

Even though I didn't want her cat, I thank her anyway. If Cookie really is a familiar—which I remain skeptical about after watching him do nothing but loaf his ginger butt on my couch all day—the gift is a significant gesture between witches. Hell, even if he's not a familiar, it's still a big deal. I know how much Minerva loved that cat.

Since my concerns about Rune and Cookie not getting along were put to rest before the new besties set their combined eight paws inside the house, I leave them zonked, side by side, in a swath of afternoon sunlight, then head out.

The walk to downtown takes ten minutes. The shops are all open and bustling, as is the norm. The temptation to duck into *The Brew* and grab a coffee almost wins, but I force my legs to stay on course and walk past the coffee shop instead. It'd be too easy to step behind the counter and help "just for a second," which would become an hour or more before I know it. The weekend crew is great and they don't need my assistance. I'd only be doing it to avoid making nice with Lexi Goodwin.

Sighing, I focus on Lexi's green-and-purple storefront with its gold *Every Witch Way* window decal. The sight of it has the usual effect, making me prickly and sour. I'm self-aware enough to acknowledge that my beef with Lexi is rooted in my personal bitterness. While my family's coven has abided by long-held witchcraft rules, the Goodwins have not. They're not *bad* witches, just...self-serving.

Lexi's business is a prime example. She infuses her products with magic, then sells them. Not just locally, either. To humans *outside* of Fate's Falls. She gets away with it because the Goodwin coven as a whole paid the price for profiting from their magic generations ago. They don't have bright-green skin because they're nature-centric witches. Their skin is green for greed. And Lexi doesn't give even a sliver of a fuck. In fact, she's one of the happiest witches I've ever met.

Of course she is. Strong magic, thriving business, popular around town. She's living her best life. No holds barred.

It's a wonder *my* skin hasn't turned green—with envy.

Drawing in a deep breath, I open the door and step inside. There are no customers at the moment, thank goddess. Having this conversation is awkward enough, I don't need an audience for it.

In all my years living here and working nearby, I've never been in Lexi's store. It's as colorful as a box of crayons and loaded with merchandise. Merchandise being sex toys. There are literally dildos everywhere. Not your run-of-the-mill dildos. Every size, shape, and color imaginable line the shelves. Some of them are human shaped, but most are not. I have no clue what species some of them are, honestly.

"Well, color me surprised!" Lexi says from behind the service counter. "Pleasantly surprised, of course," she adds, coming out to smile at me from the other side of a double-sided shelving unit that stands about chest height for us both. "What brings you in today? Personal shopping, gift shopping, or did curiosity finally kill the cat?" She winks. Not a hint of animosity toward me, despite the groundless cold-shoulder treatment I've given her for a decade and a half.

"None of the above, though it does have to do with a cat."

Lexi's black eyebrows rise as she leans over the shelf,

folding her arms along the top. Casual and friendly. "Now *I'm* the curious one."

Well, that's not a good sign. "I'm here about Minerva's cat."

Lexi straightens, her features losing their light, carefree expression. "Oh no, did something happen to Cookie?"

"Not in the way that you mean." I thought this conversation would be a quick formality. *Hey, I've got your great-aunt's cat because she wanted me to take him. Very sorry for your loss. Bye.* Instead, I'm the bearer of the bad news. It didn't cross my mind that Lexi wouldn't know Minerva had passed, but it should have. The old woman only died last night. Of course, Lexi doesn't know yet.

I've been wearing gloves around people for fifteen years. Long enough that I don't even notice them anymore. But I'm plenty aware of the thin leather right now. The comfortably snug fit suddenly feels restrictive. Removing them isn't on my personal options list, so I rub my palms against my hips to get some relief from the sweaty itchiness.

"Shay?"

Well, shit. Guess I'm doing this. "I take my cat Rune out for a walk in the neighborhood early in the mornings, before anyone's out and about. Cookie is frequently hanging out in your great-aunt's yard, and today was one of those times, but Cookie wasn't the only creature we happened upon at Minerva's house. A reaper was there. He was waiting for me, specifically, so he could deliver a request from your great-aunt that I take Cookie..." Goddess, this sucks. "Because your great-aunt has passed on."

Lexi just blinks. And blinks.

Is she going to cry? Even if we were friends, I don't have

the tools to deal with tears. It's not like I can hug her to give comfort. Too much risk of direct skin contact. "I'm very sorry for your loss. And that you had to hear the news from me. Is there anyone you want me to call for you? If you give me a list, I'll tackle it when I get home. I don't work weekends, so I'm available to help." Not what I planned to say. Or do. But it's the right thing.

Long ebony waves shimmer as she shakes her head. "Thank you, that's very kind, but I'll take care of everything from here. And don't feel bad about delivering the news. Losing Minerva is sad, of course. But she had a long, happy life, and I know she was ready to go to the other side and reunite with coven members who've already moved on."

"That's what Kohl said, that Minerva was ready and at peace." When Lexi tilts her head, I add, "Kohl is the reaper who guided her." There's a brief moment where I swear that I can see the wheels turning in Lexi's head. The familiar glint of mischievousness in her eyes.

Then she blinks again and the less-characteristic seriousness is back. "I appreciate you coming to see me in person, Shay, and so quickly. On that note, though, I better close the store and head over to Minerva's place. Stubborn woman always refused to get air conditioning installed in that house, and it really gets cooking in there on a warm day. She'd haunt me forever if I left her to bake. Isn't that right, auntie?" she says with affection, looking up and around.

"Is Minerva's spirit here now?" No point in pretending I'd know. Lexi is aware that I'm a witch with almost no magic.

Meeting my gaze again, Lexi shrugs. "Not that I can tell.

But communing with the departed has never been in my wheelhouse. My grandmother had the skill, but she's been gone for a couple of years. She and Minerva are probably having a grand old reunion on the other side."

Now that we're having an actual conversation, I see why everyone likes Lexi. Even now, having just lost a member of her family, she's easygoing and has a sense of humor. If I hadn't spent the last decade and a half being pissy because she has no issue profiting from her magic, we might even have become friends. Probably still could, since we share some mutuals.

Too bad I can't see *my* future. It'd sure be nice to know what fate has in store for *me* now.

I hook a thumb toward the shop's door. "I'll head out so you can close up. If you need me for anything, I'm not far from your great-aunt's house and I'm happy to help if you need it. Today or whenever."

"Thanks, Shay." Before I reach the door, she says, "Hey, you said it was the reaper who told you Minerva wanted you to take Cookie. She never told you her plans beforehand?"

Resting my fingers on the door handle, I turn to face Lexi. "Nope. It was totally unexpected when Kohl told me, because Minerva never mentioned it, not even vaguely. And we've had some lengthy conversations over the years."

"Oh, I'm aware. She liked to flash that info at me like a premium guilt card whenever I was too busy to say yes to her invitations to visit."

"I can totally picture her doing that, since many of our longer visits were the result of her using a guilt card on me," I say, shaking my head. Smiling a little. "But I never really minded. Your great-aunt was an interesting lady. I liked her, and I'll miss her."

"Me too." The smile Lexi gives me makes me feel like maybe this is a genuinely friendly interaction, not just a formality conversation. "You're okay with taking Cookie? I'd offer to step in, but as I'm sure you know, he's a familiar, and there are some traditional practices even I don't break." She taps an index finger on her green cheek. "Despite being a naughty Goodwin witch."

I'm pretty sure her magic doesn't include telepathy, so there's no way she could *know* my reason for avoiding her all this time. Either she got the sense that I looked down on her, which I did, or she's simply poking fun at her coven's history of playing fast and loose with the rules. Either way, she's the bigger person. But I'm ready to level up. Maybe not all the way, but start the climb.

"Cookie has already made himself comfortable at my place. I wasn't sure he and my cat were going to get along because they've always been hissy toward each other when we crossed paths, but as soon as I told Kohl that Cookie could come with me, the cats seemed to be instant best buddies. I didn't know Cookie was a familiar, though. Minerva never mentioned that."

"That's the second time you've called the reaper by name," Lexi says, ignoring the rest of my comments. The ankle-length open black vest she's wearing over a formfitting black jumpsuit flows out gracefully as she walks toward me. By the time she's in front of me, her dark eyebrows are arched high above glittering green eyes. "I've never met a reaper, and I've also never heard anyone refer to them by personal names. How well do you know him?"

I'm a maintain-eye-contact person, but I can't help glancing around Lexi's store. It's no secret that all the monster dildos she sells are created from actual beings. Rumor has it, nonhumans willing to have molds taken of their *equipment* are paid well. An upfront fee plus royalties. And the shop in Fate's Falls isn't where she and her models are making bank. It's Lexi's online business that's booming. Humans can't seem to get enough artificial monster dick.

Which begs the question: is her interest in Kohl genuine curiosity, or is she calculating the potential revenue from selling genuine reaper dildos to the human masses beyond Fate's Falls' boundaries? My goal to be less resentful toward her doesn't include helping her profit from Kohl's anatomy, whatever it might look like.

"I've met him twice," I say when I meet her eyes again. "Once, a long time ago, and again this morning, in your great-aunt's yard. There's nothing more to tell." Nothing more I'm *willing* to share with Lexi, certainly.

Her long, dark-purple lacquered fingernails drum on her hips. The witch is clearly not buying what I'm selling.

That'll teach me to let my guard down around her. I let sympathy make me soft. "The offer to help with Minerva's arrangements stands. And if there's anything I should know about Cookie, you can either track me down at my house or at *The Brew*, Monday through Friday, during the day shift."

"I'll do that," she says, waving as I open and step out the door. "See you soon, Shay."

I have a feeling those aren't casual words. And that I may end up regretting my decision to be more open-minded where Lexi Goodwin is concerned.

Chapter Three

KOHL

Many of the beings who dwell within the safety of Fate's Falls are long-living species. Much longer than humans. Some are ageless and immortal. Thus, I am not often required in the magically protected town. That doesn't prevent me from returning. Regularly. I cannot stay away from Shay.

Reaping is a solitary existence, but the *aloneness* I first experienced after leaving Shay in the earthly plane fifteen years ago is nothing compared to when I left her in the Goodwin witch's yard several days ago. After being face-to-face with her again, the frequency of my visits has increased to occupy every moment of available time. And then some.

Souls continue to call from the in-between, but I don't hasten to tend them. There are enough reapers to fulfill the duties. My brethren can guide the departed to their next destinations. The pull toward Shay is the call I choose to answer. Whatever this endless yearning is, I need to address it before it interferes to the point of failing my purpose entirely.

Nighttime's blanket is wrapped around the town already when I materialize in Shay's backyard. Lights inside her house throw diffused beams through the glass, making fuzzy bands of soft white on the grass. I stand beyond them, masked in darkness, waiting for her to step out the back door with a garbage bag, as she always does at this time of night. Part of her evening routine, which I know as well as if it were my own.

"Not happening, Cookie. Back inside you go," she says to the ginger cat who attempts to follow her outside. "I know Minerva let you wander at all hours, but that's not how things work in this witch's house."

I wait until the door clicks with the cat safely contained before addressing her. "Sounds like things are going well with your new housemate."

Shay's shriek cuts the silent air, the sound immediately followed by a loud feline yowl through the screened window where Cookie sits. Her protector's protest subsides when his feline gaze locks on my form.

"Kohl?" Shay says when I step out from the cover of shadows. "What are you doing here?" The whites of her eyes become more prominent in the darkness as she stares at me. "Oh shit, are you here for me this time? Because I'm not ready. I have to call my mom. And make arrangements for the mew crew in there." She hooks her thumb toward the house. "At least let me write a note."

"I'm not here to reap your soul," I say, moving toward

her. "Even so, it wouldn't be a bad idea for you to make those arrangements. No mortal being knows when their time in this plane will end, even a seer. Reapers can't pause the transition process to afford the newly departed time to make calls and write notes."

"Oh really? You did a lot more than pause the process for me." The challenge in her voice doesn't mask the underlying softness.

I like both tones equally. "You're unique."

"Not so unique, since you brought my friend Dela back, too," she says, continuing toward a silver trash can near the fence. "Which I'm thankful for, by the way. Dela is a truly good person who deserved the opportunity to have a happy life, and now she has one."

"I'm glad to hear it." I wait until Shay has finished with her chore and is in front of me again before I continue. "But your circumstances were not the same. The Oracle chose to give Dela the opportunity to return to her mortal life and come to Fate's Falls."

Shay's smile beams in the moonlight. "I told Dela fate had a hand in the direction her life took."

"As it does in all things, even if less directly." The words have barely left me when the realization hits. Perhaps my actions were part of the Oracle's plan for Shay all along.

"Hey, if you have any way of getting a message to the Oracle, would you say thank you on my behalf? I'm not sure why I got a second chance at life, but I'm sure fate had a reason. Any chance you know what it is?" The lightness in her voice is reflected in her expression—until I fail to respond. At my silence, she shutters her gaze, crossing her arms over her chest.

I don't have to reach for her soul to know she is raising her walls to protect herself from being hurt. Walls she had lowered for me, whether consciously or not.

"The Oracle did not direct me to return your soul to this realm."

Her beautiful eyes blink slowly. Once. Twice. Then open wide. "You were supposed to let me die that night?"

"That is what I believed, yes. A reaper's duty is to guide souls to their next place. I should not have been present at your death, yet I was called to your soul here, in this plane, while you were mortal."

Her dark, curly hair floats over her shoulders with the shake of her head. "I don't understand any of this, including why you're telling me."

"Because I want you to know."

"To know what, Kohl?"

That I love you. "The Oracle works in many ways, some direct and others, less so. Whether I truly used free will and defied the intended order of things, or my actions were subconsciously guided by the Oracle, it was the only time I have made such a decision. I chose to return your soul to your body, to bring you to Fate's Falls. Once in all of my existence, Shay."

"If it's such a monumental thing, why did you wait fifteen years to tell me?"

"It was never my intention to share this information with you."

"I see," she says, though she cannot possibly, when even I don't understand.

The casual sweatpants and t-shirt she's wearing are vastly different from the clothing she chooses for public. I've watched her enough to know the polished exterior, along with her aloofness, is a form of armor. Though always beautiful, it's her fiery spirit and the compassionate heart she works so hard to hide that call to me. Yet, when she takes a deep breath, causing her full breasts to rise and stretch the fabric taut, the parts of me which are currently *man* physically react to her exterior beauty. Beneath my cloak, my cock hardens, as it has only ever done for Shay.

"I don't know if you ever have to rest, but it's late for me, so..." She tilts her head toward the back door. No further questions or demands for answers to the ones I skirted. Just a statement of exit. Dismissal.

I do not know what I expected from this visit, or what could possibly happen between us. With nothing to guide me, I'm at a loss to say anything other than, "Goodnight, Shay," and watch her disappear into her house.

SHAY

"Is everything okay with you?" Dela asks when I follow her into the staffroom at the end of our Thursday shift at *The Brew*. "I'm starting to feel guilty for taking time to breathe because you literally haven't stopped *going* all week long. You've been on a mission every single minute."

"There's a lot to do, and I hate when anything slips off my plate."

Sitting in the chair across from me, she pauses untying her black canvas work shoes to stare at me from beneath one highly arched eyebrow. "You're the most efficient manager I've ever worked with, anywhere. Nothing slips off your plate. Nothing even gets near the edge of your plate."

"And I don't want it to. I have to stay on top of things; we're up almost twenty percent over last year's numbers." Now it's my turn to issue the raised eyebrow, only I do both, adding a wiggling motion. "Though, that bump could be from your big red demon who only began coming in for coffee when you started working here."

Dela tosses her balled-up barista apron at me. She's beaming, though. Love, happiness, and feeling truly safe looks good on her. "Raz hasn't bought *that many* coffees. Now that you mention it, though, I have noticed we're getting more daytime traffic the past couple of months. I thought it might be a seasonal thing."

"I've worked here since I moved to town, and we've never had noticeable seasonal changes in transaction numbers or revenue. Always steady growth from year to year, though this is a significantly bigger increase than any previously."

"Fates Falls does have a bunch of new residents, even since I moved here. I guess we all love coffee?" Her laughter is always light and melodic, and now is no different. The sound tapers off to a sigh, and her expression returns to one of gentle, friendly concern. "But you haven't been squeezing maximum productivity out of every minute because you're in mega-manager mode. I know what inner turmoil looks like, and even your mask slips once in a while. You've been such a good friend to me, and I want to be the same for you.

So, if something's on your mind and talking might help, you can trust me to keep it just between us."

If I can trust anyone—other than my mom, who is twenty-five-hundred miles away on the opposite side of the continent—it's Dela. Other than my mom, Dela is the only person I've risked skin-to-skin contact with since the December day I touched a serial killer's hand and saw things that changed my life forever. When I looked into Dela's future, everything was beautiful. Peaceful. Full of love. It was almost enough to make me reconsider my complete ban on physical contact. The nightmare I had later that night jolted that little dash of hopefulness from my mind.

"Walk and talk around the square before you go home?" I say when the noise from *The Brew* increases, as it does every day at this time.

The Brew continues serving coffee on the cafe side until six p.m., but the brew pub side of the business gets rolling at four o'clock. On any given weekday, the pub side will be in full swing by the time Dela and I toss our aprons in the basket, change our shoes, and head out the door.

Dela nods and returns to swapping her work runners for a pair of white canvas sandals with a yellow sunshine pattern. A gift from Raz. One of many. Intimidating as her revenge-demon boyfriend is, he's a total sweetheart for Dela. A sweetheart who would literally tear someone to pieces if she ever asked him to, but has sworn off violence otherwise.

I finish zipping my knee-high leather boots, then lead the way out through the growing crowd. I only manage the coffee side of *The Brew*, but I should ask my boss if the pub side's numbers have seen a big jump too. Or maybe I'll just ask my managerial equivalent on the brew pub side. I'd probably get the answer faster. I've seen less and less of *The Brew*'s owner since the hulking Minotaur met *his* fated mate.

Love is in full bloom in Fate's Falls lately.

Familiar faces smile, and all manner of hands, paws, claws, etc. wave as Dela and I pass. A lot of those appendages belong to romantically unattached people, a few of whom have asked me out over the years. Declining was easy. I'd made my decision and most of the time, didn't feel like I was missing out.

Watching everyone I consider a friend fall head over heels—or hooves—in love has made the solitary life sting a little. More than a little. I don't remember what it feels like to kiss someone. Or any of the other things. Solo time only takes the physical edge off. It doesn't replace the simple intimacies.

"Yoo-hoo, Shay..." Dela waves a hand in front of my face, snapping me out of my internal pity party.

Blinking, I look around and find we've walked the length of a full block. Autopilot. It's how I get through all the shitty stuff. Through a lot of life.

"It's okay if you just want to walk and *not* talk," she says when all I do is stare straight ahead. "But I'm worried about you, so I'm probably going to keep trying to help." She's a true friend. More like a sister, which I've told her before.

Except, I'm the older one. I should be the helper, the advice giver, not the other way around.

Another long stretch passes in silence. But I do want to talk. I *need* to talk this stuff out, and not over a phone call with my mom.

"I was the only seer in my family's coven," I say, focusing on the rhythmic cadence of our synchronized footsteps. "The older witches call it a special gift, but it sucks. It sucks to have no other magic when everyone around you has powers. It sucks to get visions of the future whenever I touch someone's skin."

"Of course it does. Who would want that? It sounds horrible."

"Right?" I say, turning my head to meet her eyes. "Special gift, my ass."

She tilts her head to glance at my butt, then winks at me. "Don't insult your ass like that. It's pretty spectacular."

Without thinking, I wrap my arm around her shoulders and squeeze. I'm wearing my gloves, but with both of us in short-sleeved shirts, the possibility of skin contact is still there, even if slight. I'm not afraid of what I might see because I've already looked into Dela's future. The only bad thing that's going to happen is her eventual death, and that's in the distance, after a long and happy life.

"You—you're—this," she stammers, her eyes nearly bugging out of her face. When I drop my arm, she stops in front of me on the sidewalk, waving her hands around, seeming unable to assemble the desired words.

"I should've asked. I didn't intend to hug you. It just... I guess I needed it, and you're kind of the only safe place I have and—" The next sound out of my mouth is an "oof," when Dela pulls me into a real hug. The kind with both arms wrapped around me.

Goddess, it feels good to be close to someone. To be comforted.

I am not going to cry. *Not. Going. To. Cry.*

There's no controlling it. The warmth rolls down my cheeks, unstoppable. "It's been so long since I've had a hug," I whisper against her hair. "Fifteen years."

"That's not right, Shay. You can have as many of my hugs as you want, okay? Anytime. I will always be your safe place."

Nodding, I pull away, swiping my fingers across my face before anyone in the vicinity might see. As nice as it is to have Dela's concern, I don't want anybody else's.

"Pretend you're looking at your phone while I pop into Amazra's bakery for a sec. I'll grab a couple of her Carolina reaper scones. It'll give us an excuse to have watery eyes."

Following her suggestion, I slide my phone out of my back pocket and focus on it until she reappears and hands me a scone missing its tip. The one she keeps looks the same. "Had to taste test both?" I ask.

"I wasn't sure if you'd actually want to eat something this spicy—I sure can't—so I ripped off bite-sized chunks on my way past the garbage can."

"This crafty sneakiness is a whole side of you I didn't know existed," I tease, as we resume our walk, heading for the town square.

"Therapy has helped me reconnect with the person I was before I became a spineless, quivering doormat for my ex. And now that I have Raz..." There are practically stars in her eyes when she sighs. "He makes it so easy to just be myself. But enough about me. We always talk about me. Unless we're discussing your seemingly endless selection of sexy boots."

"Boots are life," I say, and she laughs. Crossing the grass in the immaculately manicured parkette, I move my mouth in chewing motions for the bite of scone I didn't actually take. Faking is second nature. Has been since I was a young witch who wanted to feel like part of the coven instead of a useless oddity.

There's nobody at the fountain, and the gentle water noise will give some cover to my voice, so I lead us there and sit on the concrete lip.

"Short version—I left my coven, moved to a city three and a half hours away to have a 'normal' life and realized that wasn't possible because of the seer thing. I won't go into detail about how unsexy it is to see someone's future while you're *in the moment.*"

Dela's nose scrunches up, her lips pursing as if she just drank straight lemon juice. "It happens every time?"

"Yup. If there's a way to control it, I don't have the ability."

"What if you were drunk? Not that I'm suggesting you should be drunk every time you want to get intimate with someone."

"Tried it," I confess. "Turns out, seeing someone's future is instantly sobering."

Again, Dela grimaces. "That's why you stopped touching people."

"No, that was just an annoying side effect." Lowering the uneaten scone to my lap, I shake my head. Take a deep breath. "I'd decided to move back to my hometown and try to embrace my place in the coven, limited as it was. But I was literally down to my last dollar, and too embarrassed and proud—aka, stupid—to ask my mom for money for a bus ticket. So I set up a table at a psychic fair to make some quick money, which is a big no-no. A witch isn't supposed to profit from their magic. I told myself it didn't really count, since everyone would think I was just another fake fortune teller. The last person who asked for a reading—"

Good person that she is, Dela waits silently while I close my eyes, fortifying myself for what comes next. Details I've only shared with Kohl and my mom.

"He was a serial killer." I speak the words quietly, and not because anyone is around to hear. Just saying it aloud floods me with doom. As if talking about that man might summon him somehow, though, logically, I know that's impossible. Even if he found out I survived the fall that night, he can't get to me here. "I didn't just see his future, the horrible things he'd do to other women; I saw my future too, because I would've been one of his victims."

"Oh my god." Dela's arms wrap around me again. A sideways hug that causes her hand to brush my arm.

The skin-to-skin contact conjures images of Dela's happy future to slide through my mind, pushing the horrific memories away. "Thank you." Simple words that don't convey how much I mean them. But I think she can tell, because she keeps her arms around me until I shift out of her embrace.

"That's why you're in Fate's Falls," Dela says softly. "I'm so glad you got away before the visions could become reality."

This is the part that hurts more than any other. "Some of the visions *have* happened. I recognized the victims on the news."

"It's not your fault, Shay. You know that, right?"

"Rationally, sure. But every time I see another familiar face in a missing persons' report or murder case, I'm flooded with guilt. I tried to prevent *all* the visions from happening. I knew from the one of myself that he'd be waiting outside for me after the event ended. I let him believe he was successfully trailing me and led him to an abandoned train bridge over the Monongahela River. I'd explored it once, while out for a walk; I knew it had gaping holes. Everything was pitch dark—the sky, the bridge, the river. I didn't think he'd be able to see the opening. I thought he'd grab me and we'd both fall the fifty feet to the river. But he must've jumped it at the last second. I fell, he didn't. He lived, I didn't."

The gasp that leaves Dela's mouth, even with her hand covering it, is loud enough to draw the attention of people twenty feet across the green space. "Sorry," she says when they look away.

I flap a gloved hand at her. "I'd be concerned if you didn't react like that. It's a hell of a story—minus the hell for him, unfortunately."

Her big eyes open wide. "That's how you know the reaper who brought me back. He's the one who brought you back, too."

"Yeah, Kohl was there." And this is where I could end the story. It'd be enough to have a friend who understands why I am the way I am. But goddess, I could use an opinion on the feelings I'm having. "Kohl didn't just give me my life back that night. He stayed with me, shielding me from view with his reaper magic, comforting me while I cried for hours. Then he did his *poof* thing and brought me here, where I'd be safe."

"Wow."

"I know. It's a lot."

"But there's more, isn't there? All of that is backstory.

The stuff I need to know *before* the part that you've been busting your ass trying to avoid thinking about."

"Trying and failing," I say, rolling my head side to side and getting no relief for the bundles of knots in my neck.

"Well, don't even think about damming the flow now." She picks off a chunk of scone and tosses it at me. "Cliffhangers not allowed. I need the rest of this story."

"That's the thing. There shouldn't be more to the story. And I thought there wasn't, until I was out for my predawn walk with Rune on Saturday morning, and Kohl was waiting for me at Minerva Goodwin's house."

"You left that detail out of the story when you told it on Monday. You said 'a reaper' gave you Minerva's message about taking her cat. No wonder you've been distracted. Seeing him again stirred up all the horrible old memories."

I've unloaded enough heavy shit on her. No need to tell her those memories are always close to the surface. "See, the thing is...I've kind of fantasized about him over the years."

"Ooh, we've arrived at the juicy part of the story."

"Girl, please. There is no juice. My glass has been devoid of juice for fifteen long years, remember?"

"But you've thought about having a full cup. A cup filled with Kohl's juice." She giggles when I swat at her. "Tell me I'm wrong. I won't believe you, but go ahead and deny it if it makes you feel better."

"I'm not denying it." I roll my eyes when she silently makes a cheering motion. "I was sure my brain latched on to Kohl because he's good and safely out of reach, in every conceivable way."

"You said 'was.' Did seeing him again the other night make you wonder if there's more to it?"

"Yes," I say, my cheeks heating at the admission. At all the things those fantasies have included, and how those thoughts were at the forefront of my mind both times I recently saw Kohl.

Dela spins her finger in a get-on-with-it motion. "I know there's more. And that you're itching to tell me."

I simultaneously love and hate that she's on to me. "He was in my backyard last night."

Dela jerks back, her bottom lip dropping. "Why?"

"To tell me he brought me back without the Oracle's direction, like he had for you, and to say I'm the only person he's ever acted to make that choice for."

"And then what?" she asks, leaning in.

"Then I told him it was late, and I went back inside my house."

"You're kidding, right? You didn't just turn around and walk away after he told you that."

I angle my body so she has a fully direct view of my stone-cold-serious face. "Girl, do I look like I'm kidding?"

Dela's ginger hair shimmers in the late-day sunshine as she shakes her head. "And now? What are you going to do about it?"

"Do about what?"

"About your massive regret."

Scoffing, I stand and point down the street, toward *The Brew*, where her car is parked. "Right now, I'm regretting telling you." In my peripheral vision, I see her smiling at me. Not calling me out, though. She's too nice to do that.

"If you're not ready to address *your* feelings," she says as we walk, "let's analyze his. Because he obviously has some where you're concerned. There's no other explanation for his actions. Or his forthright honesty."

"Forthright, huh. You're starting to sound like your giant red boyfriend." I shoot her a smirk. "Though I'm surprised you two find time to talk."

She remains tight-lipped, but the blush flooding her face is an answer in itself. Teasing her about being hot for the grumpy revenge demon is part of our dynamic. I know she doesn't mind, but it'll keep for another day. Probably tomorrow, when Raz comes in for his daily coffee that he barely sips from. Even though they're living together now, he still can't seem to make it through her workday without seeing her.

I'd be jealous if I wasn't so happy for her.

Fine, I can multi-task. I'm jealous *and* happy for her.

When we reach her car, she leans against it instead of getting inside. Meaning I'm still on the hook for an answer that'll satisfy her.

"Kohl is a reaper. One of the first. I'm a thirty-six-year-old seer with legit intimacy issues. If there was a supernatural dating app, we wouldn't be a match."

"Because neither of you would be on it."

"True," I say, snorting a laugh.

"But you like him."

When she continues to stare a hole in me, I release a long breath. "Also true."

"And you trust him."

"Of course I do. Reapers are neutral beings. There's no reason not to trust them."

*Tsk*ing, she waves her index finger back and forth. "Don't play word games. Not 'reapers,' collectively. *This* reaper."

"Hello, Ms. Sassy," I say, crossing my arms. "Fine, put a check mark in all the yes boxes for Kohl. I like him. I'm comfortable with him. What I can see of him, I find very appealing. Even if he felt the same way, what could possibly come of it?"

She giggles. "You, hopefully. Him too, if reapers have the biology for it."

"What a naughty girl you've become. I approve, but I think your sexed-up brain forgot an important detail." I wiggle my gloved hands in front of her. "I can't touch him. A reaper is forever. I can't even imagine how many visions I might have."

"So don't touch him." She shrugs. "Sure, it won't be the same as a traditional relationship, but look around," she says, with the sweep of an arm. "If ever there was a place to embrace differences, this is it. Plus, I seem to recall someone —and PS, it was you—telling me that if fate's plan for you includes a certain person, it'll keep putting that person in your path. If Kohl is that person for you, maybe you should see where the path leads instead of running in the other direction."

Chapter Four

KOHL

After Shay's abrupt exit from my visit and our conversation a few nights ago, I have no reason to return. Yet her soul continues to call to me. Not from the in-between. She is very much alive, and my desire to share the same existence has never been stronger. Knowing the wish is impossible does nothing to diminish its potency.

Only a sliver of the moon is visible in the night sky over Fate's Falls, but the glow of a small fire at the center of Shay's backyard illuminates the fenced area. Seated in an outdoor chair, her focus snaps from the flames to my face when I become flesh in her backyard once again.

"Am I intruding?"

She shakes her head, firelight bathing her in soft amber and gold, making her smooth brown skin and long, dark curls shimmer. "I wasn't sure I'd see you again, after the way we left things—*I* left things—last time."

"I gave you unexpected, and perhaps unwanted, information. Your reaction was understandable."

For a moment, she simply looks at me. "Unexpected, yes. Unwanted, no." She motions at the vacant seat on the opposite side of the fire pit. "You're welcome to join me, but you might want to move the chair back a little so your cloak doesn't catch a spark."

"Since it can withstand the flames of hell, a small earthly bonfire shouldn't be a problem," I say, settling on the molded plastic.

"Walking through the fires of hell. That must be a trip." She makes the same head-exploding gesture from the night at the old witch's yard. "I thought you mostly stayed in the in-between and pointed souls toward their designated gate. When you're not escorting people back to their lifeless bodies or delivering messages from the newly departed, that is."

Laughing is not common for reapers because it is rarely fitting for our duty, but the sound rises from inside me, deep and full, its vibrations in my current form flooding me with relaxation and vitality simultaneously.

Shay's eyes open wide at the sound. "I didn't know you could laugh, especially like that."

"Our previous meetings didn't lend themselves to that reaction, and in truth, it's a rare one. But when I take on physical form, I'm capable of all things possible for that species."

"*All* things?" One of the perfect dark eyebrows I long to trace with my finger rises.

The stirring between my legs matches the thoughts rolling through my imagination. Things I believe she's alluding to, since I doubt she's asking about mundane physical actions. "Not all things, no." I watch her expression for signs of disappointment, and get one when her lips curve downward. "For example, I cannot die."

She snatches a marshmallow from the bag at her side and throws it at me, huffing a breath when I catch it in one hand without shifting my attention from her face. "Pretty quick reflexes for a part-time mortal."

"A supernatural perk. Lack of actual experience doesn't affect my mastery."

A snort of amusement precedes a small smile. "Quick reflexes, yes. Not sure *mastery* is required to catch a giant marshmallow from ten feet away."

"Perhaps not. But the term can be applied to all activities I undertake in this form."

She tilts her head, assessing me. "I can't decide if you're just stating honest fact, or you've mastered cockiness, or... something else."

"It is honesty."

"Of course," she says, nodding.

"And since I am being honest, I'm also attempting to be —" What word to choose? Seductive. Flirtatious. Friendly would be safest, and not untrue, but inadequate. "Playful."

"Playful. You want to have a *playful* conversation. With me." Though voiced flatly, as a statement, the wide-eyed disbelief in her expression makes it clear that she's questioning. Then the real question comes. "Why?"

Sitting is unnatural for a reaper. Even having taken physical human form, it is too constricting. Especially while bearing the full weight of her attention. While preparing to reveal long-held feelings I shouldn't have at all.

"Does it make you uncomfortable?" I ask, rather than answer her question.

"No." Unforgettable green eyes anchored to my face, or what she may be able to see of it, she adds, "I don't think I could ever feel that way with you."

Of course. "You are correct. Reapers are imbued with magic that makes us a calming force for transitioning souls."

"I'm not a transitioning soul, and that's not what I meant." Rising from her chair, she comes around to my side of the fire, stopping close enough that we could easily touch if either of us made the move. "It's not your reaper magic making me feel...the way I do. Maybe it was at the beginning, in those first moments after I died in the river, when we met in the in-between. But afterward, when I was back in my body and you held me while in your solid form—it wasn't reaper magic affecting me then. It was you. The man."

"But I am not truly a man. I can just as easily be any sentient creature. I appear in whatever form is familiar and comforting to the soul before me."

Hands planted on her hips, her eyes narrow and a huff of breath pushes past her full lips. "Arguing semantics with me is a good way to solidify your 'man' status. So is avoiding giving a direct answer."

Finding her annoyance with me appealing is very much a human response. The more time I spend in this form—in her presence, specifically—the more natural my humanlike state becomes. "Whether you embrace or reject my answer, it will change the future. Mine, certainly. Reapers don't experience fear, and yet, the possibility of being sent from your life elicits tension not only in the muscles of my temporary physical form, but in the deepest layers of my essence."

"I'm not going to send you away," she says, her gaze searching the shadows of my cloak's hood. "*Unless* you continue being evasive. Then you can poof on out of here and rematerialize when you're ready to give me a straight answer."

The muscles in my cheeks and jaw tighten as I smile. This part of my face, I know she can see. "Do you recall the other night, when I told you I brought you back without direction from the Oracle?"

"I remember," she says. "I've replayed every word of that conversation more times than I can count."

"Forgive me if I caused you distress."

"Not distress, just confusion."

"I will do my best to deliver clarity, though the actions and sensations I'm going to describe are uncharted territory for me, so I cannot speak to the accuracy of my lens."

"Good thing I'm not paying by the word for this clarity, or I'd already be at my budget with that fancy disclaimer."

Again, I laugh, the sound tapering into a pleasant vibration that seems to radiate through me. The urge to touch her is strong enough to make my fingers twitch. Her hands are bare, the fingers long and delicate where they're curled over her curvaceous hips. It's possible—likely—she will never desire physical contact. I would spend eternity without it just to be near her. That's what I should tell her. And I will, but from the beginning.

"I connect with souls in the in-between place, after they have departed their lifeless body—even in cases such as your friend's, when the Oracle has directed me to return the soul. But you... I was drawn to your soul while you were very much alive. I was there when you stepped outside of the building into a dark winter night. I watched you lead the man who believed he was stalking you to the train bridge. I saw you— no, I *felt* you make the decision to sacrifice your life so that you could end his by causing him to plummet to the river."

One hand rises to cover her mouth briefly, then it slides to her chest, her palm rubbing over the area of her heart. "You were there for all of that?"

"Yes. It was the only time in all of my existence that I was called to a soul prior to mortal death."

"Did the Oracle ever tell you why?" she whispers, moving closer.

"Knowing I had acted outside the Oracle's will, I expected fate's plan for your soul to be corrected. I watched over you, assuming your life would soon end and your soul would move on, but it didn't happen. Hours became days, then months, then years. I'd changed the course of your life, subverted the Oracle's plan for your soul. I did not dare ask how or why it was possible."

"If the Oracle believes my soul moved to the other side fifteen years ago, what'll happen when I do eventually die?"

A question I've pondered endlessly, and for which I have no answer. I am only certain of one thing. "I will be there."

"You can't be sure of that."

"Even if I have been condemned for my selfishness and have to walk through hellfire without reaper magic, I will do it without hesitation. I will find my way to you. Since the moment your soul called to me, I have been connected to you. I would have spent the rest of your mortal life watching from a place you could not see me, but the Goodwin witch's request provided reason to reveal myself to you in physical form."

She raises her hands, pressing the fingertips against her forehead. "You've been, like, stalking me from another plane of existence for fifteen years?"

"I would rather you consider it watching over you with concern and affection."

She crosses her arms over her chest. "In this realm, that's still stalking. But in your case, with good intentions, at least initially."

"Through all the years, there has never been a moment when your safety, well-being, and happiness haven't been my primary focus."

"My *being* has been safe and well since I came to Fate's Falls. As for happiness—" She makes a derisive snort. "Since you've been watching, you must've been disappointed on that front." Releasing a long breath, she drops her arms to her sides, then returns to her seat on the opposite side of the fire.

There are only two lawn chairs at the fire, so I lift the vacant one and move it beside hers, then sit. "I have never been disappointed in anything about you, though I have noted your sadness."

"I mean, I haven't been *miserable*. I have a comfortable home, a good job, great boss, and I've developed some nice friendships. The wonders of technology and magic allow me to stay in touch with my mom, even though she's over two thousand miles away. And because the psychopath thinks I died that night, my family and coven are safe. I appreciate what I have."

"But you would like to have more—what your friends Dela, Constantine, and Natalie have found. Companionship that goes beyond platonic. Someone to share life's intimacies with. Someone to love."

"And you sound like a someone who has done more than casual observing of my life." Leaning toward me, she motions at the cloak, which hides much of my face. "Show me what's under the hood. More than a glimpse of lips that belong on a *GQ* cover model, a perfectly straight, strong nose, and dark puppy-dog eyes. I should at least get a full view of who's keeping such close tabs on me."

"The rest is exactly as you think."

"Bold." A smile curves her lips. "Maybe I've never thought about how you look." Her tone and expression are playful, but her eyes give away something deeper. A longing to connect, to fill the void responsible for the loneliness she works so hard to hide from those in her daily life.

Even without *poking around in there*, as she once described it, I feel the yearning in her soul. I want to be the one who fills that void for her.

I raise my hands, but before I can reveal myself, I'm pulled from Shay's presence to the in-between to fulfil my duties. The usual peace of inhabiting my natural plane is absent. Inside, there is only tightness.

Shay won't know why I disappeared, only that I did so. Without granting her request to see beneath my cloak's hood. Without truly answering her questions of *why*. Without saying goodbye.

Chapter Five

SHAY

There will be no moping over a man who literally appears and disappears without warning and uses a lot of pretty words to say very little. A man who isn't even a man, as he was quick to remind me.

Not that his species—if that's even the correct term for reapers—matters. Every sentient being is off-limits for more than friendship. Even if their future can't possibly be laced with horrific images, I don't want to see what's ahead for someone I'm intimately invested in.

Dela's suggestion the other day that I could have a hands-off yet romantic relationship with Kohl got me thinking about the possibility. Too much thinking, because it led to hoping.

After his admission last night... bye-bye, hope.

For reasons he can't or won't explain, he went against

the intended order of things when he returned my soul to my physical body fifteen years ago. Since then, he's been waiting for the Oracle to realize my soul isn't where it's supposed to be. He hasn't been hanging around because there's some rare, fated connection between us. Kohl has been watching over me because he fucked up. He's waiting to fix his mistake.

Disappointment is a flavor I can do without. Even worse than dill pickle, and that's a stomach turner. Kohl has the right idea about one thing, though—fixing mistakes.

Kohl saved my life, brought me to create a new one. My singular focus back then was surviving. But once I was here, protected, I should've done something to prevent the killings I'd foreseen from happening. Something other than falling to my death. Talk about a plan gone wrong.

There is something I can do now that I couldn't before. Or maybe I could have, but not easily or comfortably. Though, I don't expect reliving the shit in my head to be comfortable. Not even in the company of good people I trust. But I have to try. To ask, at least.

I've been to my boss's house before. Always for work-related reasons, until his fated mate came to town. Since Natalie's arrival in Fate's Falls, I've been to Constantine's house—now *their* house—for Natalie's cousin Ro's baby shower, Natalie and Constantine's engagement party, and a paint night. Three events in a short period of time. More nonmandatory socializing than I'd done in the previous decade-plus.

The paint night was partly for fun, partly so Natalie could use her friends for a test run. Once word got out around town that Constantine's new-to-town human mate was a professional artist, residents started inquiring about her work. Buying original pieces, commissioning customs, and taking lessons. Offering those lessons in the form of fun paint-night parties was Ro's idea. Even while pregnant and abstaining from alcohol, Rosetta is always down for a good time.

Even on paint night, being in awe of how Natalie draws as naturally as breathing, it didn't cross my mind to ask for her help with *this*. That click happened last night, while I lay awake, fuming and frustrated and trying to make sense of everything. Now it seems obvious. If she's willing to do it.

One way to find out. Taking a deep breath and shoving my second thoughts about opening this can of worms as far down as possible, I ring the bell.

Constantine's deep-voiced, "I've got it," is loud enough for me to hear through the large, solid wood door before it opens inward, my big Minotaur boss filling the frame. "Shay." His heavy brow rises. "Is everything okay?"

"I should have texted Natalie before just showing up on your doorstep. If this is a bad time—"

"Not at all." Stepping aside, he gestures for me to come in. "Natalie is out on the patio. Go on through."

"Thanks, boss." It's habit, calling him that, even though he became a friend as much as he's my employer. I nod and walk past him, carefully avoiding any contact. That's habit too. Even though I know he's a good person, through and through, and he's committed heart and soul to his fated mate, who is a gem of a human, I still can't bring myself to take the gloves off.

Maybe that'll change one day. Not with everyone, but at least with the people closest to me. Hugging Dela reminded me how good it feels to have that kind of contact. I knew I missed it, just not how much.

"Hey, Shay," Constantine calls from behind me, before I reach the doors that lead to the patio. When I turn, he's standing in the kitchen, hands casually in his pockets, concern evident in his expression, even with his dark, nonhuman features. "Since you avoided answering my question, and I know you pretty well after all these years, I assume everything is *not* okay. I'm never going to pry into your personal life, but I'm always here to listen or help. Just wanted to make sure you know that."

"I do, and I appreciate it. Especially after I wasn't willing to help you when you asked."

A bullish huff of breath accompanies his head shake. "My request was way out of line. It was wrong for me to ask you, knowing how strongly you feel about not using your magic. I'm glad you refused and set me straight."

It's not the first time he's apologized for asking me to use my seer magic for a look at his future, but I nod an acceptance just the same. "All in the past; don't give it another thought. And I'm glad I didn't peek into your future because I would've hated to ruin how beautifully everything unfolded for you and Natalie."

"You're right. Things couldn't have turned out more perfect."

Envy twists its green fingers around my heart. I'm happy for my friends, but seeing them get everything they've dreamed of still drives home the fact that I'll never have that experience.

But I'm not here because of lost dreams. I'm here because of nightmares.

"If you're not in the middle of something, you can sit in on my conversation with Natalie. Might as well tell you both at once, since you're going to hear about it, anyway." I hook a thumb toward the patio door. "Want to hear the big secret of my life I've kept hidden for fifteen years?"

"Only if you want me to. I respect you and your privacy. If you'd rather Natalie not share whatever you came to talk about, she won't say a word."

"Not aloud or intentionally, but I know you two have that mind-talking thing."

Constantine's dark mouth curves upward. "We generally reserve that form of communication for personal matters."

Raising a hand, I shake my head. "Say no more. Like I've told Natalie, I don't want to know the details of my boss's sex life."

"Fair enough," he says with a deep chuckle. "I'd feel the same way if Natalie were to discuss details of her girl-talk conversations with you or Dela. Which she never has, just for your peace of mind."

"Yup, Nat's a good one."

His massive chest puffs out. If he were a cartoon character, there'd be hearts in his eyes. Then he blinks, and a more serious expression returns to his face. "With that all settled, I can head over to the brewery for a few hours, so you and Natalie have privacy." Posed as a statement to take the pressure off me, it's still obviously a question.

Mentally gathering my shit, I cross the room to join him in the kitchen portion of the open-concept house with its oversized furniture made to accommodate his bulky Minotaur physique.

"All the time I've lived in Fate's Falls, I didn't want anyone to know what happened before I came here. Why I am the way I am. It was easier to let everybody assume I'm just cold. I thought keeping my past a secret was the way to move on, but I haven't, not really. Things have come to light recently, and I realized it's time I stop hiding from what happened and do something about it. Try to, anyway. I'm hoping your brilliant artist mate can help with that, if she's willing. I'm going to pay her, of course. And I'm okay with you sitting in and hearing it all."

"If Natalie can help you, I'll make sure her creative fee is taken care of. With all the hours you've put in at *The Brew* off the clock, it's the least I can do, and don't bother arguing with me about it. You're stubborn," his amber eyes glint as he points to his muzzlelike nose and horns, "but I'm the bullheaded one."

Snorting a laugh, I shake my head. "Can't argue that."

"Good. Just one important question before we head out to see Natalie." He steps to the fridge and opens it, coming out with several cans of his brewery's craft beer in one big hand. "How many of these are we going to need?"

I extend both gloved hands, palms open. "As many as we can carry."

By the time I say goodbye to Constantine and Natalie several hours later, I have a folder of eerily accurate portrait sketches and one very solid buzz. From the beer. The friendship. Like when I revealed the ugly truth of my past to Dela, relief flooded in when I lowered the walls with Natalie and Constantine. All of it together is dizzying. Light in a way I've never felt before. It's enough to make me hum, literally, on my walk home. A random tune I must know from somewhere but can't place. Whatever it is, I like it. Then it transitions to something different. Then another song. And another, until a song I recognize enters the queue.

I cackle while walking toward my front door, nearly jumping out of my skin when Kohl appears out of thin air. "This is how I'm going to die," I say, waving my hand around in front of him. "Scared to death by a reaper."

"I apologize." He nods, and like every other time, his hood stays in exactly the same position on his head. "I was drawn to your music."

"You're shitting me, right?" I stare at him, waiting for some indication that he's joking. Nothing. Propping my free hand on my hip, I snort at the ridiculousness of it all. "Being *super* old and super nosey like you are, you must know what song that was."

"I do not."

Another cackle rolls out of me. "It was '(Don't Fear) The Reaper' by Blue Öyster Cult."

"They give wise advice. Reapers are neutral beings; there is no reason to fear them."

I blink at him, waiting for more. More words, a smile, even a hint of humor. Doesn't happen. "That's it?" At his nod, I burst into full-on laughter. The kind that makes me double over, clutching my stomach because it cramps up. It's probably the alcohol making it funny, but I don't care. It feels good to just laugh my ass off.

My neighbor, an older fairy who has lived in the cottage next door since before I moved into mine, pops her head out her front door, a loud "Oh!" carrying across the yards as she lays eyes on my unexpected visitor.

"Don't worry, I'm fine," I say, collecting my wits enough to reduce my amusement to grinning. "Kohl isn't here to reap my soul—" I whip my head over to face him. "You're not, right?"

He shakes his cloaked head.

"Nope, he's not here to take me. Just to annoy me," I call over to the kindly older fairy. "Sorry to disturb you, Mrs. Allis."

"If my presence annoys you," Kohl says when my neighbor retreats inside her house, "I will resist the urge to make myself visible to you again."

"But you'll still be hovering in the ether?" I gesture around vaguely, but it gets the point across enough that he nods. "You need a hobby other than stalking me. Whether I live to be a wrinkly old witch or the Oracle yanks my soul out of my body five minutes from now, I'm going to be fine. I don't need an immortal babysitter." Snickering, I wave my hands around as if I had the magic to cast a spell. "I release you from your obligation!" My theatrics are obviously a bit too loud, since Mrs. Allis closes her front window with a notable slam.

Kohl gives me space as I continue up the front walk, but he doesn't poof away; his currently very solid form falls in step beside me. "Do I truly annoy you?" he asks as I attempt to insert my key into the lock, which won't seem to stay still. Making a humanlike exhalation, he takes possession of the key without so much as grazing fingers.

"I didn't need help," I grumble when he makes quick work of unlocking the door. Defaulting to my usual defensiveness. Stubbornness. Pushing people away and adding bricks to the wall between me and everyone else. Old habits die hard.

Calm as ever, he doesn't call me out for being snarly, or say a word of any kind. He just returns my key in a contact-free manner.

I know he's being considerate, but it's like salt in the wound. I'm so damn tired of people being careful around me, even though *I* drew the boundary line. All I've ever wanted is to be normal.

All of that combined with his continued neutral-faced silence makes me feel like a cornered cat who hasn't had a decent meal in fifteen years. Huffing, I cross my arms over my chest. "Are you going to say anything?"

"I was waiting for your answer."

"Seriously? You're waiting for *me* to answer *you?* Oh, the irony. Okay, yes, you do annoy me, but if you're going to be floating around anyway, I'd rather see you than wonder when you're creeping on me. On that note, have you been ethereally stalking me today? Before being drawn to the reaper song, I mean. Which is kind of hilarious. And convenient. Now I know how to get your attention in a hurry— just play your *'here, reaper, reaper'* song." I semi-sing that last bit in the way someone would call their pet.

Either he doesn't get the humor or doesn't care that I'm poking fun at him. There's no hint of irritation—not that

I've ever seen him display that emotion—but also no sign of amusement. And I like coaxing a smile to his lips. They're nice lips that look sexy with a smile.

Pining for anyone is a mistake, but for a reaper? I must be a masochist in the emotions department. Though, at least I won't have to feel resentful seeing him around town looking cozy with someone else. Which begs the question, "Have you ever dated or hooked up or been in love?" I snort as soon as the inquisition leaves my mouth. "There I go again, asking questions *you'll* never answer because you just conveniently vanish instead." Making the *poof* gesture, I shake my head, push the door open, and step inside. "Good-night, Kohl."

"Leaving you is the last thing I wish to do, Shay."

The way he says my name halts my hand's forward motion on the door. The next thing I know, my lips are moving, saying words I'm likely to regret. "Do you want to come in and talk?"

"I would like that very much."

"I was sure you'd say no. If not by disappearing, then in some roundabout way, with fifty unnecessary words intended to spare my feelings."

"It will never be my choice to reject you," he says, moving to the threshold. "If ever I say no to you, it is only because I must."

Taking a step back, I open the door wide and motion for him to enter. The moment he's inside and the door is closed behind him, both cats hop off the couch and cross the living room. Rune sniffs tentatively at the bottom of Kohl's dark cloak where it grazes the floor. Cookie sits in front of Kohl, silently staring up at the reaper.

"Do not worry, friend," Kohl says to the big ginger. "All is well."

My new addition saunters off to the kitchen, Rune following directly behind.

"Were you actually communicating with the cat?" I ask, after they've hopped onto the wide window ledge that overlooks the backyard.

"He is not just a cat; he's a familiar, a supernatural creature. And yes, I can hear the truth in his soul if I listen, as his position indicated he wished me to do."

Just when you think things can't get weirder. "And Cookie was worried you were here to collect my soul," I say, though it's more question than statement.

"Yes."

"Is he going to worry about that every time you're here? *If* I invite you in again, that is. Which I'll only do if you don't leave me hanging in the answers department. No more 'poof goes the reaper,' got it?"

"If it is within my power to stay, or at least to tell you I must go, I will. There is a reason why I disappeared from your yard without warning during our last conversation."

"Can't wait to hear it." It comes out in my default snarky way. He's here and wants to talk, to explain. All things I want, yet I can't seem to drop my attitude. Even with him, or maybe *especially* with him, I need my armor.

I turn and walk to the couch. He's right behind me when I face him again. Literally a single step away. Close enough to touch without fully extending my arm. And goddess, help me, I'm tempted. I remember him being solid and warm. But maybe that was because I was so cold after he saved my dead ass from the frigid river.

Positioning myself on one end of the couch will keep him safely out of temptation range. Rather than take a seat at the opposite end and leave a cushion's worth of space between us, he brings the chair from my nearby small desk and sets it directly in front of me. His cloak flows around him as he settles on the wooden chair, not touching me, but not leaving much of a gap between us, either. There's an inch separating our knees. One careful, deliberate inch would be my bet.

"To answer another of your questions, I wasn't watching over you today. I haven't had the opportunity to do so since our last time together, and I regret the abruptness of my exit, but it was beyond my control. When I'm with you, I ignore the pull to reap, knowing one of the others will fulfill the need. That night by your fire, all reapers were needed in the in-between, making it impossible for me to resist the pull. All reapers' duties have been manyfold in recent days."

"Of course." The world beyond Fate's Falls' boundary rarely affects me, but I still watch the news. So much death overseas. And here I've been pouting because Kohl hasn't made time to pop into my yard again. "Look, forget I said anything. I had a few drinks today with friends and they make me extra saucy. The drinks, not the friends. Even without the extra sauce, I have no business asking you personal questions."

"I want to answer your questions. I very much wish to share my...personal matters with you."

Wishful thinking I can't control takes over at the intimate way he says *personal matters*. Hopefully, my face isn't giving my thoughts away. Though Kohl could just as easily poke around inside to get the truth from my soul. Maybe that wouldn't be so bad. Then he'd know my impossible feelings and I wouldn't have to admit them aloud. But he's not probing my soul. I'd feel it.

"I've had no relationships in this realm or any other. Reapers are not meant to have emotions or make connections. We were created to be neutral. Dutiful. To fulfil our specific purpose of guiding souls without sympathy, judgment, or any other bias which emotions could create. But with you...everything is different. The night I met you was the only time I have touched a mortal being while in physical form. I did so because I wanted to comfort and protect you, and once I held you, I did not want to release you. I'd never experienced such a desire—nor any other—before that night. Now that I am close to you, in physical form, the urge to touch you again has grown stronger."

All I can do is gape. Replay his words in my mind. Attempt to process it all.

"But I will not touch you. You have my word."

Me, the queen of comebacks, has nothing.

"And it wasn't the song that drew me," he says when I nod, because it's all I'm capable of. "I said it was your music, and I meant *your* music, Shay. The music of your soul. I felt your happiness rising and I couldn't stay away. The pull toward you was greater than the call to fulfil my duties."

"Why?" It comes out as a whisper, and I am not the whispering type, damn it. But I'm afraid to break the dream or spell or whatever this is, because it can't be real. "Why me?"

"That is an answer I don't have. Perhaps the Oracle knows, but I fear losing you by asking the question."

"Because my soul isn't supposed to be here." I swallow

hard when he nods. The idea of being ripped out of my life here sends a shiver down my spine. But it could happen. Even if Kohl doesn't draw the Oracle's attention to my altered course, it could happen some other way. "If the Oracle pulls the plug on my rebooted life, and my soul moves to the other side, you'll be able to see me and talk to me there, like you do here, won't you?"

"Not if the Oracle has recalled me from service for my actions."

"That sounds like a nice way of saying 'if the Oracle kills you.'"

"I am not a living being in the mortal sense; I cannot die the way you do. This body," he motions downward, "is temporary."

"What about your soul? What would happen to that if the Oracle *recalled* you?"

"Reapers do not have souls. There is no next place for us."

"If serial killers like the one whose future I saw have a soul, then you most certainly do. You say that reapers aren't supposed to have emotions, but you just told me you have feelings. So I call bullshit that you don't have a soul." Fueled by *my* emotions, I hop up from the couch, whack my shin against the coffee table, curse the fiery sting shooting up my leg, and lose my balance.

And end up in Kohl's lap.

Chapter Six

KOHL

Reapers do not experience time the way mortals in the earthly plane do. A human lifetime is a sliver compared to eons. But when Shay falls into my lap, time stands still.

The *wanting* I confessed minutes ago takes over and I close my arms around her, carefully, ensuring her skin doesn't meet mine. Even in this physical form, I do not need to breathe, yet some instinct of my temporary physiology causes me to hold air inside without exhaling.

"I'm sorry." Gloved palms flat against my chest, she shifts backward.

I should loosen my hold on her, but I don't. "I am not sorry. Not for wanting you close to me, or for enjoying how you feel against me. Not for the feelings I have for you."

"Then I'm not sorry either." Eyes that shimmer like the

earth's purest emeralds meet mine beneath the overhang of my hood. "So many times, I've thought about being with you like this. I told myself I was fixated on you because you saved me. That I fantasized about you because you were the last man to hold me, or because you were literally the most unattainable man out there. But then you reappeared in my life, and I knew it was more than that. All this time, it's been more than that." Then, as quickly as she opened up to me, her lips clamp shut. Her flattened palms curl into fists, which she thumps against my chest. "And all this time, you've been watching me, knowing I was alone, even when surrounded by people. But you didn't show yourself."

This time, when she pushes away from me, I let her go. In ethereal form, temperature does not register or affect me. But the moment Shay's body no longer presses against mine, I know what it is to lose warmth. And I want it back.

The more space she puts between us, the harder her expression becomes. "You can't explain why you were drawn to me before I died, or why you acted of your own accord to bring me back, or why you developed feelings for me. But here's a question I need you to answer, and it better be a real one. Why did you stay away for *fifteen years?* Why did you let me continue to be lonely when you could have changed everything by stepping into my world? Into my life."

I've answered this question inwardly many times over the years. Reasons, excuses, rationalizations. They all boil down to one truth. "Fear."

"Of the Oracle finding out?" she asks, planting her hands on her curvy hips. "Because that isn't stopping you now, so I don't buy it."

I rise from the chair and cross to her, leaving little space between us. "Fear that you would not want to see me. Fear that, once in your presence, I would lose control of these feelings you brought forth in me, confess my love for you, at which you would recoil and tell me to leave and never return. It was easier to long for you from the shadows than to risk enduring the pain of rejection for all eternity."

Silence falls over the room. Staring up at me, Shay's deep-plum lips part, but no sound leaves them.

"There is a place I would like to show you. A peaceful place where I have often lingered while trying to make sense of my feelings. While fighting my desire to step into your life, unbidden. Will you allow me to take you there?"

Her dark curls dance on her shoulders as she nods. "Yes." No question as to where, or how. Just trust, even after I have caused her pain.

"I will take care not to touch your skin," I say, opening my arms, then enveloping her within the flow of my cloak.

A sharp intake of breath followed by a loud "Shit!" accompany her arms wrapping tightly around my waist as the world she knows disappears from beneath her feet. Before I can revel in the sensation of her soft warm body pressed to mine, we return to solid ground, where I open my arms and allow her to step free.

"I'd forgotten what it feels like to be reaper *poofed* from one place to another." Again, her lips part, this time as she looks around at her current surroundings, an outcropping of rock high above town. "Is that Fate's Falls?" she asks, pointing downward.

"It is, but we are still within the Oracle's protection boundary up here."

"You're not exaggerating when you say 'up here.'" Chin tilted, she gazes at the night sky, extending one arm outward at shoulder height. "I feel like if you gave me a little boost, I could climb right onto the crescent moon."

"If I could do that for you, I would."

Abandoning her view of the stars, she faces me again. "I believe you."

"And the rest of my words, do you believe those also?"

Her pulse's rapid beat is visible in the graceful column of her neck. "I don't think you'd lie to me."

"Is not the same as saying you believe me."

She turns away to once again look out at the view of the town in the distance below, its streets now a web of soft lights from buildings which appear small enough to pick up between two fingers. The wind lifts her hair, and she hugs herself against the visible shiver that ripples through her.

"May I provide warmth?" I ask, stepping behind her. The small, single nod is all the answer I get, but it is enough to justify closing my arms around her again.

The tension quickly leaves her posture, and she exhales, settling her back against my chest. "One of my memories of that night is you being warm, but so much time has passed, I wasn't sure if that was another thing I'd created in my fantasies of you."

"When I take a physical form, my body has the traits of that species. This human body maintains a consistent 98.6 degrees Fahrenheit. I am unaffected by the atmospheric temperature."

"Handy trick. I could do without feeling cold. I do enjoy feeling extra warm, though."

"That explains why you so often sit by the fire in your

backyard, and why you wear boots that cover your knees. They must get cold often."

She elbows my midsection, smiling as she cranes her head to look at my face. "Now that we're in full disclosure mode, you're not even going to pretend you haven't been hardcore spying on me, huh?"

"I have not *spied*. I have watched over you in public or outdoor places."

"Not while I was inside my house?"

"Never. Though I will not deny it was tempting." Merely remembering the silhouette of her body through the glass of her bedroom window and the sounds that filtered through the screen makes me hard, a physiological response that surprised me the first time it happened, but to which I am now accustomed. Because of her, it has become a frequent condition.

Her eyebrows rise, the whites of her eyes becoming more visible as my thickened cock makes itself known against the swell of her backside. "You—you're—" She snaps her lips tight, as if forbidding more words to pass through them.

"I desire you, yes. In ways I didn't know a reaper could experience. If the present state of my physical form makes you uncomfortable, I will be mindful to position myself so you are not made aware."

"I don't mind being aware." She smiles over her shoulder, then turns until she is fully facing me. "Tonight's bombshell of information is just...a lot. You materialize in my front yard, tell me the 'music of my soul' was stronger than the call to your singular duty; that if you had it your way, you'd never leave me. You said—" Her dark eyebrows pinch together as a huff I know well to mean irritation leaves her lips. "You said you love me. What am I supposed to do with that?"

"If I could choose your reaction, it would be for you to reciprocate."

Her laughter rings out across the night air. Beautiful music. Then the sound tapers off to a soft sigh from gently smiling lips. "Are you sure you're a reaper, Kohl? Because wanting to be loved in return is the most human desire of all." She presses one palm to the upper portion of my chest. "You may not have an actual heart in there, but you definitely have a soul. And I really like your soul." Her gaze drifts over my form, her lips curving higher when her eyes return to my face. "I like the packaging it's in, too, and I'm not referring to the cloak, even if it is imbued with immortal magic."

If I cannot hear Shay return my sentiment of love, the words spoken are enough. "Have you forgiven my cowardice?"

Nodding, she brushes her leather-gloved fingertips across my hand. "You're here now."

"I would stay with you every moment if I could."

"I know," she says softly. "I also know that isn't possible. So I'm going to stop being a coward, too, and just be grateful for the moments we get."

SHAY

The Brew is always busy on Monday mornings. Even monsters need their caffeine fix a little harder on the first day after a weekend.

The nonstop flow of customers hasn't allowed any personal conversation time with Dela since we unlocked the front door. And she's jonesing for some, because in the fifteen minutes between her arrival and the cafe opening, I gave her the condensed version of my wild weekend.

That I shared the details of my past with Natalie and Constantine, then got a little drunk while Natalie sketched the faces from my visions and the serial killer who got away. My plan to get those images in front of the right people at the Pittsburg Police Department and the FBI with some magical assistance from my coven back in Gettysburg. Kohl's multiple pop-ins to my yard and the did-not-see-that-coming plot twist that he's been watching me since *before* I died—and every chance he's had since he brought me back.

By the time I got that far in my story, Dela's bottom lip looked like it couldn't drop any lower. But it did, when I dropped the tidbit about falling onto Kohl's lap, and that we sort of hugged—carefully, without skin contact—multiple times. And she honest-to-goddess squealed when I told her about the massive erection that I would've had to be numb not to feel pressed against my ass. Of course, I finished the parade of information with Kohl's claim of love. Perfectly timed with turning the sign to Open and walking away.

Just because I was excited to share my updates with her doesn't mean I'm suddenly an open book. Or that I don't enjoy teasing her. I don't get as many opportunities to do that since she and Raz stopped silently pining for each other and got together. Being in love with a red-hot revenge demon has really brought her out of her shell. I love that for her. Just like I know she loves hearing that positive things are happening in my life.

Positive things are happening in my life. The thought is like a buzzer in my mind. Only it's not an alarm jolting me from a rare good dream. It's a different kind of wake-up call. One that's telling me to stay this course and grab all the happiness I can fit in my gloved hands.

After the morning rush ends and the lineup finally dwindles, Dela pounces, blocking my way behind the counter, nudging my foot with the toe of one of her cute patterned sneakers. "And?"

"And now we load the dishwasher and clean the cappuccino machine and—"

"Oh no, you don't," she says, shaking her head. "Manager Shay's coffee clean-up list can wait until my friend Shay has spilled every drop of the weekend tea."

"There's not much more to tell. Obviously, nothing physical. I mean, even with my clothes and his reaper robe between us, it was nice to be held. It's nice that he'll never expect more. And after he stopped being evasive, and I stopped being pissed off, we talked for hours. It was nice."

"If it were any other first date, those three 'nices' would be the kiss of death." Her eyebrows wiggle, an unspoken *see what I did there?* gesture.

"It wasn't a first date. We just...spent time together. Did some catching up."

"Right," she says, smiling and nodding in a way that

indicates she means the opposite of agreement. "Catching up that included him telling you *he loves you*. Did you say it back?"

"What? No." I shake my head more than is necessary to get the answer across. "I wouldn't tell him that."

"Because it's not true? Or because it is?"

The handful of patrons sitting in the cafe release an assortment of gasps and expletives when the reaper in question materializes on the customer side of the counter. Even Dela startles at the sight of him, and she's met Kohl before.

Sweetheart that she is, she recovers quickly, smiling and offering her hand across the counter. "You probably don't remember me, but I sure remember you. Thank you so much for putting that card in my pocket the night you stopped me from crossing over. Calling that number, coming to Fate's Falls, changed everything. I have an amazing life now, thanks to you."

Rather than shake her hand, he makes a deep nod, and I can't help but feel a little thrill at knowing I'm the only mortal he touches.

"The Oracle determines the direction souls take. Reapers are merely guides," he says.

For a moment, I think Dela's going to call him out for the one time he made an exception—me. Instead, her rosy lips continue their genuine, sweet smile as she hooks a thumb toward the other end of the counter. "I'm going to clean the cappuccino machine and run a load of dishes before the lunch rush."

Though it's likely she'll be eavesdropping from ten feet away, she gets to work on the tasks, not giving us even a hint of a glance. Over in the seating area, a couple of customers rise, keeping their eyes on the reaper while making a hasty exit.

"Your presence is making quite an impression," I say, meeting Kohl's gaze. The more time I spend with him, the clearer his face becomes, even beneath the hood of his cloak. Pale—though not in a deathly way, ironically—he's handsome and chiseled, with full lips and brown eyes. But this is how *I* see him. I tilt my head toward the remaining clientele, all of whom are openly staring. "What do they see when they look at you?"

"Many different things." Vague, as usual.

Though, I suppose a certain amount of secrecy is required when your job is to deliver souls as per the Oracle's bidding. Yesterday, I would've snarked him out the door for his nonanswer of an answer. Giving him a pass is easier today.

"I apologize for disturbing your patrons."

"It's fine. If anyone complains, I'll set them straight," I say, grabbing a cloth to wipe down the counter. "So. Daytime visit to my workplace. That's new. What are you doing here?"

If the next words out of his mouth are more of the romantic, *I could not stay away* variety, it's going to be hard to maintain my cool. I'm not impervious to his charms. As it is, not smiling like a smitten schoolgirl is taking effort. Even with the reduced audience, there are enough people watching us, taking in every word and nuance, that Fate's Falls will be buzzing about a reaper in the coffeehouse. First time in fifteen years that it's happened, so it's newsworthy. All I can do now is attempt to limit the scope of that news.

"I was in the neighborhood."

I shake my head, managing to dam the snort of laughter before it exits my mouth. "From anyone else, that'd be a lame pickup line. But it's you, so I know you mean it literally. All work and no play for the busy reaper, right?"

A smile tugs at his full lips. "I am in the neighborhood because one of the town's residents required a guide to the next place, yes. As for your question, the answer lies with you." Stepping closer, he places both palms on the counter's edge. "If you are free this evening, I would very much like to play with you."

The sound of metal clattering on the floor draws every eye in the place. "Sorry!" A deep-pink blush flooding every inch of her face, Dela's lips twist into a grimace before picking up the metal frothing pitcher she dropped.

Timing *not* coincidental, I'm sure. I'm grateful for the distraction, though, because it took the attention away from me and my bottom lip, which felt as if it also hit the floor.

"I can't believe you just said that in a public place," I say, angling my body to face away from the seating area and its eager audience.

"You used the word 'play,' so I returned it. Was it wrong?"

"Not wrong, but—" A glance at the coffee drinkers confirms they're tuned-in to this conversation that's none of their business. Fuck it. They're going to talk, anyway. "The phrase you used has sexual connotations."

Any gossip that floats around now is totally worth it to see Kohl's face take on a ghostly pallor and *his* bottom lip drop.

"I assure you that was not my intention."

"Obviously." We both know a sexual relationship isn't possible. And after last night, I know we both wish it were.

"Shall I clarify the meaning of my invitation with the townspeople present?" he says, extending one arm wide, toward the handful of eavesdropping customers.

Whatever form Kohl appears as to each of them, one thing is clear: none of them want to be in a reaper's sphere of influence. His sweeping gesture in their direction sends all of them scrambling for the door. Even the seven-foot-tall demon who looks like he fears nothing can't get to the exit fast enough.

When the door hits the last customer on their way out, I burst into laughter. "Well, that was awesome. Not good for business, but awesome."

Kohl's dark brows furrow low. "They have no reason to fear me."

"Just because Fate's Falls is inhabited by nonhumans doesn't mean we're all experts about every otherworldly species in existence. And as far I know, you're the only reaper ever to materialize in town, and definitely the only one to appear for reasons other than reaping souls. So, yeah, you popping in to the local coffeehouse midmorning is likely to make the mortal folks edgier than a bucket of our strongest coffee."

His gaze shifts to Dela, currently slinking off toward the staffroom. "Your friend doesn't fear me. Why is she leaving?"

Blushing is rarely visible on my skin tone—thank goddess—but its warmth tingles in my cheeks. "She's giving us privacy."

"Because of the sexual connotations in my earlier statement about wanting to play with you?"

I choke on a combination of laughter and embarrassment, enough that I have to pound a fist on my sternum to clear my airway. "Um, no. She knows there's no chance of that happening. Here or anywhere. Ever." I've spent my entire adulthood keeping my emotions and responses in check, but right now, a long, defeated sigh at wanting what I can never have slides past my defenses.

In a literal blink, Kohl is behind the counter with me, enclosing me in a safe embrace. "My sole desire is to spend eternity in your presence, in any form or manner. Anything we share is enough."

I press my forehead against the front of his cloak, relaxing in spite of the impossibilities of our connection. "You're going to turn me into a sap, and I hate crying."

"I know," he says, running his knuckles up and down my spine. "I have heard your disdain for it many times."

I snort a laugh, shaking my head as I straighten my spine. "Your lack of shame about creeping on me all these years is next level."

When I look up at him, he's smiling, confirming my hunch that he made the comment *knowing* it'd shake me out of the woe-is-me funk. He might be out of touch with some lingo, but not with me.

The front door chimes as it opens, then closes without anyone coming in. The sound brings Dela, though, her ever-pleasant expression scrunching in confusion as she glances around the customer-less space. "There's *nobody* here?"

"Kohl scared them all away."

"Unintentionally," he says, managing to look adorably contrite.

Yep, I'm officially smitten.

"Of course you didn't mean to," Dela says. "It'll be different once people get to know you." With that, she turns her back to us, resuming the cleanup tasks. Doing what she can to give us privacy after showing full support for Kohl's presence in our workplace and my life. She's a good person, through and through, and the best friend anyone could ever hope to have.

And the part about things being different when people get to know Kohl... I thought whatever our relationship is, it'd be private. But here he is, in physical form, in public. To see me.

"I will go before I cause further disruption." Kohl's words snap me out of my internal musing.

"Probably for the best," I say, admiring the width of his shoulders and smooth flow of his movements as he makes his way to the opposite side of the counter by walking, not another poof of reaper magic. "You never said why you came by."

"I did tell you, though with poorly chosen words."

Reaching across the counter for him is instinctive, but I stop myself, tidying the napkin dispenser instead. "Under different circumstances, your accidental suggestion of playing with me would be perfect. I've thought about it. About a lot of *playful* things."

Beneath the hood of his cloak, his deep-brown eyes glitter. Reaper magic? Or something more personal?

After clearing my throat of any potential huskiness, I add, "And yes, I'm free tonight."

"Then I will call on you. There's somewhere I would like to take you, so...wear long sleeves."

Not because we're going somewhere cold. I know it's to prevent accidental skin-to-skin contact when he transports me. At least I'll get to be in his arms for the blip of time it takes to poof from one place to the other. "I'll see you later."

The Brew's door opens as Kohl poofs away, giving me a direct view of the customer entering.

Lexi Goodwin.

Dammit.

"Now that's something I've never seen before." Lexi's glossy lips curve into a mischievous smile.

Or maybe it's not, but that's how it rubs me. I'm judging her too harshly, I know, but I don't want her taking an interest in Kohl.

Standing at the counter, Lexi tilts her head toward the space where Kohl stood before vanishing. "Was that the same reaper you mentioned—by name, twice—when you stopped by my store?"

In my peripheral, I see Dela watching. Waiting. "Yep. Same one." I follow with an immediate, "What can I get for you today, Lexi?"

"Well, I'd love a cup of hot tea, the juicy details kind, but if that's not on the menu, I'll take a large pumpkin spice latte, to go."

"One PSL, coming right up." Shut down, boom. And I even smile while doing it.

Once my back is turned and I'm busy prepping her drink, Lexi's voice floats above the sounds of the equipment. "Hey, Dela. You were here while the reaper was. What's he like? Friendly, I assume?"

The prickle of irritation Lexi always rouses in me blooms into bristly brambles. Words I'll never be able to take back fly out of my mouth as I spin to face her, slamming her takeout cup on the counter hard enough that her drink slops through the sipping hole. "I may never know what his reaper cock looks or feels like, but I'm sure as hell not letting you take a mold of it for your magically infused dildo business."

Half a dozen feet away, Dela claps a hand over her mouth. In front of me, Lexi does a couple of slow blinks before a wide, genuine smile overtakes her face.

"Looks like you're serving the tea after all. And it's exactly the kind I hoped for. The reason I stopped by, in fact, though you do make a mean pumpkin spice latte." Eyes twinkling, she swipes a manicured fingertip over the escaped topping, then pops the puff of foam into her mouth. "A little too much emphasis on *mean*, but I get the reason for it. I can help with that, too."

"I have no idea what you're talking about, and have no time to play riddle games with you," I say as I pivot away from her.

"It's not a riddle or a game, Shay. I'm here at my great-aunt's request. I knew she planned to give you Cookie, and I know why. I'd like to share Minerva's reason with you, and help fulfil the purpose of your familiar."

When I turn to face her again, there's only sincerity in her expression. Accepting her offer is on the tip of my tongue, but I owe her an apology first. Another one.

The first of the usual lunch crowd rolls in, voices and laughter taking up the silent space. Lexi makes a "call me" gesture with her free hand while waving the coffee cup at

Dela and me. Then the green witch sashays out, leaving the very intriguing ball in my court.

Chapter Seven

KOHL

I have spent enough time watching over Shay in her everyday goings-on to know that tonight can be considered a date. A mortal being would have brought flowers. To do so would have required I become corporeal and visit the town's floral shop. Based on the residents' reactions earlier, I forwent the idea. Even if the shop's attendant wasn't frightened by the appearance of a reaper, this realm functions with the exchange of currency. Reapers do not possess money. Nor any other material thing.

Assuming physical form outside Shay's front door, I rap lightly on the wood, glancing toward her neighbor's home while I await a response.

Tonight, nobody watches from the house next door. Briefly closing my eyes and listening to the nearby souls confirms that my presence has gone unnoticed this evening. Everything around us is calm.

The door swings inward and instantly, everything about *me* is the opposite of calm. Shay's smooth brown skin shines in the soft light spilling from her living room. Dark hair flows over her shoulders in curly waves. The long-sleeved sweater she wears accentuates her full breasts, and even with the high turtleneck that grazes her chin, covering every possible inch of skin, she brings my cock to a full stand within seconds. I don't possess a real heart, but I swear I feel one racing in my chest.

"You are so incredibly beautiful," I say, when my senses return.

"You're handsome, too. What I can see of you." Her eyes open wide as the words leave her mouth. "I didn't mean that to come out as a complaint. I'm not being snarky, not this time, not anymore, with you. You're a reaper and I accept everything that goes along with that, including the cloak and hood and only being able to see part of your face. It's enough. And I like what I can see."

Without hesitation, I raise my hands and guide the hood back, letting it pool behind my head.

The sharp intake of her breath precedes her outstretched hand. Gloved in leather, she could touch me without direct skin contact, yet she stops short of my face, then drops her hand to her side. "You look *exactly* how I imagined." Her gaze travels over my features before meeting my eyes again. "Every hair on your head, your cheekbones, eye color, skin tone, the shape of your lips. How is that possible?"

"As I said before, reapers appear in whatever form is familiar and comforting to the soul before them. When your neighbor looked at me, she saw an entirely different being from the human man in front of you. When I met Minerva Goodwin to guide her soul to the next place, she saw me as something else. Only you see me as I am now."

"Well, your reaper mojo needs a tune-up, because this," she motions at my newly revealed features, "is not the face of *familiarity and comfort*. If my death reaper is supposed to be familiar and comforting, then you should either appear as a wizened old Black lady like all the older witches in my coven, or maybe look like my high-school Latin teacher, who was a mid-fifties white man with a soft face, a side part, and a pair of wire-framed glasses."

"I have no control over my appearance. I appear how you want me to look."

"Oh, I never said I didn't *want* you to look the way you do. I'm saying you're definitely not the picture of 'familiarity and comfort.'" Making air quotes for the last part, she raises an eyebrow. Smiles in a way that would make my pulse race, if I had one. "Do you ever look in a mirror when you're in the mortal realm?"

"No, I have not."

"So...you don't know what you look like? Ever?"

"Aside from parts which are visible from my physical form's eyes, no."

She makes one of her head-exploding gestures and its sound effects, then steps aside and waves for me to enter. "Let's get your hot self in front of a mirror."

"I'm neither hot nor cold while in physical form."

Her brief, blurted laugh is as musical to my ears as her soul. "It's not a literal thing; it's a phrase. It means very attractive or sexy. In your case, both." With a nod indicating

I should follow, she leads me to a room I haven't seen—her bedroom.

The moment we cross the threshold, my attention shifts to the bed. The place where Shay sleeps. Where she pleasures herself.

"Kohl?" Her voice pulls my focus to where she waits, a few feet away, looking over her shoulder at me from in front of a freestanding, full-length mirror. Lips I long to touch and taste curve into a playful smile. "Need a moment to critique my decor?"

Closing the gap between us, I stand behind her, meeting her gaze in the mirror. "I need every possible moment with you, but in this one, I have a confession that may change your decision to share future moments with me."

Reflected in the glass, her eyes remain locked with mine. "I don't think you're capable of any action that would make me feel that way."

We shall soon find out. "When I told you I have never watched you inside your house, that was the truth, but only in the literal sense. I have never watched you *from* inside your home. I always remained outside its walls. I never peered through your windows, but some evenings, summer nights when the glass was raised, I lingered in the area beyond, listening to your voice as you spoke to your cat or with your mother on a call, while you sang along to music. And sometimes..." Though I know it is impossible, my throat seems to tighten, as if to prevent the damning words from escaping. "Sometimes, I heard you finding pleasure."

"I see. And when you realized what you were hearing, did you poof away?" she asks, her tone steady.

"No, I did not."

"How did it make you feel, listening to those private moments while I made myself come?" One dark eyebrow rises to a distinct peak. "And just in case you're not familiar with that phrase, either, 'made myself come' means having an orgasm, which is a form of sexual satisfaction."

Beneath my cloak, my cock is the hardest it has ever been, craving the sensation she describes. "I experienced guilt for invading your privacy, but I will not lie, I was aroused. As for the subsequent times I listened... guilt was not enough to make me turn away. I was entranced by the sounds you made. I yearned to hear them."

"Guilt, arousal, and yearning. Lots of big feelings for a reaper who's not supposed to experience emotions."

"You changed me. From the first night, Shay."

"If you could, would you go back to the way you were before the night we met?"

"I would not undo the feelings I have for you if my very existence depended on it."

Still holding my gaze in the mirror, she shifts backward, pressing her body to mine. "Then what are we going to do about this attraction, this overwhelming desire we both feel, without touching each other?"

"It is only our skin that cannot touch, correct?" I say, enclosing her in my arms, taking care not to let my face graze hers, despite my urge to press my nose against her hair, her temple, her neck. I slide one hand over the front of her jeans, cupping between her legs and pressing my fingers there, eliciting a throaty gasp. "Does that sound mean this contact is too much?"

"It's not too much," a feminine yet husky snort leaves her lips, "it's not enough."

"I would happily spend eternity slowly learning your body, but there is a faster way for me to bring you pleasure."

"With my vibrator?" She smiles when a full laugh bursts from me. "I guess you know what *that* is, huh, spymaster? I'm not even mad. Not when you laugh like that, especially while I can see your whole face."

A declaration of love demands release, but I don't allow the words to pass through my lips. She knows my feelings, and to repeat them when she hasn't returned them could diminish her glow. "Do you trust me?"

"You know I do." Her eyes widen as my consciousness meets hers. "I feel you in there, poking around in my s—" Her intake of breath cuts off the rest of her words, her eyelids fluttering as I increase the pressure between her legs, rolling my fingers side to side. "You've never touched anyone; how do you know what to do to make it feel so good?"

"From you. Our connection." It's how I know to scoop her into my arms and carry her to the bed because she wants more pressure than I could give while standing. It's why she doesn't startle at the gesture or question me when I lie on my back and motion her to straddle me. Her desires and limits, her hesitation because of those things—I feel them all. "Closer, Shay. Take your pleasure. There is nothing I want more than to bring you happiness in any way possible."

"Even though it'll be one-sided?"

"I assure you, it will not be." Positioning my hands on her hips, I guide her lower, until her fully clothed core nestles tightly to the ridge of my hard length beneath the cloak. "The pleasure I feel having you like this is more than I ever expected. Take from me and give me what I have craved to witness."

Gaze locked with mine, she places her gloved palms on my chest. Then she moves. Slowly at first, rocking forward and back. The speed and pressure increase with each pass, until the motions are hard and jerky, with breathing to match.

Beneath her, an innate response raises my hips to meet her warm, soft body. My cock aches, but not with pain. With the need to be inside her. Something I have never known, should not want, but gods above, I hunger to strip away the layers separating us and root myself in her heat.

Face dewy and glowing, she moans my name. *"Kohl...* I'm going to—oh, goddess, yes..." Then her mouth forms a perfect O, her eyes close, and the most divine sounds of pleasure fill the air.

I hold myself rigid for her, committing every sight and sound to memory for eternity. Only when her posture softens and she smiles down at me, catching her breath, do I allow my muscles to relax. "You are more beautiful than all the heavens combined. Thank you for giving me your pleasure."

"But you didn't...you know," her head tilts adorably to one side, "get yours?"

"My physical form is real, but not truly mortal. I grow hard for you—easily and often—but I have never experienced completion the way a human male does."

"You have blue balls literally forever?" A pained hiss leaves her mouth as her lovely features scrunch together. "Pretty sure a lot of guys would consider that being in hell."

"Having the chance to feel this way with you is the

opposite of hell. If the moment we shared were the last of my existence, I would leave happier than I ever imagined possible."

"How did a closed-off, resentful seer end up with the most romantic and eloquent being in all the realms?"

"Fate." The answer leaves my mouth with thought; the truth of it clear now.

"I think so too," she says, reaching and pressing one gloved hand against my cheek. "I wish I could *really* touch you. Kiss you." She trails a leather-clad finger over my lips, the softness in her eyes turning to a sparkle as she winks. "And definitely make better use of your permanent hard-on situation."

Before I can respond, she climbs off of me, and I instantly miss the weight of her body on top of mine. My physical form is temporary, but my ever-evolving and deepening emotions feel more permanent than time itself.

Her eyes track my every movement as I rise and straighten my cloak, her smile diminishing when I raise the hood. "You can't leave it down?"

"Not while we travel. Though, I won't object if you prefer to stay here and enjoy more pleasure with me."

Again, her laughter lightens the room. "Tempting as that is, I already feel guilty for maxing out the enjoyment when you couldn't." Pulling her bottom lip between her teeth, she steps closer, placing her hand over the place where my heart would be, if I had one. "Thank you for coming back into my life. No matter how long it lasts, or how nontraditional it is, I want to be with you."

"Only the Oracle can come between us, and I think the opposite has been fate's plan all along." The flowing sleeves of my cloak fall like rolling waves of black as I open my arms and enclose Shay within a careful embrace. "Would you like to know where I'm taking you this evening?"

Chin pressed against my chest, she shakes her head while looking up at me. "I'm kind of digging your surprises. I've lived with my guard perpetually up for so long, but I don't have to do that with you. I know that no matter what, you'll keep me safe. Being able to trust someone completely is a luxury I didn't think I'd ever have again."

The urge to reveal our destination is almost too great to resist. Instead, I smile, calling upon my magic.

Even knowing what is to come, she shrieks as the physical world disappears from beneath her boots. Clinging tightly to me, she fills the blink of time with a shrieked, "Shit!" followed by, "Maybe we should've stayed home," as she regains her footing on solid earthly ground.

"I think you will find this worthy of the momentary disorientation," I say, opening my arms so she can step out of my embrace.

The air rushes out of her in a hiccupping sob, and she covers her mouth while looking around the backyard of the place she once called home. "Kohl, is this real?" she says, her hand moving to cover her heart. "It's been so long since I was here... Are we actually in Gettysburg, at my mom's house?"

Her question is answered when the other person she trusts completely steps out the back door of the small story-and-a-half building. *"Shay?"*

"Mom!" Shay runs into the woman's arms, hugging her without concern for skin contact. *"Mom."*

"My baby," her mother says, rocking Shay as they both

sob and laugh. "Why are you in the backyard? How did you get here? Is it safe?"

Wiping her cheeks, Shay disentangles from her mother's arms and scans the surrounding area, her bunched eyebrows relaxing when I make myself corporeal again. "Kohl brought me, using his reaper magic."

Her mother stiffens at the sight of me. "Is this a goodbye visit?"

"No, Mom, no. I'm very much alive. More alive than I've been in fifteen years. Maybe ever." She squeezes her mother's hand while holding eye contact with me, talking to me as much as to her mother. "Kohl is off duty; he's not here as a reaper, he's here as—" Her lips curve into a beautiful smile. "As my friend. My special friend?" Making a sour face, she shakes her head. "Goddess, what am I, twelve? Kohl is both of those things, and more. He's my boyfriend. One who gives the best surprises in all the realms."

My consciousness—or as Shay insists, my soul—swells until it feels as if it might exceed the boundaries of my physical form. *Boyfriend.* A term used as a sign of commitment, affection, and intimacy. To hear Shay claim me as such in the presence of the person she loves most is more than expected, more than I dared to hope.

For a long moment, her mother is silent. Green eyes that could be a matched set with Shay's stare at me. Into me.

I welcome the probing, opening my consciousness to the witch who gave life to the one I love.

The woman's eyes sparkle as our magics meet. As she sees the truth of my intentions and depth of devotion to her only child. Then her magic retreats, and she thanks me with a single nod. "You are much more than Shay's boyfriend. You're her eternal protector. Her soulmate."

"Mom."

"Hush, girl," she says, raising a hand in a casual way, though the gesture clearly holds authority, both motherly and in coven hierarchy. "It doesn't take a seer to see this reaper's future." At Shay's tight-lipped silence, the woman turns, her dark eyebrows high on her forehead when she meets her daughter's gaze. "You haven't looked." Her expression softens when Shay shakes her head. "Oh, child. Love is the ultimate reward for risking your heart and soul. This reaper has taken that risk for you."

No better endorsement exists than her mother's approval. But theirs is not a conversation for my ears. I move toward Shay, giving her my full attention, and also reaching inside, touching her soul, for the sole purpose of bringing something other than melancholy to her beautiful face.

Her gaze narrows. Without saying a word, I know what she is thinking: *I feel you poking around in there.*

I give her a wink. A new gesture for me, it causes her eyebrows to rise and a small smile to bud. "I will take my leave to give you time alone with your mother. The Oracle's magic does not protect you here, but mine will. I won't allow harm to reach you. You have only to call for me, inside, and I will appear."

From her position several feet away, Shay's mother incants a spell encapsulating her daughter within a small mobile boundary. "As long as Shay is near me, no creature, mortal or otherwise, will know she's here. I'll keep her safe while you're away." With another nod, she makes her way inside the house.

"Lucky me, having two guardian angels," Shay says. "Hey, I know I took liberties there, calling you my boyfriend."

"Take all that you desire. I am yours in every way."

Glassy-eyed, she swallows hard, nodding while walking backward. "Thank you for bringing me here. I'll see you soon."

Chapter Eight

SHAY

Well, I never thought I'd be here, and I mean that in both the literal and figurative senses.

"I hope you won't take this the wrong way," Dela says as I knock on the door that leads to the apartment above Lexi's shop, "but I'm proud of you. You're the most independent person I've ever known, so I'm sure it's not easy accepting help. But taking these steps to get more out of life is amazing. I'm so excited for you and Kohl to—"

The purple door swings open with a *whoosh* that would've startled any self-respecting cat out of my arms. Not Cookie. The big ginger doesn't so much as wiggle a whisker at Lexi's dramatic flair. Maybe he's used to her antics. Lexi may not have visited Minerva as much as the old witch would've liked, but I know she spent time there on a regular basis. Enough so that Lexi knew Minerva's plans for Cookie before her great-aunt crossed over.

"Come in, friends!" Dressed in a long, flowing black dress made of semi-opaque fabric that makes it possible to see every green curve and dip of her body beneath, Lexi waves us inside.

I nod for Dela to lead. She's here at my invitation, but being my closest friend and now the repository of all my secrets, she's aware of my unjustified beef with Lexi Goodwin. She knows how much internal crow I had to eat to call and accept Lexi's offer.

The staircase leading to Lexi's apartment is a straight shot and steeper than what you get in any modern building. By the time I reach the top, the muscles in my legs and arms are burning. Climbing while carrying eighteen pounds of tabby is a workout.

"Did your great-aunt ever mention Cookie needing to lose some weight?" I wheeze as I clear the top step.

Lexi's laugh is as easygoing and friendly as everything else she does. "Never. He's exactly as he should be, like all familiars. But if you're ever concerned about his health, call Dr. Schaefer, not the veterinarian. You knew that, right?" Her black eyebrows rise when I shake my head. "Well, no harm, either way. A veterinarian in the human world wouldn't be able to tell the difference between a feline pet and a familiar, but our vet here in town would chuckle and send you out the door if you showed up with Cookie. Dr. Daemon's heightened demon senses are great for all kinds of things."

Based on the wiggle she does, I'm guessing she's personally acquainted with his *heightened demon senses*. Or maybe she's found a way to profit from them. That is her specialty.

"Okay, you three." She motions at the assortment of living room furniture arranged in a conversational way. "Get comfortable."

Dela and I take opposite ends of a deep-purple velvet couch. The moment I'm settled, Cookie wanders out of my lap and hops onto an overstuffed black chenille armchair.

"There's not a lint roller around that'll get your ginger hair off of that pristine upholstery," I say, making a move with the intent to relocate him.

"He's perfect where he is." Lexi waves me off, scratching Cookie's head on her way to an emerald-green chaise where she lays herself out as if posing for a magazine spread. Or the opening scene of a high-end porno. "A little fur is no match for a housecleaning spell," she says, twirling a finger in the air, then stopping the stream of magic as quickly and easily as she created it. "Shay, I apologize. You probably think I'm showing off or rubbing my magic in your face, and I promise you that isn't the case. My coven's way of life is a lot different from yours, but I'll try to rein myself in a little."

"Please don't." And this is where I *outwardly* eat crow. "I've always been bitter that I was born with seer magic and no other. Winterlock witches stick pretty rigidly to a lot of the old rules, including not profiting from magic. I broke that rule when I was twenty-one and needed money fast. To say it bit me in the ass is a monumental understatement. I came to Fate's Falls to escape the life I'd scorched, and here you were, living yours to the fullest by breaking the same damn rule I had—but with no repercussions. I've been a bitch to you for years because I was resentful and jealous. I still am, if I'm being honest, but I'm working on it, and I'm sorry."

"Apology accepted." She scoots to a normal sitting position when Cookie hops off the armchair, then onto my lap. "And it's Cookie approved, too. Looks like we're all open and ready to get started."

Just like that. Without further comment or taking the opportunity to put me in place, even a little, which she'd be justified in doing. But no, she simply accepts the apology with a genuine, friendly smile and keeps going. If I can't learn whatever it is Minerva hoped I would, I can at least count this as a lesson in being the bigger person.

"We're about to link magics and do some deep digging. Things may get a little personal," Lexi says, taking over the chair Cookie vacated, which puts her nearly knee to knee with me. "But you have my word that anything that happens here stays here. Goodwin witches are excellent at keeping secrets. You wouldn't *believe* some of the things I know, and I'll never tell you a single one of them!"

Cookie chooses that moment to look up at me, and I swear he nods. Like a real nod of affirmation, not just a coincidentally timed body movement.

"Dela, I'm not sure how *familiar* you are with familiars, so I'll do a quick run-through of how their magic works."

"Oh, good. I didn't want to pry, but I have been wondering since Shay got Cookie. He just looks like a regular cat to me." She leans forward to look in the ginger tabby's eyes. "Sorry if that's an insult, Cookie."

If he understands her, he doesn't acknowledge it. Maybe

he only communicates with witches. Or maybe I've swum a little too far into the deep end.

"So! Familiars are supernatural beings, sort of a lower form of witches. The origin stories vary, as history always does. In the old Goodwin diaries, many witches had familiars, but over the centuries, their numbers decreased a lot. The books don't say why, but my guess would be humans are to blame—sorry, Dela, no personal offense there, but you mortals have had a mighty big stick up your butt since, well, forever. You don't, of course. Though I'd be happy to sell you a nifty sex stick that feels amazing up there. It's modeled from a dryad who prefers to remain nameless, and magically infused for your pleasure, of course." A playful, no-fucks-given laugh bubbles out of her mouth. "Or Raz's. Pleasure doesn't discriminate!"

"Um, no thanks." Dela giggles, a deep-red blush flooding her fair complexion.

Dela has told me some things. I know she and Raz have a very healthy sex life, and her boyfriend has literally zero inhibitions. Still, picturing the intensely stoic demon's reaction if Dela brought home a magically infused sex stick and wanted to stick it up his red ass has me snorting with unexpected laughter.

We're here because Lexi offered help, but sitting here with her and Dela, the air filled with laughter, it's starting to feel like friendship. And that's a whole other kind of magic.

"Let's get back on track," Lexi says with another easy smile. "A familiar's magic is dormant unless they bond with a witch. Even then, they're not capable of doing magic independently. Not that we're aware of, anyway." She trains her focus on the big cat on my lap. "Maybe you're keeping secrets, too, hmm?"

He croaks out a string of meows, then turns his head.

"I think he just told you to mind your own business," Dela says with another giggle.

"Wouldn't surprise me. Cookie has always been a little extra," Lexi says with a wink. "And he's a wonderful familiar, as you'll soon find out, Shay. I assume you haven't fed him yet?"

"Not blood, no."

Dela's eyes nearly pop out of her pretty face. "Blood? Is he a vampire?"

"Goodness, no!" Lexi says. "A witch bonds with their familiar by feeding them their blood. A quick nip on the finger daily always did the trick for Minerva and Cookie, but they were bonded for a long time. A familiar will only take what they need. I think you'll find Cookie very well-mannered about it. He's a very refined old man."

Refined. Not a word I would've used to describe the chunky tabby on my lap, but Lexi knows him in ways I don't yet.

"Once the bond has been created," Lexi continues, "Shay will be able to draw on his magic to strengthen her own at any time. Familiars are naturally intuitive, so he'll know what she needs before she does, and give it."

"Does it weaken them to do magic like that?" Dela asks, reaching over to scratch Cookie's chin.

"Quite the opposite, actually. The more a familiar uses their magic, the longer they live. Shay is Cookie's third witch." Lexi nods when I gape. "He was gifted to Minerva by

my great-great grandmother. Or was it great-great-great..."
She places an elegant, manicured finger to her pursed lips. "I
can never keep track of the 'greats' when it's more than one,
but you get the gist. He's been around for a long time and
has strong magic. Which is my great-aunt believed his
magic can help you control yours, Shay. But I'm curious:
why didn't your coven train you to do that?"

My knee-jerk reaction is to bristle at the question, take it
as a criticism of my coven. But that's the old me. The new
me, the less narrow-minded me I want to be, understands
that it's just curiosity, something Lexi seems to have in
abundance. "Seers are rare in my coven, and by the time I
was born, the previous one had crossed over. Other witches
tried to help when I was young, but either they didn't have
the knowledge or I wasn't open to learning." I glance at Dela
when she makes a little noise in her throat. "Yes, probably
both, and definitely the latter. Happy?"

"I'm happy that we're all here to investigate a solution
that'll open up new roads for you," Dela says.

"New roads that lead to finding out what a certain
reaper has beneath his cloak, I hope!" Lexi winks, then
presses her hands together and closes her eyes, her voice
dropping an octave as she offers thanks to the goddess and
all the witches on the other side, then requests a blessing—
for me.

Whether this evening results in me having the ability to
control my magic or not, having Kohl, Dela, and now Lexi in
my corner, I know I've already been blessed.

SHAY

It's midnight by the time I get home. Dela offered to drive me, but I opted to walk. It's only ten minutes, and after an intense evening of joining and focusing our magic, Cookie and I both needed the fresh air and to stretch our legs. Wild as it is, I actually *know* the big ginger wanted the same things I did. I can't literally read his mind, but thanks to Lexi's guidance, I'm now able to vibe with my familiar.

So many new things in my life. Great things. And it's only going to get better. For the first time in my life, I'm not just going through the motions of life. I'm alive.

The moment I set foot on my front walk, Kohl appears near my front door.

I can't hide my smile and don't bother trying. But I can still give him a little shit. I wouldn't be me if I didn't. "Either you've been ethereally following me, or you have the best timing in all the realms." All the figurative butterflies take flight inside me when he pushes the hood of his cloak back, revealing his full head.

Goddess, the man is handsome. A visual snack. More than that, though, he's good. It's his soul I love the most. Something I plan to tell him if my successful experiments at controlling my magic carry over to touching him. Even if they don't, I want him to know.

"I have not followed you in that manner since

confessing it. As for timing, I would spend every moment in this plane with you if I could. Since that is not an option, I come when your soul calls."

No point denying my soul called to him. I haven't stopped thinking about Kohl since he re-entered my life. "I'm happy you're here; I have news. Good news."

His gaze lowers to my hand as I press it against his chest. "You're not wearing gloves."

"That's the news. Part of it, anyway." I nod toward the door while unlocking it. "Come inside?"

Nodding, he follows me into the house, closing the door behind him. "I have news as well. Good news, but even so, I fear hearing it may wipe away your beautiful smile."

"Be that as it may, now you *have* to tell me. No poofing out of here until you do."

A hint of a smile pulls at his full mouth. "There will be no poofing."

"See, now I'm conflicted. Part of me is disappointed that you didn't use fifty words to say you won't leave, but you're pretty darn adorable when you use lingo."

"I prefer you find me adorable."

"Truth time?" I say, plopping onto the couch. "I always do." The sanctuary of home and Kohl's presence lowers the last of my guard, fatigue flooding me as I pat the spot beside me. "Come and tell me your news so I can show you mine before I'm too tired to have enough focus."

The couch dips under his solid form, and his leg presses against mine, our skin separated by my jeans and his cloak. The thought of removing those layers, of every part of our bodies touching, really touching, awakens every nerve ending in my body. Bye-bye, fatigue. If I can control my magic with him the way I learned to while practicing with my safety net, Dela, anything and everything is possible. It even worked when I touched Lexi's hand.

His dark-chocolate gaze tracks my bare hand as I stuff it between my thighs to prevent reaching for him. Though, maybe that would be the best way to give him my news—by straddling his lap, threading my fingers through his caramel-brown hair, and kissing those tempting damn lips.

I'm this-close to doing exactly that when my phone rings on the side table. "That's my mom's tone," I say, reaching for it and sliding my finger across the screen. "What's wrong?" Because something has to be for her to be calling at this hour.

"Shay, baby, it worked. Getting those pictures your artist friend drew in front of the right eyes, along with a solid boost of motivational magic from the coven... They got him. Pittsburg PD and the FBI. I just saw it on the news. That monster can't hurt you or anyone else ever again. They got him."

Every muscle in my body clenches. My spine feels like a steel rod; my chest and throat constricted as if by a massive hand squeezing me tight. "They arrested him?" I whisper when I can manage to draw a breath. "In the newscast, you saw him being arrested by the police? You're sure they got the right man?"

"Not arrested, Shay. Dead. Shot while fleeing."

Even sitting, the room is spinning. I fold forward, putting my head between my knees. "Are they sure it's him? Are you sure?"

"I am certain," Kohl says from a kneeling position in front of me. The hard set of his jaw contrasts the love for me in his eyes when I look into them. "That night when I was first drawn to you, I saw him clearly, inside and out. I had no control over his death, no method to foresee it, but I have continued to listen for his soul in the in-between, so I could ensure his next place is a hell in which he will suffer for eternity. It is done. He is gone, Shay, and you are free."

In my hand, my phone's screen blinks with the ended call. Mom heard everything.

So did I.

For fifteen years, I have been safe, but safe isn't free.

Now, I'm free. To go wherever I want. Be whatever I want.

But I only want one thing, and I already had it. He's right in front of me. And even if can block my magic, I don't want to limit our connection.

Love is the ultimate reward for risking your heart and soul.

This love is worth any risk.

Kohl's eyes open wide as I place my palms against his cheeks. His magic rushes through me, brighter than the whitest white, warm like the summer sunshine on my face. Pure and good and endless. "Do you see anything?"

Tears slide down my cheeks as the visions play in my mind, like frames from a silent movie. "I see me. That's all I see. You're always looking at me."

"Because you are the only future I want." The pads of his thumbs sweep across my skin, gently brushing away the tears. "I will forever be a reaper, but you are the reason I exist, Shay."

"I love you. I should've said it before, but I was afraid of the things I can't control, of all the limitations, of getting hurt. I don't want fear to rob me of another minute of loving you as completely as I can."

"I have longed for this moment," he says, cradling my face in his hands. His skin is warm and smooth, his touch gentle yet strong. "To give you all that I can. To know every inch of your body as I know the depth of your soul."

"Then know me," I whisper. "Take me to bed and love me every way you've longed to do."

He moves so quickly and smoothly, I might think he used magic, if not for the very real sensation of being up in his arms. This time, it's me he places on the bed. Gently, but I don't think he's afraid of hurting me. It's reverence. I see it in his eyes as his gaze slowly sweeps over my body while he removes each piece of clothing, as if unwrapping a precious gift.

"You are more exquisite than the heavens," he says, trailing his fingers along the inside of my leg, from ankle to high on my thigh. His brow furrows at the shiver that ripples through me. "Are you cold? I know you dislike being cold."

Goddess, he's adorable. He's also seriously overdressed for this moment.

"Different kind of shiver. The good kind. The kind that means 'touch me again,'" I motion up and down at his cloak, "but this time, do it while you're naked. Remember when I said I like your surprises? And that time you claimed to have mastery of all activities you do in this form? It's time to put those things together."

His deep laughter is like gasoline on a spark, and damn, my spark is ready to ignite.

"I have never removed my cloak."

"Seriously?"

His nod brings me to my hands and knees. His eyes grow dark and hooded as I push up to my knees alone, then run my hands over the material covering his chest, abdomen, and cock.

"I don't feel any zippers or buttons. I guess there's only one way to remove it," I say, sliding off the bed to kneel in front of him. Taking the edge of the cloak in my hands, I lick my lips while looking up at him. "Start at the bottom and work it all the way up."

The last time I was naked with a man, I was young, unhappy, and bombarded by visions of the guy's future—which did not include me—while I faked my way through the various deeds.

There's nothing fake about this moment. I'm happier than I have ever been, and when I slide my palms up Kohl's warm, nicely muscled legs, the only visions I see are of me. I never expected to be loved the way he loves me—for all that I am and also for the things I am not. Complete love. True love.

I gather the dark cloth and draw it upward as I maneuver to my feet. He raises his arms, his handsome face disappearing from view as I shimmy the cloak past his shoulders and over his head. It feels kind of weird tossing a magically imbued garment on the floor, but I chuck that sucker as far as my shitty throwing skills allow. Now that I have Kohl in his entirety, I don't want to share him with his duty. Just for a while.

"Yup, exactly how I thought it'd all look," I say, quirking an eyebrow at him while doing a walk-around inspection that includes a smack on his perfect, taut butt.

He's smiling when my circle ends with me in front of him. "You once said you hadn't thought about how I look under the cloak."

"I said *maybe* I hadn't thought about it." Gliding my hands up and down his broad, firm chest, I push onto my tiptoes and brush my lips across his. "I thought about it. Those times you heard me moaning in here?" I slide one hand down between us and circle his cock where it juts tall and hard. "I was thinking about you, Kohl."

Desire blazes in his eyes. Then his hands are in my hair, his lips pressed to mine, his tongue sliding along the seam and then into my mouth. He kisses me as if we have forever to do it and he's committing every second of it to memory. Not truly mortal, he doesn't need to breathe, and so the kiss goes on and on, Kohl's tongue stroking into my mouth, tasting me, over and over, until I'm lightheaded and weak in the knees.

"I need more of you," he says when I break away to catch my breath. "I need all of you." Again, he scoops me off my feet and lays me out on the bed. This time when he strokes up my legs, he spreads them apart, as wide as he can. "I should not be able to smell or taste, but I do. Your breath, your mouth, your skin..." He drags his nose along the highest, most sensitive part of my inner thigh. "And this, your beautiful glistening center..."

My eyes roll back in my head as he presses the tip of his nose against my clit. Moan when his tongue delves between my pussy lips.

"I could spend eternity tasting you," he says between long sweeping strokes, each one ending with his tongue working my clit. His hands slide under my butt, tipping my hips up and opening me wider for his hot, plundering mouth. Each pass is harder, hungrier. Then his lips latch on to my clit and his tongue—

"Goddess, yes. Keep doing that. Never stop doing that. Kohl, *Kohl...*" Pleasure explodes beneath his tongue. Tangling my fingers in his short hair, I writhe and rock against his mouth, until I'm panting and wriggling to put space between my hypersensitive clit and his marauding tongue. "No more," I say, pushing against his forehead.

Handsome face shiny with my slickness, he smiles up at me. No, not smiles—smolders. "You told me to never stop."

"You can't take sex talk literally. Okay, some of it, yes. Words like harder or faster—literal. Telling you I love you— definitely literal. But telling you to *never* stop eating my pussy? Definitely not literal," I say, stroking the strong line of his eyebrows as I smile.

"You didn't say any of those things."

"Yet." I curl one finger like a hook to beckon him. "I want you inside me." As much as I'd like to appreciate the bunching of his muscles as he moves up, over my body, I can't take my eyes from his gaze. The passion it holds. The love.

Hand curled around my hip, the thick head of his cock notches between my legs. "My love," he says, thrusting into me.

Tears threaten to spill free at the perfection of it all. Wrapping my legs and arms around him, I pull him deeper inside me. His body. His soul. "I love you," I whisper before drawing his mouth onto mine.

His tongue and cock find their rhythm, each perfect stroke pushing me closer to the edge. So close. So, so close.

The hand at my hip slides between our bodies and he presses the pads of his fingers to my clit, rolling the bud back and forth, back and forth.

"Harder," I pant as the bowstring tightens beneath his touch. "Faster."

And he does, sending me over the edge in a spiral of star-filled ecstasy. Buried deep, he holds himself taut as I writhe beneath him, milking every drop of orgasmic bliss.

Sated, I open my eyes to find him looking at me. *Adoring* me. And when I sigh, contented, he begins stroking into me again. Goddess, it feels amazing. Different from the first stroke, but so damn good.

He shifts our position, the new angle letting him thrust deeper. With each stroke, the head of his big cock drags against my G-spot.

I cry out as the orgasm hits like a crashing wave. Clutching at him, I pant and moan, breathless and wrung out by the time it finally ebbs.

And still, he's rock hard inside me. "Again, Shay. Take all your pleasure."

My hair sticks to my damp face as I shake my head. "Not when you can't have any."

"Being with you is the ultimate pleasure."

A snorted laugh bubbles out of me. "You only think that because you haven't experienced an orgasm."

"Then let me experience yours."

"How?" I draw a sharp breath at the sensation of his consciousness seeking mine. "I feel you in there." *Poking around* is what I would've said before. Not now. This is different. A question of the most intimate kind. "What do I need to do so you can feel my soul, too?"

"If you want me to, I will. I'll meet you there, inside."

"I want you to." Sliding my fingers through his hair, I guide his mouth to mine. "Feel what you do to me," I say against his lips as he strokes into me, stoking the still-burning embers. Goddess, it's so good. So deep and full. I close my eyes and let it happen. The coiling tightness of an orgasm. The gentle caress of his soul touching mine. *"Kohl,"* I moan as everything clicks into place and I come apart like a long, unraveling rope that ends with Kohl wrapped around me. And me around him.

Chapter Nine

KOHL

There is nowhere I would rather be than in bed with Shay in my arms. I thought removing my cloak while in this physical form might prevent me receiving the call of souls from the in-between. That is not the case.

Half draped across me, Shay raises her head from its place against my chest, resting her chin on my sternum and blinking her beautiful green eyes at me. "Maybe my magic is changing because I can almost hear you thinking."

I know she's not serious, that she's teasing, as is her way. Still, there could be some truth to her words that even she is unaware of. "Our souls are connected now. I feel yours as if it were my own. Perhaps you're sensing the pull of my duty, hearing the call of the newly departed, awaiting guidance to their next place."

"Souls need you?" She nearly springs from the bed, collecting my discarded cloak and throwing it over me, blocking my view of her exquisite nakedness. "You have to go, Kohl. I love you for everything you are, including being a reaper. I need you, but I know there will always be souls who need you, too."

With the cloak covering me, reaper magic grows until the pull to fulfil my duty borders on all-consuming. I cross to her in two strides, cradling her face in my hands and softly kissing her tender lips. "I will return to you as soon as I'm able."

Duty takes me from her before I hear whatever words leave her lips. But there is no soul waiting when I arrive at the in-between.

The Oracle is many things. All things. Whatever form or lack thereof is imagined, believed, or required by the receiver.

Every time I have been in the Oracle's presence, I have seen a woman who is long in years, soft, but not frail. That is who awaits me now.

"Come." With a gentle sweep of one arm, the Oracle draws me closer. "Do you know why I summoned you?"

"I ignored your directive with a soul. Willfully disregarded my calling to follow my desires whenever possible. I allowed—no, welcomed—emotions to enter my consciousness, and fell in love with a mortal, then consummated that bond in the flesh."

"All of those things are true, but you didn't answer the question. *Do you know why I summoned you?*"

"To end my time as a reaper," I say, taking a knee and bowing my head. "I accept whatever you deem appropriate for me, and ask no mercy for myself, only that you do not blame Shay for my actions. Whatever the consequences, they are mine alone to bear."

"Only the best souls will put the outcome of another before their own." The Oracle's ethereal touch lifts my chin, compelling me to look directly into the brilliant golden glow above. "Shay possesses such a soul, and because of it, her next place has long been decided. You, Nikohlai, were not meant to possess a soul, yet one exists within you, undeniable and worthy of reward. You are correct, I did summon you to end your time as a reaper." The light once again takes female form, the Oracle smiling down at me. "You will return to the earthly plane now, to the life you desire and have earned. I will see you again, reaper."

A funnel of magic replaces the peaceful, endless light of the in-between. Its power molds to my naked form, simultaneously cradling me and feeling as if it might tear me limb from limb.

Then I'm in Shay's bedroom again, in the same position I held before the oracle.

"That was fast; you were only gone for a few seconds," Shay says, the smile on her face shifting to a gaping O as she turns to face me. "Why are you on your knees? And naked." She darts her gaze around the room. "Where's your cloak?"

"The Oracle took it."

"What does that even mean?" Her eyes widen as she crosses the room toward me. "And hold up, are you— shivering?"

A second ripple of involuntary muscular twitching runs through me as I rise to a stand. "If this is how it feels to be cold, I understand why you don't like it." The instant she's close, touching me, warmth floods me from within. The heat is everywhere, but especially low in my groin, in my cock. I've been hard for her hundreds of times. This is different, even from when our bodies joined and her sheath squeezed me tight as she came.

Hungry for her beyond anything I previously experienced, I thread one hand through her thick curls and grab a handful of her soft, full backside with the other, then pull her tight against me and seal my mouth to hers. The taste of her lips and tongue is richer now. The temperature, hotter.

"Kohl," she whispers, pulling back enough to look into my eyes, to slide her hand between us with the palm pressed against my chest. "I see things... your future, it's different, it's..." Her breath catches, her eyes opening wide.

"If the visions are too much, don't look. Use your magic to block whatever you see."

She shakes her head, her gleaming green irises moving side to side as if watching something before holding my gaze again. "You're human. Truly and fully mortal. But how?"

"It was the Oracle's doing," I say, stroking Shay's smooth skin. "I asked only for the safety of your soul, but was given *my* soul's greatest desire—a lifetime to spend with you."

"That's what I saw in the new visions. Not just me, seen through your eyes, like before. I saw us. Young, like we are now, and old. Really damn old." The brightest smile accompanies her amused snort. "Spoiler alert: you still look hot when you're wrinkled with silver hair."

"I don't need the gift of foresight to know you will be as beautiful on our last day together as you are right now."

"Becoming human doesn't seem to have affected your

romantic eloquence," she says, wrapping her arms behind my neck, then walking us toward the bed. "But I can't wait to feel how it affects *other* things."

What we had was more than enough, but when I sink into her welcoming body this time, everything is different. Buried to the hilt in her tight, slick heat, I have to consciously hold my breath and steel my muscles to prevent what feels like an impending explosion between my legs.

Then she moves. Rolls her hips toward mine, rocking her body side to side. *"Shay."* I can barely get her name out without losing control of the tornado building at the base of my cock. "Gods above, don't move."

"Guess you lost your *mastery of all activities*, huh?" Her body shakes with silent laughter, the action involuntarily and mercilessly squeezing my cock.

"Shay, please. I don't want to ruin this for you."

The shaking and squeezing ends immediately, Shay capturing my face between her palms and looking into my eyes. "Nothing can ruin this for *us*. We have the rest of our lives to learn and grow together, in all things, including sex. I've seen it. I see it right now, Kohl. This is perfect, it's what I want. *You're* who I want, in every way, in any form. Take your pleasure with me. I promise I'll meet you there."

I pull back until only the head of my cock remains nestled inside. Then, I slide home again. Home. That's what she is. Her body, her soul. My home. For a lifetime. For eternity.

Looking into her eyes, I find my rhythm. Control. I feel the shift in her muscles. The tension in them. I hear her breathing grow shallow. Choppy. She's close to that beautiful release. To writhing under me as she rides her pleasure. To crying out and panting my name.

Sweat beads above my brow as my cock begins to throb. Not yet. Not without her.

Holding myself on one arm, I slide my other hand between us. One touch is all it takes to make her clench around me, her beautiful lips parting as she moans. *"Kohl... goddess, yes."*

Heat flares at my root, fire racing through me as I erupt inside her. A release that takes over my entire body. Pleasure unlike anything I have known, even when I shared hers.

Still deep inside her warm body, I capture her lips, the sweet taste of her breath and skin flooding my senses. Desire prickles at the base of my spine, and I feel my cock swelling within her tight walls.

"Already?" She angles her head to look into my eyes as I begin to stroke in and out, my cock getting harder with each thrust. "Maybe there's a little magic left in you, after all."

"You are my magic, Shay."

"*We* are magic. For the rest of our lives."

"For eternity. A soulmate is forever."

"Forever," she says, her beautiful eyes shining with unshed tears. With love.

Epilogue

Nine months later

SHAY

"**S**hit, sorry," I say after turning quickly causes my giant belly to bump a customer's cappuccino out of Dela's hand. Third time this week—and it's only Monday afternoon. "I'll make another one." I send an apologetic smile to the hulking rhino man at the counter. "Sorry about the wait, Cornelius." I rub one hand over my watermelon-sized protrusion. "The baby will pick up the bill for this one."

"At this rate, the baby will need a job here." Dela's giggle morphs into a dreamy sigh when her eight-foot-tall—not including horns—hell demon boyfriend walks through the door.

Fate makes some interesting matches, but hasn't gotten

one wrong yet. Not around here, anyway.

Constantine and Natalie, another of fate's love matches, come in next. My Minotaur boss usually gets Natalie settled at a table, kisses her, then either joins Dela and I behind the counter, or heads into the back office. Not today. Today, Constantine and Natalie hover in the customer area.

Which makes sense when Natalie's cousin Rosetta rolls in with her giant orc husband and their adorable little orcling son. Except... the five of them don't grab a table. And they don't leave. Just more hovering.

My nemesis turned friend struts through the door next. Dressed in one of her flowing all-black outfits, this one complete with a pointy hat, Lexi looks every bit the kickass witch she is. It's the right time of day for her daily caffeine fix, but she doesn't come to the counter.

Something's up.

When I turn to ask Dela if she knows what's going on, she's gone. But not for long, and when she comes out from the back office, she's grinning ear to ear and carrying a cake on a large, silver, rectangular platter. The kind that comes from Amazra's bakery.

If the sight of sugary carbs wasn't enough to make my mouth water, the man who follows Dela out sure is. My man. My savior. My baby's daddy. The love of my life.

A nearly synchronized "Surprise!" comes from the group surrounding me. Surrounding *us*—me, Kohl, and our goddess-isn't-it-time-for-you-to-come-out-yet baby.

"You all know I didn't want to be fussed over," I say, wagging my finger at each person in turn. "When I can move faster than an old turtle carrying a watermelon, you're all in big trouble." While everyone laughs, I grab Kohl by the collar of his shirt and tug him as close as the belly allows. "You especially."

The twinkle in his chocolatey eyes matches his smile. "I look forward to you chasing me again."

"Again? The memory part of your human brain seems to be malfunctioning. You're the one who chased me, border-line-stalkery reaper man."

"And I would do so again, in any realm, in any form, for the rest of time."

I could blame pregnancy hormones for the tears that slip down my cheeks, but I'd rather give credit where credit is due. I place one hand over the steady thump of his beating heart. "I love you now and forever," I say loud enough for Kohl's ears only.

"And I you, my soulmate." He lifts my hand to his mouth and presses a soft kiss to my folded fingers, his dark-brown eyebrows pulling together at the bridge of his perfect nose when I grimace and hold my belly. "Perhaps we should put some cake in a takeout box and get you home."

"It's just some baby acrobatics, it'll pass. My shift's not over until five."

"Actually, it's over now," Constantine says, leaning over the counter to grab a stack of plates. "Extended maternity leave with full pay. A gift from me and Natalie. Go home and put your feet up. Get some rest before the baby comes, because if she's anything like you—" His dark lips clamp shut, his amber eyes shooting me an unspoken apology. The big Minotaur looks more sheepish than bullish right now.

"She?" Kohl asks, gently stroking my belly.

"Yes." Fresh tears follow the tracks of their predecessors as I nod. "I would've told you, but you said you didn't want to know details of your human future; that you just wanted to experience it, moment by moment. A little spoiler alert, though—Winterlock witches always have daughters. So, if we have more kids, they'll all be girls."

"You said 'if.' Does that mean you haven't seen that part of our future?"

"I've seen it all, Kohl, and it's beautiful. It's so incredibly beautiful."

Human Kohl no longer has reaper magic, but he still has the strength to scoop me off my feet, into his arms. And that's no small feat with forty pounds of baby belly on board.

"Not going to warn me against throwing my back out like you did last time?" he asks while carting me off to the chorus of well-wishes and applause from our friends.

"Nah. It's going to be a lot of years before you throw your back out from strenuous activity, and when you do, you're going to tell me it was worth it."

"You saw that in a vision of my future?"

"No, I just made it up. Gotta keep you on your toes."

The rumble in his chest vibrates through me. "Naughty witch."

"Ooh, on that subject—now that you know we're having a girl, how do you feel about naming her Minerva, in honor of the witch who brought you back into my life?"

"I think it's perfect."

"Couldn't agree more," comes Minerva's voice from a place somewhere far beyond. Or maybe not so far.

If I've learned one thing in the past nine months, it's that anything is possible.

Thank You!

When I started writing the Fate's Falls series, I had no idea how many wonderful characters and stories would come to life! Thank you for reading this collection of the first three stories I wrote for this magical mountain town. I hope you loved visiting Fate's Falls, and I'm excited for you to return for more cozy, spicy-and-sweet monster romances.

Karla
♡

welcome to Fate's Falls

karladoyle.com

Want more cozy monster romances?

Go on an adventure to the secret town of Fate's Falls and fall in love with all of its irresistible monster mates! All books take place in Fate's Falls, and you'll see some character appearances and familiar town landmarks. Each book is a standalone romance with a different couple and their journey to a very happily ever after.

Mated to the Minotaur
The Grumpy Demon's Sunshine
A Reaper is Forever
The Rhino's Rose
A Dash of Demon
Hell's Belle
Orc-ily Ever After
Falling for the Yeti
...and more to come!

ALSO BY KARLA DOYLE

Doggy Style (Hope Harbor)

Resorting to Love (linked to Hope Harbor)

White Lie Christmas (linked to Hope Harbor)

King of Her Dreams (Hope Harbor)

Heart of Texas (linked to Hope Harbor)

Her Pipe Dream (Hope Harbor)

12 Days (Hope Harbor)

Puck That

Shifting Gears (Under the Hood)

Driver's Seat (Under the Hood)

Gingerbread Man (Man of the Month: Candy Cane Key)

Just in Queso (Man of the Month: Magnolia Point)

Unexpected Addition

Dating the Doubter

Gift Wrapped

Cup of Sugar (Close to Home #1)

Icing on the Cake (Close to Home #2)

Sweet as Candy (Close to Home #3)

Body of Work (Very Personal Training #1)

Worth the Wait (Very Personal Training #2)

Game Plan

More Than Words

Crossing the Line

Visit Karla's website: www.karladoyle.com

About the Author

A small-town girl with some big-city experience, Karla resides in South-western Ontario with her husband and two amazing, young-adult kids. She studied fashion design in college and spent 20+ years working in that industry before succumbing to the writing muse. When she's not writing the sexy stories that swirl around in her head, you can find her spending time with family, hanging out with book-loving friends on Facebook, or cuddled up with a book and her adorable pets.

Karla loves hearing from readers! Connect with her online, or send her an email: karla@karladoyle.com.

Join Karla's mailing list to stay up to date on all her news: www.karladoyle.com/newsletter

facebook.com/KarlaDoyleAuthor

instagram.com/KarlaDoyleAuthor

tiktok.com/@karladoyleauthor

bookbub.com/authors/karla-doyle

goodreads.com/karlad

youtube.com/@KarlaDoyleAuthor

bsky.app/profile/karladoyleauthor.bsky.social

patreon.com/KarlaDoyleAuthor

www.ingramcontent.com/pod-product-compliance
Lightning Source LLC
Chambersburg PA
CBHW070306040726
47501CB00018B/222